Romell,

Thanks for Supp[illegible] brother, but your Support has never surprised me. I appreciate the kindness of purchasing my book as you promised you would. Oh, how I missed you. I think about you always. I'm so proud and glad to have a brother like you. I hope your dreams come true like mine have. I can't wait to see and visit you. You'll be seeing me soon, bro.

Best regards,

Nadia

Relationships and love are just titles or words. The people in them, like you and me, give love or a relationship its true meaning.

An Old War among the Youth

The Sex Battle

Nadia

Balboa Press books may be ordered through booksellers or by contacting:

Balboa Press
A Division of Hay House
1663 Liberty Drive
Bloomington, IN 47403
www.balboapress.com
1 (877) 407-4847

Print information available on the last page.

ISBN: 978-1-5043-3034-3 (sc)
ISBN: 978-1-5043-3036-7 (hc)
ISBN: 978-1-5043-3035-0 (e)

Library of Congress Control Number: 2015904733

Balboa Press rev. date: 06/30/2015

Acknowledgments

Writing this electrifying novel would have been impossible without dedication or motivation. The success of finalizing this story was a challenging one. It is an accomplishment I thought was unreachable, but God has aided me in this outstanding completion. I would also like to thank my mother, Elizabeth Ross, who has showed me a great deal of assistance as she has believed in me and supported me throughout my publishing experience. I would like to thank, Romell Ross, one of my big brothers, for keeping me optimistic and focused on my goals. I want my siblings to know how much I love, care, and appreciate them: Markeese Ross, Joseph Ross, Creedell Ross, Rhonda Ross, and my niece, Kitana Ross. Hopes and dreams are things that can be fulfilled, and I'm psyched to introduce my creativity to the world.

CHAPTER 1

Erin

The Trapped Cock

I had an appointment to tutor a freshman, Ricky White, for English in the tutoring center. It seemed Ricky's large pink lips were always chapped. His hair was sandy brown, somewhat damp, and soulless. I had never seen a change in his hairstyle or his style of clothing. He mainly wore inexpensive navy-blue business suits, as if he had job interviews awaiting him before or after school. Had anyone asked me, I would have said the suits were a complete waste of bad formal attire. His brother, Mathew Henderson, one of our team's top male competitors, barged into the office dramatically after his brother rushed out of the tutoring department. Like me, Mathew was a member of the BOTS Association. BOTS, or Battle of the Sexes, was a sex game performed among male and female competitors. Those at Marshall S. King University who didn't participate in the game, whom we called norms, viewed us as a normal popularity group not divided by gender, although we were. The school saw us as a regular, boring club. I never in my wildest dreams would have imagined that the dean of our university would have managed this unforgettable game. The players were and had to be attractive but resourceful scholars. It was a shame our sex assignments had to remain a secret from the norms unless they were joining the club. I thought Mathew's aggression was shocking; his narrowed eyes scorched mine, and he further displayed his fury in other ways.

Rage and agony were responsible for causing the tightness in his lips and the shakiness in his fingers. As I blinked constantly, he came closer to me. I could easily sense the bad energy coursing through his body. I found this surprising. By the look of it, Mathew needed my enlightenment for a personal reason—a reason I couldn't clarify. I saw the need in his radiant blue eyes, which, unlike everything else, looked tender and peaceful. They were glowing beautifully. I felt like a lost adolescent in a park. I was clever and articulate, but I failed to suppress my nerves, and I failed to take part in the game he was playing with me. I couldn't explain why he was confronting me inappropriately, but I found his big, muscular hands near the edge of the desk, front and center. "Hello, Erin. I have questions that need to be answered. Now, try to think calmly and rationally about the little issue—no wrong word!" he yelled, seemingly attempting to intimidate me. Then he spoke more rudely. "This is a big-ass, major issue we have here, and you will resolve it right now!"

Did he say "we"? That was where he was incorrect. He had his own bullshit to handle. That "big-ass, major issue" was his problem, not mine.

Man, he was beyond pissed. I was curious what had provoked his madness. With curiosity in my smoky-gray eyes, I briefly hesitated.

Maybe it was Amy Robinson or Dillon Moore again. Whoever it was, she wasn't me. "What the hell is your problem?" I said at full volume. His glare was unreadable. Suddenly, his mood changed, possibly because of my unnerving reaction to his unpleasantness. His eyes appeared as soft as cushions once more.

He breathed in and out as he shut his eyes, as if his brisk mediation helped the occasion. He reopened them, taking slow breaths. "I'm going to be as polite and nice to you about this as possible." His tone was lenient. His efforts stunned me for a second as he tried to subdue his craziness. He forced a smile upon his face to offer some reassurance to something uncertain even to him. Whatever the issue was, it was personal.

"Were there any unusual obligations assigned to anyone last weekend that involved me?" he said, modifying his facial expression, trying to coax information out of me. However, I was unimpressed.

"No, there weren't any special assignments approved last weekend, because the girls would have known about it!" I said, disgusted. You fucking mood swinger.

"Well, then how in the hell did this happen to me, huh?" he yelled, unzipping his cargo shorts. His unsuppressed violent behavior was visible again. This time, his anger was suitable for the occasion.

I stood. "Holy crap, Mathew!" Where was I when this happened to him? How could I have missed this current fascination—the when, where, and why—of his trapped cock in the cage?

I couldn't stop staring. I was amused by the shame and the sentencing that had been brought upon him in my absence. I had never seen a cock cage on a man before until that moment. My mouth dropped, my eyes widened, and my eyebrows rose. The excitement was building inside me. With all my strength, I managed to hold my feverishness within. Because the cock cage was on his dick, I delicately issued a prolonged observation as I wondered. What kind of pain did this entrapment inflict on his penis? How much pain would he feel if he became aroused? As I looked closer, it seemed that his penis was irritated by the silver bars surrounding it, because it gave his penis a reddish color. It was marvelous. The image of him suffering from this incident preoccupied my mind and brought a sudden, sick joy to my heart. There it was. I couldn't have managed it any longer. A spontaneous laugh escaped from me like an explosion. I pointed at his humiliation. I would have kept this secret discreet, if I were him. What was he thinking, showing me his cock trapped in a cage?

I relaxed by returning to my seat. I rested my legs on the desk in front of me while I mumbled, grinning, "I hope you're in excruciating pain. Your dick has earned the privilege to be squeezed disturbingly against every bar in that cock cage." I smiled at the thought of the pain he would feel if his dick attempted to get stiff. Mathew stared at me as if he wanted to suffocate me with his bare hands. Visualizing him choking me brought my heart an irritable and disheartening feeling, but I thought nothing of it.

I grinned more robustly. "Now that he's incarcerated, maybe you'll stop fucking everything that has a vagina." I chuckled, continuing to dig deeper under his white skin, peeling flesh from bone. "For once, it must hurt to be—"

He interrupted me, grabbing me from my seat quickly. "Oh, hell no," Mathew said belligerently, slamming me up against the wall of the tutoring center. Thank God my manager was in an important meeting and the location of this department was mainly isolated from others.

Our eyes met. His gaze was more menacing than the one I offered. Even though he was behaving immorally and had an ugly attitude, I couldn't help but appreciate his attire, which was unlike his brother's clothing. Wearing a mixture of gray and black was genius since it complemented his skin. His black-and-gray shoes were spotless. The style of his just-fucked, curly brown hair was alluring. Unlike Ricky White, Mathew had no problems pulling his hairstyle off. I had to give it to him. The idea of him working was an even greater turn-on. He was a construction worker at his father's organization and helped him run the family business. Money was never an issue for him. He was smoking hot. For an asshole, he had a strong familiarity with fashion. He knew how to dress his ass off, so one couldn't possibly miss him, not even in a large crowd of people.

"I should bash your fucking teeth in and break your damn rib cage, but I'm not going to do that because you have the key! I need to have sex, okay! I'm going crazy without it. You hear me? If I have to fuck you to get me out of this bullshit situation, then so be it. Just know that all holes apply, especially that warm mouth of yours," he said, nodding. His overdramatic, violent behavior made him an asshole. But according to Amy Robinson, he was an attractive asshole. Because of this, my subconscious spoke to me. I was far from infatuated with the idea of his penis inside my epic lips or ass.

I pleaded, "I was just messing around with you, ok? I don't have the key to your cock cage. I promise! This wasn't a part of my assignment. You have to believe me."

He shook his head in disagreement. "Don't give me any of that 'you have to believe me' bullshit! I know and you know—and I know you know that I know—you did this or you know something about this assignment. The little posse you're in was responsible! Just tell me who is in charge for junior year, dammit?" He was a fucking psycho, a complete nut job.

"You know, I'm not injudicious enough to tell you that. It's forbidden. Plus, it's against the rules of the game." I leered demonically. Mathew now had a tighter grip on my white jacket. It was brand new and my favorite.

"Leader or not, you're going to get me out of this man-hating, nonfucking bird cage! If you don't, I will be taking all my sexual frustrations out on you!"

"You don't have to invent a new name for it. Just say 'cock cage.' And come on, Mathew—be real. There is no way you can ram me with that cage on," I said, smiling rebelliously. "No way at all."

"Wipe that fucking smirk off your face!" he said.

I dimmed my unwelcome expression.

"Don't underestimate me. Believe me, Erin—I will find some way to fuck you." He released me.

Thank God. I pulled down on my jacket and straightened out the wrinkles Mathew had created. What a horny little bastard he was. He needed to learn some self-control.

Walking in the other direction, he said, "And who the fuck makes shit like this up?" Then he shut the door aggressively.

His unexpected visit aroused my suspicions. How dare Mathew accuse our team of a false allegation? I now was the leader. There were a few things I needed clarification on. I shortly organized an urgent gathering for my team members and me. I notified them that the meeting was mandatory. Through a text message, I informed them that we would hold the meeting in the school's auditorium at 7:30 a.m., in case someone had a morning class. Because I was the speaker, I had access to the keys to every door in the school, but so did the male leader.

As I situated myself on the stage, the girls were arriving. They all sat in the first two rows on the left of the auditorium.

"How did you get access to the auditorium?" Jacky Dickerson asked. I was surprised that my right-hand chick was questioning me, yet she always was the one to talk, except when it came to speaking publicly. She was a nervous but smart and stunning African American woman like me. Jacky's skin was dark caramel, and her hair was pitch black and extremely short; it stopped where her neck started. She stood about five feet tall. She kept her hair oily and her skin moist. Jacky was the kind of woman who appreciated jewelry and the colors red and burgundy. If any one of us knew what career we wanted to select, what guy we wanted to date, or what decision was best, it was Jacky.

"I thought the gym was our territory," Jacky said.

All of the girls complained and agreed. "Yeah, Erin!" they shouted. "We didn't agree on this."

What a bunch of whiners. "We didn't want this," "We didn't agree to that," and blah, blah, blah. We all knew what criticism sounded like, and they threw out only complaints. I received no "Job well done" or anything. They were so damn ungrateful, but they knew they were under my authority, and I was standing on the stage with my hands on my wide hips. I slowly walked back and forth as my posse criticized my team adjustments.

"You all know I am investing in every one of your assignments," I said. "I am slaving to make sure you all successfully complete each duty that you all are required to! You girls know this game has its advantages! It is very constructive to us all! Do you think it's clever to be near our enemy or to let them gain advantage over us? The gym is our competitors' ground and so-called territory! Are you stupid? Don't fight them for it. Let them have it! If not, you can go down to the gym and put your homework and class assignments at risk. As your new leader, I'm responsible for how well you play this game. In my opinion, though, the women are the best of the best!" I said with a serious expression. I looked my inferiors in their eyes.

I stood at the edge of the stage, hoping the girls would understand the meaning of my lecture. "I had an unwelcome visitor no more than ten minutes ago in the tutoring center. Does anybody know who or why? I mean, I'm a little bit curious myself," I said with a concerned gaze.

The virgin of the club, Angelina Smith, who some of us called Angel, beamed as she attempted to be sarcastic. I found her sarcasm to be a bit misplaced and odd, since she didn't even have a sense of humor at times—she was the most uptight one out of us all. Angel was the definition of *innocent*. The makeup she wore was soft and sometimes unnoticeable. She was the dazzling young girl next door, but she never acknowledged it. I would have thought that being a cherry blonde had something to do with her prettiness. On the contrary, Angel was unsure of herself, her dreams, and her beauty. Her skin was slightly pale, and she was about five feet seven. Her body was her temple. Unlike many of us, Angel respected and loved her body. Long skirts and buffy Sunday dresses defined her main summer attire. For the winter and fall, she had several sweaters and turtlenecks. Angel didn't like showing a lot of skin. "Jeez, well, it all depends. Was it a guy, Erin? Did he hurt you?" she joked with a half smile.

I was furious. "There is no time for fucking jokes, okay? It was a top competitor, so of course, it was a guy," I hissed. Inquisitiveness lingered on their faces as they stared at one another.

"What did this somebody want? Did he mention anything specific?" Tia Long said, scratching the back of her head. A small portion of the auditorium smelled like sweet strawberries, or it could have been cherries. Someone's perfume reminded me of the strawberry fruit snacks I had demolished when I was a child. I gradually inhaled the familiar fragrance while I looked at Tia untrustworthily. I walked off of the stage and down the aisle.

"It was Mathew Henderson!"

My team whispered his name to one another.

"He is freakishly furious for some absurd reason. Someone in this very room planted procedure three on him."

They all laughed uncontrollably. Someone's laughter was more forceful.

Amy repeated while laughing, "Procedure three. Ha-ha, his dick is trapped in a cock cage. That's some extremely funny shit!"

There was plenty I could have said about Amy. In my opinion, she was crueler than I was, yet I often found her victim role amusing, especially her desire to seek out revenge. Her irresistible light brown eyes matched the color of her long Shirley Temple curls, which made it past her shoulders. When it came to makeup, I didn't think there was a time I had seen her without it. Amy was five feet nine. As good as Amy looked, she was twice as bad. She was a crazy bitch.

Jacky composed herself. "That assignment did not get approved. The last time I checked, the cock cage most certainly wasn't meant for him."

That's my girl. At least someone was keeping up with me. "Yes, indeed, Jacky. Potentially, it was meant for the new speaker, and he is just too cool and reckless to withhold such a demand over the others. However, someone had to secretly speak to the male helper of the BOTS Association, because this individual knew she needed his assistance to get the cage on our selected competitor. This woman probably posed as me, since the male helper has not met the new female speaker. This person claimed the highest superior ranking—my superior ranking!" I frowned. "One of our teammates accepted the duty and said, 'Fuck the meaning of this obligation! Fuck this team, and you know what? Fuck that caramel-skinned cunt that refers to herself as the speaker!' I'm the new chief of this posse! Now, I'm going to ask one time and one time only. Who was involved in this?"

Tia started coughing as she stood. She looked at her imaginary watch on her right wrist. "Hmmm. Oh, darn it! Look at the time!" She made an irritating sound with her mouth. "Well, what do you know? Time flew by, didn't it, girls? My class just started. It's time to blow this Popsicle stand," she said, rushing to the exit. Tia was a white woman and a total slut, though she was the funniest one I had ever met. She barely cared about anything, especially the consequences of her actions. She would fuck anywhere at any time. Strangely, her confidence was higher than Angel's and Amy's. Sex completed her in the way that some girls felt love completed them. Her dark brown hair was the longest of us all, but mine took second place, and Angel's secured third. Tia's makeup was erotic and dramatic, her clothes were the tightest and the shortest, and her body was partially fit. To me, her ass was, however, small. Tia was five feet eight.

Amy giggled, twisting her lips. "Well, that's bullshit, because we have Internet marketing together, which starts in a few hours. What color is your watch? Because we can't see one. Well, at least I can't!" She grinned.

"Tia, get your flat ass back here, or I promise I will terminate your missions myself." I rolled my eyes briefly. She stopped instantly.

The crew readjusted their heads to scrutinize Tia's expression. Tia turned in the opposite direction to face us. She held her black Gucci purse tightly with both hands—the same purse I'd let her have. She rudely tapped her right foot, shattering the silence in the room. My eyes viewed my flawlessly polished red nails as I wondered. How could she have followed through with such a proposition? There was no way she had planned this heinous act alone. I walked up to her, cleaning my middle and index fingers with my thumb.

"You're covering for someone, aren't you? You are not bold or bright enough to pull it off alone. No offense, Tia." I coughed.

By Tia's expression and tone of voice, I could tell she resented my clarification, but she agreed. "I guess no offense taken." She shrugged.

"So who did it?" I asked.

Tia avoided my eye contact. She inspected the ceiling and floor in the room. She nibbled on her bottom lip. "I know this is difficult to believe, but I was the only genius behind this crime, so I will take the full blame for what occurred in your absence," she said.

I eyed her up and down in disgust. I escorted her out of the large space, folding my arms. "You want all of the credit for this thoughtless act? Then you got it. You're suspended until further notice." I removed my hand from Tia's shoulder and sealed the doors behind her. Although another lecture wasn't necessary, I repositioned myself back onstage. I glared with confidence to seal the deal.

Angelina said, "Why are you smiling, when we have a serious confrontation on our hands?" She shook her left leg in the chair.

"Yes! Angelina does have a point," Jacky agreed as she munched on pieces of pineapples.

I fooled around with my light brown hair, twisting my small curls with the tip of my finger. "Nothing. Mathew is looking so good today. Personally, he isn't my type, but you all know that I am intrigued by the good appearances of men. I would adore riding his handsome face." I blinked. The girls maintained their composure. I had to dig deeper into the barrel.

Amy said, "Sounds like you have an obsession to me, Erin. You should really go talk to someone—like a psychiatrist, perhaps—about your stalker-like tendencies. You don't want to end up naked and spying on a guy, because you seem like the type who hides in guys' bushes." I wasn't surprised that Amy was responding to my statement about Mathew.

I looked at the wooden floor. My shoulders fell hopelessly. I put my right palm on my forehead. "Since you're a child with a bitchy attitude and already labeled as a stalker anyway, I will ignore you. Oh my God, you guys. I forgot to tell you something important about Tia. In fact, I heard she fucked Mathew, and she has been having sex with him on the down low for almost a week now, I think!" I grinned to tease Amy.

Amy's eyebrows rose. She stood instantly. "That fucking bitch-slut nutcracker! That dirty cunt. I'm going to pull every string of her hair out," she said quickly, trying to wander off. She vulgarly brushed up against Jacky as she strolled down the aisle. She knocked Jacky's leftover pineapples on the floor during the assault. Jacky snatched her right arm determinedly.

Tia busted open the door. "That's not true! What'd I tell you about calling me dirty? I wash my ass just as much as you do. I never had sex with Matt, because I am your best friend!" She began to mutter. "I mean, I thought about it a few times on numerous occasions, but I never did, because you were always around. You see, you never gave us enough time to do anything like that anyway," she said, blinking frequently. Then she mumbled while gliding her finger across her chin, "I do wonder what the sex is like." She smacked her lips, arching her upper lip. "I don't think he's interested in buttering my muffin anyhow."

"What the hell did she say?" Amy tried to escape Jacky's custody.

"Let me go, dammit!" Amy said. She darted at Jacky. "Just let me knock her out. I promise she'll fall straight out. It'll be over before you know it," she whispered to Jacky.

"Why are you getting so worked up? It's not like you heard a word she was whispering. Plus, I'm not allowed to let you do that. You know that. We are going to get down to the bottom of this," Jacky said.

Amy smacked her lips together. She crossed her arms. "I'm not dumb or deaf. I can hear just fine."

Angelina disagreed. "Yeah, then what did she say?"

Amy hesitated. "Huh, mmm, shit, who the fuck knows? I do know that she was referring to my boyfriend, you uptight, white, lonely, dry virgin!"

Tia laughed and then waited patiently for me to respond to her. I signaled her with a head gesture. She did as I demanded and shut the door quietly.

I said confidently, "Calm down, Amy. She is definitely and most certainly not interested in Mathew. You aren't supposed to be dating him in the first place, let alone taking him seriously. I specifically ordered you not to get into a relationship with him."

"Dating him? Bitch, please. We are in love; we will be spending the rest of our lives together. We will end up having a big house, a used Lexus, and little, pretty human people." She grinned.

Oh, look at how dumb she sounds. "Just listening to the sound of your irritating voice makes me wanna cry and is starting to make my skin inch."

Jacky said, "Little, pretty human people—I think those are called children, Amy."

Angelina said, "I would like to add something. You do know that Mathew isn't the marrying or the boyfriend type, right?"

"Of course he is," Amy said, nodding.

"Apparently, you don't know the deceptions of Mathew. He was the same guy who recently threatened to stick his long john in every hole I have, my mouth included. Creatively, he is planning to do it with the cock cage on him if I don't get him out of the mess you put him in. So yes, he is the boyfriend type and a good one at that, Amy. You have such great taste in men," I said sarcastically as I clapped.

Jacky was curious. "Oh, really? How was he planning to pull that off?"

In a deep voice, I mimicked him and our prior conversation. "Isn't Amy's new man creative? He was all like, 'Believe me—I will find some way to fuck you.'"

Amy jerked her arm away from Jacky's possession. She rolled her eyes. She chewed on her gum even more. We all heard her smacking loudly from a distance. "You're a liar!" She chewed while speaking. "He would never say something like that to you while he's with me. You should be ashamed of yourself for even mentioning such a misconception. Whatever you were planning won't suffice," she said. She put her hands on her hips. I separated myself from the stage again.

I leered at her. "Look, we're all friends here despite the characters we have been assigned this year." While laughing, I said, "I was and am not planning anything against you. Nonetheless, for breaking my rules, you will end up hurt as a result of your silly and inconsiderate engagement with him."

Amy laughed at my outlandish announcement.

Angelina said, "How did you get the belt on Mathew, anyway?"

I walked up to Amy.

"Our male helper—you know, the male assistant of the game—planted it on him after he knocked him straight out," Amy answered and giggled.

Jacky glanced at Amy because she misunderstood her. "While he was sleeping? What? He actually trusted you with a key to his apartment?"

Amy searched for her dark blue Prada bag. Once she detected it, she grabbed the bag immediately off the chair. "See, you bitches get on my nerves with that 'I know Mathew' bullshit," she mentioned rudely. "That's why I don't hang with this damn team. The last time I checked, it was our apartment, okay?"

Angelina interrupted the conversation. "How did you get the guy to contribute without visual proof of the assignment?"

She snickered as we exited the auditorium. "That is where Tia came in. She provided sexual services for him."

Jacky saw that Tia was nowhere in sight. "Where did Tia wander off to?" she said, reviewing the hallways of Marshall S. King University.

We split up the moment we journeyed into the halls. I entered my classroom before my class started. When I proceeded to the rear of the classroom, the students found me conspicuous, probably because I was an important part of the most-popular group at our university. Actually, all of the popular students were involved in our famous club. As my classmates gazed upon my arrival, the sides of my mouth curled up. Thank God our new professor was also late.

Dillon Moore, an attractive white woman who was my secondary chief, was sitting in the chair next to mine. Her skin was flawless. Although Dillon possessed a look of maturity, she had just turned eighteen, and she was about five feet eleven with dark brown eyes. Dillon adored scarves and had a deep appreciation for music. Most of the time, she had headphones stuffed in her ears. Her hair was as short as Jacky's, but the front and center of Dillon's hair was about five or six inches longer than Jacky's, and her hair had streaks of burgundy and platinum. To me, what made Dillon unforgettable was her skill at applying and enhancing her beauty with a slight touch of makeup. It was never too much. Her inquisitive personality was another plus. However, when it came to love, she was the weakest of us all. Dillon, in my opinion, was easily manipulated by men, which was obviously a dangerous weakness. Dillon came off as bitchy as I did because of her bossy and stubborn attitude. Somewhere deep down within her, she was just afraid, trying to find better ways to protect herself mentally.

"So where were you? There was a meeting that brought awareness to every member, except for you, as usual." This was a time of seriousness.

She hesitated to respond. She was attending to an assignment given days ago. "As you can see, I had more major responsibilities to attend to than a meeting for your club."

I rearranged my upper body so that I could stare directly into her dark eyes. I put my hand on the edge of her desk. "You may be secondary chief, but my substantial position outperforms your small ranking. So in other words, I'm allowed to knock you off your two feet any day of the week. Just try me." I smiled. "In fact, I'll strip away all of your fucking privileges."

She narrowed her eyes at me as if I had lost my mind. Maybe I had. As she glanced at me with a devilish smile, our eyes met. Dillon's leer indicated she was faithfully testing my leadership, as if I were bluffing. She leaned closer in my direction, popping her Doublemint gum in my face. Her grin widened.

"So what did I miss, missy, that was so important?" she asked.

I slowly returned to my seat. "Amy manipulated Tia into agreeing to become sexually involved with the helper to pass the third procedure," I said.

"What was our third procedure?" she said bewilderedly.

And she called herself the team's secondary chief. "The assignment you were ecstatic about—the male chastity belt."

"Ah, yes, the famous cock cage. I remember, but let me guess. It happened over the weekend. Who was the selected competitor?"

"Mathew—Mathew Henderson, her new boyfriend. I ordered her not to go down that road," I said.

"Now, you have to keep in mind that you are the speaker. Unfortunately, not every member will listen and follow your every instruction," she said.

I quickly said, "They—or she—probably won't. As a result, they will be punished or eliminated from the games, and you know how everyone desperately desires to be a participant in our sporting event, although they know nothing of what we do."

I knew that more difficulties would eventually materialize between my team members and me. Although they yearned to achieve their assignments independently, I felt tempted by them, except for Jacky. The rest of them were trying to make my job more challenging. It only motivated me to take advantage of my dominant status by helping them through it. After the class partook in a reading exam, I immediately fell asleep. I fantasized about climaxing all over Mathew's face. Why did I think of Mathew above all of the other guys in the school and in the competition?

Oddly, James Gordon interrupted my lunch in the cafeteria. He was another top competitor and member of our popularity group. As I ate my mashed potatoes, peas, and steak with gravy, which was dry, he put his muscular hands on my smooth shoulders. He gently massaged his way down to my hips. I leered in suspense but secretly. His massage felt enticing; it seemed like an angel's touch. There was a rumor going around that he was great with his hands. My conscious mind freely admitted to the enjoyment he was providing for me. I would have never admitted that feeling out loud. James's wardrobe smelled renewed and hygienic. As he invaded my privacy, I slowly sealed my eyes. I inhaled the scent of his freshly washed garments. I loved inhaling enchanting fragrances. I joyed those few seconds of relaxation.

I finally said, "James, get your dirty hands off me!" He laughed while he sat in the seat across from me. "What do you want?" I scowled. He impolitely placed his left hand in my plate, reaching for my chocolate cake. I spanked his hand quickly. I didn't know why he was playing with me. He knew how much I loved chocolate cake. I stared at him, and James glared at me, looking at my breasts and then at my pink lips. "What, James?" I said before sipping on my Pepsi through my straw. It was cold and refreshing.

He was light skinned with tattoos marring his immaculate skin, but the colorations massively enhanced his sex appeal. His T-shirt was as white as snow, his jeans were black, and his jacket effortlessly matched the color of his pants. James's Nikes were white as well. He was six feet two and intelligent but manipulative. He took advantage of unfortunate and spiteful situations. He creatively established dilemmas and turned them into something extraordinary and beneficial for him. I knew not to get involved with him.

He seductively planted saliva on his lips by licking them. It seemed as if he were trying to seduce me. "I want you and me to settle on a constructive and resourceful agreement, one that would be satisfying for you and me," he said. He rubbed on some hand sanitizer that introduced me to a strong odor, a vanilla scent.

I deliberately ate tiny bites of my chocolate cake. I finished chewing before speaking. "What is this supposed to be—a diversion or a bullshit bargain? It won't work. Thanks, but no thanks. In fact, that's your cue to leave me alone," I said.

A sound of laughter departed from his small mouth. "I'm plotting a diversion or a scandal? Is that all you can come up with? I'm here to distract you. Yeah right, I'm not going anywhere, not until you at least hear me out. It is absolutely legitimate and simple, if you'll let me elaborate on it," he said. His infectious gaze was entangled with mine.

I nodded. "Okay. Clarify your limited proposal, will you? I'm just dying to know what you have prearranged for us," I said ironically.

Softly, we conversed. James was an advanced whisperer. Additionally, he swiftly welcomed himself into my private territory. He was sitting beside me, spoiling my left ear with his suggestions. James was freakishly courageous.

"I learned that your team was responsible for putting a cock cage on one of our teammates. Whoever this person may be, he's not talking or bringing this to our attention. For the girls, this means your posse has advanced over to the fourth task. Now, you may have developed a theory that I'm a traitor, but I'm willing to volunteer as a participant to help you."

I looked directly at him unpleasantly. *Yeah, probably for sexual favors, I bet.* "What gave you the assumption that I need any of your support? I don't even trust you with a simple outline of our project, let alone trust you enough to confide in you," I said.

His head gesture indicated a sign of agreement. "Yeah, you're right. What if I easily brought to your knowledge a hunch we have concerning the identity of your leader? What if I included the knowledge that they are planning to place a chastity belt on someone on your team even if they are not the speaker, like you guys probably did?"

Oh no, I most certainly can't allow that to happen. This dispute had gotten more serious. A critical problem had emerged. I attempted to conceal my concerned expression. Should I call out another urgent gathering? Should I agree to an unfamiliar prearrangement and possibly put my team in jeopardy of a punishment? Unsure what to do, I scratched the back of my neck. Furthermore, I was uncertain about his intentions.

I breathed out. "What would you desire in favor in return?"

He grinned, and I watched as the sides of his mouth curled up. "Give me Tia," he said after swallowing a mouthful of Coca-Cola out of a can.

I stood in revulsion. "What the hell do you mean by 'Give me Tia'?" I said, mimicking him. "She doesn't have a shiny red bow glued to her fucking head. There isn't any snow outside. I refuse to pass her along. She's not a damn Christmas gift you pass along to guys!" I said.

I couldn't stop myself. I kept babbling. He laughed and then grinned wickedly. I stood over him, trying to restore my breath. Preparing to leave the lunch table, James patted me on the back. He dismissed the ruckus I had caused.

"Calm down. Calm down. Everything will be all right. Just relax, and don't get all worked up for nothing," he said in a soft tone. "I'm so sorry, and you're right—how rude of me. She's not a damn Christmas gift. In my eyes, she needs to be treated better than that. That is why it would be much, much better if she was my birthday gift instead, since it's right around the corner," he said. "What do you say, huh? Do this for me. Trust me. You're going to need a guy friend on your side."

I thought about it all as he exited the cafeteria. As I dumped my tray, his offer was on my conscience for the remainder of the day. Would I honestly take James's settlement into consideration? Well, dammit, I would. His offer did sound desirable. He was apparently a traitor, no doubt about it. If we collaborated on a proposition, I would be a traitor as well. My mind repeatedly replayed his words proposing the idea of exchanging Tia for two assignments. Would that make a huge difference to Tia? Under those circumstances, maybe she would agree without knowing what I had done. We had done countless unacceptable things. This was just the start of it.

CHAPTER 2

Tia

A Visit to Mathew's

I was comfortable with my sexuality. But because I was less discreet about my sexual affairs than the other women around me were, my reputation preceded me. The norms of Marshall S. King University respected and looked up to the rest of the members of our popularity club, and I wanted the same treatment and honor, but instead, they belittled and disrespected me, especially the women. It didn't matter that I was one of the highest-playing participants our junior year. One could have said that my careless but erotic behavior was responsible for my messy reputation. Things like having sex or going down on a guy in a bathroom stall steered my status in the wrong direction. Additionally, some students and members might have said I abused the meaning of the word *sex*. Angelina said that for me, "Sex had lost its meaning." I was having what she believed to be reckless sex with Latino, white, and black men, like it didn't matter to me. Well, she was right. It didn't trouble me one bit.

I never noticed how much sex I was having until someone finally told me to take a long look in the mirror. In my eyes, I was experimenting. My sexual engagements were fun and harmless. Sex wasn't dangerous. Sex was hot and amusing. It was funny that my mother used to tell me, "You're not living until you have convinced yourself to live dangerously." I was sure she wasn't referring to sex, but I thought, *I only live once, right?* What was wrong with that? Yet for three special sophomore girls, everything was wrong with my sexual acts, but men were like automobiles to me. I loved taking automobiles for long rides, since causal sex was all I desired. I felt that love was useless because love was how people got their little hearts broken. Without love involved,

I wouldn't cry, feel any pain, or break down pathetically, as women in love did in the movies when they found out the truth about the guys of their dreams. From my perspective, relationships and faithfulness were things that didn't exist.

At that time, I couldn't help that sex was my drug of amusement. During those hours, I felt as if I couldn't survive without it, as if I needed it all the time. All I wanted was a nice, big dick inside of my wet walls. I often saw my sexual relationships as a way to stay in shape as well. The only negative outcome from having too much sex was being called a whore or, in my case, the slut of the school. Every woman was a slut, in my book. Because I was more honest about my actions, I was a ho. What did I do in public that those other little bitches didn't do in private? Everyone did slutty things every once in a while, to God only knew how many people. Shamefully, some people were embarrassed, while others, like me, were not. If men and other girls didn't judge women, I felt they would have slept around more than they did already. Yet no other man or woman would have cared about being called something offensive. I loved having sex, and I wasn't ashamed of it. It was what they hated most about me, though—my carefree attitude and reckless behavior. But in my opinion, my behavior gave them no position to judge me. Or perhaps they'd never heard the saying "Never judge a book by its cover." Girls continued to mistreat me. I would stroll down the hallways, and those same three bitches proceeded to throw more gasoline on the fire. As their rumors about me increased, their names escaped me, because I could never recall them, or maybe I just felt they were that insignificant.

I ignored the rumors that the girls spread to incite chaos. They were jealous of my carelessness and me, but the loud commotion of my high heels click-clacking against the tile floors helped me to glance straight ahead while they muttered psychobabble bullshit. I thought they hated the way I acted and the way I talked. It seemed to me that their ice-cold shoulders and attitudes also came from my choice of attire. I wore short skirts, half tops to expose my firm abs, and small dresses to piss them off further, and it did more than I had ever imagined. My appearance was intriguing. I believed my long, dark hair and clear skin had something to do with it. My pierced ears and belly button enhanced my physical look, especially my luxurious features.

I despised school with a passion. I found myself leaving regularly. I guess it was childish to have my teammates in suspense about my whereabouts. The sex assignments that the girls were planning to execute were nothing compared to the men's duties. I knew it. I bet the boys' tasks were fun and witty. Since the male competitors already had my interest, I wanted to give them my devotion. Their assignments appeared to be more challenging than the girls', or maybe I liked them more because they were men. As a matter of fact, if it weren't for the opposite sex, I wouldn't have wasted my precious time dealing with depressed instructors, stressful homework, or classroom assignments. Our regular work was fucking boring, and it sucked. Angelina wanted to make the normal work easier for me. I was convinced that a little tutoring was what she had in mind. Instead, she gave me the answers to most of the quizzes and tests we took. She didn't mind letting me cheat off of her, which came as a shock to me, but the boring times I was spending in class were not. One day, I was so bored that I was banging my head on my desk because I was imprisoned in my biology class.

"It would be quicker if somebody just killed me already," I said aloud as my migraine developed. Above everything, I still hated Angelina for what she was: a virgin.

Eventually, biology came to an end. I swiftly ran to the door before I died of boredom. Entering the hallways, I examined Mathew and Michael Harrison conversing outside of my classroom. I was partly curious about the topic of their conversation. Had Mathew finally become exhausted with his situation enough to make some alterations? If so, this meant drama for his girlfriend, Amy Robinson, and me. I marched up to the two competitors. I couldn't stop looking at Mathew Henderson. I stood facing them both as their scents invaded my nostrils. One of their colognes was more robust than the other, but I still liked both of the fragrances.

"So the two of you are undoubtedly plotting something diabolic against us. What is it?" I said, wrapping strings of my hair around my finger.

Mathew looked me up and down in repulsion, as if the sight of my existence made him sick or something. I feared he was still angry with me for helping Amy. Yet the assault wouldn't have been my desire. He immediately wandered off in a different direction. He oddly walked down the hall, holding his private parts. He widely parted his legs, as if segregating them would support his imprisoned cock. At least that was what I believed. His penis surely wouldn't be piercing my pussy anytime soon, I thought to myself. Eventually, he would have been fucking me soon. I forgot Michael was beside me—he believed I was ignoring him on purpose, which I was, but that was not the point. Fantasizing about Mathew had me preoccupied. Michael's existence was never any of my concern—my fantasies of Mathew were my main concentration. Suddenly, he snapped his fingers in my ear to gain my undivided attention.

"I said can you take me to Mathew's house so I can grab my wallet?" he said, arranging his hands in front of my face. How rude, right?

I said aggressively, "Hell no! I can't do shit for you. Ask Mathew. It is his apartment, remember? Or did you forget that?" I said, bolting down the hall. Michael was walking beside me. *Oh my God. Please harass someone else! Go away. Go away, please.*

"Don't you think I asked him already?"

Please stop talking to me, Michael, because I really didn't care. I rolled my eyes as he informed me of Mathew's unsettling behavior.

"He's got issues, and he's also been frustrated and cranky for no reason. We can't figure out what the hell's his problem."

Oh, there is a reason all right, you dumbass.

"It's not like I care personally—his problems are his problems. I have my own shit to deal with."

Mathew had allowed his predicament to overcloud his judgment. His friends would have surely laughed and joked about our female victory. But the boys, without a doubt, would have been supportive and a great deal of assistance, since a bunch of heads was greater than one. Whatever made my job easier was fine with me. Lesser work was always a step away from complications, yet this vulnerability would have brought me a step closer to my own triumph.

"Even if I could drive you there, I can't, because I don't have a car," I said.

He stopped. "Well, thanks anyway. You've been helpful," he said sarcastically.

I peeped back at him. I looked into his eyes. The disappointed expression on his face produced a feeling of generosity in me. It wasn't his fault Mathew was being a hypersensitive bastard. Secretly, the fault was mine to carry. I shook my head. This was a fucking trap designed by Mathew. I knew it. It had to be. I guess Mathew had wanted me after all, so I decided to play his little game for now.

"I'm not promising you anything. You got that? I'll see what I can do for me. I mean you."

He smiled from ear to ear.

Aw, wow, now you're smiling.

Other than Mathew, I couldn't figure out why I would foolishly go along with their scandal. I didn't even like Michael, and there was no way I wanted his tongue or you-know-what anywhere near me. I couldn't help but believe this as I sat down in Philosophy 447, another unstimulating classroom. I was just trying to get closer to Mathew by helping Michael obtain his so-called wallet. I covered my face for a moment and sat behind Dillon. She looked kind of decent in her little long-sleeved dress. It was a denim button-down shirtdress with a collar and side pockets, and she wore a black leather belt. I turned to the side and found Angelina in the seat to my right, wearing a light pink turtleneck and a pair of white jeans. Boy, did she love her sweaters and turtlenecks. I then looked straight ahead as I listened to the silence in the classroom. Though it was only the first week of school, I needed to get the hell out of there. I had only entered the class no more than five minutes ago to get Dillon's car keys. While Dillon was working on one of her BOTS Association projects, I kept glancing at her purple handbag.

She was so into finishing her assignment that the keys to her red Lexus ES 350 were now in my custody. My glare traveled over to Angelina, who appeared to be having some abdominal pain. She turned to her right to lay her head on her desk. She started to fall asleep while

Professor Turner wrote our assignments on the board. I crept to the exit, and then I left the building. I sent a message to Michael's cell phone. Afterward, I waited outside by Dillon's car for him. As I watched him leave Marshall S. King University, I kept thinking about Mathew and his hard cock going in and out of me—and the whole situation with him having his dick trapped in a cock cage. I opened the car door, climbed in, and put on my seat belt.

Michael accompanied me. He shut the passenger's door and pulled down his seat so that he could get more comfortable. I started the car and drove off. As I breathed in and out, I inhaled Dillon's new-car smell. It was nice, and during our travels, all of my thoughts were purely sexual. When I stopped at red lights, I glanced down at Michael's crotch without him noticing. I cleared my throat again and again. I was curious about the size of his penis but not because I was interested. I was in a state of wonder. My hormones sometimes had a way of manipulating my mind and arousing me in the craziest ways. Was his cock big or small? I rolled the windows down. I was feeling hot. My body was sweating—in between my thighs mainly. *Dammit.* The cool breeze from the window didn't do anything for the warmness under my sky-blue skirt. To take my mind off of things, I stared out the window instead of at his crotch. Mathew lived in a beautiful and friendly neighborhood. The people in his community cared about keeping their neighborhood safe. His block seemed peaceful, and Mathew's street was the cleanest block in their community. He lived in a one-story apartment that had other residences attached to both sides. Michael warned me to slow down, as we were about to reach our destination. Finally, Michael told me to stop. I listened and turned off the car. We exited, and I locked the doors. I waited for Michael to show me the way. I watched him grab Mathew's house keys from out of his right back pocket. He eased closer to an apartment made of gray brick that had white windows and a beige Welcome Home mat by the door. Michael unlocked the glass storm door and then the door to his apartment.

Mathew's apartment looked like a home that a fabulous carpenter or a home designer had recently finished. He had antique hardwood bamboo flooring; creamy beige walls; white windowsills; and beautiful, long dark brown single-panel polyester blackout curtains in every window. For a one-bedroom apartment, his home was larger than I'd expected. He had done well for his first apartment, and I was secretly impressed by every foundation and detail of his home, especially his furniture set. In Mathew's living room, he had a stunning North Shore living-room set and a large light brown rug in the center of his floor. I walked into the kitchen, which was a tad small, but I figured Mathew had made it his dream kitchen somehow. I wasn't shocked to see a black kitchen-table set. The table and chairs gave his home a casual and contemporary style. His apartment was my dream home. Everything was intact. There was only one thing missing from the equation: me. When Matt and I were little, we'd planned to share a home like a happy family. I would go on and on about how I wanted bamboo flooring: single-panel polyester blackout curtains and a North Shore living room set for my first apartment. His home equipment explained the details of my dream home. The details of his apartment were ideas he stole from me. Instead of living together, I was not included. This was a situation decked out for him and Amy. As I roamed Mathew's apartment, wishing it belonged to us, I dreamed that we were living in a home exactly like this one.

"Thanks for giving me a ride. I really appreciate it."

Aw, shut the fuck up. He could cut the whole "I appreciate it" act. It was phony. I knew he'd brought me there to fuck me. Michael wouldn't appreciate my kindness until he was in between my thighs. Maybe because Michael had given me the opportunity to see where Mathew laid his head, I would give Michael the closeness and compassion he was attempting to trap me for, but this agreed intimacy would be a game of my choosing.

I knew he was speaking, yet I wasn't listening to a single word that left his mouth. He continued babbling. Inspecting Mathew's home was my occupation, and Michael searched for his supposed-to-be-missing wallet. I searched for Mathew, though he wasn't there. I then looked into his bedroom. By the looks of it, it was the cleanest area in the apartment. Mathew had a large bed with silky black sheets. The dresser appeared brand new, and his two nightstands were new as well. In the center of his tile floor was a glass table holding his thirty-two-inch flat-screen TV. There were pictures of him and his family in the center of his dresser. I speedily detached my silver-laced sandals from my feet. I shut my eyes, smiling.

I touched his cold, silky black sheets, attempting to create warmth. I gently slid onto his bed, spreading his cover and sheets over me. With my eyes shut while underneath his cover, I undid my black nylon-and-spandex lace-back push-up bra and slid down my sexy, strappy black Chantilly lace thong. In the background, I could hear Michael babbling again. Despite the fact that he was calling my name, I proceeded to stay in my world of imagination. I was reminiscing about my last sexual encounter. I got utterly aroused, breathing substantially. I couldn't resist the temptation. Small noises left my mouth as I separated my legs. I couldn't resist the urge to touch myself. The moment I fantasized about Mathew's solid and lengthy dipstick inside my kitty cat, I was awfully wet, basically heated.

I bit my bottom lip. My masturbating had matured to the anticipation of being fucked or rammed toughly by Mathew. *Whoa, yes.* I extended my fingers on my left hand inside my slippery walls, and how slippery they were. The other hand was massaging my clitoris.

I spit on my fingers, and I then rubbed the top of my pussy smoothly. I whispered a bit. "Hmmm, yes. Yes. Oh my." In the process of playing with my honeypot, I sucked on my perky, small breast as I groaned. "Ohhhh, my sweet Mathew."

I stopped the movements of my hands the second I heard the bedroom door squeak. I knew Michael was watching me. I had counted on it. My eyes searched for him. He was staring at me from the doorway. As I concealed my body with the cover and sheets, he walked into the room.

"Get the hell out, Michael!" I continued to secure everything.

He smirked. "Stop fronting. You knew I was watching long before your reaction. Plus, you haven't even finished cumin'." He bit his lip. "Please don't stop on my account," he said, yanking the cover and sheets from my grip.

I reluctantly shook my head, trying to keep my body parts sacred, and said, "You got your stuff. Now, let's just go."

He shook his head, glancing down at me. What a stare. He exposed his chest, removing his gray button-up shirt. His pistol was completely stiff, and it was sticking out of his pants. *Lordy, Lord, Lord, Lord, why me?* He certainly wasn't small either.

"You didn't think I would let you leave without fucking you, did you?" he said, unfastening his zipper, watching me.

I thought to myself that this was the scenery I needed. "I'm not in the mood."

He jerked on my legs to pull me closer to him. "Yeah right, Tia. I heard you are always in the mood to fuck."

I told you my reputation preceded me, but nobody wanted to listen to me.

I involuntarily wrapped my legs around his torso. His stare was courageous. I begged once more. "Please don't, Michael," I murmured. I loved to plead against the occurrence of an affair I secretly yearned for.

"Stop begging me not to do something you obviously love." He laughed.

Aw, dammit, he knew. How did he know?

He didn't listen to me. He kissed my oversensitive neck. His kissing technique was sweetly tempting and dominated the slut in me. In other words, I was fucked—royally fucked. *Oh my Lord, not the tongue. Not the licking, sucking, and swirling of his wet and fragile tongue.* My vulnerability emerged when a simple touch, kiss, or lick was brought upon my skin.

Michael whispered into my ear, "If you're the girl I hear you are, then resistance isn't a suit you wear well. You like saying no and pretending. You and I know you want it. Just submit since you will eventually."

I listened because pretending was a waste. I showed proof of submission in my gaze. There was no denying something my body was aching for. He bit on my thoroughly hardened, perky, small, Hershey-shaped nipples. I groaned, "Hmm." I did what I did best. I was positioned on my knees, caressing his thrill drill back and forth with my right hand.

I licked my bottom lip. "Tell me what you want me to do with him," I said.

He controlled my head with his left hand. "Ohhh, baby—you know what I like," he said with a smile.

I touched myself once more. "Whoa! Say it to me. Tell me you want me to suck it," I muttered. "I wanna hear you say it to me."

He forced his stick into my mouth and said, "Stop talking. And suck on my—ohhh!" I silenced him with my superior technique. His large banana befriended the deep, wet, dark corners of my warm mouth as I kept spitting on his dick and sucking on his balls. He tilted his head back, especially when I was deep-throating his dick, taking him all in. His eyes were relaxed. My hands were planted on his legs, which were moving around in response to the pleasure he was receiving. I loved that I was causing him to shake like a bitch.

"That's, um, good. Ahhh." It was difficult for him to structure a sentence. His words were shaky. "Oh, fuck." He moaned. The sound of his dick leaving and reentering my mouth was an honorable announcement.

"You like that?" I said, giving him the nastiest blow by blow. He shoved me onto the bed. Suddenly, he smacked the outer layer of my wet muffin with his big prick.

"Yes, I liked that. You feel so, so good." With his shaft gliding against and massaging my clit, I got even wetter. I was leaking onto his sheets badly.

Enough with the teasing already—just fuck me. I began breathing heavily again. "Just fuck me! Dammit!" I said, grabbing the back of his neck. He grinned. He entered me with command and deliverance. My pussy was slippery. I loved how she never disappointed. I put both of my legs on his shoulders so that his prick could serve a greater purpose.

He groaned in my left ear, but his groans were minor noises competing against my mournful cries. "Um, hmm, yes, yes, I want every inch of you!" He, thank God, went deeper and deeper inside me. My voice stretched to a high pitch. It expanded higher and higher.

I cried out, "Oh, sweet, sweet Jesus!"

The bed squeaked. The headboard went into battle with Mathew's beige walls. When Michael stroked left to right, his balls came into contact with my anus. "Yes!" the whore in me screamed. Sweat trickled down our bodies. We were inhaling and exhaling, begging to restore our lost breath. His movements were quick. He fucked me roughly and recklessly, and I enjoyed every minute of it. Michael was exhausted. I laid my fingers on his cheeks to motivate him to accelerate his speed. He did as I desired. My kitty cat purred to the readjustment. I laughed momentarily, attempting to obscure the fact I was a little embarrassed by the sound. I screamed repeatedly. My legs quivered uncontrollably. My body hardened. All thoughts were motionless. Nothing mattered but my spectacular climax. The withdrawal was a liberated one.

He collapsed beside me. Silence surrounded us, except for Michael's breathing, which was a disturbance during my moment of relaxation. His hands were on his chest, and his eyes were shut. I appreciated Michael's presence during sex, but sadly, being around Michael or any other guy after sex got to me badly, like an itchy spot on my back that I had to scratch. Some might have said that this meant I regretted it or got caught up in the heat of the moment. Besides this little voice in my mind, I couldn't break free from the feeling of remorse. I ran to the bathroom to erase all evidence of what had just occurred. Washing my belly with a washcloth wouldn't exactly cleanse away my faults. While I was running a hot bubble bath, Michael startled me. He knocked on the door for my attention. I jumped. I twisted the knob and opened the door wildly and found a welcoming drink of water on the other side of the door.

Michael stretched out his right arm. "I know you're probably dehydrated, so here you go. You must be thirsty."

Without hesitation, I seized the water and slammed the door. After I got what I wanted, I couldn't stand being around him, and Michael was the third person I'd had sex with in the group. Michael was a cute white boy who wore too much cologne sometimes. His blond hair ceased at his shoulders. He stood about six feet tall. He wore jackets with hoods on them, long shorts, and his favorite gold chain around his neck. He wore a lot of dark colors, which went with his dark brown eyes. His humorous character helped his popularity and his designation as a participant his sophomore year at Marshall S. King University.

I swallowed a mouthful of water before getting into the tub. Soaking in the hot, steamy water, I could visualize what Erin and Dillon would say if they tricked me into another one of their interventions: "You can't seem to keep your legs or mouth shut, can you? I don't think you can get any sluttier." I sipped on the remainder of the water in the glass. Eventually, when I was finished, I tried to reach for the long red towel touching the sink. I fell because there was no rug on the bathroom floor. I heard Michael laughing at me.

"Are you okay?" He chuckled.

I responded, "Yeah, hmm, I'm fine."

The floor was slippery. The mirror was foggy, and the room was steamy from the hot water. Leaving the bathroom, I felt weak and lightheaded, and my vision was blurry. I stumbled up against the walls, barely making it back to Matt's room. At that moment, I stumbled over my own two feet. Unexpectedly, Mathew saved me from my fall. I was distracted by his exquisiteness. I touched his smooth face. I had known he would come—well, sooner or later.

I was trapped in his mesmerizing, gorgeous blue eyes. I delivered an apologetic smile for my former action. I hoped he would smile back at me in forgiveness. Mathew smiled innocently at me. At last, he'd accepted my apology for the cock cage we'd planted on him. My heart was beaming with content. She was grinning proudly, and I was a character in his romance movie, a film only he knew the ending to. I attempted to move, but my body was exhausted. My eyes had grown outrageously heavy. For some reason, I couldn't stand up straight. Mathew acknowledged my struggle, so he scooped me up and carried me to his bed. Michael had done something to me—he'd put something in my glass of water. *That little bitch.*

"Where is Michael? He drugged me, Mathew," I said, holding my head.

Leaving the bed, I tried once more to make a sudden movement. Instead, I ended up on the floor. Michael bolted out of the bathroom, wet and glistening, with long black shorts on. They had silver and blue lines on both corners. He aggressively situated me on his right shoulder and threw me back onto the bed. My head was dizzy. The dizziness advanced into a migraine. I had had enough with being tossed the fuck around.

He grinned for a second time. "I just contributed a little something to knock you out for a little while. That's all. Don't worry."

I shook my head in shame. My eyes inspected Mathew. He was comfortably leaning against the wall, inches away from his desk. He was calm, cool, and collected. My wrath reached the surface.

Mathew pouted and became hostile. "I guess I'm supposed to be sympathizing over your situation. I think you look exceptionally contained, I might add. Did you really think I was going to let what you and Amy did just go?" he said, holding his crotch.

I proceeded with negativity. "Fuck you—the both of you." What was the worst Matt and Michael could possibly do to me? Nothing shocked me. Who knew? Maybe I would relish it. I grinned. Mathew massaged my scalp with his fingers.

Mathew chuckled. "Oh no, never. It's not sex."

He wasn't telepathic. How did he know what I was thinking? It must have been my flirtatious smile. I pouted. *Dammit. Dammit. So close, but not quite.* "What are you going to do to me?" I said.

"It's nothing fun, Tia. Too bad you won't be conscious to see it," Michael announced.

My eyes lost the battle against the endless feeling to sleep. I kept falling in and out of consciousness. The next morning, I couldn't remember much. Not knowing what had happened was scary and frustrating. I woke up in my bedroom with my all-white pajamas on, although I enjoyed sleeping naked. When I moved briefly, I discovered something disturbing. My hands were on my pussy. *Oh, Jesus Christ, holy cow.* I screamed myself into a migraine. I screamed at the top of my lungs again and again for about ten seconds. A few minutes later, I started searching my room for Mathew's assignment. Maybe they had gotten so big headed that they'd taken the written paper with them. *What a bunch of dumbasses.*

Eventually, looking on my light pink desk, I retrieved the paper stating an assignment. The duty had been greater than I, because of my feelings for Mathew, in my opinion. In fact, I'd failed to successfully stop a competitor from finalizing his mission. They'd collaborated on an assignment against me. At the bottom of the sheet, my signature was required. I grabbed my favorite black pen and unhappily wrote my signature on the line. If I wasn't in trouble before, I was in trouble now. I would probably get punished for this. My decisions had jeopardized everything we'd worked for.

At least I'd found out one thing: Michael wasn't the guy I was looking for, the guy with the gray scorpion tattoo on the lower half of his stomach. He and I had unfinished business to discuss regarding Amy's lies and misbehavior. I took a look underneath my pajama pants and saw a T-shaped stainless-steel female chastity belt with a highly adjustable waist size. I tried my best to get out of it, yet removing the belt was impossible without having the key in my possession. I cried and shook as I tightly squeezed the first gold lock on the stainless steel, aggravated. This bullshit between us and the boys wasn't over by a long shot!

CHAPTER 3

Angelina

Sun-Death

I could hear them outside my closed window that beautiful September morning. I smiled while I quickly opened my eyes and strolled to my large window to open it. I continued to leer with the feeling of the acceptable weather pressing against my skin. I listened to the small birds chirping in a particular pattern and rhythm that sounded like music to my ears. It was like a song they were singing only to me, and it was a wonderful sound to wake up to at nine o'clock in the morning. Their art aided me in getting out of my full-size bed. Normally, my alarm clock would do me justice, but that day was different. I couldn't help but feel blessed and jolly. While the hot water ran in my tub, I slowly stripped out of my red Mickey Mouse pajamas and my panties that said "Welcome, Mickey." I looked at my nakedness in the huge mirror in my bathroom, which was connected to my bedroom.

As beautiful and popular as I was, I should have been having tons of crazy, stupid fun in college, but I wasn't having any fun at all. I was bored at the time, and people had the nerve to say that the students with the most popularity points were the most liked and lively scholars in the school. But of course they would mention something as silly as that. Stupidly, they believed everything they heard from us and other norms. *What a bunch of idiots,* I thought as I stopped the water before it overflowed. I buried myself in the tub. Out of all of us, Tia was the wildest, especially when it came to sex. Knowing her made me happy to know who I was, because for me, there was nothing wrong with being a virgin. I understood the difference between the slut, Tia and me, the virgin. I knew what everyone in the groups, male and female, were thinking about me. Why would a virgin join a secret sex club, especially with my sentimental thoughts about losing my virginity to someone who wouldn't cause me to regret it? Well, every woman that's fucking started off as a virgin like me. *What was wrong with being untouched and wanting and waiting to give my virginity to someone breathtaking?* I thought as I soaked my almost-flawless skin. Oh, what I would have done to have dreamy, lovable skin. I grabbed my white bar of mild soap and began scrubbing my face, arms, back, legs, breasts, and behind. I soaked for a half hour. I got out of the tub, gathered my belongings, and threw them onto my bed.

I slid on a short white dress that hugged my body and stretched the length of it from the bottom. There were shiny silver buttons on the left side of it. *How cute.* They gave the dress more of a personality. I put on my see-through heels with straps tied to my ankles. Pinning up my hair was the finishing touch. That style was endearing to me. I peeked into my spotless mirror, brushing my white teeth and then rinsing my mouth out with Listerine. I yanked my white jacket off the hanger in my closet, and I scooted to grab my big white purse from under my bed. I left immediately. Guys were staring at me in a way I had never been exposed to before. It was inconvenient for me. I liked to think my dress had something to do with the attention I was receiving. I wasn't used to hot guys looking in my direction. It felt astonishing to be seen. The sun was shining, and the wind was exceptional. Boy, I was feeling gorgeously confident. While waiting at the bus stop, I noticed Dillon sitting on the bench.

"Dillon! Hey, Dillon, over here," I said, but she gave no response, so I snatched her blue headphones out of her ears.

"What the hell, Angel? They are fragile!" Her voice was sad and antagonizing—what a mixture. "If you break them, you will be paying for them. I promise you!" She stood with a malicious expression. I slid closer to her with my hand on her shoulder.

"What's wrong, Dillon? Because I know you're not really angry about me snatching some cheap headphones out of your ears."

She looked at the ground. "Tia's what's wrong with me! She stole my fucking car keys right out of my purse yesterday like it was nothing for only God knows why!" she whined.

I understood why she was upset with Tia. "Yeah, she was surely in the wrong, but you know Tia will give them back to you, right?" I rested my right hand on her back.

"You're damn right the little cunt is giving them back to me. I'm just so sick and tired of her thinking the world revolves around her overextended vagina or her ass, which is probably overflowing with semen right now!" she said with narrowed eyes. "I kept texting and calling her cell phone. The little human blow-up doll just kept rejecting and ignoring me. Don't worry about it, though. I have something very special planned for Tia—the semen holder!" Her tone was vengeful. I said, "Something planned for her—Dillon—like what?"

She nodded. "She will definitely see."

I removed my right hand because my iPhone 5 started vibrating in my purse. I struggled as I searched to find it. I sat on the bench, and Dillon followed me as she sat alongside of me while I continued searching for my phone. "Who is it—one of our teammates?" she asked.

I pulled it out of my purse yet refused to view it with Dillon over my shoulders. She was nosy. I wanted to tell her to mind her business. I didn't, though.

I frowned. "One of our teammates? How do you know it isn't a guy who's texting me, Dillon?"

She giggled. "Are you having sex or plan on doing it anytime soon?"

I bit my lip and then smiled. "Uh, yeah, I'm not a virgin anymore. James and I went out during the summer, and it just kind of happened so quickly." *Damn, what was I thinking? Jeez.* It was the first but worst name that clouded my brain. Dillon glanced at me as if my response were unbelievable.

She twisted her lips up at me. She gave me the stupidest look ever, as if I were lying. "It just happened, huh? Right out of the blue? You are having sex with James Gordon?"

"Yes! Don't tell anyone, because I am trying my very, very best to keep this a secret, Dillon," I confessed. "You have to know that James is amazing!" I yelled with pleasure. "Oh my and that tongue, hmm," I said, shaking my body as if I had the chills.

She snickered. Speedily, Dillon said, "You are still a virgin, aren't you?"

"Yeah, pretty much," I responded immediately while nodding and shrugging. She and I rose, as the bus was approaching. I took a quick peek at my text message from Andrew Walker, the sexiest one of them all. He was twenty-two years old and a perfect distraction for women like me. He was white and had small lips. They were definitely kissable, and that skin of his was perfection. His eyes were green like Smokey Robinson's. Green was one of my favorite colors, so his eyes were dreamy to me. His face was pleasantly structured. His expression was the definition of purity, but his personality was sexy and confident, and his body was athletic.

Let every member from the team know we need to have a coed meeting at 7:30 a.m. in the gym to discuss complications. We will end this assignment in sun-death.

Dillon and I found our way to the back of the bus, where Erin sat. Walking toward Erin, I kept thinking about Andrew's message. He had to be texting me straight-up bullshit. There wasn't going to be a sun-death, because it was very rare. Sun death was an opportunity for teams to retrieve more credit added to their additional points. Sun-death only occurs if a male and female opponent is influenced by the same assignment at the same time, like having a male and female chastity belt, situated on both of the players. From my knowledge, we didn't have a member that had on a female chastity belt so it had to be a lie. Because of this, I thought nothing of it.

Erin chuckled. "Dillon, you're the last person I expected to see on the bus. Where's your car?"

I crossed my legs and sat beside Erin. Dillon, on the other hand, sat quite a distance away. "Long story short, someone in the group is stealing shit that doesn't belong to her."

When the bus driver stopped at the next destination, a homeless man boarded the bus but didn't pay for public transportation. *When in the hell did bus drivers start letting people on the bus for free?* My eyes traveled to the front of the bus, which wasn't crowded. He and the driver had a short conversation. All I could see were their moving mouths. Judging by their mannerisms, they must have been acquainted already. After their dialogue, the man came limping toward the other customers. I noticed he had a small supposed-to-be-white cup in his hand. He was limping as if he were suffering from a recent injury. As he pleaded for change, he shook his cup to steal the attention of others. The passengers refused to be of any assistance. They were everything but courteous. What a shameful world it was. As he passed, people looked disgusted by the awful smell he carried. Many secured their noses in their hands or jackets. The shaking of his cup progressed.

The black homeless man only had one dirty brownish shoe; the other one, on the left side, was missing in action. His dark gray sock exposed a gigantic hole that was publicizing his big toe to the world. His brown shirt was torn, as if he'd recently had a fight, and his hair was as nappy as could be. His clothes were sabotaged by stains, and his pants were badly ripped at the bottom. Finally, he reached the rear of the bus. I knew Erin would cause a needless commotion. She thought homeless people were revolting. To make matters worse, he stopped in front of her, yet she seemed distracted by something of more importance on her BlackBerry. It wasn't a shocker that Erin's reaction was overly dramatic and ill mannered. Her expression was demonic and strong.

She suddenly tightened her lips in an unattractive way. "Oh Lord, what the hell is that dreadful stench?" she said seriously. Erin looked up at him standing right over her. "Oh, oh, hi." She forced a glare upon her face. I glared at her, giving her an "Are you stupid or something?" look. Continuously, he shook his cup.

He was grinning while he danced, shaking the cup. "Please," he begged. "Please spare change." His voice was serene. Erin suffocated him with her smoky gray eyes.

I whispered to Erin, "Are you giving him some change or not?"

She mumbled, “Hell no—for what?” She was now holding her nose with her hand. “Why do I have to give his smelly ass some money? Why can’t he give me some change?”

“He’s homeless. You’re not, stupid.” I said.

She rolled her eyes, twisting her lips upward, and then she smacked them together. “You don’t know that shit. He probably was just swimming in a pool of money. His ass was maybe more likely rolling around in the dirt outside. He probably has more money than you and me put together.” Erin again smirked at him while she continued to babble. “But you want me to make his ass richer. I bet he owns a nice car parked a few blocks away, too. Your white ass can give his homeless-pretending ass some change if you want to.”

She properly crossed her legs. Her lecture was downright not surprising, yet it wouldn’t register in my brain. I couldn’t believe the way she was belittling him. There was no way that babbling speech had come from her mouth.

She smirked into the homeless man’s face while whispering to me, “I’m just not giving him any of my hard earnings.”

I laughed. “Hardworking money from where—working in the tutoring center?” I smacked my lips. “We all know the real hard earnings are your mother’s money.” I snickered.

“Actually, if my sorry excuse of a mother can work her old ass off, he can, too. And even though that lying bitch has all that money, I don’t want one red cent of it!” She folded her arms.

The homeless man reacted as if he’d observed every word Erin spoke. Erin purposely ignored him, hoping he would take his business elsewhere. He penetrated her with his distasteful eyes. Their expressions were reciprocal. To diffuse the hostility between them, I generously placed twenty dollars in his hand.

He was still standing over Erin. He now smiled in her face. “And, ho, please—I didn’t roll around in dirt. I don’t have a pool filled with money or a car parked a few blocks away, so that was an insult. It’s one block away, I have two pools of money, and this dirt was specially manufactured for me, you little bitch. You’re broke anyway,” he murmured. He then shortly proceeded elsewhere. Erin's cloudy grays reunited with my baby blues. I shrugged.

"I fucking told you, I told you, I told you. His African-American ass is loaded. He's probably on his way home, planning to wipe his balls clean with your twenty dollar bill. And I bet you want your money back, don't you?" She shook her head, folding her arms.

I coughed. I didn't know what to believe. "Girl, you upset him. I would have lied to you, too." Dillon removed her headphones from her ears. Erin and I stared at her. She shrugged at us. Instead of paying attention to us, she had been listening to her music during the entire scene.

When we reached our destination, Erin, Dillon, and I exited the rear doors of the bus. Marshall S. King University was an enormous college for the best students, the smartest scholars in the state of Illinois. No school uniform was required, thank God. Some students lived on campus, but none of us from BOTS Association stayed in the dorm rooms, though I loved my university. As we walked on campus, I was happy to be around friends. We marched past students doing work on their laptops or relaxing with laid-out towels in the green grass and significant others making out on campus. We also saw some students on the track team stretching. We all entered the school fiercely. Everyone stopped and stared, as people normally did. Most of them spoke to us, some just continued to watch, and the rest of the norms smiled at our presence because they wanted to be like us, even though the norms didn't know what we were. At that moment, I reminisced about the text message Andrew had sent to me. I considered informing Erin and Dillon about Andrew's potential scam. I grabbed Erin's right arm suddenly.

She jumped at the coldness of my fingers. "Your fingers are freezing, Angelina! Get them off of me."

I murmured, "I need to show you something that was sent to me when I was at the bus stop."

Her glare was a considerate one. I retrieved my phone so that Erin could read the message. She was now upset. Was it because I hadn't told her about it sooner? It seemed to me that trouble was already slithering its ugly head in our territory. The darkness was rapidly spreading. I thought Andrew was attempting to drown me in his lies, but his lies were actually the truth. It was difficult trying to keep up with Erin and Dillon. Dillon was texting on her phone. She was likely informing Tia, Amy, and Jacky of the monstrosity that was arising that day.

I had a strange feeling that Tia was responsible. I couldn't wait for her punishment to be issued. What sort of troublesome predicament had she gotten us into now? We traveled toward the guys' region, the gym. *Oh Lord. Look at the sweat dripping from their bodies from them playing basketball.* It was a three-on-three match: Jeremy Waters, Andrew, and Michael versus Mathew, James, and Christian Bell. Christian's Puerto Rican with short black hair and a toned body. He was twenty years old. His big shoulders, muscular arms, and six-pack were the most interesting things about him. He was a knucklehead to me because he treated women like dirt, so I knew to stay away from him. Only Dillon was crazy enough to fall in love with him. As I gazed at them, I realized how handsome they were, but my wide baby-doll eyes were mostly on Andrew. He glanced at me as if he were studying me. I froze. He was staring. I thought, *Look away! Look away!* The eye contact was too intense to tolerate but I loved those eyes of his.

As we approached our competitors, Andrew removed his brown shirt. His veins were popping out of his arms, accompanied by tough sweat. As a result, his muscles were glistening. I swallowed a mouthful of saliva while looking at my beautiful toes, sticking out the front of my see-through heels. Tia, Jacky, and Amy arrived shortly after. At that second, the guys stopped their basketball game, which Andrew's team seemed to be winning. James smiled at Tia. The same process occurred with Mathew and Amy and with Christian and Dillon. On the other hand, Jeremy Waters, a handsome African American male, had his eyes on Jacky. Jeremy was twenty-one years old. He loved wearing jackets and hats. His body was toned but not too athletic. He was maybe two shades lighter than Jacky, and Aaron was three shades lighter than Jeremy. Jeremy was the sort of guy who liked classy women, not sluts. He wanted something serious, so I could see why he was beaming in Jacky's direction. I snapped back into reality when Dillon charged up to Tia and snatched her car keys from out of her right hand. She whispered something in Spanish with an attitude: "*Desagradable perra flaca*." Michael and Andrew beamed lusciously at me. I started to feel violated by their penetrating eyes. My expression was evidence of that feeling.

Erin said, "Are we all just going to grin stupidly at each other, or are we having a meeting, or what?" After Erin's announcement, pleasure was put to rest, and business was the focus.

Michael said, "Sorry, Tia, I'm a little shocked right now. I never saw your mouth sealed for this long before. It's usually all-day easy access to us." They laughed briskly. They were so immature, I thought.

"Well, Michael, that is a funny story, because it seems your little sister and I are having that same exact problem." She leered. "I heard she's been swallowing lots and lots of semen these days."

I giggled loudly. When Michael looked my way, I immediately placed my hands over my mouth. I cleared my throat after and held in my laughter.

Mathew smiled wickedly while pointing at Tia. "Where's the assignment I completed yesterday, Tia?"

All eyes were on her. She was quiet at that moment. Erin was pissed that the same individual was responsible for yet another unpleasant confrontation. Erin repeatedly blinked her eyes. Tia slowly marched up to Mathew, and he aggressively regained his assignment sheet.

"Now I forgive you," he said. Mathew folded the sheet and tucked it in his back pocket.

Dillon spoke to sustain the confidentiality of the true leader. "There will not be a sun-death. You cheated," she claimed, absent proof. Her tone was far from mild and low.

I secretly smiled at Andrew. His green eyes were compulsive. Christian chuckled. "Oh, there is definitely going to be a sun-death."

My subconscious was cheering on the chaos she knew would reappear.

Erin interrupted. "We're willing to negotiate on other terms."

Andrew smiled. "Well, well, well, Erin, what do you have to bargain for?" he said sarcastically.

Jacky mocked Andrew. "Well, well, well, Andrew," she said, "what the hell do you want?"

Amy was reunited with Mathew, smothering him with tender kisses. *Get a room, seriously,* I thought. We were trying to discuss business. *Go pleasure off somewhere else.* The entire team beamed at me like the Joker in the movie *The Dark Knight*. The phrase "Why so serious?" had me bewitched. It was insulting.

Shaking my head, I said, "Uh, no, no, no, that most certainly will not happen!"

Christian smiled. "Well, you have to lose it sometime! It may as well be with one of us." He bolted up to me and whispered into my ear so that I was the only one who could hear him. "Or all of us, if that is the kind of thing you're into. I heard virgins are the freakiest."

"You knuckleheads are gross! I promise you that you horny little losers will never—and I mean ever—do that to me!"

He whispered again. "It looks like a train may be something you might like. I bet a thousand dollars your little, tight ass would be into it." He winked his left eye. Every word just made me sick. I was surprised I didn't throw up after.

I frowned. "I'm not that kind of girl, okay? I will never be that kind of girl, no matter how much you guys want me to be!" I said, pushing him far from me. "No one's contagious, wrinkly, saggy dill pickle is going to take away the one thing I cherish most!" I wept.

Jacky comforted me, muttering into my ear, "Relax, Angel. It doesn't have to happen today. You know that. They are just trying to piss you off. Remember that." Her arm was around my shoulder. Well, it was working, since running a train on me was nonnegotiable. There was no way they could convince me or us otherwise. It was obvious those knuckleheads were trying to turn me into a ho and that, I wasn't.

Jacky muttered, "What did he say to you?"

I murmured everything he'd said to me, word for word.

Jacky responded, "He's sick."

I agreed. "Tell me about it. And Dillon likes him."

Erin said, "You can have—"

Jeremy interrupted. "Nobody wants the slut of the group. That's final."

Tia lowered her eyes.

Michael was infuriated. "Everybody had Tia, so what are you bringing her up for?" he said belligerently.

Erin, with her hands on her waist, said, "Yeah, I doubt everyone slept with Tia." Erin looked at James. I noticed James smiling at Erin.

The guys privately conversed among themselves. They huddled as if they were professional athletes about to start a football game. My subconscious booed in contempt. On the contrary, the cheerleader in me voluntarily cheered on one particular athlete—Andrew—since he was damn mouthwatering. *Focus, Angelina, focus.* I had to snap out of the luscious fantasy that was Andrew Walker. They rejoined our conversation. Amy was still hypnotized by Mathew's presence, of course.

Michael announced, "Since neither of you will let us fuck the virgin, this matter is now nonnegotiable. No offense, Tia, but we don't want to work hard for something everyone has already had many times over. She is also a questionable problem we won't need to be dealing with again."

Tia was fed up with Michael's insults. She walked up to him and slapped him across his left cheek.

Amy and I laughed. "Whoa!" I yelled. "Ha-ha, boy. That's what you get!"

"Ow, you bitch!" he said. Poor Michael—I felt the sting from the loud sound of him getting smacked. It was quick and shocking to everyone, especially Michael.

"You're a sad excuse for a male competitor. You couldn't even effectively take care of your business in the bedroom. Your tired, pathetic ass couldn't last more than three minutes up in this. To be honest, the size of your wanker is just another disappointment to me. I know who and what I am, yet I accept and embrace it. There is nothing you or anybody else can say to discourage me from it. And your no-pussy-getting ass is going to be calling me discreetly for a private affair, so how about showing me some fucking respect in public?"

I had never witnessed her angry side before until now. I found it absorbingly bold. Everyone laughed. How hysterical was that? Tia charged out of the gym room. *Way to go, Tia. Way to go.* James followed after her.

A half smile had grown on my face. "I guess she told you," I murmured. Amy and Jacky were still laughing. Talk about public mortification. Michael left soon enough, rubbing his face.

Erin proclaimed, "You can't have Angel, so sun-death was correct. The first person who takes someone's virginity wins. We select James."

Mathew responded, "Okay. We choose the virgin."

I frowned. "What? You're insane. No! That's not fair. I'm not doing it!"

Dillon captured my arm. "You have to, Angel. You must do this for the team," she ordered.

"No. I'm discussing this with Erin," I whispered.

Dillon escorted me out of the gym. "I advise you not to do that! There are plenty of little virgins who would be happy to substitute your station and do the things you refuse to! You have to make sacrifices for the team! We all do. Get active, or you'll be detached from your status!" Her voice was intimidating. Suddenly, she slammed the door in my face. I flushed.

They wouldn't actually strip me from my classification if I weren't eligible for my position, would they? I knew that in the long run, my virginity would have to be deflowered, but this was too soon for me to handle. I scowled. Being a pure little angel was a part of my mission. What a bunch of heartless cunts. However, I honestly did consider fulfilling their request to escape my nightmare. Sadly, I didn't want to be a norm, because they did normal, boring projects and classroom and homework assignments. Unlike the norms, I had been rewarded with my outstanding position.

This was the only place I belonged. I felt welcome and not like an outcast. The game was the only place a virgin like me could be popular under all circumstances. After the meeting, I lost my appetite, though it was lunchtime. Instead of eating, I sipped shyly on my fruit punch. The cafeteria was tremendously rowdy. I thought about the ruckus of my teammates and competitors. *How could* my friends do this to me? What did I ever do to disappoint them? Nothing whatsoever. I didn't have to do a damn thing! Who does Dillon think she is? "There are many other virgins willing to happily gain your spot. You must do it for the team. Be active, or be replaced."

I chuckled temporarily. I took problems too seriously. I was stressed out for unnecessary reasons. Even making a move on Andrew was a problem for me. *Oh my God, he looked scrumptious in his gray-and-white shorts. They nicely hung off the sides of his hips.* From time to time, I swore I couldn't bear to speak to him properly. My tongue sometimes felt tied up, and nothing would come out of my mouth. It seemed like my throat would dry up, causing me to choke when I was around him.

His appearance and disposition could have had something to do with it. I wasn't shocked that every girl viewed him as either her fantasy or her dream guy—well, almost every girl. Sexual opportunities had no problems knocking at Andrew's door.

Oh Lord. He was headed in my direction. I had to remember to relax and breathe. I figured that my virginity probably was less stimulating to him because he was experienced and I wasn't. My palms started to sweat since I was nervous. The closer Andrew got, the more my nervousness increased.

I hoped I wouldn't be too clumsy. I would be flushed if I started choking again. This time, I feared that another embarrassing situation in the presence of Andrew would be nonredeemable. He sat across from me. My eyes rejected his gaze. I could feel his unavoidable stare demanding my attention. It was the kind of attentiveness he possessed without sweating or worrying. I refused to stare into his eyes. I thought it helped to diminish my anxiety. Everything appeared all too easy for him, and he liked to toy with the dominant advantage he had over me. I wished I could have given him a glare of dominance or confidence altogether, but he knew it was difficult for me to resist his gorgeousness. I resented my lack of ability to fight wanting him. He stroked his short blond hair, still looking at me.

"Angelina, you seem a little off the edge, stressed out even. Is everything ok?" His tone was objective, and his expression was unfamiliar.

"Oh no, I'm far from it. I'm not annoyed or stressed out. Why—do I seem frustrated or annoyed to you?" I said with my lips twisted, shaking my head mildly. "Absolutely, as a matter of fact, you look very sexually frustrated," he said. I couldn't believe he said that to me.

I rolled my eyes. "I'm not sexually frustrated!" I shouted subjectively. Some students in the cafeteria stared in our direction as if I were insane. What the hell were they looking at? *Relax, Angelina. You don't need to draw anymore attention to yourself.*

He smiled. "Yeah, you are. You know, there are things you can do to alleviate some of that stress of yours."

I said, "Yeah, like what?"

He smoothly rubbed my right arm in a circular motion. "You need to get a really good massage. For me, sex does the trick. Maybe masturbation would do you justice." He admitted straightforwardly.

What! How dare he say that to me? "Well, I never did either of those things before," I whispered.

He snickered slightly. "You never masturbated before? That's why you're so uptight and nervous."

"I'm not uptight and no! I haven't, and I'm not nervous. Why is the fact that I never masturbated before so shocking to you?"

He shrugged. "Well, if you have or haven't. Gotten fucked or played with yourself, I mean, that's completely up to you," he whispered in my ear. "Like you, we all started off as virgins, Angel." His whispering sent chills down my spine.

"I know exactly what you're trying to do." I breathed out deeply. "I can see beyond that poison like charm of yours. I'm not having sex with you—or anyone, for that matter," I assured him.

He stood, smiling down at me. Our eyes met directly. "Every guy isn't after your virtue." He paused. "Perhaps, it's not me that desires you."

Not once did the thought of him not desiring me cross my mind, yet something in me was convinced that he did want me. Therefore, there was no need for masturbation. I was appalled thinking about it. Why touch myself, when Andrew's gropes were all I fantasized about?

Besides, how much fun could I possibly have on my lonesome? To be honest, I wished this assignment would disappear somewhere beyond my reach. Better yet, I wished another teammate would willingly announce to the members that it would be better served as someone else's duty. That way, I could tell my bitchy little teammates to fuck off!

CHAPTER 4

Erin

Forgetting Evan

There was no way we could substitute for Angel. She would have to have sex soon enough. It would strengthen the team if she did what was commanded of her. If she disappointed me with one ounce of failure, I would terminate her and replace her with another virgin. Her replacement would have to willingly or reluctantly follow my orders. Furthermore, Tia needed to be punished for her foolishness or eliminated from the game. Her actions were putting my team in jeopardy once more, and I couldn't allow it. Our chances at winning the competition were decreasing. James and I, on the other hand, finally fell upon an agreement. It was a Friday when I gave in to his persuasion. It had been weeks since Mathew's unwelcome visit to the tutoring center. I was in bed. I attempted to finalize a decision to help us complete our fourth assignment: public humiliation. Michael was apparently the best candidate for the position. As my imagination wandered off into action, my phone started to ring.

"Hello, Angel. It's a little late for calls, don't you think?" I said, stretching my legs.

"Erin! It's only four o'clock. It's still light outside," she argued.

"Well, it's late to me. That is beside the point, though." I coughed.

She hesitated. "So I was wondering if—"

I interrupted. "No."

She started stuttering. "Wait. You haven't heard the entire question."

"I don't need to. I'm Avant." I said in a deep voice. "I can read your mind, baby." I laughed. She was silent. See, I told you. She had no humor. I exhaled. "I'm sorry, Angel. Another member isn't allowed to accomplish such a critical task for you, not this time. You need to accept that there is only one solution. Just do what is asked of you, or resign from your station," I explained.

"Everything Dillon said was right. If I refuse, I'm gone, correct?"

I hated to be the person to spread the bad news, but I had to. "Yup. Pretty much." I yawned.

She was quiet for a second again. "Okay, tell me what I have to do."

"That a girl, Angel. That a girl. Your opponent is James, but perhaps you need a softer touch. They know your vulnerability lies with Andrew. He's the only advantage they have over this assignment, but we also have an advantage over them. The sooner we get you prepared, the better," I said.

"By preparing, do you mean masturbation? Andrew was talking to me about it. Is this what you're talking about?" She seemed embarrassed to ask the question.

I laughed. "You've never masturbated before, have you?" Oh my, this was too good to be true.

"Why are you laughing? And no, I haven't, nor do I look forward to it in the future." Her tone revealed shame. She would be participating sooner than she expected.

"I'm sorry. This is not a laughing matter," I said, laughing once more. "It's normal. It shows that you have a perfectly healthy sexual appetite, so there is nothing wrong with it."

"So do you, you know."

I said proudly, "Sometimes, yes."

"What about Andrew?"

Boy, she sounded nervous when she talked about him. *Is she serious?* I wondered as I rolled my eyes. "What about him, Angel?"

"What am I supposed to do about him? He has this power over me. I can't control it."

Yeah, he has that influence over many girls. "Like a gift you wrap, girl, you give him that power over you. Don't give in to his charms. Be the girl that turns him down. Show him he needs to adapt to a new atmosphere—your atmosphere. It's time to make him feel uncomfortable and a little nervous for once."

"Okay. I will," she said gloomily.

She won't, I thought. I exhaled calmly. "Don't stress yourself over this assignment. There was a reason I carefully chose James, and I will talk to Andrew, so don't worry about it. You will do fine."

"Okay, okay," she said with relief, and she hung up the phone.

The first thing that interfered was my conscience. She didn't know what the hell she was doing. We were fucked. Her lack of sexual experience would cripple our opportunity, and there was nothing I could do to really help her. Amy was trapped in the role of pleasing Mathew. The predicament was fucking sad. I couldn't have catered to and pampered a guy with the Amy I-love-you-so-blindly approach. Dillon was in the process of completing an individual assignment, and I doubted she would complete it anytime soon. Jacky, perhaps, could coach Angel with accuracy, I thought as my eyes concentrated on my white ceiling.

Before long, I was peeking at the picture on my dresser of my older brother, Evan Wilson. He'd committed suicide before my freshman year in college. The image of him deeply affected me. I couldn't look at him for much longer. A tear dropped onto my left cheek, and a second tear chased the first. I knocked the picture down on my dresser because I hated remembering the tragedy. I remembered screaming myself hoarse as I discovered him hanging by his neck in one of our closets. The image was seared into my brain—rewinding, fast-forwarding, and playing like a marathon. I had never plucked up the courage to face my nightmares of his death. The repulsive image of him dangling in the closet paralyzed me head to toe sometimes. Truthfully, the expression on his face petrified me the most. It had haunted me for years. Unfortunately, it still did. My mother interrupted my recollection as she gently tapped on my door.

"I heard a ruckus. Are you okay in there?"

My business wasn't any of her concern, I thought. "I'm fine!" There, a response for the mother of the year.

"Okay, sweetheart. I know things are hard and very rough between us, from losing your father to Evan committing suicide. It's just you and me now, and we have to take care of each other," she said.

I cocked my head to the side as I opened the door. I had a serious issue with subduing my emotions. Tears trembled from my eyes. "Is this what you tell yourself so you can sleep better at night, while my nightmares of them welcome me in the most painful ways?" I yelled. I leaned on the door, scowling with frustration.

She paused for a few seconds, touching my shoulder. "You know that's not true, sweetheart. We are going to make it through this. For your birthday, I was thinking we could go to the Bahamas or Hawaii, like you always wanted." She didn't care about what I wanted.

I pulled away hostilely. Her expression was impassive. "Yeah, I did. But as a family—you know, when my brother and father were still alive. I blame you for the burden that was randomly tossed on my heart for your selfish reasons of prostitution. The divorce is the reason he boarded that plane to California. If you just would have been a good wife, he never would have been on that plane, and my brother would still be here with me. Now I'm just stuck in this nightmare with you." I slammed the door in her face. I listened by the door. I could hear her breathing and crying outside my door. Good, I wanted to hurt her just as much as she has hurt me and our family. I wanted her to know the pain I felt because I loved her as much as I hated her guts. I listened until she eventually walked away like she always did.

For the entire weekend, we argued nonstop. Boredom and unfriendliness consumed me. She left me to drown in my loneliness, as usual. I drove her away with our weary conflicts. Running was what Shante, my mother, did best. Like a coward, she could never conquer her fear and be a real mother to me after the great loss we'd experienced. Understanding each other was our major failure. I despised her for being arrested numerous times for prostitution in her former years. Shante was now working in the fashion and modeling industry in New York City. She used to fit into one category. Now it seemed she was fitting into multiple modeling categories, especially for magazine catalogs. She was six feet three, thirty-three years old, and thin, meeting the exceptional requirements of a model working in the fashion industry.

I needed love, but instead, Shante sent me money to fill in my pain and emptiness. All the money in the world wasn't powerful enough to save me from my reality. All that night, I had nightmares about my brother's death. Before I knew it, it was Monday morning. Before my English 135 class started, I grasped Jacky's right hand and secretly supplied her with her next two assignments. Along with her missions, I slid an antivirotic into the pocket of her black jacket.

She seemed concerned. "What is required of me?" she asked.

I planted my hands on both of her shoulders, standing behind her. "You are equipped to strike for mortification."

"Who?" she questioned.

I smiled while whispering into her ear, "Michael." He needed to pay for going after Tia the way he had. Although she was a slut, she was my slut. I wasn't about to let anyone fuck with a member of my team. Sure, she was in trouble, but it didn't mean I would stop watching her back. We had to stick together.

I stood beside her. "He has a Band-Aid on his upper lip. Most likely, it's a cold sore, but you know what they say about cold sores. What you have in your jacket is some antivirotic. Your task is freakishly light. Remember that. Your assignment is to just embarrass him, publicly. That's all, Jacky."

"Nice," she said, glancing at the front of the medicine bottle. "Wait—even his information is plastered on it. Where did you get it from?" She looked at me oddly.

I raised an eyebrow as well as both of my hands. "Well, it doesn't belong to me, silly. Amy volunteered to help you out."

She looked deeply into my eyes. "Can I postpone this, or is it urgent? When do you need the assignment finished?"

"Just get it over with today, please," I said. "If I were you, I would be spending more time on my second one, which is a homework assignment, because it holds a maximum amount of difficulty and consequences."

She crossed her arms after scratching her head. "What's the assignment?"

A serious expression materialized on my face. "Seduce a professor, and get him or her to sign where his or her signature is required," I explained shortly.

"And I thought challenges didn't exist anymore." She glared. "Sounds like fun to me."

We entered our first class of the day. I sat at the rear of the classroom. Jacky observed the class in search of Michael, who was situated next to the huge window to the left. Our hot professor was late, as usual. Jacky used this opportunity to finalize her first easy assignment. She charged up to Michael, smiling darkly at him. I assumed she was inspecting his hidden cold sore. She buried her hand in her jacket to expose the antivirotic. She slammed the medicine onto the desk. He stared oddly at the medicine she'd brought before him.

He snickered. "And what the hell is that?" He folded his hands.

She leered. "It's your medicine, silly!"

"What the fuck are you talking about? That's not mine, and you know it, if that's what you're implying."

Their eyes darted devilishly at each other. "You dropped this yesterday in the hallway! I saw you!" she said seriously. "And all I know is, that thing on your lip that you're hiding is disgusting!"

He swiftly touched where the Band-Aid was positioned.

"Who did you think you were fooling with that pathetic excuse for a Band-Aid?" Jacky teased him. "It doesn't cover the whole thing. You've got herpes, and it's screaming for exposure, now, isn't it? How long have you had herpes, Michael? Are your breakouts rare? Judging from that herpes sore, I would say that you got it real bad." she said, strolling to the back of the classroom. She sat down in the seat across from me. The room was utterly quiet.

Michael said, "You're a liar. What is this—an assignment? It's probably your medicine!"

Jacky laughed evilly. "An assignment—what— are you referring to the assignments we do in school or you know what?" she asked, blinking at Michael with a clueless expression on her face. Jacky was having fun with her first task. "Whatever do you mean by that—an assignment? And for the record, the medicine can't be mine, because it has your name on it," Jacky said, applying lip gloss to her lips.

He eagerly collected the medicine, shocked at her accusation. She'd proven the allegation. He was surprised his personal info was listed on the medicine Jacky had brought to class.

From Michael's point of view, throwing the medicine in the trash wouldn't be an intelligent action to take, since we would recollect it and expose it to the rest of the school. Leaving it on his desk for others to view it would have also showed a lack of intelligence. Having it in his possession was the worst possible thing Michael could do, because it would appear he needed it. Either way, his situation wasn't good. Michael investigated the classroom. The students whispered in suspense while staring at him. Jacky and I laughed as a result.

I said sarcastically, "Jacky, herpes isn't a laughing matter." We burst out laughing again. "We should help him instead of tease him about his little condition. I'll let you know if I just happen to find any more of your special medicine, Michael," she said while giggling.

Jacky played along. "You're absolutely right, Erin, but if I had herpes, I would just kill myself right here in front of everyone. You better stay away from him, girls. He's highly contagious." We laughed once more.

He spontaneously charged out of class. *Nicely done,* I thought, grinning. Later, Professor Rodríguez stole the girls' attention with his glorious arrival; his appearance was challenging to ignore. We all weakened at his presence. He was a Puerto Rican with short black hair and dimples that could drive any female student wild for him. He was a twenty-five-year-old English instructor who was muscular. He had an appealing voice that saturated your underwear instantly. Girls couldn't forget those small lips that they wanted suffocating their skin. He was the kind of English professor female college students fantasized about every day. Jacky's eyes met mine. I recognized exactly what she was thinking, and I nodded in agreement. Suddenly, we both leered at Professor Rodríguez.

"What is your plan of seduction?" I said.

"I can tell him that I need help with citing—you know, paraphrasing and quoting. We do have a research paper due. I think this is the perfect time to ask him for tutoring sessions after school. Let him teach me beyond the educational level."

I pretended to work on something constructive, writing mumbo jumbo on my white sheet of paper. "Let the instructor instruct you privately. I like it." Then I warned her in my most-serious tone of voice, "Be exceedingly cautious. This assignment can prove you legendary or simply stain your reputation." I frowned. "I will have no use for you if this happens. Have patience, think critically, and be very persuasive," I concluded with sadness.

"You dealt with his duty before. Even though you failed, I won't mimic your error. I promise you." She nodded slightly. "What are you working on?"

I tilted my head down in shame, rejecting her eye contact. "It's a breakup thing. My assignment isn't senior material," I said.

"You're not a senior. This is your specialty, Erin. You're good at it. I think you should stick to what you know."

"I want something different. I want to conduct a senior project junior year because the BOTS Association would remember it." I scratched my neck, which was itching intolerably. I felt relief as I scratched my neck. *Ah, yeah, that's the spot.*

"You're trying to become a legend. I want in."

"Quiet down, Ms. Dickerson," Professor Rodríguez ordered.

"Sorry, Professor Rodríguez, it won't happen again. I promise," she said seductively. Everyone looked at Jacky.

"What?" she yelled at the students who were staring at her.

I murmured, "Way to sound like a naughty schoolgirl, Jacky. You call that keeping a low profile? Don't be flirtatious in public. Keep the soon-to-be affair at a minimum."

I recognized that every duty needed my supervision. I didn't have time to focus on my teammates' stability and still finish my requirements at the same time. My subconscious screamed for an extra hand. I thought of the whereabouts of our competition as I rushed to the girls' bathroom. When I finished washing my hands, I glanced helplessly in the mirror. Suddenly, I heard unusual sounds coming from one of the stalls in the bathroom—slurping and sucking noises. I followed the sounds to the last stall. I peeked through the cracks and saw a girl on her knees. *Oh my God.* I hoped this wasn't what I thought it was. The noise grew louder and louder.

"Aw, Tia, that's disgusting. You're doing this in the girls' bathroom? Really?" I shook my head. "Class has not even started yet! Well, at least it's not an opponent!" Christian bolted out of the stall, zipping up his blue-jean shorts and readjusting his black T-shirt. "Look at that. Great, it's a competitor. What a fucking shocker!" I glared hopelessly at Tia.

She arched an eyebrow, shrugging as if she had done nothing wrong. "What? I am having a little fun. It's not my fault you rudely interrupted me!"

I left her to wallow in her loneliness. What a disgrace she was. She had a lustful motive to sleep with every guy we were going up against. She was the true definition of the word *slut.* My subconscious stated, *Let the slut run wild,* but she always ran recklessly with or without my approval, and she had since day one. Maybe Tia was too erotic for my taste. Our afternoon class started. Jeremy, Andrew, and Mathew were present. *Oh boy.* They were looking in my direction. What had I done now? *Oh, wait—Michael. Jacky convinced our fellow students he has herpes.* I laughed. Well, Oops, my bad. I wondered what evil plot the competition had brewing against us. I thought my actions had them bewildered. When it came down to the facts, I was highly concerned. Nonetheless, I was worried about what they had planned next.

When I was in that particular room, I was more troubled by a baldheaded and uptight biology instructor and what his old, cranky ass was up to. He went by the name of Mr. Ford. He was more intimidating than my male competitors. He entered the classroom. He knew he was just an evil old bastard with a beer belly and a long gray beard. Boy, did he look maliciously angry. I believed he liked ruining his students' lives. He enjoyed seeing us fail and panic. He had a humor that was petrifying; it was anything but humorous, especially to me. However, he seemed to keep himself busy with his own amusement. One of his sources of entertainment was sending students to the dean for no good reason. He was a sick old bastard. Mr. Ford was writing our assignments on the board, singing old, junky classical music. Amy attempted to sneak her way into class. She successfully situated herself in the seat in front of me.

Mr. Ford babbled quickly. "Ms. Robinson, you're late. That's why you are going on a little field trip to the dean's office—and don't let it happen again!"

Amy stood. "Go visit the dean? For what—just being a minute late? You're fucking crazy. That's not fair. This isn't high school, Professor. We are free to make our own decisions."

He smiled harshly. "Watch your mouth, young lady. And no. For being two minutes late, Ms. Smartass! There's a huge difference. You can either write me a five-page paper on Monday or spend some special time visiting the dean."

Amy rearranged herself in her seat. She frowned and reluctantly said, "Well, I guess I am seeing the dean."

"Great! That's bold of you to choose to see the dean and to write me a paper on Monday about tardiness and calling your professor names."

"Wait—I said I would visit the dean," she argued.

"You took three seconds of my life away—three important seconds that I will never get back, Ms. Robinson. During that time, while you were guessing, I decided for you."

He stood in the center of the room, smiling. *Oh Lord.* He had something wicked up his dirty sleeves. The room was silent. I couldn't control my breathing, because the situation caused me to panic. He slowly walked back and forth, pacing in the classroom. He rubbed his chin with his index finger and grinned from ear to ear. His behavior was beginning to annoy me. He pointed to the assignment on the board while bending down to sit in his wooden chair.

"Surprisingly, that assignment is for my humanities class!" He breathed in deeply. "I guess today you lucky little bastards have a free class, but do something constructive with your time. I don't want to hear any talking, or I'm going back to the chalkboard! Understand me?"

What? Nothing to do? Did I fall asleep? Because I must be dreaming. Did he say we were having a free class? Mr. Ford had to be ill. All of the students cheered loudly. Some of them jumped out of their chairs. Mr.

Ford was scandalous. Immediately, he silenced the applause with his laughter.

"I'm sorry! I can't do it. You should have seen your faces! You all looked so damn happy. What a bunch of idiots." He laughed to the point of choking. All of the students were disappointed and sad.

He tried to restore his breath, but he continued to choke. "Of course you fuckers have to work!" Only a twisted person could collect enjoyment from others' crushed hopes and wishes. He was tasteless. The students started yelling, mainly Andrew and Jeremy. They were the loudest of us all.

"That wasn't right, Mr. Ford!" the students agreed. "Yes!"

Jeremy said, "You're a sick, sick man. You know that?"

Jeremy's response caused Mr. Ford's facial expression to change, and it didn't look good. "Well, since I'm so sick, you can be my doctor and cure me in the dean's office. And, Mathew?"

"Yeah?" Mathew responded.

Mr. Ford smiled delightfully, not maliciously, which was welcoming. "You can go see the dean too, for being so damn quiet and sneaky. It's always the quiet ones you have to watch."

Mathew exhaled. Biology was the worst course I had ever taken. Finally, class ended, and my subconscious repeatedly broadcast the "free at last" speech. I noticed Jeremy walking confidently down the hallways. His optimistic personality was attractive. Eventually, a girl with a fitted red dress and medium-long brown hair approached him. While I passed them, they held hands passionately. Plus, they were locking lips like lovebirds. Who was she? What was her name? She was probably a norm. I figured I could seek her out to manipulate her so that I could get what I truly wanted. *That's a little cruel, don't you think?* my subconscious said. It was not as if I had never done it before. Besides, destroying Jeremy's relationship would be fun.

CHAPTER 5

Tia

I Am Who I Am

I hadn't been able to stop thinking about sex or the guy with the scorpion tattoo ever since Amy had mentioned him one night when I'd persuaded her to drink with me at my eighteenth birthday party. However, she wasn't much of a drinker, and Amy had become insanely intoxicated that night. When she became a little chatterbox, she straightaway began unraveling her paper and ribbon to expose some of her jaw-dropping secrets. They were the kind of secrets people would have died to know. I wondered what Mathew would do if her secrets suddenly unraveled in his hands. At first, I couldn't believe that she was withholding scandalous information from me, and the little info Amy revealed to me was like a small teaser, which led to my dissatisfaction. Like sex, I had to have more. I had to have more details about her alluring one-night-stand confession and the guy who'd raped her in a motel room. What I had learned about this tattooed guy helped me to fantasize about the thought of him touching me. Because of her unfaithfulness and drunken confessions, I was now trying to chase and fuck a ghost. I strongly believed this guy was a competitor. I would have done anything to find out who this guy was. Because I had already fucked the shit out of Michael, I knew he wasn't the guy. Michael didn't even have any noticeable or hidden tattoos. What was I thinking? I also could scratch Christian off the list, because I sucked his dick enough to know he was not the guy. Jeremy definitely wasn't him. I did fuck him my freshman year, although nobody knew about it.

It seemed I was waiting for this special discovery. Yet my current situation would have made fucking him impossible anyway, since I was trapped in a fucking chastity belt. Thank God I could use the bathroom. There was no way they would have handed me the key for personal reasons anyway. From what I'd heard, this guy had given Amy much pleasure. I was trying my best to find him, yet I was doing a poor job of figuring it or him out. Not having sex certainly wasn't contributing to the discovery of this mystery guy. How could I not think of sex and want it, when everything around me was a reminder of sex? It had been two days, and my actions were preposterous. For some odd reason, I couldn't function properly without my normal dose of the python. I missed it. Two days, for me, seemed like two months or two years. It was pitiful. My subconscious was ashamed of the anxiety I felt. All I yearned for was a couple of inches inside of me. *A few inches—who was I kidding? I need the entire dose—a big, juicy dick—because a portion wouldn't suffice for me.*

This was the wickedest arrangement Michael and Mathew could have planned for me. I would have preferred a double penetration to this virgin-protection device. At least my body could have gotten something out of it. I wanted and needed someone inside me—anyone with a penis. Some people would have said that I was addicted to sex. I probably was, but all I knew was that I couldn't concentrate on school, and it was supposed to be my first priority. Education didn't fascinate me, nor did it make me cum. Speaking of cum, amazingly, the taste of Christian was still on my tongue.

I went to my geometry class, though I despised it. To add to my misery, I was trapped with the virgin of the group. By the looks of it, she would be one of those eternal virgins. *Just look at her.* The unhappy cheerleader in me cheered for a sexual awakening. My sex life was now in the hands of a damn virgin. She was probably in a purity club. *Jeez, how did I get so lucky?*

I hoped she wouldn't infect me with her innocence. I stared in her direction. She welcomed me with a cheerful smile and a friendly wave. *Just look at her.* I was disgusted. I shook my head. Her happiness made me fleetingly miserable while she attempted to spread her friendliness. Although I rejected her courtesy, there was one thing I required from her. She needed to hurry up and get fucked so that I could preserve my daily exercises. Every decision constantly came down to them, the virgins. What was so damn unique about them? Shit—absolutely shit. Sex was wonderful. Who didn't like orgasms? They were beautiful to me. The virgin was beaming at me once more. *Look away, Tia; look away.* To eliminate confusion, she tapped me on my stomach.

I glared at her in frustration. "Ouch. That hurt," I said, even though it didn't.

"Sorry. Look, I know we don't get along. God knows I have tried. I'm sweet, and I have feelings for someone. I actually like one person. And you—you're different. You sleep with a lot of guys. You give blowjobs in the bathroom before class starts. You probably masturbate frequently. It's not necessarily a bad thing," she said seriously. "You're constantly adhering to the same mistakes, but I completely understand."

Oh, hell no. This pale, certainly dead, eight-year-old-small-breasted virgin bitch did not say that. But yes, she had. "Itty-bitty-top virgin bitch that can't get no kind of dick, what's your point? And it's during class, not before, by the way. There's a difference!" I said.

"Hey! You didn't have to insult me. What was with all the bitch, virgin, bitty-itty, no-penis statement?" she said, pouting. "I have spoken only the truth about you."

Was she fucking kidding me? She had to be shitting me. She had to be. "I didn't say *penis*. I said *dick*, and your announcement that a girl constantly masturbates, gives out blowjobs, and has countless sex affairs isn't an insult?"

"Well, sure it is. But for you, there was no other polite way of saying it. I could have said much, much worse. Believe me."

She was right. And boy, the truth hurt. After her lecture, my subconscious daydreamed of squeezing her windpipe with both of my hands. I smirked delightfully.

"No, you're right," she said, "It was full-blown negativity. It was unsuitable."

Damn straight.

"I'm sorry," she added. That was unlikely.

"I guess," I said with an unreadable expression.

She smiled. "I need your help with something."

I knew it, I knew it, and I knew it. I hoped for her sake that she was joking. She had to be shitting me this time. I was surprised she wanted my help. "Why should I help you? I don't even like you," I said.

"You want to have sex again, don't you? Or did you already forget about—you know?"

Right, the belt—I forgot for about a minute. My subconscious thanked her for reminding me that I was no longer sexually active. I smiled aggressively. "Well, how can I assist you, Angel?" I said happily, as if she were a customer I wanted to satisfy.

She twisted her face up. "I need to be more open, if you know what I mean."

Of course I knew what she meant.

She smiled. First, she needed to learn how to loosen up and relax. Sex helped me to relax. But what could help her? I didn't know if I particularly liked her smiling at me, yet I felt pleased to bring happiness to someone without having to open up my legs or mouth. My subconscious was stunned. Her innocence shaped her beauty. My smile wasn't unique. My beauty was far from pure and fragile. My personality wasn't jolly. All of a sudden, Angelina snapped me back into reality.

"Tia, Tia! Hello?" she said. She knew how to mess up a great moment.

It was disrespectful for her to snap her fingers in my face. However, the problem wasn't important enough to confront, so I decided to let it slide before any unnecessary drama took its course. For the members of our sex club, it was lunchtime. Angel, Jacky, Amy, Erin, Dillon, and I sat in the center of the lunchroom. Christian, Andrew, Jeremy, Michael, Mathew, and James always positioned themselves in the back of the cafeteria. From time to time, we stared at them, wondering what their next plan of attack was.

Jacky had the most exciting assignment, seducing a teacher—a homework assignment I would have been honored to complete. Dillon was constructing something boring, Angelina was going to be deflowered, and Erin was to become familiarized with Jeremy's fun parts. I was left out as usual. This game was boring. I ate my fruits and vegetables to eliminate my hunger. The only food item I had left was my banana. I was about to eat it, when an idea emerged. I stood and walked over to Angelina with a perfect strategy to tease and tempt Andrew.

I whispered into her ear, "Go to the boys' table, and tease Andrew."

She shook her head repeatedly. "Tease him with what—a banana? Oh no, most certainly not. I don't see how doing that will help me be more open to my sexuality."

I said, "Before you play, you have to learn the rules of the game and how it's played. You should tease before you make an effort to please him." I swirled the banana around in my hand.

"I can't," she whimpered. "What if I choke or something and end up looking stupid in front of everybody—in front of Andrew?"

It was funny she mentioned choking in front of everyone. I would have been looking forward to it. "Look, you asked for my help, and now I'm helping you. You want to be more sexually ambiguous, right? This is the crawl you should make. Plus, Erin said that's an order anyway," I lied. She stared down at Erin. Erin leered slightly. It was a perfect smile at a perfect time.

"An order is an order. Okay, I'll do it," she said, breathing in and out with shaky hands.

How marvelous.

She stood as she held the banana in her right hand. While slowly walking, she peeled the banana. She was nervous. I could tell by her shaky fingers. She landed herself between Andrew and Jeremy. Before relocating for a better inspection, I warned the team to watch her poor performance. I positioned myself behind Angel, precisely across from the boys' table, ears locked and loaded to collect info. Andrew beamed instantly. Jeremy, on the other hand, wasn't pleased with Angel's company. Everyone at the table was watching her. They were quiet.

"Oh, um, don't mind me. I'm just enjoying my lunch." She grinned.

"Well, go enjoy it somewhere else," Mathew said rudely.

"I'm sure I can stay, right, boys?" she murmured.

Jeremy said, "You should go eat elsewhere." The others agreed.

She hesitated. "Don't you guys like bananas? Because I do," she said seductively. She placed the banana in her mouth and started softly sucking and licking on the tip of the banana. She stopped for a second as she leered at the boys.

"I would really like to stay. Don't make me go, when my place is right here with you guys."

"No, no, you can stay!" they agreed simultaneously. "Yeah, we like bananas." They all were drooling in their own anxious way.

She sucked on it lightly, placing the entire banana in her mouth. What a liar she was. I mocked her in my mind: *I can't! I can't do it. What if I choke?* It didn't look as if she were choking to me. She was sucking on it like an expert.

"It's so tasty," she said. It was just a banana, so how tasty could it have been?

Andrew agreed. "Yeah, it is." He breathed.

Angel grinned at Andrew, who was now vulnerable to her. Eventually, she ate the entire banana. It was hot. Her technique was superior, and it was more than what I'd expected from a virgin, who was supposed to have no experience.

She frowned. "It's all gone." She exhaled sadly. "I have nothing to suck on now. I guess I'll find something else to put into my mouth. Later, you guys." It kept getting better and better. Where had that come from? I was even a little impressed.

Virgin, my ass. I had never seen a virgin suck like that before. She left their table with confidence. I looked at their faces. Andrew immediately tried to follow her, but Jeremy ordered him to compose himself by pulling on his shirt to reposition him back in his seat. He did as commanded. I smiled. Jeremy had to be the team's speaker. It was always a privilege to discover something new. Angel and I rejoined our regular lunch table with my arm over her shoulder. "Good job," the others said, but she wasn't going to receive congrats from me.

"Wow, I didn't know you had it in you," Erin said. Angel was now sitting next to the head chief.

"What are you so wowed about? So you made a few losers drool. So what?" Amy said. "Who can't suck on some fruit?"

Erin whispered something into Angel's ear and then my ear. "I'm having a small get-together at my house. You and Angel are invited."

I hissed, "For what reason, Erin?"

"James and Andrew will be there."

I hissed again. "I don't want to come to some boring gathering! All you care about is you. If it wasn't for your selfishness, I wouldn't be trapped in a belt, now, would I? I'm not coming! You hear me? You're the worst leader ever. I don't want to go, and I'm not coming! There is nothing you can say that will change my mind." My tone was solid, and I turned my back to Erin.

"You will be having sex with James. In other words, your belt will be removed," she said.

I turned back around and hugged her enthusiastically. "That's all you had to say, sugar tits. Sure, sure, I would love to come! I'm so glad you asked," I said. I grinned from ear to ear. "I knew somewhere on the inside you would make a good leader."

She had had it with me disappointing the team. I had seen the evidence distributed all over her face. I figured that if I got to have sex, why shouldn't I go? But why did I have to have sex with James? Out of every competitor, why was I stuck with him? Why not Jeremy or Mathew? In the hallways, Mathew had the nerve to reach out to me.

"Hey, Tia, how have you been, and how is your afternoon going?" He could have cared less about my feelings or how my day was going. I decided to stay quiet. He would be having a conversation with himself. However, his tone was hospitable to my ears. I embraced his pleasant voice. He was leaning on the wall in front of me.

"So you—"

I immediately crossed my arms. "Aww, cut the shit, okay? You couldn't wait to bust me out in front of everyone. You embarrassed me."

"I didn't think you would ever get embarrassed, but I apologize if I embarrassed you in any way."

"There shouldn't be any *if*—you did. You embarrassed the hell out of me. I'm just better at hiding the way I feel." I stared at him.

"And I'm sorry for setting you up for an assignment, but you did do the same to me."

I rolled my eyes, since I was far from intrigued by his apology.

"Thanks for apologizing, but apology not accepted, you idiot," I said, leaving him on his lonesome. He followed me, of course.

"Look, I only did it for payback. You can't just go around locking a guy's dick in a cock cage, and have him not be upset about it, Tia." he complained. "But I can forgive you if you can forgive me. You made me mad as hell at first, yet all can be forgiven, and we can go back to being friends, like we used to be." He winked and smiled at me.

I stopped walking. "You stopped being my friend a long time ago. This conversation has nothing to do with us. It's all about you," I said.

"How do you figure?" he said while his eyes penetrated mine. I moved in to kiss him, and he pulled back from me so that our lips wouldn't meet.

"When it boils down to it, look at that. All I see is a guy who would do anything because he is sexually frustrated." I turned again and bolted in the opposite direction. He gripped my left hand.

"You are right; I am sexually frustrated. See? You know me so well. Now, I know you're going to be with James later on tonight. All you have to do is get the key from Erin for me."

"No. Maybe I don't want to." I placed my hands on my hips.

"Please, Tia. If it was for you, you know I would help you without even blinking," he said desperately. He begged and begged. He looked more sexually frustrated than I did. His pleading sort of turned me on. "Oh, please, please, Tia. Help me." We conversed while walking down the hallways. My moment with Mathew had finally arrived. I leered at the thought of it.

"So you're telling me you want me to steal the key for you?"

He nodded. "Yes, yes, that's exactly what I want you to do, and James will do the same for you. You know I haven't forgotten about you," he said eagerly. His facial expression was awkward.

"No, I want more. What else will you do for me?" I smiled shyly.

"What do you want?" he asked.

"You know what I want," I said. It was obvious. I bit my lip and blinked twice.

He sealed his eyes tightly, gently leaning in to kiss me; I shut my eyes, repeating the same process. For a second, I was briefly staggered, my anxiety disagreed with me, and the flying butterflies in my stomach were attentive. My heart shined brighter than the stars sparkled, my jaw dropped, and I was shocked. I kept my eyes sealed for him to kiss me. At that moment, I experienced excitement, wonder, and happiness all at once. It was exhilarating. The unbearable sound of my heart beating accompanied the emotions piercing my existence. I leered at his presence. We both smiled. I was blushing like a twelve-year-old girl.

"I'll think about it," he said, gliding my hair behind my right ear. Why would he leave me waiting on a kiss that wasn't going to happen?

My elated feeling was ruined the second he opened his mouth. "Yeah, I see," I said, pouting.

How was Mathew capable of making me feel like one of those animated characters on TV? And then came the feeling of unfulfillment at the expectation I had for us. He never had an ounce of passion for me until he displayed signs of despair. He traveled down the hallways, leaving me to consider his desperate plea. It was obvious he was using my sexual desires to his advantage. I wanted the day to expire. Suddenly, I was free to visit Erin and the others. After all, sex with James had stolen my concentration.

At Erin's house, I noticed how stunning her place was right away. For starters, she lived in a rich and fine neighborhood. If I felt safe anywhere, it was in Erin's hometown. There were small mansions on every corner and block. It was the cleanest community I had ever seen in my life. Everything about her neighborhood was gorgeous, especially her home, a three-story white-brick house. The first story had many large windows, exposing the living room, kitchen, and dining room. Before reaching the door, I looked through her window and saw her beautiful white marble floors, which also was on the ground around the front of her house and probably a huge swimming pool in the back. I believed as I rang the fancy doorbell. The sound of it ringing was sophisticated. Erin opened the door and welcomed me into her home. *How come I never saw her mother's house before? Wow, oh my God.* Their home was fascinating and beautifully decorated with items of significance. The white marble floors covered the entire first story of her home. Everything was clean and intact. Everything was organized, so I concluded that I wouldn't mar her valuable belongings by touching them in curiosity. Because of how expensive everything appeared to be, I planned to keep my hands to myself—unless I was touching James. I didn't have the finances to replace her personal items.

I looked over the entire house. James and Angelina were already there, having a conversation in the kitchen, eating fruit from the large clear bowl in the center of the table. Angel was talking while James laughed about Erin and her bus experience. "James, I'm not joking. And then the homeless black guy said to Erin, 'Actually, I have two swimming pools with money, and my car isn't a few blocks away. It's down the street, you dumb little black bitch!'"

James hit the table as his laughter proceeded. I couldn't stop looking at the clear bowl in the center of the table. There were grapes, pineapples, mangos, and cherries. There was a glass-and-silver chandelier dangling and sparkling above their heads. In the living room was a sixty-two-inch television, and the dining room seemed to be just as flawless. I couldn't help but wonder what Erin had planned for us that evening. James and Angelina joined me on the living-room sofa after she finished her story. The furniture was black. I had never been aware of how attractive James was, especially when he made time to smile. I blushed, giggling on the inside.

Every member on the opposite team had some sort of attractiveness. Erin entertained her company with her arrival. I couldn't help but notice her wide hips. The red dress she was wearing was a little inappropriate for the occasion. It was tightly hugging her curves. What was she all dressed up for? James was for me, and Andrew was for Angel, but I thought he should have been for me, too. I looked at Erin. What was she wearing, and who the fuck did she think she was? She stood in front of us with her wavy curls. *Whatever, whatever.* I rolled my eyes at the thought of her beauty. She hadn't told Angel or me to dress suitably for the event.

"James and Tia, you have an arrangement to attend to. Beforehand, Angel, Andrew is running fashionably late, so it would be impossible to do anything without him," she said, standing like a professional, looking classy.

I gently shook my head at her. *What an attention whore.* "This is some bullshit," I whispered. And then I said, "Why do James and I have to wait? I'm not a patient person. The delay could be long. I don't have all night." I arched an eyebrow at her.

"You can't interact or any way communicate with James until Angelina's task is finished. We don't cheat."

Yeah, since when?

"It's forbidden for anyone else or me to eradicate your chastity belt without the fulfillment of an accomplished assignment. After we help Angel, you will focus on James, okay?"

I stood. "Focus on James? What about me?" I said bewilderedly.

She smiled. "I never said sex with James was for your pleasure. James is the punishment for your stupidity leading to intolerably absurd behavior that has created plenty of issues for us. Whatever he decides to do to you or with you is your business. It is an issue you must deal with. And if you disapprove, then you can just quit the game and lose the chances of winning those gifts at the end of the year."

I frowned and said sadly, "A punishment? For what—just being the character I was assigned to be? I thought—"

She walked up to me. "That's what you get for thinking. You think too much. Thinking is such a difficult task for you. Your mind is messy and completely unorganized. Let me think for you instead. You have gone far beyond your scheduled limitations, and your character is highly insupportable." Then she murmured in my ear, "If I was you, I would be more interested in gaining the knowledge of what tremendous activities are plugged into James's method of pleasure. Look beyond that gorgeous face of his. Haven't you heard rumors about him?"

Erin then grabbed Angel's arm and guided her up the stairs to one of the bedrooms. She was right. I wasn't concerned about the plan James had for me. He could have been a sick person, a complete and total pervert. My mind became wrapped in distasteful imaginings. I anticipated the worst. I sat beside him, even though I was frightened and fearful of his desires. I needed to know his purpose for my company, but I was too scared to ask him. It was awkward for me. I blinked shortly.

Erin said, "Happy nineteenth birthday, James. She's my gift to you."

I hesitated, thinking nothing of what she'd said. "So do you have anything special planned for us?" I said after clearing my throat. I rubbed the right side of my neck nervously. I toyed with my fingers. His expression was unreadable. He gently planted his hand on my thigh.

"I'm really not the type of guy that likes to talk about sex. I would rather just show you."

He was relaxed and calm to the point that it made me highly irritated. So basically, he was a pervert. Surprises terrified me. I didn't like not knowing what the hell to expect. Somehow, the mystery crawled deeply underneath my skin. *A surprise, huh? Okay.* My mind wouldn't accept his response. I was extremely uncomfortable. *Someone—anyone—please rescue me.* I inhaled and then exhaled loudly to diffuse my frustration. He passionately kissed me on my neck, which generated chills down my spine.

"Relax," he whispered seductively. "This is for me." He smiled erotically. I felt exhilaration. My heart began beating uncontrollably.

CHAPTER 6

Angelina

Masturbation

Masturbation should have been easy. How difficult could it be? I just had to position my fingers inside of my pussy and work them back and forth, in and out in a circular motion, right? It, in fact, seemed doable. I smiled while I stood in the mirror in Erin's guest room in my purple lace underwear. I was impatiently stalling for time. What or whom was I waiting for? Andrew? I lay on the bed with apricot crisp sheets and peach covers wrapped around my body, which were consumed of small hypnotic white and silver diamonds. As I rubbed my middle and index fingers against my pussy, making myself wetter was my only concern. Placing my middle finger inside of me, I breathed out as I masturbated, but something was missing. I didn't understand what was wrong. Something didn't feel right to me, but I refused to give up so easily, so I tried again. At that moment, I shut my eyes as I thought of my latest sex dreams and the unexplainable cravings that followed along with them. I needed to focus on my fantasies or someone specific. I wondered about what Tia had said to me yesterday about my deepest and darkest desires, which, for me, included Andrew. The moment I started fantasizing of him and his luxurious body, my body warmed up to the desire of being groped and fucked. Suddenly a tingling feeling came over me. I wished I could hear his whispers and feel the sweat that was dropping from his hot body. I suddenly became horny. I rubbed my pearl and groaned quietly. Unexpectedly, Andrew burst into the room. I stopped because I was a little bit embarrassed. His presence somewhat stunned me. For a second, when I was playing with my pussy and thinking of him, he all of a sudden showed up. But then again, I was excited that he was there with me at that second. I noticed he was holding a small white bag. I wrapped the covers around my naked body. As much as I wanted to show him my gorgeous body, I instead covered myself like a pussy. I was shy, and he wasn't. His confidence and boldness were attractive.

"This looks like you touch yourself to me," he said in shock while shutting and locking the door. "What's the problem?" he asked.

I was ashamed to say it, but I did. "I'm no good at this—you know, playing with myself. I don't even know where to start."

He leered wickedly, as if my lack of experience intrigued him. "Would you rather I touched you?" He could have asked me that again and again. He sounded hot.

Oh my, temptation was calling me. I savored those and the other enticing words Andrew said to me that night. I stored them in my little box of pleasures for mental orgasmic reasons. Of course I preferred to have him touch me. *Yes, yes, and yes.* I feared that if I responded, small rosy spots would appear on my cheeks, mortifying me.

"Yes, I would probably enjoy it more if you touched me instead." I flushed.

What girl didn't want to be groped by Andrew Walker? I did. My insides were screaming for attention, pleasure, and pain. He joined me on the bed, laying the white bag behind him. I was now wondering what was in the bag. His fingers traveled underneath the covers, and oh my. I jumped with a pounding heart busting through my chest. His hands were cold. I could tell his hands had been on something extremely cold before. His eyes and right hand penetrated me. I gasped. My gasps progressed when he decided one finger wouldn't suit me. I tilted my head back as he added an extra finger inside my walls. His fingers felt great in me. I had become more open to him and his sensational touch. I wanted to let him in me, so I opened my legs even wider for him. His gaze had grown darker on me, but it excited me considerably. With his other hand fondling me like an expert, he continued to stare me down. It was so seductive that I stared back at him lustfully. I wanted to speak, yet my tongue was knotted up, mainly tangled because of those hands of his. It felt astonishing when he moved around in me. When I slightly lifted my bottom half, he was able to work his fingers in different angles at a greater speed. He went faster and faster, and I slowly rocked my hips; he knew exactly what he was doing. Finally, I yearned for him to cease his hand motions. Still, if he had stopped, I would have pleaded for him to carry on under any circumstances. With his continuous groping, I bit my lip a million times over. I would have gotten on my knees and begged for more. He shouldn't have shown any mercy whatsoever for me. It would have just been more of something I couldn't take at the time.

He spoke softly. "Women talk too much sometimes—wouldn't you agree?"

I nodded. "Yes, we do." I groaned. "A lot." I breathed.

"Shush, and I bet you're one of those women that likes to talk." I continued to agree in silence. "You want to speak now, don't you?" he said, and I groaned, shaking spontaneously. His fingers went even faster than before. My lower body rose more gradually. He was now leaning more toward my body.

"When a girl is quiet and speechless, that is how a guy knows he's doing his job right," he said. "Your expression and the sound of your quietness shows me how good I'm making you feel," he whispered.

Oh my, what was he doing to me? All I could hear were his words. All I could feel were his fantastic fingers ramming me into a seductive obsession.

"Fuck the loud moaning noises, because they're fake. Now, your body posture—the shaking and curled-up toes—are the real signs of pleasure. Do you feel my fingers inside you? Here—taste them," he said, forcing the fingers he'd fucked me with into my mouth, demanding that I suck on them. I did. I tasted like nothing.

Instead of putting his fingers back inside me, he rested them on my clit. He gently rubbed my clitoris up and down. I had exhaled loudly. I loved to watch his reaction, but I was too busy shutting my eyes, trying to concentrate. His fingers accelerated faster and faster. *Stop, stop,* my subconscious yelled, full of pleasure. His words were lingering in my ears. They had stayed with me faithfully. He continually talked nasty to me, and his choice of wording only made me more orgasmic.

"I wonder what kind of crazy faces you create when you cum," he said. "I want to see you cum, Angel."

You and me both, baby—you and me both.

"You want me to fuck you." Yes, I did. "I can tell. Nothing personal, but I don't think you can take it."

I moaned repeatedly. "No, I can take it. I can take it, Andrew. Give it to me."

He went deeper and deeper. I jumped and screamed in excitement. How much deeper could he have possibly gone? "I don't think you can. Just imagine if I was inside you—I would probably break you. You can barely take me finger fucking you, so I doubt your tolerance for every inch of me would be bearable. Plus, I don't make love or have sex, Angel. I fuck," he said aggressively.

I couldn't take it anymore. My legs tightened. The room, all of a sudden, was extremely hot and heavy. The moment I succeeded in an orgasm, my mind froze up, and my body was stiff. I didn't care much about my good reputation, my average grades, or being kicked off the team. I couldn't move an inch. I forgot to breathe fleetingly. It was the greatest feeling I'd ever explored, and I desired more. The expression on Andrew's face seemed to say, "Mission completed." I happily turned onto my right side, ready to drift to sleep. However, I saw Andrew pull out a clear seven-inch dildo with a realistic head. *Oh no.* He handed the dildo to me.

As he attempted to leave the room, I asked, "Can you?"

"I can't. I only did this because Erin asked me to. I was just supposed to give you an orgasm."

Wait—now I'm slightly confused. You did this for me for Erin? "Would you still have done it if Erin wouldn't have asked you?" I said, not wanting to know his actual answer.

His voice was manly yet smooth and comforting to the ear. "Honestly, Angel, I probably wouldn't have."

I scowled. *You wouldn't have, not even for me?* "Why? Is spending time with me that bad?" I asked sorrowfully.

"Yeah, actually, it is. I'm trying to stay away from you."

"I want to get to know you. You, however, are trying to stay far away from me. Is it so bad being around me? Why did you really do this? Because you like someone else—Erin, perhaps?

"I did it for you. I can see your frustration lingering all on your face. I wanted to help you relax."

"Well, if you want to help, you should understand that your fingers are a little small for pleasure, don't you think?"

"They were big enough to make you cum, now, weren't they? I really have to go right now, okay?"

"Why?" I asked quickly.

"I can't control myself when I'm around you. If I stay here with you for another second, I'm going to fuck you against every wall in this room, and I'm not ready to do that to you. Sucking on that banana the way you did that day made me fantasize about you being my sex slave, but I'm bad for you," he confessed before closing the door.

So he did want me. He was just convinced that he was no good for me. It was because I was a virgin, wasn't it? It was the reason I had to do this myself. I didn't want to do it myself, though. I didn't want to do it at all. After Andrew left me alone in the guest room, I gently slid the dildo inside of me. It was uncomfortable and weird. It introduced my stomach to an odd feeling. It was sickening and nothing like what I had recently experienced with Andrew. I was indifferent to the sensation. I had to open up my mind to engage in my first sexual proposal with myself. I had shut my eyes to dream. I wanted to feel spectacular and sensational.

In my imagination, I let go by accessing the hot and nasty urges I buried underneath my innocence. I used the words of Andrew as motivation, savoring them. I slowly opened my current box of pleasures. My mind traveled to the occasion of his fingers ramming me into a seductive fixation. I stopped because I observed a small amount of blood on the dildo. Surprised, I continued to masturbate. I experimented with the functions and different levels of vibrations on the dildo.

I pushed the last button, and the ears on the rabbit started vibrating instantly. I liked that. The sensation felt incredible on my clitoris. The feeling was more advanced than my encounter with Andrew. The vibration from the rabbit ears bouncing against my pearl left me speechless. I elevated the speed of the long rabbit ears. Andrew had been right about something: moaning and groaning wasn't an indication that a woman was receiving real pleasure. I now knew this to be true, since moaning wasn't a thing I did much of when I was masturbating on my lonesome. I bit my lip again and again. I couldn't handle the aggressive force massaging my pussy. The evidence of its power was displayed in my toes, heavy breathing, and intense shaking. There it went again, that untouchable and unreachable longing feeling. It kept going and returning. But the more it came and went, the closer I was to reaching that feeling completely. Every time I retained the joy that my body cried out for, the feeling was more durable than the last time.

I needed and wanted it. I wouldn't stop the moment from happening. I placed the speed at the maximum level, and my body captured the feeling moments later. It felt like a tropical heaven, and my body didn't want to exit the gates. I focused on one important thing—that feeling—which only lasted for about one minute. It was over. I assumed that masturbation would always feel that way. For one minute, time stopped. In the next, it disappeared far beyond my reach. After I put the dildo in a ziplock bag for evidence, I slid my clothing back on and headed down the stairs. Sadly, Andrew was gone. I wasn't surprised. James, Erin, and Tia were waiting for me to return. Tia couldn't have looked weirder or more impatient. Erin grabbed the bag from my possession to inspect the blood on the dildo. Finally, James viewed it, since his observation had worth.

"Where's the assignment sheet?" he said.

Erin pulled the paper out from her bra. James quickly glanced over the assignment and then rewarded us with his signature. I sensed a small sigh of relief. I was glad the challenging part was over. An enormous weight had been lifted off of my girlish shoulders. However, masturbating was nothing like I imagined. I would definitely do it again. I wanted to keep the dildo that was in James's ziplock bag. I was too afraid to ask for it back, though.

James and Tia charged up the stairs. By the looks of it, Tia was joining James unwillingly. She stared directly at me with frightened eyes. I guess not knowing what to anticipate alarmed her. Maybe she would learn that sex served a greater purpose. Not all sex was great sex, no matter how appealing a guy looked. I was somewhat scared for her. Who knew? Maybe she would enjoy it.

CHAPTER 7

Tia

A Deprived Father

He released me from my belt, and then he tossed it onto the floor. I was relieved to hear the sound of the belt hitting the floor, since it freed me of my imprisonment. "Take my shirt off," he ordered seriously.

Jeez, he could have given me a break, I complained inwardly, but I did as commanded after hesitating for a short duration. Then again, it was a big mistake.

"Next time I order you to do something, don't hesitate. Do you understand me?" he said, stroking his fingers through my hair lightly.

Oh, fuck me. How can he be so direct and self-centered? What about my needs and interests, you self-serving bastard? I said, "Yes, understood." *What did I get myself into now? Some unidentified trouble.* I closed my eyes because I was nervous. Then I ran my fingers down his stomach to distract myself.

He tilted his head to the side. "I didn't ask you to touch me or move, did I?" he murmured while sucking on my earlobe. James was all kinds of weird.

I didn't like it at all. It was creepy. I didn't know whether it was too kinky for my taste or why I hated it that much. What made sex fun for me was that I made my own rules and regulations of seduction. James had formed his entertainment, and I was the victim of his pleasure. Judging by his tone, he enjoyed pain. He pulled a ribbon with a red bow from out of the front pocket of his jeans. He tied it around my head—for decoration, perhaps. I recalled Erin saying happy birthday to James. *Oh, hell fucking no.* I wasn't an object, yet Erin had sold me to James as if I were a damn Christmas gift. I had the red bow to prove it. He seemed greatly amused by my attire for some reason.

"Close your eyes, Tia," he demanded in a dark tone. It was going to be a long night, and his bossy, you're-mine-tonight attitude gave him the form of a dominatrix.

I listened. I was too afraid not to or to show signs of hesitation. Reluctance upset him. He blindfolded me with a tie he retrieved from the same front pocket. He left me standing by the door.

"Can you hear me?" he asked smoothly. He was fucking toying with me. What a child he was.

Touching the tie, I said, "Yes. I can hear you."

"Good. Come here," he ordered. As I started to walk, he said, "No, I never said walk to me. Crawl on your hands and knees—slowly."

His tone darkened as he spoke to me. It was unnerving. *"Don't walk like a human. Crawl like an animal." Nice, Tia. You were about to sex a fixated control freak, a depraved bastard.* What in the hell did he think I was—a little, cute pussycat or something? I got on my hands and knees and crawled to the sound of his voice as erotically as possible.

"Come here, kitty, kitty, kitty," he said repeatedly while I crawled helplessly to him like a toddler on the ground. The coldness of the floor caught the attention of my hands and knees. I was trying to listen carefully in order to find him in the room. I figured that the more I moved, the quicker I could get the fuck off of the floor. His voice seemed louder to my ears with every step I took. I got as close to him as possible. James began producing hot noises with his mouth, and my hands searched for his feet or legs. My hands found him, and I finally smiled through my blindfold.

He helped me up. It was the only generous thing he had done for me that night. "What took you so long?" he said, placing my hands on the desk wildly.

I don't know. It could have been that slow fucking turtle crawl you ordered me to do a second ago.

I was again uncomfortably bewildered. He had lost his damn mind, I thought. I had to remember that all of this was for Mathew. I repeated that notion in my head. James boosted me up and immediately turned me around. I recalled seeing a mirror in the room before James stripped away my vision, and I knew precisely where the mirror was stationed.

According to our centered position, we were standing right in front of it. I easily made the assumption that he wanted to inspect us fucking in the large mirror, which was bolted onto the wall. My heart was pounding out of control. James was too busy breathing on the nape of my neck to notice my discomfort, or he didn't care. Shockingly, I could feel his gloomy gaze on me.

"Bend over. Stick your behind up and out as far as you can," he commanded. I temporarily hesitated and then followed his order. He spanked me hard for not acting quickly. It stung.

"Stop hesitating." His tone was unfamiliar and unlikable.

I gasped heavily. I shut my worried eyes. He pulled down my brown shorts. His fingers tickled the sides of my thighs and legs as he did so. He grabbed my white panties and stuffed them into my mouth. *What the hell? No, he didn't.* My behind was in the air. He tore off my brown shirt. It was my favorite.

"You don't need this, do you?"

I shook my head. What good was my shirt now?

"Play with yourself," he said, and I hesitated once more. "You don't listen, do you? That's okay. You'll pay for it." He bit my left cheek. I jumped mildly.

He said, "Play with yourself," before he spanked me harder. I coolly positioned my hand on my clitoris. Every occasional spank added more painful bruising. He pierced me with his fingers. I spit out my underwear, and I moaned loudly. He aggressively covered my mouth with both of his hands, tilting my head back.

"Quiet," he ordered into my ear. "You don't get to moan out loud. Hold it in," he commanded. I moaned again. He bit my cheek again, harder this time, and spanked me.

"Whoa." I gasped.

Although the shit stung, it still got me wet, and James took advantage of the opportunity. He pierced my pussy with his dick. I arched my behind against his erection more, so I could feel him deeper inside me. He was about average size. He was gyrating inside me while pinching my nipples. His other hand was playing with my clitoris. *Good boy.* James fucked me roughly from behind. He felt remarkable inside me. He rapidly threw both of my legs up onto the desk. I groaned uncontrollably, and he smacked my behind. He hostilely readjusted my body. I was facing him. He lifted me off the desk, fucking me in the air with my arms wrapped around his neck. *Jeez, when will it cease?*

"Get on top," he said.

After all of the biting and spanking, I acted instantly. I bent down with caution because of my sore ass cheeks. They were bruised, but finally, I was in control. Riding was my specialty. I bounced on top of his long john. I moved my hips around and around while I bounced up and down. My cheeks smacked against his stomach. He had a perfect view of my behind.

I moaned. "Aw, yes, yes, I'm about to come."

He startled me with a quick spank on my left cheek. "Quiet!" he yelled.

I bent over with my behind in the air. He followed to reenter me. He fucked me harder, faster. *Jeez, fuck much?* He slowed down briefly because he was exhausted and needed to recuperate. I finished him off the moment I began riding again. He was shaking. He was exhausted, lying on the floor. He removed the tie from my eyes. For a second, I had forgotten about giving Mathew the key to his chastity belt. It had been a long time coming and was a lesson well learned. It was truly a punishment I would always remember. I rushed to gather my belongings. As for me, I had learned my lesson.

He smiled proudly. "I wanna go another round."

I had never truly hated having sex with anyone until I slept with James. He brought back the memories I was running scared of—memories of my father. I had to go rest from the pain he'd helped my mind reactivate. The pain was excruciating and discomforting.

"I can't. I have to go do something. It's an emergency," I said, shutting the door. My pussy was still wet. I stayed wet as hell. I was interested in another round. Actually, my pussy could handle a lot of rounds. It was rounds that I fantasized about doing with Mathew. Sometimes, though, I felt that I couldn't control myself. The more I had sex, the more I felt I needed it and the more it was difficult to stop, I thought.

I almost got lost with all of those damn doors in Erin's hallway when I was trying to leave. I finally found the stairwell. I slipped while rushing down the stairs, trying not to be seen. Erin and Angelina were nowhere in sight. I put on my ripped brown shirt. I was thankful that my breasts were tiny. I quietly closed the front door. By accident, I bumped into Erin, who frightened me. She caused me to jump. "Jeez, Erin, you startled me," I said, walking past her, heading for the bus stop.

"Where are you going in such a hurry?" she said with her hands on her hips.

"I have to be somewhere else right now," I said, making an effort to leave without having a conversation.

"Aren't you forgetting something?" She leered wickedly with an extended hand. I approached her. She moved her left hand.

"What's that in your hand?" I said.

"The very reason I invited you and the very reason you came over—the key. You seem to be more interested in aiding Mathew. Have you not learned your lesson?" she said. "Even with you helping him, the girls will win."

I rolled my eyes lightly. "What makes you so sure? The boys could still win in the end." I smirked.

She spoke once more. "I doubt it. I can promise you. Your actions will leave your so-called best friend and future boyfriend scarred." She opened her hand and revealed Mathew's key. I snatched it from her hand and continued heading to my destination.

Everything I had done was for Mathew. It wasn't love, but I obviously cared for him. I didn't know why I had just done things to jeopardize my rank and next posting. My teammates had known I was a complicated individual the moment they'd signed me up for the team. I had disappointed Erin countless times—on accident, of course. I was in this competition for the pleasure, not for the assignments, not to win. During the time I was traveling over to Mathew's apartment, I was anxious. I arrived at Mathew's door. I hesitated. If James had been there, he would have spanked me childishly. I knocked loudly. Mathew answered the door after a few more knocks.

He was stunned by my arrival. "Come in."

I entered, hoping not to discover the presence of Amy.

"Where's your girlfriend?" I said, looking around.

"She's with Dillon. They're having a sleepover at Jacky's."

I stared at him with questions that needed to be answered. I was scared of the truth. I was petrified of the feelings he might have for Amy. She was living in my dream house with my dream guy.

"Here—make yourself at home. Would you like anything to drink?"

I was thirsty. On the other hand, the last time I had accepted a refreshment, I had been drugged with God knew what. I was not going to be drugged again. I was smarter than that.

"Sure, I would love something to drink—thank you!" I smiled, not caring if he drugged me anyway.

I stooped down to sit on his sofa. I buried my nose into his couch. I could smell his cologne all over the sofa; it was similar to Cool Water by Davidoff, and it was perfection. I could have buried my nose in his couch all night. I inhaled. *No Amy. How delightful.* Mathew and I could have a heart-to-heart conversation without any interference. Mathew passed me a glass with four ice cubes in it and a Pepsi. I sipped on it, and it tasted flat. My first sip was my last.

"How deep do your feelings go for Amy?" I said. He was stunned by my question.

He arched an eyebrow, "Where did that come from?" He beamed.

I scratched my neck and crossed my legs. "I don't know. I guess I'm curious about your relationship."

He laughed, breaking eye contact. Then he gazed back at me. "Believe me, it doesn't go that deep." Why was he with her if he didn't love her? He probably did love Amy Robinson. She was pretty. What guy would argue that perception?

"You do care about her, though?" I said sadly.

He tilted his head back. "Of course I care about her." His answer almost made me burst out in tears. I frowned, putting my head down in shame for everything I had done for him. He lifted my head with his finger. We were quiet for a few seconds.

He met my gaze. "Nowadays, I have been more worried about you."

"What for? I'm fine. You don't have to worry about me. I came to say good-bye and to give you the key to your cage. I can't keep doing this with you."

"What is it that we have been doing?"

"Nothing, Mathew. It doesn't matter anymore."

I reached in my front left pocket and gave him the key. He removed his shorts to escape from the cage. Then he was free at last. I turned to the door, grinning, and caught a glimpse. I was weary from my day and his games. I walked to the door and twisted the doorknob; he gently grabbed my hand.

"Why do you do the things that you do? I miss you—you know, the way things used to be," he said. Where had this question come from?

I looked back at him, forgetting I'd never given him a brief explanation for the purpose of my sexual behavior. "What do you mean? You're interested in knowing why I am a bed hopper?" I said with crossed arms.

"That's an ugly way to put it," he said, glancing at the floor with his hands in his pockets.

"You can't even look at me while answering the question, can you? Isn't that what you and everybody else think of me as? I don't think there's a classier or a nicer way to say it, so it's fine. I don't care. I know you do because of the way you gaze at me."

"I'm not disgusted by you." Sure he was.

"Yeah, Mathew, you are." I froze, thinking there was no way the truth would part my lips. I giggled. "You want to know why I do what I do." I expected to mislead him. The truth about my past would destroy him. "I do it because I like it. Actually, I love it. It's all about the feeling of an orgasm, holding it for as long as possible and doing it again and again. It doesn't matter who it's with. An orgasm is an orgasm." He looked at me as if he were disgusted. *There is the stare I was planning to see.*

"Can you blame me? Do you listen to the disgusting shit you say out of your mouth?" His voice was cold and dissatisfied by my choice of wording.

"No! Don't you stand there like your trash doesn't stink. You have problems just as much as I do!"

"A long time ago, we were friends. Now I don't know who the hell you are anymore. That girl I knew is gone. I don't care anymore about how and why you became the slut that you are today."

I frowned. "You're an asshole!" I said, pushing him. "Ask me. Ask me again what happened to me and why I'm so damn damaged!" I kept shoving him forcefully, but he was barely affected by it. His balance was firm.

He yelled in my face. "Why the fuck are you this way, huh?"

I glared unkindly at him. "It's your fault I am all fucked up in the head and use sex as a way to forget, but I can't forget! I will never forget." Tears poured down my cheeks. I sniffled. He stared down at me in confusion. He placed his hands on my shoulders, trying to pull me closer to him.

When he touched me, the sensation unleashed images of my father raping me over and over again. I could feel and see him smiling at me. I was stuck in my past. Mathew brought me closer to the devastation of my nightmares. I froze as my mind recalled the tragic situation of my father and me. I could see his sickening face and those devilish eyes penetrating the pure and sweet girl I once was.

"Stop, Mathew. Stop! Don't touch me. Don't touch me, please! I blame you!" I screamed, balling up into a corner as I cried.

He appeared to be frightened by my reaction to him touching me. "What, Tia? What happened to you?" he said, attempting to hold me.

"You are what happened to me! You! I'm hurting and remembering things I can never forget because of you—because of us and everything I had." I gawked while unwanted tears fell from my eyes.

"I still don't understand what you're saying to me," he said with a weird expression on his face. A tear fell from his sorrowful eyes.

A small part of me hated yet cared for Mathew. I tried to smile at him to keep from crying and laughing to keep from frowning. It didn't alter the fact that I was angry with him and with myself. I wept and shook. How could I forgive Mathew, when I couldn't even forget the man who was hiding in my shadows? I couldn't let go, because I didn't know how. I had believed I was over it.

"I don't want you to feel this way. I'm sorry you're in pain. You know my only wish is to be here for you."

I stayed with him. He continued to hold me to cease my crying.

I wiped my nose. Exhausted, I was in his bed. Tears rolled down my cheeks. Sleep, surprisingly, came easily to me. I woke up feeling thirsty in the middle of the night. I was about to go to get something to drink from his kitchen, when I heard moaning coming from the living room. I peeked outside his door and saw Mathew fucking a girl on his couch. He fucked her harder from behind as he pulled her hair. She groaned even louder, and he pulled her closer to him by yanking on her hair. She lifted herself up, and he placed his hands around her throat while whispering, "Bitch, shut the fuck up. She doesn't need to hear your fucking mouth. Do you understand me?" He let her neck go. She coughed. They continued, and then I could hear him smacking up against her ass again and again. I began to breathe hard. My pussy started dripping. Moments later, my panties were soaked. Just thinking about how hard his dick was from fucking her got me even hornier. I shut the door quietly. I returned to his bed and masturbated about five times before he returned to his bedroom. I couldn't stop touching my pussy. I needed more, so I was prepared to go for about two more rounds. Just as he was entering, I started playing with my pussy for the sixth time. I stopped when he positioned himself on the floor to go to sleep. He could have fucked me. But instead, he did otherwise. I was as horny as he was. I was always ready to fuck. I had never in my life wanted to get fucked by anyone more than I wanted to get rammed hard by Mathew. I wanted him badly. I couldn't sleep because of my desire. Finally, when he fell asleep, I stormed out of his apartment.

When James had touched me, it had been a reminder of my father's forced invitations in my room. His hungry gaze, the amusement in his voice, and his sick smile had defeated the little positive energy I had left in me. I was damaged goods, ruined by my father's sickening touches. *Somebody, please—please heal my open wounds. Fix me. Cleanse my sores. Restore my health.*

This Lifeline

This lifeline is seriously tangled with curly knots,
Scarred forever by scratches
And marked with unwanted tattoos that can't be hidden.
This lifeline of mine is dried up with blood
that will remain in my darkest history.
Somebody, fix me.
Heal my wounds;
Cover my bloody sores.
Because there is no pretending to be blinded by the truth.
I'm cursed by my stupidity and pain.
Most of all, I'm haunted by the memories of my sickening secrets,
The secret of how my ill father corrupted me.
They are the most difficult to manage.
This lifeline of mine is damaged and buried with
chains, slowly breaking down my possibilities.
I tried to protect them from being revealed,
But every single day, it gets more challenging to keep it concealed.
This lifeline is tangled with curly knots,
Scarred forever by scratches,
Marked with unwanted tattoos that can't be hidden.
Why is it so permanently thin and spoiled rotten to the core?
Fix me.
Heal my wounds;
Cover my bloody sores.
Because this lifeline of mine transformed my scratches into scars,
My old, dried-up blood into stains.
Sooner or later,
Everybody will know my secrets.

CHAPTER 8

Jacky

You Got Herpes, Boy

I admired Erin. She was a leader—and a great one at that. I was her most trustworthy participant. Maybe at the end of our junior year, I would be rewarded with the authoritative status of team speaker for senior year. Erin needed to approve the new year's ranking leader. With her permission, we would vote for a new chief. Dillon's actions ensured there was no guaranteed upcoming leader. Angelina or Amy could be my chief for our final year. Before I could dream of the activities for next year, we had to finish our junior year. Unlike the rest of my teammates, who were fond of boys their age, I loved men who had already matured. Professor Rodríguez, the youngest instructor at Marshall S. King University, was a man of maturity. Besides, I had no intention of having sex with him once. *No way.* What would one affair do for a young woman like me? Why once, when I could have him again and again like an unstoppable marathon? From what I'd heard, older men gave the best sexual experiences.

It was Monday morning, and I was anxious for my first class of the day to begin. Because I was highly impatient, I arrived in class earlier than my instructor had anticipated. Professor Rodríguez's morning services could be of great use. Today had significance. According to my plan, I was attired for the occasion, a naughty schoolgirl ready to be led astray by her instructor. My hair was in pigtails, and I wore black glasses like those of a librarian. My uniform also included a dark blue tie, a tight red jacket to match my miniskirt, and pumps. My dark makeup nicely contributed to my look. My pumps clicked loudly against the tile floors. As I arrived in Professor Rodríguez's classroom, the door slammed behind me.

"Ms. Dickerson." He paused. "You're early," he said slowly, staring down at my miniskirt. He coughed. "You look"—he paused again—"different."

I grinned. "I know I'm early, Professor Rodríguez. I was wondering, if you aren't occupied after school, if you would tutor me. I require some extra assistance with citations and paraphrasing," I said with an innocent smile.

"I don't think you need any help. You're doing great in my class," he said with his hand on his chin, misunderstanding.

"I don't want to be great, Professor Rodríguez. I want to be outstanding or swell. Please? You won't regret it. I promise," I said.

He smiled. "Sure, right after school, young lady."

"I swear." I giggled.

A good tutoring session with my instructor was something I needed. I was surprised he didn't recommend the tutoring center to me. It was designed to help students with their classes, because most professors didn't tutor students after school, not like high school teachers, I believed. I walked effortlessly to the first seat near the door. I purposely slipped on the floor, dropping my English and biology books onto the ground.

"Shit, my foot," I said, holding my ankle. He rushed to my rescue, making an effort to assemble my belongings. "I got it—thank you."

He smiled.

"Don't make this problematic. It's fine."

I regained my supplies. And then I softly groped his hand. His eyes met mine. He pulled me by both of my hands to lift me off the floor. I stood and then assertively fell back down to the ground.

"Oh boy, oh boy, oh boy, my ankle," I complained. "It hurts!" I shouted.

He carried me from the floor to his iron desk. "Which ankle, Ms. Dickerson?"

I sobbed. "Shit, the right one."

He carefully removed my pump from my foot. He gently touched my ankle. My foot was hypersensitive. I held in my giggles with difficulty.

He smoothly rubbed and massaged my ankle. His muscular hands felt fantastic. *That was nice.* I tilted my head back.

"Well, it's definitely not broken, but you probably sprained your ankle," he said seriously. "Here is a pass to see the school nurse, to be sure it isn't serious," he said, writing down my information on the pass. I didn't want to leave, and I was not looking forward to visiting the school nurse. I stooped to sit in my assigned seat.

"Don't be ridiculous. Thank you, but I'm sure I am fine. I really appreciate the kindness," I said.

He leaned back in his chair to continue grading tests. "Okay, but if you happen to change your mind, the pass is up here for you," he said smoothly.

"Okay, thank you." I smiled again.

Erin and a few more scholars entered the classroom, including Michael. He stared devilishly at me while sitting in his seat. I sneered delightfully at Michael. I guess the "You have herpes" prank was unforgivable as well as unforgettable. *Get over it.* I glanced at my teacher. Professor Rodríguez was dressed in a nice black Armani suit, a black vest, and black Stacy Adams dress shoes. *Oh my.* I treasured his professional appearance. My subconscious smiled. *Bend me over and spank me silly, Professor Rodríguez.* The remainder of the students entered the class before eleven o'clock. All girlish attention was on Professor Rodríguez. The girls glanced seductively.

"Good morning!" he announced. "How was everyone's weekend?"

"Fine," the women said all together.

"Take out your homework assignment, and have it in your hands for me to collect before you leave," he said, writing our class and homework assignment on the green board. I tugged on Erin's arm.

"Provide me with the info. What did you discover?" I said.

"He's single with no children. He was married to a much older woman but soon divorced for financial purposes—so I heard." She raised an eyebrow. "When he was married, let's just say he believed in infidelity. He committed adultery."

Mr. Purity obviously wasn't covered in righteousness after all. Disloyalty was his close companion. He didn't strike me as a man who fell into the category of adultery. Professor Rodríguez quickly accumulated our homework assignments and slowly glanced over our work.

"If you throw the ball, say, on the first pitch, you'll a hit home run." She signaled me by tapping on my arm. "Today go for the home run."

"Okay. What do I do?"

"One or all of the above—whichever gets the task done," she said.

"What if neither of those strategies works?" I frowned.

"Do you see the coffee on his desk?" She pointed.

"Yes," I said.

"He will be very cooperative," she murmured.

I smirked. *Good.*

The professor said, "Complete the reading assignment on page ninety-three, do all ten questions on page one hundred one, and copy down your homework assignment. It needs to be submitted first thing tomorrow. Any questions, anyone?"

I ran my fingers through my soft hair. He sipped on his coffee and then rested it on the desk.

"Okay. Get started. When you're finished, get a head start on your homework, or just remain quiet during the remainder of the period."

He proceeded to calculate the scores on our tests. He quietly tapped his foot. I opened my English book, glanced over the story, and anxiously finished the ten questions about the boring Oedipus story. I started working on the homework assignment on a blank sheet of paper. When my pen left the paper, my classmates started leaving, and I patiently grabbed my belongings with my questions and homework assignment in my hands. I smiled as Professor Rodríguez grasped the sheets of paper. I gazed into his eyes and at his smooth lips. He leered at me unforgettably. Out of nowhere, Michael rudely bumped me.

"My apologies, Jack the Rabbit. You look different today—erotic. Tia's slutty tendencies must be rubbing off on you. You look like all kinds of fun."

I gave him the finger and kept marching. Unfortunately, he followed.

"I love how smooth your legs look. I see they are sealed firmly right for the moment." He beamed. "They were just open a minute ago. What time do those doors reopen?" He blinked twice.

Get a life.

"Fuck off, Michael," Erin said.

Michael traced Erin's steps. He put his arm over Erin's shoulder.

"Want do you want, Michael?" she said.

"That was a nice little stunt you pulled with the medicine and the I-got-herpes thing. I just happened to have a cold sore that day, so congrats on the assignment." He clapped.

"So what—congrats to us for treating your herpes problem?" Erin said.

He clapped louder. "It was pretty degrading for me, but if I was you, I would do some research on the Internet—Google, perhaps."

I shoved him. "What the hell did you do?"

He laughed. "Someone's good at *Playboy*." He said with narrowed eyes. "She should consider being a *Playboy* Bunny." He chuckled during his departure. "It's the true definition of the words *public mortification*."

"Erin, who is this pertaining to?" I peeped at her. Her expression was unreadable. And then it was filled with unawareness.

She shook her head. "I don't know. It may have been Tia or Amy." She walked in the opposite direction. "I'll find out ASAP!"

I relaxed my shoulders. "What about Mr. Ford? He will make you see the dean for skipping class!"

Shit. It was time for Mr. Ford and his devious acts. Without Erin entering class with me, my brain was in my stomach. I marched slowly into class and sat in the closest seat. I started breathing deeply to cease my panic attack. Mr. Ford entered the class with his arms crossed. His head was shinier than usual. He had huge bags under his eyes. He exhaled deeply as he stood in the center of the classroom. We all gazed at one another. A student was coughing in the background. Erin suddenly joined us in the classroom. She sneered at Mr. Ford. His expression concerned me. He looked evil. However, I was surprised Erin didn't have to visit the dean.

Today students had to deliver their presentations. The purpose of the assignment was to improve our public-speaking abilities. I hated speaking in front of audiences. I communicated with my fellow peers but did so one or two students at a time. My heart was thumping out of my chest. All I was capable of hearing was the sound of my heart pounding in my ears. All of a sudden, I was dehydrated. During the middle of my presentation, my nerves manipulated my performance. It was horrible. My lack of confidence in my speech and lack of rehearsal made me sound as if I had amnesia. I should have practiced more—or at all, for that matter. Lack of preparation was the reason I fell flat on my face. The humiliation was finally over. I sunk lower in my seat, hiding from everyone. I wanted to die.

After Mr. Ford's class, the day went by swiftly. Professor Rodríguez was nodding off when I visited him in his classroom. I locked the door behind me and pulled down the shades for privacy. I set my purse on his desk. I placed my hand between his thighs while placing soft kisses on his neck. He smelled hot and manly. He was in the chair with his head entirely tilted back. I ran my fingers through his soft, dry hair. His chest was moving from his light breathing. My facial expression darkened to desire at his weakness from the drugs. My eyes filled with a hunger wanting to be satisfied. I situated my black glasses on his desk. I slowly removed my red jacket and blue tie, dropping them onto the floor. I unbuttoned my tight white button-up shirt, exposing my breasts, while looking down at him. I delicately rubbed his python through his dress pants. He was bigger than I'd imagined.

Oh, Professor Rodríguez, I finally get to feel you inside me. On all those days when I made you weak, you were just as vulnerable as I was, but today is the only day the desire to peek is allowed. He wouldn't remember anything, and my mind was running ridiculously. The situation made me horny immediately. I kissed him on his neck again and then on his chest and stomach while positioning myself on top of him. I opened his mouth with my hands to stuff one of my breasts into his mouth. I forced his head between my breasts, and I shook them in his face. I captured his hands and placed them on my ass cheeks. I made him smack them. Later, his hands fell because I had grown tired of controlling them myself. I glided my princess against his companion. I bounced on it for laughs.

I whispered into his ear. "I'm going to suck, fuck, and ride you until I get tired. You hear me?" I said, licking his neck.

Later, I scrunched up my panties and tucked them in his right pocket. I slid in between his legs and unzipped his dress pants. *Oh my God.* He stood tall and proud. I licked his shaft and sucked on the tip. I placed his entire erection in my mouth.

"You like that, Professor?" He didn't move a muscle. After I carefully situated the condom over his length, I regained my position on top of him. The feeling of him inside me was relieving and mind-boggling. I rolled my eyes at the tightness of his penis inside my pussy.

"I'm going to fuck you hard and rough."

I thrust my hips, and I looked at him as I took him all in. As he was tightly introduced to my walls, the introduction was gratifying. The drugs Erin had given him made him weak and vulnerable. Momentarily, he was going in and out of consciousness. His movements were not powerful enough to make a substantial difference, so I kept riding him in the chair. I stared at him, watching the heaviness from his eyes become more difficult to overcome. I sucked on his bottom lip. I went faster and faster, holding onto the back of his seat, and I didn't care if we fell from the wild and hot ride I was giving him. I was too excited to have his dick inside me to show concern or fear of getting caught. I'd wanted him for so long, and he was mine now. I was exhausted, but I wanted an unlimited amount of him, so I continued. I wouldn't let my exhaustion take away from my exhilarating experience, but I needed and wanted more. It was a craving that only his touch could fulfill. I was displeased.

I wanted him to fuck me. I valued rough, kinky sex. I liked a man in control of the situation, dominating and punishing me—it excited me. I wanted him to ravish my being, fuck me spontaneously. I was fond of erotic surprises. I thought, putting my breasts in his mouth. *Suck it, yes.* "I'm your dirty little slut. Yes. Aw, Professor, I feel you," I said naughtily. I held the back of his head. I leaned as far back as I could go. My behind smacked against the upper part of his thighs.

"Jeez, Jesus Christ, oh Lord, yes," I murmured. "I'm your nasty bitch."

I came. I stopped and urgently readjusted my skirt, fixing it. His pants were down to his ankles, and I kissed him on his left cheek to leave a red mark. I grabbed my purse and pulled my purple camera from my bag. I snapped some quick images for evidence. I zipped up his zipper.

I whispered in his ear, "You can keep my panties. I want you to have them. When you smell my underwear, I want you to reminisce about this moment with me—a moment you won't remember."

Before I left the classroom, I snatched my personal items from the floor and my glasses from the desk. I forged his signature on the dotted line and slammed the door behind me. I couldn't have imagined this scene in my wildest dreams. It was incredible. After today, I looked forward to more private sessions with my instructor. But next time, he would remember every dirty little detail.

CHAPTER 9

Erin

Naked Images

I quickly powered up my Apple laptop. I typed in the password. My bet was on Tia. I entered her name into the Google search bar. Oddly, there were no images of her on the Internet. *Good girl.* I typed Angelina's full name next. *Clear.* She hardly disappointed me. Next, I looked up Amy Robinson and found modeling images. *Okay.* Finally, I typed in Dillon Moore's name, and my jaw dropped. *Dammit, Dillon. I had high expectations for you, and you blew it.* I exhaled to release my frustration. There was no looking beyond this. Everything was publicized, from her facial features to her toes—the whole birthday suit. I shook my head. Her boyfriend—or, should I say, ex-boyfriend—had no boundaries, no limitations. As with Tia, her reputation preceded her. She was now excluded from her future status. "Shit, shit, shit!" I beat the desk. I stared directly at the screen on my purple laptop. *How humiliating.* I yanked my cell phone off the desk and speedily dialed Dillon's number while fragilely tapping on the desk. It rang momentarily.

Someone responded, yet it sounded like a devastated adolescent. She spoke in a low and hesitant voice.

"Jeez, I can't hear you. Hey, speak up," I said, adjusting the volume on the phone.

She whined. "What happened wasn't my fault," she said. "I was asleep when he took those pictures."

"Fact or not, that isn't significant. It's all bad either way. You have sabotaged your reputation indefinitely for ranking leader."

"What! No. You can't do that!"

"I'm sorry, Dillon. Tia has higher chances of being senior chief than you."

"Absurd. Tia's reputation is worse, so I strongly doubt that."

"Perhaps you should see the naked images of yourself, which are plastered all over the Internet. Last time I checked, the exposure of Tia's birthday suit isn't on Facebook. We need a girl that is eligible for your position to temporarily substitute for your station until all of the commotion boils down."

"You can't replace me. I won't allow it! This commotion will never truly boil down. You know it!"

I knew she was right. I just needed an excuse for a replacement. However, it was nothing permanent. "We're having another meeting tomorrow morning. It's the last one you will be able to attend; I expect you to be present. Inform the girls through text messages."

"After everything I've done for you, seriously, Erin. You are fucking annihilating my junior year!" she said, her voice cracking.

"I have a higher ranking, Dillon. Do as I ordered." She was quiet. I added, "Word of advice: I would kick that lame excuse of a boyfriend to the curb."

"Yeah, okay. Whatever. I will consider it."

I hung up the phone. *Oh yeah, she should be considering it all right.* He was the reason she was in this mess in the first place. *Dump his no-good, lazy ass.* I tossed my phone onto my bed. My stomach started growling. I rushed down the stairs to prepare breakfast for dinner. Tonight, though, I wasn't hungry for food. I sustained a deeper hunger for sex. I missed sex. It had been such a long time since I had been sexually satisfied. I ate eggs, bacon, and three small pancakes without syrup or jelly. I drank a mouthful of orange juice. *Tasty.* I smacked my lips together, sucking the remainder of the juice from around my upper lip. It was cold.

At that moment, creativity invaded my brain. I had a glorious but evil plan to conclude my challenging obligation. It would test my strength of independence. I needed some magical strategy to get Jeremy to confide in me, so I could pursue him to indulge me. It was intelligent. The timing was perfect, because we required a replacement. Perhaps I could manipulate or persuade Jeremy's girlfriend to assist me. I could easily gain knowledge pertaining to the strengths and weaknesses of their relationship and use it to my advantage. What female student at our school didn't want to become a member of our BOTS Association, although they knew nothing of our sexual acts?

I was positive that the girl, whoever she was, would be part of the destruction of her own relationship. I removed my clothing as I looked in the mirror. I stood there gloriously, embracing every feature of my body. I proudly admired my temple. While I peeped, my eyes were incapable of remaining open. I collapsed onto my bed, and I was completely naked. However, I couldn't sleep. I thought of my older brother. My emotions, at that period in my life, were overly sensitive. We had shown our affection through arguments, which had sometimes resulted in thoughtless fights. They were purposely designed for a greeting or good-bye.

I covered my head with my pillow and my body with a blanket because of the coldness from the central air conditioner. I cried. I hated that he had committed suicide. Our playful confrontations, his laughter, and our unconditional love had sustained my sanity. Great sex preoccupied my mind to try to push away my uninvited memories. My last sexual encounter with Lucky had been well deserved. I moaned and made reassuring, loving faces. His head was in between my thighs. His tongue was situated at the tip of my element. As the process proceeded, he thrust his fingers inside me. I adored the assault.

I cried out mournfully. I slightly lifted myself to support closeness. He kissed the insides of my thighs and gradually moved up the sides of my stomach with heated, juicy kisses. My lips quivered. My body couldn't befriend stillness. I giggled at the fragile feeling of his soft and sweet touch. It tickled me silly throughout the invasion. He fondled my breasts and sucked on my hard nipples. I peeped up at his dreamy ocean-like eyes. I was trapped in the sea and lost, trying to map my way back to reality. *How did I arrive at this destination, my sweet, sweet Lucky? How did I get here?*

"You want me, Erin."

"Yes!" I said, tired of struggling to deny it. "Yes, Lucky, I want you."

He unbuckled his jeans and exposed his—cock cage. My mouth dropped open.

"I told you I would fuck you somehow with this cock cage on!"

I woke up screaming and breathing out of control. *Holy Moses, he was coming for me.* My heavy sweating awakened me. *Stop panicking; it was only a dream.* I wiped my forehead. *That horrible nightmare could have given me a heart attack, Mathew Henderson—seriously.* I released the tension from my shoulders. They were stiff. I rolled them backward and forward. Exhausted, I regained my position in bed and slept dream free.

It was time for another boring meeting in the auditorium, and I was in charge of it. I needed to recap the situations that had previously and recently occurred. Amy and Tia were sitting beside each other. *What a predicament.* Tia was trying to steal Mathew from her, and she knew nothing of it. Tia was insane to maintain their friendship and quietly date Mathew behind her back. It was a cowardly and bitchy thing to do.

Angelina was texting—or sexting—Andrew on her phone. *Good luck with that one.* Dillon was scowling with her lips sucked in. Secretly, I found it funny. In fact, I smirked at her. She glared back at me. Jacky was the most isolated one out of the group, sitting closest to the back. She was eating pineapples. What was with her eating fruit? I wonder as I befriended the stage once more. As the investigator, I was studying my colleagues' unpleasant habits. I raised my eyebrows, pacing in the center of the stage.

"Someone inform us of the former and recent activities that have happened." The pitch of my voice rose. I cleared my throat. Tia gave me a look. "Yes, Tia. You can be the year's informer. What happened, and what's happening?" I said.

"Well, let me see. Angelina popped her own cherry—good job. At least you're the only girl in this room who couldn't say she lost her virginity to an asshole who doesn't love her—because the asshole would be you. To change the subject, I had sex with James as a chastisement; I guess I learned my lesson. Mathew was released from his cage. Would talking about everyone's relationship be applicable to my discussion?" she said with large eyes.

"No, it would be irrelevant," I said. "Is there anything else?"

"Jacky drugged and raped Professor Rodríguez—nice, Jacky," she said, winking at Jacky. "Oh yeah!" she screamed. She reclaimed her seat and then stood up again. "I almost forgot—Dillon's the slut with the dirty pictures on Facebook, in case someone didn't recognize her." They giggled. "That clarifies the activities; no further events, Erin."

"Stop with the teasing," I ordered.

"You're the one who's the slut that is fucking everyone!" she said hostilely. "*Apuesto a que tu boca está infestado de enfermedades de transmisión sexual, que polla adorador*!"

"That's enough!" I said, creating a fist for no purpose. I thought Dillon had just said something about Tia having STDs in her mouth.

Jacky changed the subject. "So this means a replacement is in order."

Angelina said, "It's a temporary replacement so that the chaos can decrease! No one is permanently replacing her!"

Amy said, "Calm down now, Angel. Ever since you plucked yourself, you two are so gay for each other. Relax. It's her station; nobody wants it anyway." She rolled her eyes.

Jacky and I laughed. Dillon was quietly babbling her comments in Spanish: "*Espero que ella recibe herpes genital, chlamydia, gonorrhea, syphilis y trichomonasis tener un derrame cerebral lenta y morir al instante. Odio esto, odio esto, odio esto.*" She was such a child.

Tia joked, "I guess you won't be ordering me around in the future, thank God." They applauded, except for Angelina. Dillon mocked them by cheering along with sarcasm.

"Okay, okay, okay, everybody. Let's discuss a more suitable strategy for substitution. I am aware we choose the most eligible and relevant individual for ranking, yet I have made alterations for our advantage. I need someone to eagerly collect twenty-one signatures instead of twenty."

"I'll volunteer to collect," Amy said immediately. Every member left the room except for Amy and Dillon.

"Good. Save the last spot for someone special. Draw a line at the bottom of the list after the signature has been given."

"What is the girl's name?" Amy said, ready to put her pen to the test against her pink notepad, but I didn't know the answer to that question.

"Good question, Amy. I need you to find it out for me; it's Jeremy's girlfriend."

Amy roamed into the halls. I walked closer to Dillon.

"Again, I am sorry, Dillon. You would have been a good leader." She was silent. "I will talk to you soon."

The expression on her face was annoying. There was nothing I could do. We had to proceed without her. It felt sort of awful leaving her behind, but I didn't make up the rules; I just followed them. Who knew when her mess would resolve itself? Of course, Dillon would always be an important part of our popularity group. Her responsibility wasn't finalized, just postponed.

In the hallway, James strolled up to me. "I wanna see Tia."

Well, good for him. I exhaled, exhausted. "Yeah, and I wanna see Jesus and own a blue magical pony, but that probably won't happen either."

"Come on. Stop tweaking, and just do it, okay? You may have seen this as a punishment, but I doubt she saw it that way," he said, retaining a grip on my right arm. He just loved to touch me.

"Look, whatever your dick and Tia's ass, mouth hole, and pussy want to do with you is your business. But let me tell you this: you have no leverage to carry out my interest anymore," I said, snatching my arm away. "It was tolerable entering into a partnership with you. On the other hand, your time has expired. I no longer want your services."

"Yeah, right," he argued. "Soon she'll be begging for it. I doubt she will be able to stay away!"

"Yeah, because that will be difficult," I said ironically.

It was risky to deny the fact that Tia had had enough of James. From what I'd heard, he was a controlling maniac sexually. If he desperately craved another sex session, he would personally have to bring it to Tia's attention. Tia was obsessed with Mathew, and so was Amy. There was no way drama wouldn't bite them in the ass that year. It was just the beginning.

There I was, sitting in Mr. Ford's class again. We were watching him teach the bullshit of the century: history. History wasn't bullshit; his teaching method was. He was an appalling instructor. Boredom pervaded our atmosphere. I was fond of history. Mr. Ford, however, annihilated the topic. His bald head reminded me of the animated character Mr. Clean. He stood in front of me, scratching his balls. *That is fucking gross!* Did he really have to do that right in front of me? *Sit in the back next time,* I told myself. Talk about provocative or mildly inappropriate.

His tone was deep, hoarse, and creepy, as if he were a depraved person clandestinely living in our neighborhood. "Today you're going to be working on a lab project."

For me, everything he said went through one ear out of the other. By the look of the monstrous grin on his face, which was the creepiest and most awkward grin he had revealed yet, apparently, he was just getting started with boring me to death. I didn't know whether or not I hated his maliciousness or him personally. Judging by my own character, I had no right to criticize him. On the outside, I was as hard as stone. But on the inside, I was a lonely, heartbroken, evil, sexually frustrated, jealous, man-stealing bitch, so no judgment there.

The guy I was in love with, the guy of my dreams, had feelings for another. Without him, my dreams would be transformed into a nightmare. And now I was preparing to organize the same nightmare I was most frightened of. In addition, I would leave this school a legend my junior year. Being a female legend was something I wanted desperately. I had forgotten about being loved and having the happy fairy-tale story that girls wished for pathetically. I had forgotten about being nice and being liked. Who needed to be loved, when I was going to be remembered by a sex game? Only leadership created a leader's level of remembrance and intelligence. Now it was my time to shine. Nobody had seen anything yet.

I watched the clock as our class time dwindled. When class ended, I left the room sparkling like a star on the inside. After class, I decided to get a little something to eat because I was hungry. Downstairs in the cafeteria, I searched for any of my teammates. All of them were sitting toward the rear of the lunchroom. I felt a small pain occurring at the right side of my tummy—cramps. It was just what I needed—stomach pain—but I managed, of course. Amy arrived at the table with a young girl.

"Erin, I would like you to meet—"

"Thanks, Amy. I got it from here. It's nice to meet your acquaintance," I said, extending my hand, waiting for her to speak her name. She displayed mutual appreciation and shook my hand shyly.

She smiled purely. "Josephine Young."

Josephine Young—her name was catchy to me. She had potential beauty. With the right guidance, she could have been one of the prettiest women in school. She wore glasses and had a mouthful of braces. I thought they were unattractive on other people, but strangely, her light pink braces gave her a touch of prettiness. She was a nerd but a hot one. It was odd for me to think so. She was the girl I had seen Jeremy kissing some days ago in the hall. That day, her clothes were baggy. It was downright disgusting how loose her clothing was. I guessed Josephine was probably nineteen years old or maybe even younger. Amy handed me the sign-in sheet. With my index finger, I moved down the list, thoroughly searching for her name. Her signature was the last name on the list. I folded my hands together. Amy had done what she was told.

"Well, it looks to me like we have twenty signatures before yours. I don't even think you have what it takes for a membership."

She scowled. "Yeah, I probably don't."

I laughed. "Then why are we having this conversation, Jo?"

"It's Josephine. And because I should be qualified to be a member," she said with a serious expression.

"For qualification, you need a high percentage, so how high is yours?"

She had a blank expression on her face. She was clueless. She stared at the table, pausing. "A fifty-five percent," she said confidently. She was lying. I didn't like prevaricators. She was lessening the probability of our transaction.

"Wow, fifty-five percent. Not bad—too bad it's a lie," I said without blinking.

"Okay, okay, a thirty-five percent." She had finally spoken the truth.

"Raise your percentage. Then you and I will discuss prerequisites for joining our little club. Remember, you can't become popular by association."

"How do I do that?" She shrugged.

"By the exposure of your coolness—let it be natural. Don't try too hard. Don't try at all. Get out of that shyness of yours. Because if you want to be in this club, you will be engaging in activities you never thought you would engage in before. It's the kind of things some people end up regretting."

She paused, folding her arms. She smiled at us and informed us with confidence, "Some regrets are worth making, some opportunities are worth taking, and I am looking forward to being engaged in the activities."

I loved every word. Her statement sounded like something I would have said. I rose. "Keep thinking like this and you will be a member in no time," I said. I extended my right hand to her. Jacky and Angelina laughed. I shushed them. Suddenly, they were silent. Jo shook my hand. I positioned myself back in my seat.

"Is there anything else I can do?" she asked.

Yeah, I wanted her to get the fuck out of my way so that I could fuck her boyfriend. She could have done that for me. I'd let her have him back after I fucked and dumped him. I strongly doubted the stability of their relationship, especially because I had plans for him to fall in love with me. What a demanding bitch she was. All the same, I liked her.

I waved her off. "Just work on being cool." This was all too easy for me, like cutting a piece of cake. All of my arrangements were set in motion. I would trap Josephine in my webs of deception.

CHAPTER 10

Angelina

Liking Andrew

What the hell was wrong with me? I was always thinking and dreaming of those beautiful green eyes. I felt I had a serious predicament up my sleeves. Every night after Andrew had led me astray, I fantasized in my dreams about him touching, kissing, and caressing me. The thought of Andrew catering to all of my mouthwatering and darkening desires turned me on. It had a tremendous effect on my behavior. What was happening? Anytime I was in his presence, I got strangely aroused. He was tormenting me. He knew how much I wanted him. It was obvious he yearned for me and knew the way my body was aching for him. The desperation in my eyes was readable. He was playing hard to get. I had never chased a guy before. It was a masculine behavior, and it wasn't attractive; it was confusingly unnatural for any woman. Instead of him being all over me, I was all over him, practically begging for it. *What a tease.* This was my first encounter with a guy who was a tease. I had to do the teasing, which meant I should have been the teaser. A voice inside me said, *A male teaser is motivating.* But motivation was the last feeling flowing through my mind. He provoked me, yet I was the one publicly humiliated.

Tears continuously flowed down my face. I concealed them the moment I sat down at a table in the cafeteria. I needed a minute away from Erin, the posse, and the assignments. I was supposed to remain with my team, but I didn't need permission to spend some quality time alone. Sometimes the situations of the game were overbearing for me. I couldn't tolerate the pressure on some occasions. The overpowering thought of my father's absence produced tears like a waterfall. I folded my arms around my face so that I could finally weep in peace.

Unfortunately, the distractions would not allow me to cater to my depression. Andrew Walker tapped my shoulder insistently. His cologne smelled like Armani Code. I called it the panty dropper. Every second the fragrance invaded my nostrils, I dreamed of him touching me for hours.

"You couldn't sleep last night, huh?" he said.

I lifted my head in Andrew's direction.

His voice and face conveyed seriousness. "What's wrong, Angel?"

"Oh, nothing. I hate these assignments. I hate this school, and did I mention that I hate these assignments? Nothing. I'm tired of everything. I miss my father. And that special boy at my house—we should have never adopted him."

"Whoa, I thought Tom was your biological brother."

"He is, but he should have been adopted. That way, when I permanently change the locks, I won't feel as bad for locking his ass out."

"What's really upsetting you?"

"Do you never get exhausted of this game? Everything we do consists of sex—sex this and sex that. On a daily, this is what every popular college student is doing—an assignment based on sex."

He gazed into my eyes while listening, smiling to soften me like oil at room temperature. I was liquid.

"You're feenin' badly, ain't you?"

Oh boy, I'm feenin'? No, I was definitely not, not anymore. He was not the addictive substance my body was crying for. Plus, I needed a taste to be addicted, right? It was tempting—that was all. "No, you're feenin'," I said, shaking my legs, and he laughed. "What do you want from me?"

He shrugged. "Nothing. Maybe I find you amusing."

Maybe you find me amusing? He was burying me in confusion. "How fascinating." I scowled.

"You know want I think?" he said.

That was the problem. I never understood what the hell he was thinking. On one occasion, he was burning hot, and on the next, he was ice cold. I hated it. It was as if I were trying to anticipate the weather.

"No. I'm sure you're about to tell me," I said.

"I think you're one of the most gorgeous girls in our school. Your frustration has caused you to think unclearly. You want to be with someone that loves and understands you. All the pleasure in the world doesn't mean anything without doing it with the person you feel you can't go on without."

I snickered. "What do you know about love? I bet you don't even know how to treat a woman," I said distastefully.

"I'm realizing what the real issue is with you. You don't really know what you want. You are confused. Do you just want sex with me, do you want love, or do you want both? You know that love is something that I don't want. You know that sex is the only thing I'm looking for."

"I'm not confused, Andrew! I know what I want, ok. I just want sex with you," I said, staring unkindly at him.

"You are beautiful. But somewhere deep inside you, you really don't believe that. Do you? I bet you stare in the mirror to justify it—your beauty, I mean. Even when you confront it, you still convince yourself otherwise, even though your reflection is reliable proof of it. You're waiting on someone to love you and to make you happy. I don't care what you say, Angel. You just don't want sex. And because I don't want that at all, you want it even more. I'm a challenge for you. You think if I have sex with you that I will change my mind about what I want."

"I don't know what you are talking about. I think you're the one who is confused," I said, throwing my wicked eyes in his direction.

"I know why you chase me, but you don't know why you chase me." He smiled. "Although I just want sex, I barely act like it. I can stare directly into your eyes, because it's a sign of respect, meaning you're more than that. I can tell you how beautiful you are without completely coming on to you. You like me because I'm not weak or desperate to sleep with you. I see the woman in you. You can't help that it turns you on, Angel."

"You think you have everything all figured out. Don't you? I know why I pursue you. I don't need you to justify anything to me," I said.

"I think you can't stand liking me. You like that I respect you and I haven't tried to seduce you. It keeps you guessing, but you're also confused. Does he like me or not? You can't really tell. The confusion between us keeps you interested in me. You like the way I make you feel and think, but you also hate it. You can't explain it. You wanna call, but you're hoping and wishing that I will call first. I bet you stare at your phone while you wait. I care for you too much to become that asshole that makes you cry every night, though I really do want to fuck you. I just care about your feelings too much."

He bit his lip in the bottom left-hand corner. *Oh boy.* I envisioned him kissing me kindheartedly. I was daydreaming that our bodies were intertwining on the cafeteria floor. I wanted him to fuck me on every table. Something striking and spectacular would transpire. I was sick with eagerness and elevated expectations pertaining to him and me. Without thinking of the consequence, my heart took action. I leaned in, puckering my lips up nicely for him, seeking an unforgettable kiss. I waited for the passionate entanglement to ensue between us.

Nothing happened. I opened my eyes and discovered that he'd disappeared. The situation was embarrassing. I had hoped for something endearing but had received nothing of the sort. What was happening? I was completely tangled in knots. I didn't understand any of it. Why would he embarrass me like that? It was a horrible feeling. I didn't like it one bit. One second, he wanted me, and the next, he teased me as a woman did a man. Was Andrew worth it? I was more puzzled about a guy than I'd ever predicted. Besides school and the unsettling game, Andrew took up all of my thoughts. In a sense, it was pathetic to me—for anyone. I was bewitched, and I loathed it. Dillon visited me at the table.

"Why aren't you sitting with us?" Her tone was thoughtful and friendly.

"Nothing. I need some alone time to think." I pouted.

She teased me. "Alone time to think—blah, blah, and blah. You didn't need some alone time a few seconds ago."

"What are you talking about?" I blinked twice.

"Um, I saw you talking to Andrew. I also saw you by yourself, looking stupid with your lips poked out in the air. From a distance, I thought I saw a small waterfall, but it was nothing. You were just over here drooling," she said, poking her lips out strangely.

"That's not funny!"

"Relax, relax. I'm joking," she said kindly.

"I don't understand what I am doing wrong," I said, covering my face.

"Stop running after him. Women don't chase men for a reason. He got you straight stressing, chick. You will grow wrinkles before you get a chance to even think about climaxing. You are very frustrated. You need to smoke or splash out some waterfalls, if you know what I mean." She winked.

"I'm confused, Dillon. What should I do?"

"Good sex will solve all of your problems." She laughed. "You need to get rammed. Trust me," she said.

What the hell was her deal? *Good sex? No, no, no, I need to be loved and held.*

"You don't need love. You need great sex," she said, thrusting her hands back and forth around her vagina. She had issues. She needed to get out of my head.

"You know what, girl? Fuck Andrew. He isn't that damn fine to be chasing anyway." I could see her thinking about her statement. "No, he isn't that cute. Okay, yeah, he is, but don't chase him. Let him chase you."

Let him chase me, my subconscious repeated.

Jo added, "Don't call or text him." She smiled.

Who in the hell invited you? It sure wasn't me. No calling and no texting him? It was impossible. I hadn't asked either of them for their opinions or advice. They were staring at me for some reason. *Please stop staring at me.* It was weird and awkward. Why was Josephine there?

"Why are you even here right now? You don't mind if I call you Jo, do you?" I stared back.

"First off, I do mind. I prefer to be called by my name—Josephine," she said.

"Sorry about that, Josephine. So, Jo, why are you here?" I hissed.

"It's Josephine, and I'm here because I was told you were the person who would be training me."

"Training you? What in the hell for?" I rudely gazed at her.

"I don't know," she said. "Or maybe informing me of what the club is really about."

"Look, I don't mean to be a bitch or come off as bitchy, because I'm usually sweet, but fuck off!" I said, leaving the lunchroom.

Dillon and Jo followed behind me. She wanted me to train a girl who only had a 35 percent. There was no helping her, nor did I want to. It wasn't beneficial to me. The halls were packed with students.

"You have to excuse her for being bitchy. The cooch still hasn't been penetrated by a real male penis. We're working on getting those dry panties dropped to remove some of those spiderwebs, right, Angel?" Dillon teased.

Spiderwebs? Was she serious? I stopped walking down the hallway. Why was everyone fucking with me today? It was Fuck with Angelina Day—it had to be. Jo walked in front of me with a hopeless expression on her face.

"Do you know what wanting to be popular feels like? Because I do. I want to be popular. I want to feel like I belong somewhere—anywhere. Please help me with this, and I will never ask you for anything else," she begged.

I saw a small portion of myself in her, wanting and feeling the need to belong somewhere. "Okay, okay, okay! What's first?" I smiled. She began suffocating me with an energetic hug.

"Thank you, thank you, and thank you!" she said.

You're welcome. I felt someone else hugging me from behind. I lifted my head.

"Christian, get the hell off me!" I said, pushing him into a wall.

He spoke sarcastically, blushing. "Oh my God, don't leave me out. I thought we were having a girl moment." He blinked while snapping his fingers.

Jo pulled on my arm as if there were an emergency. "I have to host a party. I have never thrown a party before." She panicked.

"Calm down, Jo. Calm down. It's fine. Breathe a little. It won't hurt to do so."

She inhaled and exhaled roughly. I could feel her heart thumping. She was nervous and freaked.

"When is the party?"

She was still breathing heavily. "Next Friday. I need to be finished by next Friday."

"You have plenty of time."

"I don't have invitations, decorations, or food," she said.

"Seriously, Jo, don't be a nerd. We don't waste time making invitations anymore."

I searched for Andrew in the hallways. He was speaking with Mathew and Jeremy. I grabbed Jo. She was even more nervous and confused about what I was doing. She needed everybody's attention, and I had to support and coach her. I smiled at her because she was so attractive, the most beautiful woman I had ever seen. Staring into her eyes made me a little nervous. I had never kissed a girl before. If I ever kissed a woman, that girl had to be Jo. I wondered what it would be like to lock lips with another chick. I felt embarrassed about wanting to experiment with Jo. I would have never admitted to being bi-curious. I was planning to kiss her for Andrew's attention, experimental purposes, and Jo's introduction.

"You should give your announcement after we do this. Everyone will be watching and listening, and all you have to do is tell them about the party you're about to host for me," I muttered.

She had an insane look on her face. "What do you mean 'after we do this'? Do what?" She blinked twice with a raised eyebrow. "Angel, I don't understand any of this!"

I ran my fingers through her thick hair. "You don't have to."

She gazed at me bewilderedly.

"Trust me. Close your eyes."

She listened. As her eyes shut quickly, I kissed her as I'd wanted to kiss her the moment I'd first seen her. However, while kissing her, I dreamed that Jo's lips actually were the lips of Andrew. I sealed my eyes and thought of Jo as well as Andrew. She French-kissed me back. I was shocked because her kissing technique was promising. She used the right amount of tongue, and instead of leading me, she followed, and she knew when the kiss was about to end. She didn't mind my hands resting on her waist. I enjoyed the feeling of her fingers moving down my slim waist. Our brief involvement was passionate. This attachment made me forget about fucking a man. It stirred me in the direction of women for thirteen seconds. We were mistaken for temporary lesbians. I acted like a lesbian for Andrew and curiosity, and she acted like a lesbian for popularity. People didn't have boundaries or limitations anymore at Marshall S. King University.

"Look, man! Check it out. Jo and Angel are making out." Mathew gawked. I peeped down the hall, and Andrew was watching, as I'd planned. It was perfect. We stopped locking lips; I touched her face and moved down toward her neck slowly. It was quiet in the halls.

"Now tell everyone about the party," I murmured in her ear.

She smiled and faced the students in the hall. Her voice was low and timid. "Um, okay, yeah, I'm giving—I mean, I'm hosting a gathering Friday."

"You mean tomorrow?" Christian said.

"Tomorrow? No, on Friday—the party is Friday."

"Tomorrow *is* Friday," a girl with red hair said. They laughed.

I explained, "Jo's throwing a kick-ass party next Friday night at her house! There will be liquor, marijuana, and all kinds of other shit to get us fucked up! Who's with her?" Every student in the hall screamed and applauded.

She held my hand. "Thank you. There is something else I need to ask you," she said. Her eyes were drowning in questions unanswered.

"Sure. Shoot, Jo. I mean Josephine," I said.

She hesitated. "Above all the girls, why is Erin the leader of the females? What's so special about her?"

I smiled, thinking about the years that I had known Erin. "You want the Erin story, huh? Okay." We lightly walked down the hallways.

"Yeah, actually, I would love to hear it," she said, stopping me with a serious expression.

"Erin was the first person to date a senior with the highest ranking and most popularity points in the school her freshman year. She was the youngest girl ever to be awarded a sophomore and junior assignment and then secondary chief during her sophomore year."

"Wow, Angelina. What was the assignment—the junior assignment, of course?"

"It was the teacher seduction."

She had grown more eager for knowledge. "So what happened? Did she pass the assignment or not?"

I smirked while I shook my head. We proceeded to stroll down the halls again.

"I'm confused now. I don't understand," she said, disappointed.

"You want to know why she is so special. Before she came here, we all were doing individual assignments, which she completed the most of. She's the reason there is a Battle of the Sexes."

Her mouth dropped open because of my statement. "Then Erin is a legend," she said while both sides of her lips curled up.

"No, not quite, but it's a start."

Andrew was smiling at me. Suddenly, he approached me. "You're a lesbian now, I see." His glance was erotic.

"Maybe I am," I said in a jolly tone. "Why? Are you jealous?"

He laughed. "Jealous for what? You're not my girlfriend. Favorably, you look hot kissing another girl, though."

I pouted. "But I'm not your girlfriend—yet."

"Plus, it looks to me like you already have one."

"What?"

"A girlfriend." He stared again. I pulled him by his collar, kissing him strongly. He agreed with me.

"Don't you ever leave me hanging like that again," I said, scowling. He was mine and mine alone. I felt like a lucky girl who was about to get even luckier.

CHAPTER 11

Amy

Home Invasion

Among the teams, everything was organized in an orderly fashion. Jo replaced Dillon's Spanish-talking ass, hopefully for next year as well. Erin was our controlling and lonesome leader. She seemed happy without a fuck buddy or boyfriend. I guess Angel and Andrew were finally dating. Even if they were together, I bet she was still a virgin. Nonetheless, my mind was stuck on the concept of Jacky fucking her teacher. She was a lucky bitch. Tia, all of a sudden, had become busier than ever. I wondered what the hell she was doing. I, however, entered a world full of drama. Mathew was cheating and fucking around on me again. He tossed his deceitfulness in my face by staying out partying all night with whichever cunt he was with. I was there in our apartment, waiting for him to come home to me. I was again glancing at the time. He would probably be a no-show that night. It was twelve o'clock. I watched the time pass by.

I texted Tia to kill time, yet she didn't reply back to me. I waited awhile. Still she didn't answer me, not with a call or a text message. I was expecting some form of communication between us. I couldn't manage the night without talking to her, but my request was denied. I ate the leftover chocolate ice cream melting in a small plastic bowl on the kitchen table. I paced in the front room. I stared at my cell phone, hoping Tia would respond. I watched the door, hoping Mathew would walk through it any second. The truth was that he wasn't coming. I locked him out just in case he decided to arrive at a later period.

It was over between us—so fucking over. Whoever the bitch was, she was going to get acquainted with my fist. While lying down in our bed, I wondered who she was as I cried myself to exhaustion and eventually to sleep. Had I not learned anything yet? There was no way a guy as handsome as Mathew didn't already have skeletons in his closet. Unfortunately, my skeletons were more of a monstrosity. I wasn't lying to him, but I wouldn't be called to the stage for an award in honesty either. There was something I didn't know how to talk about, so did it make me a liar either way? I was as destructive as Mathew. On the other hand, losing him would have devastated me. This was the first time I'd ever admitted that to myself.

I was tossing and turning, sweating in my sleep. It was hot in the apartment, so I hurried to crack open the window. The wind rushed through the window the minute I opened it. It was cold, breezy, and comforting. I paused at the window, smiling at the fact that the wind was blowing. I shut my eyes while standing there, taking everything all in. By the window, I lifted Mathew's black tank top over my head. Eventually, I buried myself underneath his comforter and silky sheets. Tonight, with the coolness traveling through the window, I was guaranteed to get a good night's sleep. It was dangerous for me to leave the window wide open the way I did. But shit, I was burning up.

"What the hell? What the hell? What the hell?" I repeated, screaming out of my sleep. Around three o'clock in the morning, I woke up screaming for a number of reasons. One reason was because of an unsettling feeling I was experiencing. I was in pain. The second reason was because I was stuck in a catastrophic and dangerous situation. But most importantly, the main reason was that I was tied up like a fucking sex slave—you know, the way that women were being fucked unwillingly by thousands of men and chained up by the one fucked-up guy responsible. So as a woman, what did I do? I did the only thing a girl could have done in that situation.

I screamed again as loudly as my tonsils could stretch. "Help me, please!" My roaring seemed loud to me. My yelling would have been more powerful, but I could barely breathe. I was panicking, and a pillow was in my face. I struggled to move around, because my hands were tightly knitted together behind my back. My ankles were tied up as well. The tight ropes were rubbing against my skin.

I breathed out as my voice stretched. "Ahhh! Aaaggghhhh." The ropes were way too tight. I cried as I thrashed around on the bed. My movements were pointless. My skin was already irritated, and I continued to yell at the top of my lungs. My skin was bruised. "Ouch," I complained. A man wearing all black exited the bathroom. It was too dark to recognize who the person was, and he was wearing a black ski mask. He rushed to remove the pillow from around my face, and then he covered my mouth with his cold hands.

I was scared for my life. There were countless mistakes that I needed to fix. I hadn't seen my mother in a week. In that moment, I missed her, because the last conversation we'd had was an argument. I wondered if I would have a chance to correct it. I wished I'd had an opportunity to reveal the secrets I was keeping from Mathew. This triggered me to shake nervously. My heart was rising in my chest—*thump, thump, thump*. I thought about the first time I had been drugged and raped and woken up in a motel room the next morning. I wouldn't survive it this time. Tears fell down my cheeks. I yelled underneath his hands.

His first words to me were "Shut the fuck up," but they weren't the last. The tone of his voice was disturbing and intimidating. I was afraid.

On top of this, I was extremely fatigued. I felt like an idiot for leaving the window open. It was one of my biggest regrets of that night. He was behind me, doing God only knew what. He boosted me up so that my behind was in the air. His chilled fingers were now removing my cotton bra, and he lowered my cotton panties to my ankles. What was wrong with me? I felt him touching me now—why couldn't I feel his filthy hands on me when I was asleep? Why, Lord? I hadn't felt anything at all. I should have felt something—anything. On the contrary, I'd felt nothing. If I had, would it have made a difference for me?

"When I remove my hands, don't scream! You got that?" He watched. I nodded and agreed with him in fear.

I said softly, "Please, please, untie me. These ropes are too tight against my skin." I cried. "Let me go, and I promise I won't say a word to anyone about this. I swear. You don't have to do this to me!"

He was silent. *Please speak to me. Say something,* my subconscious said in desperation.

He spanked me aggressively, moaning in the background. "Shit, girl, look at that ass." His spanks hurt. He did it again and again. I jumped every time in pain. My behind became bruised.

His voiced sounded strange. "Just keep begging." My pleading and shouting seemed to turn him on, but I was screaming because of the pain. He proceeded to spank me.

I cried. "Stop, stop," I said frequently. He wouldn't listen, and he covered my mouth again. He pulled my hair for the first time, but it wasn't the last. I tilted my head back. "Ouch, ouch, ouch," I said.

I was whining like a child, and the fact that I felt tired wasn't helping me either. I stood still as I kept crying. He groaned as he groped my breasts and pinched both of my nipples. He positioned himself on the bed behind me. He opened my legs and placed his dick in between my thighs. He yanked on my hair. His hands gently and tightly rubbed alongside my stomach. He then wrapped them around my neck. His cock was resting on the outer layer of my pussy. He stroked his dick with his other hand still around my neck. *Please stop. Please,* my subconscious begged. I swirled around like a small worm once more. I cried out at the feeling of uselessness. He kissed my neck. My body was enjoying his kisses, but I pulled away from him. He squeezed my ass cheeks together bellicosely.

He said, "Shush!" He tightly gripped my breasts as I experienced his cock enlarging on the lips of my pussy. It got stiff as he glided and swirled the tip of his dick against my pussy. I couldn't help that my pussy was so wet, and my nipples were no longer soft from him groping my breasts. I lowered my behind. He yanked on my hair because of my reaction. "Lift it. Lift it back up," he moaned.

I cried out while breathing hard. He pulled harder, and I lifted my ass back up. With his dick massaging in between my pussy lips, he repeatedly stroked his dick as he rubbed it against my pearl. I listened to the sound of his python rubbing between the lips of my wet pussy. I couldn't help but get aroused from the feeling of his anaconda rubbing on my clitoris as well. I got wetter and wetter. I was unexpectedly wetter now than I had ever been with Mathew. He continued to swirl the tip of his cock on the top of my pearl persistently from almost every direction and angle. He moaned and sucked on my ear as he leaned closer to me. His body was so close to mine. I hated that I liked it, and I was confused that I was slightly enjoying the things this man was doing to me.

"Shit, your pussy is so fucking wet." He exhaled. "Whoa—oh, fuck."

He walked in front of me, placing his dick in my face. He lowered himself, bending down to stare at me. I dropped my face into the pillow. He got on his knees by the bed. He lifted up my face and forced his fingers into my mouth to open it. He toyed with my cheeks, slapping me slightly. I spit on him, and then I screamed for help. He wiped my spit off of his face, and he laughed as he stroked his dick in my face.

"Have you sucked dick before? If you suck me off real good, maybe—just maybe—I'll let you go, but you have to show some serious skills. Now, open that warm mouth of yours," he said, attempting to insert his cock into my mouth. He suddenly slid it against my top and bottom lips. I sealed my mouth. I shook and moved my head in the opposite direction.

I looked at him. "Fuck you, you coward!" I paused and then screamed. "Fuck you! Fuck you! Fuck you!" I shouted at him again.

He gripped my face. "I love the way you scream, but come on—just suck on the tip." I remained silent. I didn't listen. He grabbed my jaw. With the other hand, he stuffed his fingers into my mouth to extend my jaws.

"Ugh." I shook. "No, stop it. Stop, please." He gripped my neck. I could feel his fingers pressing aggressively against my windpipe. He released. I started coughing. When I caught my breath, he attempted to force his dick into my mouth. I shut it.

He said smoothly, "You know you wanna wrap your lips around it. Come on, baby. Suck it for daddy!"

He was gliding his dick against my lips again. He gripped my neck tightly. I couldn't breathe for a second time. I unwillingly opened my mouth. He placed his knees on the edge of the bed and bended them to effectively put his cock into my mouth. He rearranged my head. "Aw, yeah," he said. "Just like that." He grunted. He firmly rested his hands on my head to ensure that I sucked his dick the way he desired.

I kept gagging, though. I gagged and gagged. I couldn't help it. This eventually upset him. He breathed out loudly. There was no doubt he was annoyed by my lack of participation. He unfastened the ropes on my hands and ankles. I was surprised and still scared, my eyes wide, yet I was relieved he was doing so.

"You can go! You're fucking boring me!" He paused. I was curious, but I'd dreamed those words would leave his mouth. I was hesitant to move. "Did you hear me? I said go!" He pointed to the door. "Go!"

I charged to the door, trying to go left. He blocked my path. I went right, and he followed me. He smiled. I cried out. "Please, please, just let me go! I want to go home!" Tears dropped from my eyes.

He marched up closer to me, laughing. "Then go. Are you deaf or stupid?"

I tried with all of my strength to run past him. He yanked me by my neck. I screamed, and he covered my mouth while laughing. I yelled underneath his hands.

"Don't do that. Crying just turns me on even more," he confessed. He tossed me onto the bed, and I balled up in a corner.

I rocked back and forth, and I shut my eyes tightly while praying. "Our Father, save me from sinners, for I am a true child of God. Deliver me from evil and evildoers." Again, he pulled me by my hair. "Ouch! Stop it! Aagh!" I yelled.

I slapped him, making an effort to battle against him. He liked it. I swung my arms wildly to fight him back. He captured both of my wrists. He pinned them down with his hands. I tried futilely to bite and kick him. He had me right where he wanted me. He was on top of me, in between my thighs. Suddenly I gave in. I didn't want to fight him anymore. I couldn't, and he knew it. He placed himself inside me. I gasped and jumped at the feeling of his dick entering me entirely.

He muttered and groaned in my ear. "That's how I like it."

In time, his moans turned me on. He continued to pin my arms down tightly. My body, without a doubt, now found his voice and touch familiarly arousing. As I rudely removed his ski mask, I discovered that it was Mathew who was giving me a rough time. I felt stupid that I hadn't recognized his voice, although he sounded completely different.

During that entire time, I had never once thought it was Mathew doing this to me. I felt betrayed and deceived. I quickly started attacking him by slapping him in the face. He proceeded as if he had done nothing wrong as he recollected my hands.

I screamed, "You son of a bitch! Why would you do this to me? Why, why, why?" He kissed me and kissed me. "I hate you so fucking much!" I shouted at the top of my lungs. I cried. "Get the fuck off of me, Mathew! Get off!" I yelled. I could hear my voice weakening. It was sore, and my throat was burning from all of the yelling and whining. I saw that all of my protests were unnecessary.

He stopped, and I paused. With his thumb, he rubbed my cheeks, wiping away my tears. He had nearly given me a heart attack. I hated him for what he had done to me that night. He ran his fingers through my hair, and he French kissed me. I didn't return the favor. How could I after what I'd experienced? I had been raped before, and I believed it was happening again.

"You liked it the entire time. I know you did," he breathed.

He thrust his dick back inside my pussy. He groaned mildly, assuring me of his pleasure. "Aw, aw, fuck, Amy." I attempted to keep groaning discreetly at his dick leaving and reentering me. The way he was fucking me had my pussy drowning in wetness. Suddenly, I moaned aloud. "See, I knew this dick felt good." I wanted to rub my pussy. The feeling was like no other pleasure I had experienced. He went faster and faster.

"Oh my goodness. Oh my goodness, Mathew," I moaned.

"Fuck, Amy. Shit," he moaned. His grunts were sometimes unexplainable. I liked listening to him being satisfied.

He traveled deeper, moving back and forth hard. Two minutes later, he came quickly, but he pulled out of me in an instant. He was on top of me, squashing me with his body weight. I felt as if I couldn't breathe. He roamed to the bathroom. I listened to the sound of water running in the sink. I pulled the cover over me and turned onto my right side. I felt him leaning on the bed. He situated himself beside me, facing in the opposite direction. I felt relieved. I was overwhelmed. What had I done to deserve this? After ten minutes passed, I was asleep. I knew there was no such thing as a perfect relationship, but ours was over because of this sex club. I had accepted all of his bullshit. My love for him had blinded my judgment. *Look at what he has done to me, what I have done to myself.*

Yet a week later, the day of the party, another issue emerged. I was playing a basketball game on Mathew's cell phone without his permission. He was asleep, snoring his morning away. It was a beautiful Friday. Suddenly, an unknown number called his phone. I looked at the number and wondered who it was.

"Hi. Who is this?" I said in suspense.

"No, who is this? Isn't this Mathew's phone? I need to speak to him!" She coughed.

"This is Mathew's girlfriend." I said. "You called me. Who in the hell are you?" I replied rudely.

"No, see, that's where you're wrong. I didn't call you. I called Mathew, not you," she said with a hoarse voice.

"Look, I don't know or care why you're calling him. If you're not family, don't waste your sick, weak fucking fingers dialing this number, okay?" I said rudely.

"Well, if it isn't the famous I-have-been-cheated-on, too-pathetic-to-leave-him Amy girl I have heard so much about," she said proudly in a sick tone.

"You don't know shit about me! I would watch what I say if I were you!" I yelled.

She chuckled momentarily. "Aw, what are you going to do to me, Amy? There is so much I would like to say to you. Do you remember your special night in the bar with that perfect stranger or your relationship with a guy with the scorpion tattoo on his lower hip?"

I was speechless. How did she know that? Fuck, how did this bitch know that? "Who are you?" I yelled while pacing in the living room.

"Now, wouldn't you really like to know, Amy darling, the girl who is a slut for no reason?" she joked.

I shouted, "Are you sleeping with him?"

"Sleeping with him? Oh no. I have done no such thing. Your skeletons have stopped me from doing it, and what dark skeletons they are. Don't you think? You're just as dirty as the bones hidden in your closet."

"I don't know what you're talking about! I don't have any fucking skeletons! You must be a nobody, a real dirty little norm cunt whore. And I'm true perfection! Don't ever forget it!"

"Are you ready to bet Mathew on it—the guy you love? I can't wait to expose you to everyone." She laughed. Seconds later, she coughed again.

"Fuck you! That's why you got the Ebola virus, you sick, stupid, silly little tramp. Don't call this number anymore. You hear me?" I shouted with big eyes.

"I hear you crystal clear, Amy, but the question is not what I want with him. It's what he wants with me."

"You're a liar. Mathew doesn't want anything to do with you."

"According to whom?" she said. "There is so much more that you are hiding, and I'm going to figure it all out very soon."

"When I catch you, you're going to wish you never knew me," I said.

"Well, start running before you get too fat for the chase," she said.

Did this bitch just call me fat?

My heart clenched in my chest at the bitch having knowledge of my private events, and her humor was insane. Who was the cunt? How did she know? I had been careful. No one knew my secrets—not Erin or Angel and certainly not Tia. If someone knew my secrets, this could sabotage my relationship. The shithead had to be bluffing. She had to be. Nobody knew—and I planned on keeping it that way. I couldn't help but ask myself who the bitch was. How did this tramp know Mathew? Did I know her? Had she and I ever had a conversation, excluding the encounter that had just occurred? Did she go to Marshall S. King University? Was she popular or irregular?

After my last statement, she didn't reply to me. She was afraid to organize a little meeting to share words with me in person. I would have been afraid too, if I were her. That was okay. Even though her whereabouts were unknown, I could take my anger and frustration out on Mathew, since I was now holding him accountable for her call. He was still asleep. I quietly entered the bedroom and looked down at him with fire in my eyes. They were burning red with hatred. Anger was coursing through my body, and all that energy and disappointment traveled down to one special place: my right hand. I slapped him forcefully across his face. He reacted aggressively as he woke up to my unhappiness. "What the fuck, Amy? Shit!" he shouted. He sat up as he covered his face with his hands. He had a tiresome look on his face. Her call was something that had to be addressed. It was a fucking emergency, and he had some serious explaining to do. I tossed his cell phone onto the bed.

My voice sounded a little hoarse. "Your little sick puppy called you while you were fucking asleep, Mathew! How stupid are you? We are so over. You hear me? Over! I hope little Ebola bitch was worth it!"

He laughed. "Like I have not heard that lie before. And what did I tell you about slapping me? You slap me just one more time, and I swear you will be hospitalized before the day starts." He threatened me while he rubbed his left cheek. "Shit," he complained, but he was lucky that was all he was getting. I was happy I had slapped him in his sleep. I ignored him, and I started throwing my clothing and shoes into a duffle bag immediately. I stomped my feet like a child while packing. I checked under the bed and in the closet for the remainder of my belongings. There was nothing else lingering around that I saw at that moment. Then he stretched and stood up straight.

"Why are you packing?" he asked with a half grin. I wanted to smack him silly again. But if I did, as he'd said, I would probably end up in the hospital. I didn't know if he was just talking bullshit or if he was serious. I didn't want to find out.

"Because I should have never come here in the first place. I regret ever taking you seriously. I should have listened to Erin."

He wiped the corners of his eyes. "Yeah, I totally agree with you."

I glared at him in shock. "Fuck you!"

"That can be arranged. Just come here, and I can give it to you just the way you like it." He smiled.

I gave him the hand. "I don't think so, since you are still messing around on me and lying to me about it!"

"Here we go again with the false accusations. You tend to overexaggerate things. You know that, right?" Another smile crossed his face. He was fucking with me. What a twisted fuck he was.

"That is open to your interpretation. There is no need to try to mislead me with false information. Oh, it's accurate. The evidence is your cell phone," I said, and I slammed the door.

I stood at the bus stop, weeping with an ugly brown bag in my hand. Out of nowhere, Mathew ran up behind me, trying to catch his breath. There was nothing he could have said to make me change my decision. I started to tap my right foot impatiently.

"Where are you going?" He breathed. "Home?"

I stepped forward, waiting for the bus. "Far away from you, and that is the only thing you need to know. What I do no longer concerns you!" I ran my thumb and index finger against the top of the bag while he spoke.

He scowled. "Oh, so that's it. We're over just like that." He looked at me with questioning eyes.

I crossed my arms and responded, "Duh. What did you think? I would forgive you? Well, you have another think coming!"

"Well, it's obvious what we had meant absolutely nothing to you," he said, attempting to cross the street.

I reached out for him. "Wait! It meant everything to me—the world." I cried. I threw my arms up for dramatic effect, dropping my bag in the process.

He returned to me. "Prove it, huh? She just called because she needed my help. That's all. You made a big fucking deal out of nothing. She's a sick girl and has no one supporting her, not a leg to lean on. She lost her mother awhile ago, and her father is in jail, but I don't want her. If I was trying to mislead you, she wouldn't have known anything about you being my girl, because that was precisely the last thing I was telling her about. I have no interest in her. If I did, I would have slept with her, and I didn't."

I felt foolish for going off on him. "I'm sorry, Mathew. I didn't know. How was I supposed to know her father was in jail and her mother was dead?" I said with sorrowful eyes. I tried to touch him, but he was far from my grasp, and it didn't seem as if he longed for my touch.

"Yeah, well, that's what an erroneous assumption without facts will get you, but we're over, right? Isn't that what you said, Amy? Our relationship meant more to me than it ever meant or will mean to you. I changed so much because of you, Amy. You know exactly how I was. Do you remember what I said when you asked me where I saw myself in five years?"

I laughed as I remembered. "Yes, you said you saw yourself going to college with a basketball scholarship, having fun, hanging out with friends, and having sex with a thousand—I mean two thousand—girls, including me."

He was serious for the time being. It was heartwarming. "Now ask me where I see myself in five years or more."

I gazed into his blue eyes. They reminded me of the sea. I stared harder as he came closer to me. I was swimming deeper and deeper in his blue eyes. If I went any further, I would drown in his ocean of love and compassion.

"Where do you see yourself in five years or so?" I said, hoping for a more suitable answer.

He grabbed my hands passionately. "In five years, I see myself laughing and smiling like I am right now with the girl of my dreams, her hands in mine. When I graduate from college, I still expect the love of my life to be around, living with me, having my children, and getting married someday. I wanna live in this moment forever, Amy." I smiled as he continued. "No girl will ever compare to you—ever. Starting now, I will be the guy I need to be."

With my left hand, I rubbed the right side of Mathew's face. Now I remembered why I was madly in love with him. I fell for his lack of predictability. It was the sweetest and most beautiful speech anyone had delivered to me. I believed every word. Maybe he did love me more than I loved him. Once again, he had stolen me and saved me from drowning in an ocean of misfortune. Without realizing it, I was back in our apartment, wanting and needing to be ravished by him like never before. We were filled with passion. And oh, how affectionate I was after he poured out his heart to me.

Our bodies were close, skin against skin, chest to chest. Each touch moved me in unimaginable ways, and my skin was highly reactive to his touch and kiss. Those hands of his had a mind of their own. And his lips kept mine engaged. He kissed me everywhere—but mainly in one particular place. He was down between my thighs, kissing my girlish parts. The moment was intense and bellicose but likable. We barely made it to the bedroom. We stumbled over every possible thing in our path, but we wouldn't and didn't stop. He undressed me while I stripped him of his white shirt and navy-blue shorts.

We were all over the living-room floor. He sucked on my companion. While traveling down even further, he slurped on the juices trickling down below. *Yes.* He took me all in by swallowing my wetness. I gasped at the welcoming of his skilled tongue. *Yeah, eat it. Eat me.* He was gulping on my pink ocean, and he did it well. I was bedazzled by the action and sucking of his tongue. I looked at him. His lips were showered with the sparkles of my shiny, clear waterfall. I kissed him to taste my own sweetness. He grabbed my behind and squeezed my cheeks together tightly, because they belonged to him. He licked on my clit, pushing his finger inside of my walls. What a delight it was.

Before situating a condom over his impressive length, I was in between his thighs to place his entire python in my mouth, but beforehand, I spit on his dick to get it nice and slippery. His prick was almost at the rear of my throat. I choked slightly while saliva covered the hairs surrounding his private parts. I watched the wetness tremble down to his balls. I locked on tighter and tighter as I continued to suck intensely. I suckled firmly while my jaws pulled on the skin of his python. The use of my tongue was highly beneficial. I massaged his anaconda with my hands smoothly and effectively as I took him all in. He tasted delicious, and he was mine. Five minutes later, my jaws had grown tired. He then boosted my right leg up.

I was ready for him to enter me. He asked, "You want me?" I nodded, and he said, "No, I want to hear you say it. Say you want me." He liked knowing that I longed for him.

"I want you, Mathew. I do," I said seductively. I was impatiently waiting for him to ram his dick inside me.

"What do you want?" He breathed.

"I want you to fuck me." My hands were wrapped around his neck.

He entered me, and boy, I felt him all of him. The sex was outstanding. Practice did make perfect—Mathew was evidence of it. Inconveniently, the passionate, meaningful touches from Mathew ceased in what was supposed to be our remarkable moment of making love. I was a girl who climaxed from his gentleness and his love, so he knew to be gentle with me. I was sure. However, instead of making love to me, he fucked me hard, as he never had before. There were no feelings involved in this act. I felt like a stranger having sex with some random guy. He was anything but the perfect lover in our time of intimacy. Where was he? What happened to the tender kisses and the smooth, soft gliding of his fingers against my creamy, warm skin?

His hands were also strangers in the darkness. I thought I had once known and grown fond of them. They were heavily buried along the sides of my back. He rammed himself in and out of me with the force of a monster. I feared his hands would leave red prints on each side of me. All I heard was his breathing, longing for more of it. The sound reminded me of the wind blowing behind the backs of both of my ears. Who was he? Mathew Henderson, for me, was temporarily gone. However, so was I, as I attempted to clear my infected mind of the thought of Mathew's unexplained and unexpected transformation. The sex creature had overtaken the guy swimming in compassion, because he was interested only in pleasuring himself. The love in him had died, and it wouldn't battle the maniac in him. Suddenly, he came and lifted off of me, removing his condom.

"What the hell was that?" I yelled with disapproval.

He laughed. "What?"

He- always believed everything was a game. "Don't 'What?' me. You know what. It was like you were having sex with me as if I was a total stranger you randomly approached at a bar!" How could something start off so well and end so badly?

He grinned with carelessness. I hated that fucking expression I saw before my eyes. It robbed me of my cheerfulness. "And how would you know what being approached at a bar is like?" He had thrown his shirt back over his head. He searched for his shorts. He bent down and grabbed his shorts from the floor. He shortly put them back on as well.

I stared with anger. “I wouldn’t. I was speaking hypothetically.” I fidgeted.

He looked back with a seriousness that was troublesome. *Oh boy, that is not good.*

“Sure you were.” His expression was now unidentifiable.

“Is there something you want to ask me? Just say it!” My right eye twitched. I couldn’t control it.

“My short, durable event—your so-called humanity switch—was my final good-bye fuck to you. If you really want me to be specific, we are over.”

I held back my tears. “You don’t mean that. Tell me you’re joking.”

“Yeah, actually, I do mean it,” he said calmly.

“What happened to everything you just told me, huh?” I yelled at him. I blinked twice.

He ran his thumb around his chin. “Um, now, what did I say? Oh, right, I remember. What about it?”

I moved closer to him. “You said you wanted to be with me, get married, have children, and grow old together. You said those would be the steps we would make in the future.”

“Yes. That’s exactly what I said.” He smiled, and I returned a friendlier gaze. I wrapped my arms around him, smiling with the heart of a bright white goddess.

“Not once in my speech did I mention that the girl was or would be you,” he said, removing my arms from his shoulders.

My smile fell to a place unreachable and difficult to find. I slowly sat down on the love seat. He searched for his dark blue jacket and put on his all-black Jordans. I cried. There wasn’t any way I could hide the pain he’d caused me any longer. The tears sprouted out of me.

“You are beautiful, Amy, but you are also whiny and bitchy as hell. Please have all your junk packed up before tomorrow night. I am sure you left some bullshit feminine product behind.”

I stared with hatred while he shut the door. My eye was twitching again. Moments later, he reentered the apartment, falling forcefully as he entered the living room. My head was tilted downward.

"Um, uh, I was supposed to ask before I dumped you, but it slipped my mind. Can I borrow twenty dollars? I'm out of gas," he said.

After everything, he had some fucking nerve to ask me to borrow some money, then or ever. *Hell no,* my subconscious screamed. I wanted to kill him, so I stared at him as I envisioned myself decapitating him repeatedly.

"Fuck you, Mathew!" I answered with a frown.

"I don't understand. So"—he paused—"is that a no?" I ignored the bastard while staring more wickedly. He blinked twice, glancing at his watch in irritation. "Well, I'll take that as a no."

He shut the door again. I couldn't believe what had happened that morning. I broke down in tears again with twitching eyes. I was still shocked, sitting there with a dumb-ass, surprised look on my face. I couldn't believe Mathew. I didn't know who he was anymore. He'd played me like a fool. And now I felt stupid.

I kept thinking about what he had done. As naive as I was, I thought this bullshit must have been a joke—but who was laughing? No one was.

I waited for him to come back. I waited and waited. I knew he wasn't coming back, at least not that night. Plus, Jo was hosting a party, so he undeniably would be a no-show. There was a joke, and I finally understood it. The joke—the big laugh—was on me.

CHAPTER 12

Erin

The Party at Best

It was party time, but it wasn't going to be relaxing for any of my teammates or me. There was no peaceful way to escape our duties regarding our present and future assignments. As the year progressed, so did our obligations. Because I was determined to win, I was sure we would achieve more than the guys would. They were strangely unorganized and clueless about strategies against us because they were too busy trying to fuck every opponent. During the party, my plan was to make sure they would do just that. The males had to believe it was a simple gathering to alleviate the stress formed by the game. With Angel and Jo, the sweet and pure girls of the group, hosting the party, no one would suspect anything. Because of this, I allowed them to structure the event themselves. But honestly, they were a diversion.

Jacky's task, on the contrary, was to supply us with drugs. Her task was the most significant in order for us to accomplish this operation. I was secretly impressed with Jacky's performance thus far. With my arrangements, my team didn't know what I had organized for Jo. I was a difficult speaker to comprehend, yet I was planning my activities in an orderly fashion. Unlike the boys, I felt it was preposterous to let the chips fall where they may, so I placed the chips right where I needed them. I had an obsession with dictating everything or at least making an effort to do so.

At my house, Jacky and I brought our own supplies. With the location of the party changing on the day it occurred, the boys wouldn't have time to react efficiently. Our beauty was our biggest weapon. The more beautiful we were, the more we became a serious distraction to our competitors. Did they actually want to win? Who knew? They were boys seeking easy or complicating methods for oral and sexual intercourse, so we had to look even more mesmerizing than usual. Jacky and I were in my room, doing each other's makeup. Pink and black were the colors she selected for the enhancement of my beauty. The look was different but interesting, better than what I had imagined the outcome would be.

Shockingly, the look gave me an image of mysteriousness. My attire concentrated on conflict with the makeup, because the colors on my dress were lighter than the colors she blended in with the tone of my skin. I had on a long, fitted tropical-flower-print dress in shades of purple, from light to dark. It had small images of wildflowers—violets and orchids, to be exact. As for my hair, Jacky created feathery bangs over my right eye. How hot was that? In addition, she curled the remainder of my hair thoughtfully into submission. For the finishing touch, my pumps were light purple, my favorite color. I darted to the mirror in my room and stared back at my reflection. I smiled at Jacky's bountiful art.

"You look pretty, Erin," she said, taking my focus off of the mirror.

I opened up my arms to her. "We both look exceptionally beautiful." We hugged each other.

She exhaled. "Let's go over the plan again to be sure."

I released her. *Oh no, not again.*

She was now by my bed. I followed her. We sat beside each other. "The party is supposed to be happening at ten o'clock, right?" I said.

"That's correct. But see, everyone—at least the popular kids—will start arriving somewhere between ten thirty and elevenish perhaps."

"Yeah, they probably will. We have to get the addresses to the party changed like yesterday, and all it takes is a little communication."

She stood to add more makeup, as if I hadn't applied enough blush and eye shadow. "So people won't show up at Jo's house, right?"

"Exactly," I said, nodding. "We need to text someone to start the chain from one person to another and so on. We need someone that is not involved in the game, though." I paused for a few seconds. "Wait a minute. Do you know Ricky—Ricky White?"

She paused for a moment and turned to face me. "Yeah, wait. Where did I hear his name? Ricky White," she repeated. "Isn't he's Mathew's little brother from his father's side?" She continued to look in the mirror. She rubbed her left cheek to feel the smoothness of her skin.

I snickered. "Yes, he is. All we have to do is text him, and we are set."

She stopped again. "Okay. Say what exactly? What should I do?" She was alarmed.

While attaching my high heels to my feet, I said, "I don't know. Just be creative. I'm sure you will think of something. Once you do, everything will be ready. Leave the rest of the work to us."

I looked into her eyes while responding to her. I was saddened that she modified her makeup, but it was a huge improvement on her part. Jacky's appearance was as stunning as mine. Her bone structure was irresistible and now electrifying because of the makeup's enhancement. She was wearing a short, strapless golden-yellow-and-lime-green dress. The colors blended considerately against her brown skin. The color of her makeup was similar to the colors on her dress. Her hair was pinned up, with a few strings hanging down where her neck started. She wore silver earrings that dangled when she moved. Her shoes, which she'd borrowed from me, were white boutique sandals. My doorbell rang. The visitors were all girls wanting to be members of BOTS Association. I opened the door to welcome my guests.

"Hi. We heard from a little birdy that the party is jumping off here," one girl said, peeking beyond my doorway and pointing inside my house.

"What nerd did you hear that from?" My right hand was resting on the doorknob, and I was slightly leaning on the side of the door.

The short girl, who had an all-white dress on, said, "Tom."

I immediately noticed her accent, but I couldn't figure out where she was from.

"No, it was not Tom. It was Benny Boy," a girl with black hair stated.

Benny Boy, I repeated to myself. *What kind of nickname is that?*

I made them some room to enter. The leader spoke. "No, you both are wrong. It was Ricky something," she corrected, throwing her left hand out as she responded. She was right.

"The party is supposed to be at Josephine's house," I said.

"We don't know any Josephine. I would have thought you were hosting the party from the jump anyway."

"If you don't know Jo, you will!" Jacky interrupted.

The leader seized my arm, pulling me into the next room, the kitchen. "We haven't been properly introduced." She rested her hand on her chest. "My name is Catherine Brooks." She forced a false smirk upon her face. "My friend with the white dress and British accent is Arabella Strauber, but I call her Faith. The last one, with the extremely dark black hair, is Chloe Myers," she said, pointing.

I laughed freely. "You pulled me over here for a group introduction?"

"No," she muttered. "I pulled you over because we are all interested in a membership."

Some of the names from the list began to pop into my head. I pointed mildly. "Your signature is the first on my sign-in sheet, and your two friends took the second and the third spots on my list. I remember you." I heard the doorbell ringing frequently throughout our conversation. People eventually started rushing into the kitchen for refreshments and alcohol.

She rubbed her neck. "There will be a meeting for the substitution of Dillon's station next weekend, right?" She was clueless and uninformed about Dillon's replacement. There was no denying she was misinformed, so I decided to have a little bit of fun.

I laid my hand on her left shoulder, walking her back to the front room. "Yes, of course, there will be! Tell your friends the meeting is Monday evening, because I know you want the spot for yourself!" I said cheerfully.

"Will do, Erin, and thanks a lot," she said with optimism.

I started searching for Jacky. The doorbell continued to ring repetitively as I rushed to open the door. The music was now playing, and people were dancing and drinking like there was no tomorrow. I charged up the stairs. I opened every bedroom door, attempting to find

Jacky. She was in the showroom, making sure everything was intact. I barged in while she was conversing on the phone with Angel.

"There's been a mistake or something. Erin and I were getting ready at her place, and people started showing up with food and drinks," Jacky said.

"That's crazy because we announced the party would be at Jo's house!"

"For some reason, I don't think anybody knows who she is or where she stays."

"I knew we should have passed out invitations!" Angel said disappointedly.

"You're absolutely right. Since everybody is already here, you and Jo can bring your refreshments and everything else over here."

"Okay, we are on our way!"

"Okay," Jacky said, ending the conversation. She hung up.

I barely heard a thing. "So what happened?" I said, strolling up to her in suspense. She noticed that the back of my dress was out of order. She readjusted it by pulling on the hemline.

"They bought it, and they should be joining us shortly. Boy, I'm exhausted already." She collapsed on my bed wildly.

I joined her. "What about the electronics and all the other equipment for Dillon's assignment?" I said, concerned.

She popped up quickly. She paused to think with caution. She ran her fingers across her bottom lip. "Everything is organized. We are just waiting for the competitors and the team to arrive."

I left her to attend to the showroom and get the equipment set up. I went back down the stairs so that I could keep an eye on my guests. The bell rang again. I immediately answered the door. It was Andrew. I hadn't expected him to join us. When I opened the door, he wore a charming smirk. His eyes penetrated me deeply, gray versus green. "Are you going to just stare at me, or are you going to let me in?" he said.

"No. None of the above, because I'm hoping my distasteful glare sends you running in the opposite direction. You're not invited to my party. I would like it if you turned around and partied elsewhere." Both of his hands were in his pockets. He thought he looked charming in his black True Religion jeans and white Hollister shirt.

"You know, you remind me of this one white rose in my mother's garden." He smiled again. "It's surrounded by thousands of flowers, like red roses, wildflowers, lilies, daisies, and orchids, like the ones on your little party dress there." He entered my house. I looked down at my dress.

"You think you're pretty fucking charming! Well, you're still not invited!" I said.

He ignored me. His eyes scanned the living room, and then he peeped into the kitchen. I followed.

"Chill out, Rose. I'm already here! I might as well enjoy the party you threw for me!" he said, dancing around me to the music.

What an idiot. "Don't call me that! You know my name, so use it!" I said with a serious expression. I was in the center of the floor. He danced around me in circles. I folded my arms in all seriousness. My expression was solid. As he continued to dance, I started to laugh at him, warming up to his humorous character.

Angelina interrupted when she danced up to Andrew. The sound of the doorbell continued to capture my attention. This time, it was Christian.

"Just the guy I wanted to see!" I said wickedly. He already smelled like alcohol.

"I thought Joey was hosting the party," he said, leaning on the wall by my doorway.

"Yeah, we all thought that. You do realize the person throwing the party is a girl, right?"

He chuckled loudly. "Who names their daughter Joey?" He belched.

Lord, he was disgusting. "I think you're dumb. There, I said it, and her name is Jo for Josephine."

"Well, that name isn't any prettier. Now, is it?" He walked into the living room. "Where are the drinks?" he yelled. He raised his left hand. I quickly grabbed it and led him into the kitchen. He took a bent-up notebook from his back pocket and threw it onto the table.

I scratched my arm. "What's the green notebook all about?"

"Nothing. Just some signatures—we're voting for the team speaker for senior year." He poured himself a drink.

I opened the notebook while leering. "Can I sign?"

He hesitated and then responded. "Sure. Go right ahead." He collected another cup. I read the names. I placed my signature underneath Jeremy's name. He snatched the book from me. He came closer to me, pushing me against the wall in the kitchen. What was wrong with him? He didn't have to snatch the book away from me like that.

He whispered into my ear while glancing at me, "Look at how big and pretty those gray eyes are, and those lips are just as big!" His breath smelled as if he had been drinking all day. I covered my nose with my right hand. He put his hand behind my neck. "I bet your throat is deep! Did you choke your first time? Perhaps not—you look like you can swallow!"

I beamed disturbingly, and then I smacked him bellicosely across the face. His reaction was priceless. He touched the side of his face and suddenly rubbed his cheek. He laughed and said, "Well—then again. You probably did choke your first time, huh?" *What a pig.* I looked back at him. I left him in the kitchen, and I went up the stairs again to isolate myself from the others. Before my departure, with a simple head gesture, I signaled Dillon to attend to Christian. I went into my bedroom to prepare myself. Mathew entered the room. He startled me.

"Mathew, you scared me to death!" I breathed out. He shut the door.

"I didn't mean to startle you. I just came to see how you were." His voice was genuine.

"I'm fine, Mathew. Thanks for checking up on me." I sat on my bed and stared out the window. He sat beside me.

"When you were tutoring my brother for English 112, I'm sorry for the way I was acting. I was, how you say, caught off guard." We laughed together.

"Now you find it funny?" I said, watching him.

"Yes, it is a little, I guess. I had some good laughs and giggles about it."

"Or shits and giggles, as Jacky puts it," I said, thinking of her.

He stood. "I wasn't planning to do anything to you."

I inhaled and then exhaled quietly. "I know, Mathew. I know. You were angry. I don't know any guy who would have been fond of a cock cage." I stood, trying to walk past him. He stopped me.

"Is there something I can do for you?" He caressed my face with his right hand cautiously. It was warm. It sent chills down my spine.

"What are you doing?"

"Have you ever felt you wanted to do something, but you just decided not to?" He positioned his hands on my hips. I didn't respond. He murmured into my ear softly, "Answer the question."

"Yes," I answered gently.

He tried to kiss me. I pulled away. "I see you, Erin. I see everything you're about—the pain you feel, the love you seek to fill that big hole in your heart. I know you, Erin, and I like every part of you, even your indecent side. You don't have to pretend to be innocent and timid with me, when you're bold and heartless just like me, but I can't help but find it interesting. I understand the lies you tell, the secrets you keep, and the games you play. It's what makes you the rarest and the most dangerous woman at this university. I also can't help that I want you, Erin. I want you so badly."

I waited, and then I leaned in to kiss him forcefully. He held my behind. He squeezed my checks firmly. I shook my head. "This is ridiculous, Mathew. What about Amy—you know, your girlfriend?"

He stopped. "What about her? If this is your excuse to stop, it's a funny one. I like you more than I like Amy right now. I don't care about Amy," he said, desiring to kiss me again.

I yanked my body away in the opposite direction. "What about Tia then? I know you care about her. Do you really want to risk losing her—whatever you have with her—for us?" He paused, and I said, "I didn't think so." I rearranged my dress to look presentable. I wasn't stupid enough to dive head first into the same pool as Tia and Amy. *No, thank you.* I had my own issues to recuperate from first.

I sealed the door behind me. Amy brushed up against me. She proceeded to look around in the halls. I collected her right arm. She seemed upset; I could tell by her appearance. Mathew was probably troubling her. Amy was solid and robust. She should have felt relieved about leaving her unhealthy relationship. In a hurry, she relaxed her hand on my shoulder, and then she exhaled rapidly.

"Have you seen Mathew?" she said, walking back and forth like a crackhead.

"He's in my bedroom. Relax, grasshopper." I pointed to my bedroom.

"Is some sick bitch with a real bad cough with him that I should know about, or is he alone?" She was panicking.

"I don't know, Amy. Go check for yourself," I said shortly.

Tia walked up to us and rudely snatched Amy from me. Amy dropped a book. I followed behind them to return her property, but Tia slammed and locked the door. It was Amy's diary. I secured her possession, placing it in a dresser in Shante's room. I ventured off into the kitchen to get a drink. I swallowed it immediately. The drink smoothly traveled down my throat. Jeremy was at the table, watching Jo dance with Angel in the living room. I wondered why he wasn't dancing. I sat on the right side of him.

"Do you see her?" he said.

I rested my hand on my face to support the weight. "Who?" I stopped and looked at Jo. "Oh, her. I guess that was a dumb question."

"When she dances, she burns because she is fire. I consider her to be dangerously elegant and beautiful. As I touch her, I start burning from our fiery entanglement. Her love has subdued me. Without her, I'm blistering in flames, because she is the reason I am warm. She sizzles like fire."

I gazed into his eyes. "Slow your roll, Shakespeare Junior. Although that was sweet of you, you scare me when you say shit like that!"

He smiled. "Too sugary sweet, huh?"

"Yeah, it seems to me that you like her a lot." I touched his shoulder.

"No." He paused. "What if I love her?"

"You're likely overestimating your emotions. What if you don't? What if you're an obsessed serial killer or a 2015 black version of the Ted Bundy rapist?" I yelled over the music.

He laughed, and then he was quiet, reconsidering his thoughts. "Seriously, Erin, you're going to compare me to Ted Bundy?"

I shrugged and added a clueless look. "I don't know. That poem was definitely a line that helped Ted Bundy profess himself as a gentleman!"

He chuckled slightly. He exhaled, glancing into my eyes. "Erin, I—"

"Don't say anything. Just know that the wind will continuously blow. The storms will severely sabotage your shiny days with her. The rain will proceed to linger and pour cruelly. It will damage the petals that are keeping your flowers intact, as well as the grass below her feet. And so your blue sky will adapt to the clouds, as the skies are gray. True love will heal your gardens and renew your sky. Your love, if real, will never die! Even in confusion and pain, your garden of love will continue to blossom for a century's time."

He looked confused. "You wrote that?"

"Yes, I was in love once, but he left me for a girl I left him for."

He licked his lips enticingly. "Wait, what? Are you, you know, a bisexual?"

"No, I was experimenting. It went terribly wrong, and I don't want to talk about it. I would appreciate it if you kept this to yourself. I'm a little embarrassed by it."

"I'm sorry that happened to you," he said with sympathy while fidgeting in his chair.

"I said it was wrong, but some mistakes are worth making. I never said I regret doing it. Life is too short to regret and hate every error that was probably beyond our control." I chuckled as I stared at him.

"What does the poem mean?" He arched an eyebrow at me.

How cute. "A planned destruction or a spontaneous occurrence will prove and faithfully test your love. Your love will go through difficulties not foreseen, but if it's real love, nothing and no one will be able to break it, because true love is unstoppable."

"It's a test of love, loyalty, and commitment." He stood happily.

"Exactly," I said.

Josephine danced up to Jeremy. He grinned charmingly. They danced alongside of Andrew and Angelina. The music's tempo was quick. Suddenly, the songs were slow and fragile. I could feel the music coursing through my veins. Every word pierced my soul deeper and deeper as the song persisted. I was in the kitchen with my eyes closed, rocking and mildly swinging to the music. R. Kelly's "Slowdown" was persuading me to mutter the lyrics, singing to my fulfillment. Even my toes were dancing to the rhythm and soft beat. While sitting in the chair, I ate a few refreshments from my grandmother's crystal bowl on the table. Dillon was heartbreakingly dancing with Christian. She knew I had proclaimed she was misspending her engagement with Christian. If she wasn't planning to do what we'd rehearsed for the renewal of her station and reputation, her presence was fruitless to the games.

Judging by their encounter and assuming her interest, she had an amateurish intention for him. I would be indifferent to her personal accomplishment, because it would be another reckless experience for her. There was a commotion occurring at the center of the living-room floor—Andrew and Angel were arguing like a married couple. He isolated himself from her. She sat on the sofa.

He charmingly smiled his way into the kitchen. Our eyes were entangled. "Would you like to dance, Rose?" He proceeded to refer to me as a flower, a white rose in his mother's garden.

I took his extended hand. "Yes, I would love to," I said, grinning.

Jeremy peeped over at me. He smirked at me, so I smiled back. I was wishing that Jeremy had asked me to dance. However, he hadn't. We were dancing beside Jo and Jeremy. Andrew's body was close to mine. He looked as great as he smelled. I rested my head on his chest. I was proud of him for finally putting the moves on Angelina. They inflicted jealousy on the people in their surroundings, including Dillon who was throwing her jealous eyes in their direction, but the real question was why?

CHAPTER 13

Dillon

Embarrassing Christian

I didn't know if I was madly in love with Christian. Despite the mess we had been through, I hadn't anticipated having such deep feelings for him. Maybe it was love; maybe it wasn't. One thing I did know was that I truly did care for him from the bottom of my heart. Sadly, I longed to see him pay for the suffering he'd inflicted upon me. People didn't inflict pain on the ones they loved—well, not normal people at least. Because I was daydreaming about revenge, I knew there was a possibility that I'd never loved and would never love him. I'd meant to. I wasn't blinded by love, as my teammates presumed. I was only interested in redeeming my reputation.

While Christian and I danced to the slow music, Erin was growing impatient with my venturing to spare him from humiliation. I still couldn't do it, though. The task was eating at my subconscious, and Erin realized it when her dance with Andrew was over. By the way, Angel didn't like them dancing one bit. It was innocent because they were just dancing; it meant nothing more and nothing less than the assignment I was about to confirm. It would serve no greater meaning, and Christian was drunker than drunk, so what would this mean to him? How would it affect him? Well, none of that was essential anymore, since Jacky reached out to me. She whispered direct instructions into my ear.

Without drawing too much attention, we were able to walk him up the stairs successfully. To include the participation of Erin, I came back downstairs to discuss important matters with her. She was correct about my mission going unnoticed at her party. In all honesty, I could never fully accept her as our leader, because I envied her station, and I was jealous of her authority and her persuasiveness. Yet she had to be envious of my potential to steal her authority, and Tia was as nosy as could be, since she'd interrupted our little chat for more knowledge.

Tia noticed three girls standing in the corner. They were pointing at me. Suddenly, they laughed pitifully, as if something were hysterical. The main follower, the one in the background with the black hair, had a scary look on her face.

I pointed with my eyes. "Tia, do you know those girls standing over there in the corner to our far left?"

Tia and Erin both answered me concurrently. "Yes, I know them."

Erin spoke independently. "They were my first visitors. The one in the middle, Ms. Prissy, is the leader. Her name is Catherine. The one on the left with the white dress on is Arabella, and the one behind them—I forgot her name!"

I touched Tia's arm. She frowned. "Those are the girls that criticize me and try to make fun of me, but instead, they end up looking stupid themselves!"

Tia grasped my arm eagerly. "So let's approach them!" She beamed innocently. We walked over to them confidently, and then she tapped me on the back, signaling me to speak my mind.

"Does any one of you have a problem with me or maybe have something they want to say to my face?" I said, blinking my eyes twice. My tone was disrespectful and nasty.

Catherine said, "Yeah, as a matter of fact, we do! I think you're unfit to be in a club—the both of you!" she said, also sharing her evil eyes with Tia. "Let me start with you first, Dillon. I think you're sad and weak! How and why did you let that loser wrap you up around his finger the way he did? He's got naked pictures of you on the Internet, like the inappropriate whore that you are! You're dancing with him to love songs as if everything is all peachy! You're the dumbest chick in this club. I can't wait until I replace you." Her friends were staring at her. "I mean, until one of us replaces you!"

"Catherine, I got this one," Chloe said, interfering. "You, Tia, have no purpose for living with your overly stretched-out vagina. I'm surprised any guy would want to be with you after how many guys were in you. As for the rumor about Michael, I think it's true, but I bet you're the slut that gave it to him. Herpes, I mean. I heard you trapped him in his apartment and raped him!" The two girls agreed by laughing. Swiftly, they all made an attempt to bolt away.

Tia snapped her fingers in Catherine's face. "Wait. You're not leaving without my input, now, are you? How rude of you—the both of you! Dillon, do you have anything you want to say before I devour these bitches?" she said bluntly.

I laughed. "Yeah, Tia, thanks for letting me go first—how nice of you." I moved closer to Catherine. Catherine quickly crossed her arms. "You." I paused. "Cathy, or whatever your name is, you don't exist. You're the real loser, because you're nobody to us—just a ghost in our hallways, ignored by important people like me. You are just some simple, nerdy, slutty, pale tramps whose only mission in life is to do my homework and beg to sit at our lunch tables. Then again, I don't even think any of you can do geometry. None of you skinny bitches are going to substitute my station, because there is already a substitution in order."

Catherine rolled her eyes. "We will see Monday morning."

Tia mocked her. "'We will see Monday morning'—man, you sound slow. Save the slow people and me from your lack of education, and just shut the fuck up, okay? Your voice is starting to cause my skin to itch. Now, you, Chloe darling—I remember you now. I was wondering why you looked so familiar to me. I know why you hate me, why all of you hate me! I slept with all of your boyfriends. What were their names? Jim, Paul, and Tommy, right? Now, if I have herpes, guess what—all you bitches got it too! So you shouldn't hate me because your men love friendly pussy!"

We went back to our business and continuously searched for Erin. She was nowhere to be found. We relocated. She was in the bedroom upstairs. We entered the room. Christian was handcuffed to the bed, blindfolded, and gagged. He was stripped down to his boxers, which were blue with small white parallel lines on them. *They went too far. Look at my baby.* My first thought was to release him. He was moving, but his movements were minor. His ankles were also cuffed to the bed railing.

"Is all this action and equipment necessary?" I said with aggressively.

Jacky was setting up the video camera. "Believe us—it's all necessary." She grinned at Erin.

Erin was watching him from the view of where the camera would be set up.

"What's the video camera for? When we talked about this, you didn't say anything about recording it!" I said.

Erin said, "Yeah, I did fail to mention a video camera to you, huh? Oops, it must have slipped my mind!"

Jacky burst out laughing. "This is one of the greatest junior assignments created. For evidence, we need a video as a visual aid for maximum points."

I started panicking, breathing strongly. "I can't do this. I can't do this!" I repeated. I sat on the bed next to Christian. He struggled to get my attention. I avoided him.

"Don't change your mind on us now! This is the assignment you have been working on for weeks! I just gave you the ammo you needed to perform in front of an audience. We are doing this with or without you. It's your choice. I thought since you were so in love with him, it would have killed you to see him with one of us," Erin said.

Jacky said, "I can do it. I can do it, because all of a sudden, you don't have the balls for it!"

"No! I have the balls, okay? It's my assignment. I won't let anybody get the glory for my work!"

Erin said, "When you said 'balls,' I hope you didn't mean it in a literal sense, but that a girl, Dillon. Make us proud. Fuck him until he is exhausted, so that way, it will be difficult for him to pitch a tent. Then, like somewhere around twelve o'clock, turn on the video camera. We and everybody else will be watching from the showroom. I bought some brand-new costumes that are in the closet, if you really want to play house and have some fun!" she said as she lifted her eyebrows seductively.

Eventually, she glanced at the clock on her phone. After they left, I paced back and forth in the room. I removed his blindfold and gag. He yelled for his teammates, calling out for help. I immediately wrapped my left hand around his mouth and climbed on top of him.

"Stop screaming, Christian," I said, but he continued to make an attempt to scream underneath my hand. "Stop it before I call Tia in here to ride your fucking face! Believe me. You don't want to go there." In an instant, he was quiet. Threatening to force Tia to ride his face was effective, considering the guys she invited to her bed.

I entered the closet. I slowly searched through Erin's new sexy uniforms. "The nurse outfit is boring, the sexy police officer doesn't fit the profile I'm going for, and the hot bunny rabbit outfit is foul. Christian, you have a choice between the teacher, the student, and the punisher."

He didn't respond to me.

"I wonder where Tia is nowadays!"

"The teacher, okay? Put the teacher costume on. You'll look sexy in it," he murmured in the presence of stress.

"See, that's where you're wrong. I could pull off any one of these costumes." I returned the student and teacher costumes to the closet. Christian needed to be punished for what he had done to me. It would bring my heart pleasure to humiliate him in front of everyone. He could refer to me as his female dominatrix for the night.

I stripped out of my white blouse and the remainder of my clothing. I unfastened my red bra from behind. I dropped my panties to the floor. "I remember when we first had sex. The first time you finished before me—and the second, the next, and the last time as well. We never did rounds because of your low-ass stamina. I never got the chance to finish. It's selfish of you, so tonight you get to come again and again. I'm going to give you one big ejaculation right after another. Let's see how much pleasure you can take all in one night."

"I don't care what you do. At the end of the night, you will still love me, and I still won't care about you. This is what it all comes down to—me not giving a shit about you. I get to sleep with you again. Except this time, I don't have to listen to you talk. It's not a punishment. It's a reward. Come on. Make Daddy come while you will be left dissatisfied," he said. "Again."

He grinned. The truth hurt. Every word he said was a fact contributing to my pain. It all was true. I brushed his honesty off my concerned shoulders. I went into his boxers, searching for his little friend to distract myself. I rubbed some lotion on my hands. I caressed his dick, rubbing the tip. I rubbed my thumb against his head frequently and began to jack him off. I increased the speed of my hands. I stroked him harder and faster. He groaned, trying to hold it in. He jumped at the feeling of my touch. Six minutes into a serious and solid stroking, he grew impatient toward my method.

He stiffened. "Come on. Just suck it already!" he said, rolling his eyes with irritation. He laughed. "Do that thing I like with your tongue on my balls."

I stopped, thinking of the technique he was pleading for. I looked up at him. He was swirling his nasty tongue around. I went back to my original tactic to frustrate him even more. He exhaled loudly. Four minutes later, he came. He groaned quietly, as he was able to hold his sounds of sexual enjoyment within. The majority of his semen was on my hands and fingers. I collected a napkin from Erin's nightstand. I wiped my hands clean of his heavy, thick semen. I forced more lotion into my hands and rubbed it in.

"What the hell are you doing now?" He stared.

I told him. He knew my objectives for that night. I found it hysterical that my hand jobs led to his irritable behavior. He hated them. Because of this, I loved giving them. I grinned. "What? Did you think I was joking when I said I would give you one big ejaculation right after another? I was so fucking serious." I stroked his dick again.

His tone was fragile. "Come on. You know I can't come that many times like that. Damn. You're going to overwork me!" He was breathing like a fatigued person.

"That's the whole point. Then you won't be able to get hard."

I caressed his dick more considerably. He moved his right hand. "Dammit, Dillon. Shit." He groaned as he registered a few minor movements. Eventually, he was hard like wood, much stiffer than the first time. The veins from his dick were easily visible. It was long and juicy. By rubbing and staring at it, I got horny. I imagined his dick going in and out of my pussy recurrently. Thinking of the feeling of his dick sliding against my walls got me massively damp. I tried to hide the fact that I was tempted.

He chuckled. He revealed a surprised expression on his face. “Stroking me is getting you horny, isn’t it?” I softly rocked back and forth while attending to his upcoming ejaculation. “Look at you. I see you’re feening for it more than you ever have. Don’t worry, babe. Daddy will let you taste it. All you have to do is ride him.”

I stopped and moved away from him, wanting to resist my urge to fuck him. Avoiding fucking him was my plan.

“Don’t fight it. Just think about how good I feel inside you. Do you remember the time when I had you bent all up in the corner?”

Shut the hell up, my subconscious said, because she felt it was necessary. I exhaled to preoccupy my unwanted thoughts and his words of encouragement. Jacking his dick off was the only sexual method I wished to sustain. I couldn’t let Christian change and tempt me, as he had in the past. As my touch persisted, I avoided eye contact, but watching my hands pull his excess skin up and down made me more vulnerable. His dick curved upward, and I was sure this was rare. It had an arch that motivated me to believe his friend could potentially make me climax if situated correctly. He could easily hit my G-spot. A good orgasm would certainly have reduced some of the tension I was feeling.

“And while you were bent up in the corner, you screamed and moaned, so I’m sure every neighbor heard me inside of you,” he said with an arousing smile and sealed eyes.

Yeah, I screamed, but only so you could feel like a king in the bedroom. However, there had been something remarkable about the first taste. In my opinion, the first penetration had been the most appreciated and memorable.

I had him right where I wanted him. I could continue to fuck him even when he finished, because I was in control. Fucking him would be nonstop for me. In fact, there was a high probability of his dick becoming my best source of stress alleviation for the time being. I could squirt and trickle away all of my difficulties, frustrations, and dissatisfactions right on that filthy face of his. I could do it for all of the embarrassments he'd caused me and for all of the pain I had endured because of it. Everything could have ended there with my initial orgasm.

Suddenly, he was blowing kisses in my direction. "But the reason you were cramped up in that small corner was because you were really running from me, because you can't take dick. You never could. Now you know he's too big for you," he said.

"What? I could and can take it, you cocky son of a bitch!" I lost it. I had to recollect myself. I started pacing to distract myself from his cocky attitude.

He was stunned. "Yeah, then come prove it."

Did he just dare me to take his dick, as if I can't tolerate what his dick is capable of? Did he convince himself that the way he fucks is just too fucking astounding and worthy for me to swallow, as if that is the purpose for my resistance? I would prove him wrong in a heartbeat. I couldn't wait for him to watch me.

I took a condom from the left pocket of his pants and walked over to the bed. I patted his penis to be funny. What did I ever see in this asshole? Shit. Absolute shit, my subconscious said with honesty. I grabbed his penis while sitting with my legs on top of his. I gripped his dick with both of my hands. I leaned down to place the condom over him. He watched me, but he said nothing. He licked his lips. I sat up and reseated myself on top of his dick, taking in every inch. I leaned closer to him to put my breasts into his mouth. He sucked on them, nipping on my breasts, as he usually did. I wrapped my arms underneath and around his upper body.

I held on tightly while leaning to relax my head on his right shoulder. Meanwhile, he sucked on my neck, which caused me to become wetter and wetter. I started to ride him quickly with intense force. Every time I moved for a sexual expression or to fulfill some sensual request, the sex became a little more aggressive. The bed squeaked at my forcefulness. And then I was grinding to recollect my energy. I immediately realized my exhaustion, and I lifted up so that he could use some of his physical strength. He was beating my pussy up from underneath. We could hear the sound of his dick and balls and my pussy overpowering every noise in the room as his balls slapped hard against my ass.

My legs became weak. They started to shake, and I suddenly fell down and broke my position. His mouth was open wide, head tilted back, and his eyes were sealed in satisfaction. I screamed, trying to hold it all in. Him fucking me from underneath was one of the greatest positions I had ever experienced. After this action, the juices really dripped from below. I rode him once more, overwhelmed at the thought of continuing. I leaned down to kiss his chest and those small muscles of his. I then locked my fingers behind his neck firmly to support my balance. I rode harder and faster. Moments later, he came. As a result, he grew soft. His heavy breathing matured. I stood still on top of him in disappointment. He inhaled and then exhaled in relief.

He smiled. "Boy, I'm tired. Wow, that was a hell of a ride, huh?"

Oh fuck no, my subconscious screamed. I wanted to proceed. It couldn't be over. I wanted more. I repositioned myself at the bottom half of the bed. I removed the condom. After sucking his dill pickle to get him up and running again, I repositioned another condom over him.

"Damn, this again, Dillon. Shit, I'm tired. You are going to overwork him!" he said, exhaling.

I lowered myself onto his penis in a kneeling position. "*Me importa una mierda porque eres mi perra*."

He stared at me as if I were insane. "Who in the hell are you calling your little bitch?" he yelled. I just smiled.

I kept my knees pressed against the bed. This time, I curled my feet around the insides of his legs. Meanwhile, I also leaned forward, and my hands had a firm grip on the sheets underneath him on both sides. My feet were now wrapped around Christian's calves. I moved my hips in small motions while tilting my pelvis and squeezing my butt to achieve a better result. Boy, it was compelling. Changing up my actions gave me better leverage.

I continued to move my hips in a steady rhythm. I swirled around and around in a circular motion so that his dick could reach my G-spot. I went right to left, left to right, up and down, down and up. I repeated this precise routine continuously. I discovered a sensitive area, but Christian's penis felt remarkable reaching a specific spot inside of my companion. I tilted my hips more to the left. I felt as if something were coming—maybe it was a sexual peak building up inside of me. The exhilaration and strong feelings of pleasure, partly due to my lack of fulfillment over the years, needed to be unleashed through an intense outburst.

I didn't stop, because I liked the unexpected feeling of it. There it was—the encounter I had been longing for, the orgasm of my dreams. In my costume—which included a deluxe black-and-silver Venetian mask, a black fraternity paddle, silver heels, and a sexy PVC leather halter lingerie set—I continued to fuck him until that pleasurable feeling ceased. It numbed my entire body, but the pleasure generated from below traveled all over my body; even my toes and fingertips seem paralyzed. The sensation visited every location in my body as well as my mind. I was free. As my enjoyment concluded, Tia barged into the room. She slipped as she made her way into the bedroom. I recollected myself and nervously jumped off of him. I replaced the gag over his mouth.

"I'm okay," she said. "No need to stop knocking good boots for me because I broke something or anything. Nothing is broken, though. I assure you." She detached her heels from her feet. "My foot and ass are literally sweating from this party." She pulled her underwear from between her cheeks. She rushed up to me happily. "You look so hot, Dillon—oh my, my, my."

"I look okay," I said with boredom.

She hugged me for reassurance. "No, you look sexy." She touched my face with both of her hands.

I looked her up and down. "Are you going lesbian on me now? You got that I-like-you look on your face."

She leered at me strangely. "I think you're forgetting who I am. To change the subject, are you ready to overtake Christian?"

I hesitated while staring down at the ground and back at her. "Yeah, I'm ready," I said sadly.

She said excitedly, "Well, it's showtime." Then she whispered in my ear so that Christian wouldn't be exposed to her words. "Don't be angry, but Erin has suddenly made a slight change to your assignment."

"What change?" I said, troubled. "What now?" She opened up the door, and there were five girls waiting at the door. "What do they want?" I closed the door in their faces. I tapped her shoulder.

"They're waiting for cunnilingus from him. Do you accept the readjustment?"

CHAPTER 14

Tia

Live Sex Performance

"Do you accept the readjustment?" I said once more.

It would have annoyed me to restate it again. I was waiting for an answer. She appeared to be empty. Her heart was thumping out of her chest. She was drowning in her own nervousness, panicking on the inside, battling to uphold this change. I could tell from her eyes and shaky fingers that this new proposal was a problem. She blinked. If this situation had been about Mathew, I wouldn't have hesitated to respond, nor would blinking have been necessary, because I could and would not do it, not in a million years, not for a game. She was slowly debating. During her deliberation, she started to pace in the room. I cleared my throat for an answer. She didn't get the hint. She was quiet. I guess she was arguing with her subconscious. I sat down beside Christian, who attempted to move. I rested alongside of him. He was babbling underneath his gag.

I played with his gag and large ears. "Blah, blah, blah, blah—I can't hear you," I teased. "Chatter, chatter, chatter!" I laughed. From this angle, he sort of looked like a monkey. I made funny faces at him, teasing him to get a reaction.

"Yes, Tia. I accept it."

I left the monkey alone and quickly turned to face her. I couldn't believe she'd accepted. She would regret this. I knew it.

I looked deeply into her eyes. "Are you sure you're okay with this?" I reworded the question to be certain before she made an error she would be unable to correct.

"There are naked images of me on Facebook because I trusted and cared for that jerk! Of course I'm sure! What? Men are allowed to embarrass us, but women can't do the same?" She was upset. I could comprehend it. I exhaled and placed my hand on her shoulder, hoping it would calm her down. After all the yelling, she still wasn't sure. I shook my head.

"Okay. If you say so," I said as she turned on the video camera. "Make us proud. Remember, in fifteen minutes, we will be watching."

I shut the door. The five girls were waiting for my response. "She agreed, so it's on, ladies!" They screamed as if they'd never received head before.

Meanwhile, I entered the kitchen and popped some popcorn. I opened the refrigerator and grabbed Pepsis for Erin and me. Eventually, I headed to the showroom. It was huge, like a movie theater. There was a large TV on the wall, and there were about a hundred seats. They all were filled. The remainder of the competitors had been thrown out or were sexually occupied. I knew because my duty was to make sure of it. The showroom was crowded, loud, and full of laughter and personal conversations. I was located in the center of the theater to watch Dillon overtake Christian. Erin was stationed in the center of the ruckus, as always. She was giving yet another unnecessary speech. *What an attention whore.* I thought she liked hearing herself speak aloud. I ripped open my bag of popcorn. A large amount of it fell onto the floor. Erin whistled at full volume. *Here goes the big speech.* Everyone grew silent.

"The female popularity group really knows how to party! Is everybody having a good time?" she yelled. Erin had a way with words. My popcorn went down the wrong hole. I choked on it, and then I started coughing during her announcement. I cleared my throat.

I sipped on my Pepsi. "I'm okay." They completely ignored me.

"Hell yeah!" they all screamed while hopping out of their seats and spilling portions of their drinks.

What a bunch of animals.

"Come on, guys. Our male popularity group has Tia screaming louder than that! That's just pitiful. I think you can do better!" she said, screaming at the top of her lungs. I hoped her voice would be hoarse the next day. They reacted to that outburst, and Erin was happy about that last statement. *Whore.*

I frowned. *What a bitch. What the hell was her problem?* I was at the edge of the building, and Erin was pushing me off the cliff. I was tired of being mistreated. *"Tia is this; Tia is that," they say. Do they ever get weary of harassing me?* I scowled again while babbling underneath my breath. The audience yelled more forcefully. Why was she so loud? It was not necessary. *Somebody, please shut this bitch up, and look at her damn dress.* It was every color in the magical fucking rainbow. I burst out laughing. She looked like a black superpower rainbow bitch, a fucking Power Ranger or a bag of magical Skittles. My laughter interrupted Erin's public dialogue. The noise reduced, and everybody stared at me because I was a disturbance.

Their stares didn't stop me from releasing the remainder of my giggles. I stood and clapped, and then I waited shortly. "My bad, Erin—I thought you were finished! You look like you have to shit, and I bet you have been holding it since you've been up there!" I said in an unfamiliar voice. I cleared my throat once more. I muttered, "Do you have to shit, Erin? Don't hold it. Sometimes you got to let the shit go!" Some students laughed behind me.

"Why in the hell are you speaking like this? Dillon is waiting for us!" she said, frustrated.

"I just need to know if you have to shit. Because if you do, I can finish your speech and shorten it up for you, since they are always so fucking long!"

She was embarrassed. "No, Tia! I don't have to shit, okay? Are you happy now?" she said with wide eyes.

"Very much. Please continue!" I said, chuckling as I sat back down in my seat.

Her hands were on her hips, and she beamed innocently. "Our junior scores have been raging through the roof! If you like Jo's party for the drugs and alcohol, boy, do we have something fucked up in store for you! Watch, and enjoy a live performance from one of the top members of our BOTS Association! This is a taste of what our club is all about!" she yelled to the norms.

Boy, was her ass overly dramatic with those big-ass speeches. I ate my popcorn slowly while Erin joined me. I passed her a Pepsi. She snatched it from my hand and popped it open. She watched me intensely. I looked away to avoid discomfort. I made small noises with my mouth.

"Tia," she called.

She looked pissed. Mama Bear wasn't happy. "Huh?" I dug into my left ear while slowly turning to face her awkwardly.

"What was the purpose of you asking me to use the bathroom in front of everyone, when you knew I didn't have to go?" She eyed me.

"Erin, I don't know what you're talking about. Oh, look at Dillon—the video is on. Look at how slutty she looks. Her costume is so not sexy," I said, changing the subject. The sound of the video was outrageous, like at the movie theater. It was loud, and I loved it. We were watching nonstop. The room was suddenly quiet. Dillon had everyone's eyes on her.

Dillon was on top of Christian in her punisher costume, touching all over him. His gag had been removed. She smacked him confrontationally. She slapped him again and again. It must have hurt. *Get it, girl. Beat his ass. What a pussy.* Every time she assaulted him, it was more pugnacious. Christian had an argumentative expression on his face.

"What the fuck?" he yelled. The audience laughed at his reaction. "Aw, no, this bitch is crazy! Ho, you must have lost your fucking mind! You don't be hitting me!" He paused between every word. "You're not going to be slapping me around like I'm a bitch!"

She struck him to substantiate her domination. She was getting it. She was strangely attaining pleasure from antagonizing him. It was sort of a turn-on for me as well to see him being abused. He turned his head toward the video camera sharply. He looked shocked at his exposure to an audience.

"Aw, naw," he whined. "People sitting there watching us and not about to help me? I know motherfuckers are watching! This shit is not funny now. I'm in the next room! Come save me!"

Dillon laughed, so we followed along with her and laughed as well. She was popping her pussy in his face. Then she started riding his face. He made a series of hysterical sounds. As awkward as they were, I became excited. He might have been an idiot, but he was a straight-up comedian. I was breathing heavily, as I lusted to be touched.

My hormones were racing absurdly. This show was unbelievably lustful. I exhaled because I was highly stimulated. I curled up my fingers, battling my urges. I didn't want my sexual appetite to be transparent to the others around me.

She moaned. "Suck on it."

I shook as my body ached impatiently. My panties were wet. *Oh no, not again.* I was leaking out of my underwear. This was the second time it had happened today. I glanced in between my legs. *Hot fudge,* my subconscious said to my wet underwear. Dillon kept riding his face, but this time, she was more forceful. Watching them made it worse for me.

Erin pointed and said, "He's not even hard! What a total fag!" Everyone giggled except me.

Dillon left the room after she was finished. One of the girls waiting patiently at the door entered the room, taking Dillon's spot. She—I no longer could recall her name—had long, curly dark brown hair. She was tall, with a nice, toned shape. She hesitantly danced her way on camera to the music. She peeled off her clothing to show us her nakedness. Remarkably, Christian was still soft. I envisioned her sweating to maintain his weariness. *What exactly did Dillon do to exhaust him?* I wondered as the girl seductively crawled to him. She sucked on his stomach and journeyed up to his neck. Eventually, she duplicated Dillon's actions. She aimed straight for Christian's mouth, as if her vagina were his dinner. She suffocated him with her pussy to keep him occupied. Then an even taller beauty named Diamond, who had pink-and-black streaks in her hair, rode his face aggressively. She took her mission seriously and added on some extras to what was required of her.

I heard Erin, but I was estranged from her and from Dillon's audience. I visualized myself riding Mathew's face, like the fantasies I imagined in my dreams. The music was loud. Diamond grinded on him briskly. She shook unbearably as she groaned again and again. I mentally journeyed back to my erotic experience with Michael, wishing it had been with Mathew. I flashed back to our affair, and the images of every moment came dashing back, further arousing me. The memory stimulated me beyond my control. I sealed my eyes while my thoughts continued to ambush me. I remembered getting frisky with my pearl and fantasizing about Mathew, not Michael, shoving his dick in me, although Michael could fuck.

I loved the way Michael yanked on my legs to pull me closer to him. My legs were glued on top of his shoulders. When he kissed my neck with caution, I weakened as I finally accepted the encounter. In fact, everything he did turned me on even more. The juices streaked down my legs heavily. I inhaled quickly but quietly. The memory of him biting my small nipples and of me masturbating had stolen my full attention. I gripped the arm of the chair on the left side at the memory of us fucking like maniacs. I loved how he teased me, because the tease was my true motivation. Him gliding his cock against my clit felt spectacular. I purred like a little kitty and cried out mournfully when he thrust himself inside me. I needed to leave the showroom because watching them didn't help me one bit. Something unexplainable hit me.

I shook and muttered, "Erin, do you feel that?"

"Quiet, Tia. I'm trying to watch this," she said, shushing me.

That bitch. Why did she just up and shush me? I charged out of the sorry excuse for a theater. I slammed the door. I rushed down the stairs to the nearest bathroom. Andrew was in the bathroom, and I mistakenly intervened. Peeking over at his size, I noticed a tattoo on his lower hip.

"Andrew," I said, surprised.

"I'm finishing up. I'm about to leave, so it will be all yours," he said, taking a leak. His head was tilted back, and his eyes were shut. I locked the door.

I moved closer to him. "You have a tattoo on your lower hip."

"Guilty as charged." He fastened his zipper. He looked at my legs. "I see the reason why you rushed in here. You didn't even make it to the bathroom." He laughed. It was not funny.

I glanced down between my thighs. I quickly grabbed some tissues by the sink. "That's not what you think it is, okay?" I wiped between my inner thighs.

He stared. "Okay. What is it?" he said, washing his hands.

"Nothing. Forget I said anything."

He dried his hands with the huge green towel hanging up by the end of the tub. "I'm not stupid, Tia. I knew what it was the moment you came rushing into this bathroom. I just wanted to hear you say it."

I gazed into his eyes. "It's nothing. I spilled a little water on me. That was all." I crossed my arms.

He laughed. "Water, huh? Is that what you're calling it nowadays? Okay, whatever you say, Tia. To be honest with you, it looks to me like you got so aroused that your so-called water is trickling from in between your legs. From how wet you are, I bet your panties are soaked."

I closed my legs. He stared again, shaking his head at me. Why was he distracting me?

"You're saying this to distract me from my question." I rested my hand on the sink. I was serious. Andrew was an attractive, distracting, and charming guy—but only to Angelina and the other females in our school. I could resist him. At least that was what I thought. He couldn't wait to prove me wrong.

We were close to the point of kissing. "What question was that?" With his finger, he curled my hair behind my right ear. I breathed more heavily. Without a doubt, he noticed it.

"It's a question about your tattoo and Amy." I was now against the wall. He had trapped me in the corner. Unfortunately, I didn't mind. It felt nice.

"What about it?"

I lost my train of thought. I tried to remember my question. I coughed. It was far from my reach. His fingers were attached to mine. He slowly slid my hands up against the wall, extending my arms to the maximum.

"You had sex," I said, "with you know, and she's—"

He gazed strangely at me. "Look at you. You're all tongue-tied. How cute. I have never seen you so nervous before or even at all. Your nervousness is almost attractive. Now, I'm guessing you forgot what you wanted to ask."

I hadn't forgotten, but it was difficult for me to say it aloud. He placed his left hand between my inner thighs. I gasped as I closed and then reopened my eyes. It was wonderful—well, at least my pussy thought so, because another major leakage was occurring in my panties. I needed to learn some self-control. He licked his lips, and I watched him do it.

"I knew it. Your panties are soaked." He smirked. He left me in the bathroom. He'd fucked me mentally, and it had been great, yet I was disappointed I hadn't gotten anything useful out of our conversation.

I needed to get laid. I washed my hands thoroughly before wiping myself all over again. The moment I shut the door, Mathew approached me. I gazed everywhere else except at him. I felt him looking down at me. I avoided his stare and ignored him. I walked around him. He followed and captured my hand.

"You ask too much of me," he said with a serious facial expression.

I snatched my arm away from him. "I ask nothing of you. Keep your friendship. Enjoy the party, Mathew." I tried to escape him.

He gripped my arm again, harder this time. "Have you heard? I broke up with Amy."

I grinned. "Good. She's a bitch, and you broke up with Amy for a friendship with me?"

"She's your best friend. You seemed to like her just fine to me." He eventually released my arm.

"We were friends like you and me, but things change. There's a difference. It's something you can't seem to grasp."

He was staring once more. "Go out with me."

I snickered as if he were trying to be sarcastic. "What did you say to me?" He laid his hand on my face. My expression was unreadable.

"I owe you one for helping me out the other night."

When he finished talking, I started to frown at him. I rolled my eyes and marched in another direction. "Whatever, Mathew. Do whatever you want to do."

I poured myself a drink in the kitchen and then two more after the first. Amy entered the kitchen. She was scowling at me. The alcohol burned my throat. I coughed briefly.

"I have to talk to you about something," she said with her head down. Her tone was fragile.

I exhaled, exposing my irritation. "Not now, Amy. Not now."

"Look, I really need you right now. Please, Tia. I can't think straight. I just need to talk to someone I trust about this. It's about where I went wrong with Mathew. I cheated on him, Tia, many times, but only because he wasn't being faithful to me. I did it since I was hurting."

I turned to face her in shock and interest. "Now is the perfect time to get that excess baggage off your shoulders." I smiled.

Jacky interrupted. "As you can see, the party is over. There is a meeting happening in Erin's room. You and Amy should join us."

I blinked with disapproval. "Thanks for asking, but Amy and I were having a conversation before you rudely interrupted with your announcement from Erin." I was angry at Jacky's interference with Amy's confession. The bitch was just about to reveal her dangerous set of problems. *Nicely done, Jacky—nice.*

She giggled. "Tia, I wasn't asking you."

We walked up the stairs. I mocked her as we traveled to the room.

Erin said foully, "It's nice of you to join us."

What is everyone's problem around here? I said, "Who—Amy or me?" Everybody was lying on the floor on top of blankets.

Erin was twisting her hair around with her finger, as usual. She shrugged. "Both of you."

"You call this a meeting?" I looked around.

She looked oddly at me. "I never said this was a meeting. Did you hear me say that?"

I directed my hatred at Jacky. She beamed purely as I said, "So what is this about?"

Angelina answered. "We are planning to open up to each other and share our feelings."

I stared at all of them. "That's a little gay, don't you think?" I said disgustedly. "Don't be pathetic. Feelings are for girls. No one wants to share feelings—not me at least."

The others said simultaneously, "We *are* girls!" Amy and I joined them on the floor.

"So who would like to go first?" Amy said.

Jo raised her hand, smiling. "I'll go. I have heard so many things about this club. They are all rumors. Well, probably some of them. It's the reason I haven't told Jeremy that I am a part of the team. I love him. However, our problem is we don't talk to each other the way that we used to. He cares about what people think. He is easily deceived by rumors. I hate that about him!" she said with aggression. "I wish I could have more time with him."

Erin gave her advice. "Sometimes people need their space so that they can have a little time to miss each other. That way, they know what their relationship is worth."

Dillon said, "Why doesn't he want you in the club?" She scratched her ear.

Jo exhaled. "He feels the game and the players will corrupt me. I don't believe it. He's afraid he will fall out of love with me." She lowered her eyes.

Jacky said, "I like Professor Rodríguez."

"What?" Amy said. "Oh yeah, tell me what girl doesn't, but all you're doing is having sex, I'm sure."

Erin said, "Amy, you can't be too sure of anything with them. Just don't get caught, please."

Jacky said, "I don't plan on us getting caught."

I beamed at Erin. "You know what I think, Jacky? I think you would be more sexually compatible with James, since you like that *Fifty Shades of Grey* and dominatrix bullshit. James would make a great light-skinned Christian Grey," I joked.

Jacky said disgustingly, "I don't think so."

Jo said, "So how about you, Tia?"

I stared at her with hatred for mentioning my name. "That is none of your business and shouldn't concern you—any of you." I rolled my eyes.

Angelina spoke. "Come on, Tia. Share something personal—something we don't know about you."

They all agreed. "Yeah, share with us!"

They were pissing me off. "Okay, where do I start? Whoa, I know," I said in a jolly tone. "I was just in the bathroom with Andrew. He noticed how wet I was. He went up my inner thigh to see how soaked my panties were, and he was so surprised. I wanted him to fuck me right there, and I was speechless. I don't think anywhere in that equation I was thinking about Angel's feelings."

Dillon said, "You have issues, Tia—some very serious issues." They agreed again.

I laughed. "You know what, Dillon? Christian was the first guy I ever gave a blow job to in the girls' bathroom at school. It was an every-Wednesday thing for me. He does this little turtle-shell thing with his back before he comes, but I'm sure you already know that." I smiled lustfully.

"You're a bitch!" Dillon yelled.

My subconscious snickered at her remark of unfriendliness. "Would anybody else like me to open up to them? I would be happy to oblige," I sneered.

Jo said, "No. Exchanging your thoughts and opinions for ours is no longer necessary." The rest of my teammates shook their heads.

Good, because Jeremy was next. I blinked in Amy's direction. "Amy, so would you like to share something with the group?" I blinked again, waiting for information.

She had jumped into Erin's bed. "No. I can't seem to think of anything that I would like to share. Maybe you should come back to me."

That little bitch. "Are you sure, Amy?" I said, waiting for the truth.

"Wait. I do have something I would like to mention. Mathew broke up with me for some nasty cunt. The trashy whore called his phone, looking to get busy with a hoarse voice," she said. I laughed.

"I'm sorry about that Amy, but is there anything else you would like to tell us?" Erin said.

"I did something horribly, horribly wrong and didn't know it. I don't know what I was thinking."

Jo said, grinning, "Well, that's great, Amy. Erin, tell us about you. Is there someone special in your life?"

She answered, "No. Not yet at least. I'm not looking for someone to be with, but I believe that special someone is looking for me. They say people often find something when they are not searching for it. One day, somehow, love finds them. I know I will make some girl very happy someday," she said in a pure tone.

What the hell? Was I hearing this bullshit correctly? She wasn't a lesbian. My eyes locked on Erin. I shook my head. That was a damn shame. *What a fucking liar.* A damn lesbian—who was she trying to misinform? I looked at Josephine. She was smiling fondly. Erin and Jo smiled shyly at one another. She was planning to pursue Jeremy and Jo. I knew she was pure evil. There was nothing sweet about her future unrighteous act. It was sick and insidious. But boy, I was anxious to watch the drama of the game unravel beneath Erin's feet.

As she stood, she handed us individual diaries. "What are those for?" I asked.

She said, "They are diaries, Tia. I'm guessing we are supposed to write in them." She continued to pass them out. "From now on, these diaries are yours. Write what you want in them. This is something new that we are trying out. When the year is over, maybe we will read each other's diaries. Remember, don't write your names in them. Let it remain a mystery." She jumped into her bed.

CHAPTER 15

Jacky

Teacher–Student Sex

What was Erin doing? I knew her intentions for Josephine's presence. We all did. But why was she flirting with Jo? Unfortunately, Jo flirted back. Jo caught her gaze. Erin provided her with an inexplicable reason to blush. Their affection was discernible. What Erin had planned was madness. It was so deviously intelligent that I wished I had thought of it for her. Jo and Erin conspicuously relocated to the left side of the room. They conversed among themselves. I could see why Erin was on the road to becoming the first female legend of the sex game her brother had manufactured. It was too bad he was long forgotten. Now she was the creator of a game between the sexes.

I unbolted my diary and began putting my pen to paper. It was quiet for once. Everybody else mimicked me. I wanted Jo to remain in Dillon's position. She never would be awarded the position of our new speaker for next year. Everyone had her moment, but this was my time to shine. I wrote my darkest and dearest secrets in my new diary. I kept thinking of Professor Rodríguez. He still didn't know about our previous affair. I fidgeted with uncertainty, imagining his future reaction to my inappropriateness. The thought was unsettling. I could have kept the knowledge from him, but I needed more for my personal stimulation. I allowed my imagination to fulfill my sexual curiosity. My desire was to be dominated by my teacher on numerous circumstances in any particular setting. I envisioned him fucking me while he discussed the history of literature and poetry. Imagining his hands touching every part of my body excited every inch of my girlish parts and every hair on my naked skin.

His eyes scanned the classroom. He decided to return our first drafts of our research papers. The assignment was about the treatment of animals and why their living conditions affected meat eaters. When my paper was in my possession, I took a glimpse at my score. I frowned. A 66 out of a 100 percent—are you shitting me? I read his comments at the end of the paper. The bell rang, and students rushed out of the classroom. I was stuck, perplexed.

"Professor Rodríguez?" I said timorously. "I don't understand what's wrong with my paper. I have my thesis and blueprint." He took my paper and scanned his writing on it.

"Ms. Dickerson, your thesis isn't a precise opinion on a limited subject. If your purpose isn't argumentative, there's no debate. Your thesis shouldn't be a fact, because it needs to be debatable."

"Why shouldn't it be a fact?" I said.

"There's no point in trying to convince or persuade readers of a true statement."

"Can I ask you something?" I fidgeted.

"Sure, ask anything you like, Ms. Dickerson," he said, tossing his papers into his dark brown briefcase.

"Do you ever get tired of teaching?"

He cocked his head to the left and grinned lightly. "No. I don't get tired of doing something I love. When you discover your passion, you go with it. It's suitable to get paid to do something that you love and what you are good at, as opposed to something you hate."

My heart was pounding nervously. "Out of all of the years you've taught here at Marshall S. King University, have you ever fantasized about fucking one of your students?" I said seductively, eyeing him.

He quickly turned to me, shocked. He was insulted by my question. "You shouldn't ask me those things! That is out of line and extremely inappropriate, Ms. Dickerson! I would like you to leave my classroom now!"

"Come on. Just answer the question. Say, 'No, I don't want to fuck any of them, but I do dream of fucking you, Ms. Dickerson.'"

He was motionless. After a while, he held the door wide open, signaling me to leave. I approached him to close and properly seal the door. "You have to stop this," he said. "You are my student! That's all you will ever be to me! Do you understand me?" he yelled.

"I don't like your tone of voice, Professor. I'm twenty-one years old, which makes me perfectly legal. Anything that happens by chance with me will be completely confidential." I extended my arm to touch his face.

He twisted the doorknob's handle. "I won't let you destroy the one good thing I have in this life!" he said. He surely misunderstood my intent.

"Professor Rodríguez, I don't want to threaten you, but you're a fool if you think I'm intimidated by your choice of approach. You have misinterpreted the reason for my allurement."

He listened with an open mind. He stationed himself in his black leather chair.

"Every day, I battle wanting or longing for you, because I'm not allowed to see you this way. But then I see you fighting the urge to peek between my thighs and underneath my small skirts and dresses. I noticed that every morning, you lose that battle."

I was sitting on top of the desk with my legs separated. His hungry eyes were buried underneath my skirt, expressing his vulnerability. My legs were open enough for him to see one of my favorite pair of white panties. I hesitantly undid the buttons on my purple short-sleeved sweater. "I'm saying you don't have to peek anymore, because now you have the opportunity to look freely. My body is in full exposure to you. You can do whatever you want with me and for as long as you require me."

He urgently pulled down the shades. He blinked and rubbed his finger against his chin. "Anything I want for as long as I want you?"

I groaned. "Anything you like."

He folded his arms, smiling at my generosity. "You look like you want it rough," he said, writing on the board.

"It's the only way I take it." I bit my lip.

"Good, because that's the only way I give it anyway." He continued to write. "Don't read it yet," he ordered.

"Yes." I fussed and crossed my legs at the same time.

"From now on, you will address me as Daddy, so try that again."

"Yes, Daddy."

He watched me. Then he removed my heels from my feet. I unzipped his pants. I peeled off his white-and-baby-blue tie and his all-white button-up shirt. Meanwhile, he placed my right leg over his shoulder. He lifted me. I wrapped my legs around his neck. He squeezed my cheeks and smacked them individually. Oh boy, did I love the strike.

"Once I eat you out, start reading."

He peeked at me, smiling. I moved closer so that he could get me wet and aroused. My thighs covered his ears. He held me up. He pressed both of his hands against my behind, pulling me nearer to his lips. They felt better than I'd imagined. He was in between my legs exclusively. His veins jumped out on his arms and neck. I made seductive sounds as he slowly sucked on my index finger. *Hmmm, he could do that again.*

"Oh, shit, Jacky." He teased me with his tongue.

Don't stop, dammit—don't stop. I jumped, overreacting to his mild teasing. He licked me slightly, and now my pussy was moistened, and my toes curled because he was elegantly swirling the tip of his tongue in a circular motion. I leaned toward him more hostilely. He decided to cease and toy with me even more.

He sucked repeatedly, moving his skillful tongue in every possible direction. How much more could his tongue paralyze me? My pussy was speechless. No worries or questions crippled my mind. His tongue bounced off of and then back on my pussy. I moaned again. I tilted my head back. I started to read his writing aloud from off of the board.

"I have been a very, very bad student. Because of this, I need to be fucked and spanked like the naughty slut that I am, Professor." I clenched my teeth because of his unpredictable suckling and slurping. He ate me out perfectly. I screamed with pleasure.

"Read the entire thing," he said. I liked him ordering me around, and I listened.

"For anything I do that is irrelevant to your demand, I will be punished with your stiff, big, and powerful dick." I stopped to embrace the pleasure. "Fucking and satisfying you are now my desire. Do with me as you please."

The muscles of his arms expanded when he bounced my pussy on his lips. *Mmm, eat me, Professor.* I was surprised at how high my ass was extended in the air. I kissed him from his neck to his balls slowly in order to tease him. I locked my mouth securely on his companion. Then I sucked him back and forth from the head to the shaft, the shaft to the head. I had to reward him for his outstanding cunnilingus. I sucked on his dick with great force, paying attention to every inch he was blessed with. His gifted dick was also my blessing, so I was appreciative for having the opportunity to be fucked with his miracle. I spit on it and eyed him. His eyes were sealed solidly. He smelled manly. He placed his finger inside me.

"Aw, fuck."

"You're tight and wet. How long has it been since you've been fucked?"

I shook my head. He stopped to slide a latex condom over his penis. Then he boosted me up, holding my body weight with his arms. His actions were unexpected but deserved. My walls were smothered during our first insertion. He pierced me smoothly. All of a sudden, he was bouncing me around on his dick. My breasts were slapping against his chest. I screamed at the unbearable enjoyment. He lifted my right leg in order to go deeper for our bliss.

"What are we gonna do about that nasty little grade, huh?" he whispered.

Why was he whispering? Even his whispers turned me on. Unlike him, I couldn't speak, not now. He proceeded to fuck me. But then he decided that fucking me wasn't enough. A dialogue while fucking would be an improvement.

I shook. How could I speak when I was too busy taking his stick drill? I couldn't.

He spanked me. "Answer me. You're gonna get that fucking grade up, right? I'm talking to you."

If I had tried to speak, the only thing we would have heard would have been my moaning at the feeling of his cock. I shook when thinking of responding to him. He spanked me for a response again.

"Yes, yes. I promise," I said, barely squeezing the words out of me, because I was preoccupied with his cock.

He smacked my ass for a better answer. "You can do better than that. Yes what?"

He started pounding me harder for communication. "Yes, Daddy. I'm going to bump my grade up—yes, yes, yes." I moaned as I made a fist.

I could now feel him in my stomach so deeply that I was dick whipped already. "What are you going to get on that next grade, huh?" he said, spanking me yet again.

I screamed, "Oh Daddy, I'll get an A. Yes, yes, yes, I'm getting a fucking A-plus—a hundred fucking percent!" I shook once more while shouting. My lips quivered.

My body tingled at the feeling below. I had generated a fondness for his sweet and hard strokes. The physical sensation tangled my spine, and my groans blended in with my laughter. He resumed the titillation. He gradually thrust deeper and deeper while entering me. He put me down and bent me over entirely so that I was touching my toes. I jiggled and wobbled my behind up in the air. He spanked me because of the tease. I embraced the strike and longed for another. I patted my pearl and massaged it tenderly. He struck my ass again. I cried out, weeping pleasantly.

"Yes, Professor, I'm your A-student, spank me. You son of a bitch, do it harder," I said.

He stood behind me, teasing me again. Boy, did I love but hate being teased. He spanked my pussy with his dick repetitively. I grinded on it from the rear, and he smacked my right cheek. I arched my back.

"You like being naughty because you want me to punish you. What are you?" he questioned.

"Yes, Daddy. I'm your teacher's pet," I said quickly.

I was still in my position, waiting to be fucked. He lowered himself, thoroughly rubbing his dick on my pussy, front to back, back to front. He sucked on my neck and groaned in my right ear. He placed his other hand in front of my vagina to enhance the feeling while slipping his dick onto the outer layer of my pink lips. He teased me to the fullest. I tilted my head back, fantasizing about the time I'd raped him when he was drugged. He laid his hands on my neck, gripping each side. Then he ran his fingers through my hair and quickly penetrated me. I almost lost my balance. He pulled my hair as he continued to force his dick inside me. I arched my back for effect. He then locked tightly onto my neck.

Suddenly, the juices from my vagina began running down my thighs and legs. The deeper he penetrated me, the more the liquid trickled from in between my thighs. His penis was drowning in my wetness. He shifted left to right and right to left. He released my hair. I peeped underneath to watch him fuck me, to watch his dick leave and reenter my pussy. He grasped my breasts and played with my hard nipples. He traveled a few inches north and to the right. I moaned louder than before. I tightly sealed my eyes, focusing on the feeling. He leaned nearer to me, swirling his behind around. My legs weakened. I deliberately lowered to the floor. My phone started to vibrate forcefully. He mimicked my movements, following me to the ground. He twirled more bellicosely.

My voice was shaky. "I'm about to come," I whispered.

"Aw, yeah, come for me, baby—come." He spanked me once more.

He ameliorated his speed, smacking himself against my behind, and ejaculated. He softened, eventually stopping completely. He leaned on me to relax and catch his breath. I inhaled and exhaled. Someone knocked on the door, startling us. I immediately made myself presentable. I buttoned up my sweater and adjusted my black skirt. I looked at the board and ran to it to erase his writing. I peeped back at him. He was ready. Then I searched for my white panties, which was on the floor the last time I checked. I couldn't find my underwear at the time, and I smelled nothing but sex in the air. I was afraid of getting caught. I needed my underwear, so I looked on the floor, but I couldn't found my white panties. Then, at that moment, I thought hiding in the closet would be the smartest thing for me to do. I really didn't want us to get caught.

Before I roamed over to the small space, he smiled at me. "No need to keep looking for your underwear, it belongs to me now," he said. Then he stared and whispered, "What are you doing?"

I opened the door to the closet. "It smells like nothing but sex in here, Professor. What would you assume? I meant it when I said I am not trying to cause you any trouble." I smiled and winked. Someone knocked on his door again and again. I shut the closet door. It was stuffy and uncomfortable inside. The space was tight.

Professor Rodríguez opened the door. "Professor, I'm shocked you're still here. I was unsure about the homework assignment and wanted to make sure I'm right." Her voice sounded familiar.

"Okay. I'm listening."

"The instructions say, 'Read the love sonnets by William Shakespeare. Identify the pattern and format. Lastly, write your own love sonnet.'" It was Tia, and she probably was waiting for me. For some reason, the closet smelled like fresh paint. I kept my hands on the doorknob.

"That's correct. Just make sure it follows the same rhyme and format as William Shakespeare." He grabbed his suitcase and jacket from out of the closet. Finally, he turned off the lights and shut the door. I exited the closet, brushing the spiderwebs from my shoulders. *How disgusting.* I hoped a spider was not crawling on me. It would have sent me roaming the halls.

It was dark, and the lights were off. I peeked down the hallway. I saw Professor Rodríguez and Tia conversing. I left his classroom, hearing parts of their dialogue.

They walked down the hallway together. "It smelled kind of"—she paused—"odd in the classroom, Professor." Tia said sarcastically, "Or nutty perhaps."

He laughed at Tia. "My room smells nutty? I'm sorry for laughing, but that's a new one for me, Ms. Long."

"Professor—you know, like Corn Nuts," she said seductively, "I love Corn Nuts." She eyed him slowly.

He stared at her strangely. "Yeah, Corn Nuts, I have to remember that one. Would you care for me to walk you out, Ms. Long?"

Tia shook her head. "No. I'm waiting for a friend. Thanks, though." She smiled as he left the university.

I started to walk behind her. I bet she could hear my footsteps. "Jacky, Jacky, Jacky, I see you're still taking advantage of your former assignment," Tia said.

I laughed. "Of course I am. I would be an unwise woman if I didn't. But now I'm starving."

"Yeah, sex in a classroom with your professor will do that to you. So I have to ask. What is it like?"

"*Delectable* is one word to define it. He really knows how to throw down when it comes to every part of the word." I gazed delightedly at her.

"I guess I have to see for myself."

I felt offended by her comment. He was mine and only mine. I stopped her instantly and eyed her. "Stick to Mathew, Andrew, Christian, or whatever victim you added to your fuck-and-suck list. He is off limits, so don't mention anything like this to him or anyone," I threatened with confidence.

She said, "You are keeping him all to yourself, I see. How very greedy of you, Jacky. If I want him, I can simply have him. And as for my fuck-and-suck list, I'm sure you and every other woman has one of those." She managed to take two steps toward me.

I gripped her by her arm before she took another step. "One more student will eventually lead to our discovery. Do you want to get him fired?" I said while we exited the building.

Dillon drove up to us in her car. Amy also came along for the ride. We both got in, and Dillon drove off recklessly. Amy was drinking some Remy from a glass bottle. Amy didn't seem like a drinker to me or the type who could handle her liquor.

"Hi. How are you, Amy?" I said. She smelled like alcohol. She didn't respond to my question. I raised my shoulders. Tia shook her head.

My stomach growled. "I'm starving, and I'm thirsty, Dillon. Let's get something to eat."

"Me too," Dillon agreed. "I am starving. I haven't eaten all day."

Tia said, "There is a Leona's Restaurant straight ahead to our left."

"I see it," Dillon said, and she parked in the lot.

"Damn, Dillon. You still can't park," I teased.

"Fuck you. At least I have a car to park."

Amy laughed. She left the bottle of Remy in the car. Dillon locked her doors. We stepped into the restaurant, waiting for a waiter to approach us so that we could sit. I felt dirty and needed a hot bath. Had Professor Rodríguez and I really had sex in his classroom? The cool breeze journeyed underneath my skirt. My panties were absent. *It was real,* a voice inside reminded me. I was happy, glaring unbearably. A Mexican waiter who looked to be in his late twenties arrived a few seconds later.

He was energetic and optimistic. He glanced at us and said, "Table for four?"

Dillon stared flirtatiously. "Yes, a table for four."

"Follow me, please." We trailed behind him, especially Dillon.

He grabbed four menus with his left hand. I skimmed the restaurant. It seemed cultural and professional. The atmosphere gave me a mellow vibe. The white marble floors were so shiny that they sparkled. My heels clicked against the floor. I stared down at my reflection. The waiter searched for an available table. He finally stopped at one of the back tables in the right-hand corner. We sat. Tia decided to sit beside me. In front of me were Dillon's big, beautiful dark brown baby-doll eyes. Her mascara, light brown smoky eye shadow, and black eye liner made her eye color stand out. She was peeking at the waiter. He was nicely situating the menus on the table in front of us. He later brought four full glasses of water to the table.

"Someone will be with you shortly." He directed his friendliness mainly at Dillon. We realized their mutual attraction.

"Thank you very much"—she scanned his name tag—"Nick."

The cold water was fogging up the glasses. I pulled mine closer to me, eager for a first sip. I placed the glass at the tip of my lips. I was dehydrated. A middle-aged woman acknowledged us. She had a high ponytail, small heart-shaped earrings, and a gold necklace to match. Her hair was sandy brown. She blinked but then sneered brightly.

Her voice was fragile, like soft petals on a red rose. "What can I get for you, or do you need a few seconds to scan over the menus?"

Dillon said, browsing the selections, "Yeah, I have no idea what I want."

"That's fine. I'll be back in a few." She was jollier than Angelina. I couldn't help but feel intrigued by her character. Unexpectedly, it snatched my focus.

I slightly raised my finger for her attention. I cocked my head while smiling. "I know exactly what I want," I said, handing her my menu. "I would like the lasagna. I prefer a salad with ranch over a soup, extra butter for my bread, and lemonade—a small one." I paused momentarily. "That will be all, Nancy. Thank you." It was quiet at the table but loud elsewhere in the restaurant. Nancy finished writing down my order. She looked happy.

Dillon spoke up. "Yes. I would like the same, but change that salad into a chicken noodle soup. I don't want lemonade. I prefer a Coke and no extra butter for my bread. Unlike Jacky, I'm not trying to have my arteries all clogged up with fattening butter. That's all."

I mocked her in silence.

The waitress added Dillon's order to her pad. "And anything for the two of you?"

Amy frowned with a disgusting attitude. "Nothing for me—my ass is already fat enough as it is!" She rolled her eyes spitefully. Her bitter remarks and foul disposition were pissing me off. Her eyes were engulfed in distastefulness. In fact, her negativity worried me.

Nancy arched an eyebrow. "How about you?" Her eyes advanced to Tia.

"I already ate." Tia grinned politely. The waitress departed from the table. The restaurant was crowded and full of conversation, laughter, and cheer. We avoided asking Amy what was troubling her.

"Do you see that Puerto Rican guy sitting there by himself at the table behind you?" Amy whispered. I presumed she was talking about the table behind me.

Tia and I turned to look behind us. "You mean the guy with the red Hollister jacket and black T-shirt?" I asked.

"Yeah, the guy with the jacket. I want to take him home with me," she said tenuously.

I took another look behind me. "Have you lost your fucking mind? What's wrong with you, huh? You don't even know him. So you are going to take him to your bed. There's no telling what he has or what he will do to you while you are snoring his ears off!" I gaped.

She laughed. "There is nothing wrong with me. You need to control your thoughts. I recommend you keep your unwanted comments and concerns to your damn self."

"This is the reason girls like you are human-trafficked and end up having some incurable sexual disease. Refusing my advice is the reason you're fucking stupid!" I stood. Tia grabbed my right arm, pulling me back down to my seat.

"Amy," Tia agreed, "I don't think that's a good idea."

Amy folded her arms. "You've got some nerve. You've got somebody new in your bed every night!"

"Just do whatever the hell you want! From this point on, we are no longer friends!" Tia said. Other customers began staring at us.

Amy rose. "I don't give two fucks about losing our friendship!" She looked at everyone around us. The customers watching us caused Amy to return to her seat.

Dillon shushed them rudely. "People are starting to stare, and you guys are embarrassing me," she said, covering her face. She smiled and waved at the other guests. The waitress strolled over to the table with our orders. We were quiet as she properly organized our dinners in front of us. She beamed joyfully, humming softly to herself. She left again.

I tasted my lemonade, which was sweeter than I'd anticipated, yet it was delicious.

Dillon broke the silence. "Are you sure this is something you want to do, Amy?"

She smiled innocently at him, looking over my head. "I never have been surer." She poured some of her water into my glass. She spiked her water with a roofie. I glared in amazement.

"You're going to drug him? How do you know he won't go willingly?"

"I don't want him to go willingly. What's the fun in that?" she said earnestly.

I grabbed my fork. "You're stupid," I mumbled under my breath.

I ate my lasagna, thinking about her thoughtless remarks. She wasn't bright. I felt sorry for her. I was just trying to protect her from her own stupidity. I isolated myself from her and her disastrous character. I was getting a bad vibe from the predicament that was about to occur. The only thing I attended to was my dinner. I spread some butter on my bread and sliced my lasagna up into small pieces. I loved lasagna, and the red sauce was perfectly prepared. The cheese, sauce, and meat were delightful. I sipped on my lemonade. Amy disposed of her smeared makeup and reapplied it. She quickly brushed her hair.

"How do I look?" She boosted up her perky breasts as if they were not already perky enough.

Like a damn idiot, my subconscious said.

Tia saved face. "Like you recovered from your previous misery."

"Very funny, Tia." She stood. "Who is coming with me?"

I ignored her question. Tia copied my tactic.

"I'll go with you," Dillon said.

How brave of her.

She locked onto Tia's arm. They smiled while walking to his table. Amy held a glass of water. While finishing my dinner, I couldn't help but notice Dillon distracting him while Amy switched the glasses of water. I despised what was happening, yet my eyes couldn't resist watching them. I kept to myself and remained silent. I wiped my face with a napkin. They rejoined the table with her guest. The waitress handed me the check. Dillon and I split it equally, leaving a generous tip.

Amy was practically smothering him with her affection. She introduced us to her guest for the night. "José, these are my other two friends, Veronica and Ericka." She pointed as she introduced us to avoid misperception. I guess my name was Ericka.

Tia shook José's hand. "It's very nice to meet you," she said sweetly.

I avoided all physical and verbal communication with him. I looked at Dillon exhaustedly. "I am frustrated and tired. I'm ready to go home and take a bath!"

CHAPTER 16

Josephine

Erin or Jeremy

I spent the night with Erin. She was beautiful and sugary sweet, like melted marshmallows cooking over a hot fire. I slept beside her in her king-size bed. We conversed before she started to doze off on me. She made me blush to the point where I was blossoming rapidly and delicately like a daisy. She didn't touch me—but I wanted her to. At the party, I liked the idea of writing our private thoughts in our diaries. Eventually, Erin fell asleep on me, and I agreed I would record my most intimate secrets in my new diary. As I introduced my pen to paper, I smirked at memories of Jeremy and me. Because he was busy being a spoken leader, he didn't have time to pamper or shower me with his undivided affection. Sure, he loved me, and I loved him. The truth was that I wanted him to need and desire me. We had grown too comfortable and bored with each other, in my opinion. We were uninterested in one another's company.

I was in my underwear, and so was Erin. She looked hot—partially naked and slumbering. Red was attractive on her. She smelled like freshly bloomed roses. The party had been outstanding, and the best part was that I'd received popularity points for hosting it—with the assistance of Erin, Jacky, and Angelina, of course. I scampered off into the kitchen to attend to my hunger, wrapping Erin's purple robe around me. I heard classical music playing. My eyes browsed the living and dining rooms. I listened carefully. The sound was the doorbell to the house. It was four o'clock in the morning.

"Who is it?" I screamed while walking to the door. I looked into the peephole and saw Dillon, Tia, Amy, and some guy. He was cute. I opened the door, and they proceeded into Erin's house. The guy looked drunk. Amy helped him inside. I closed the front door.

"Josephine, this is my friend José," Amy said, aiding him to the sofa.

Dillon stood beside me. She muttered in my left ear as she walked past me, "He's not a friend. We just met him at a restaurant. She drugged him and plans to rape him, probably on that couch over there." She pointed, and I turned around for a moment.

I couldn't believe my ears. My eyes widened. "What?" I chuckled. "You are kidding, right?"

She stopped to look at me and spoke in a serious tone. "Do your eyes deceive you?"

I saw how Amy was physically guiding her supposed friend, who appeared to be leaving consciousness. The bell rang again. I stared at the door wearily. Tia marched to answer it. Jeremy and Andrew had arrived. They were disturbing the peace and the vibe. *More people are exactly what Erin and I need,* I thought sarcastically. I was overwhelmed by the number of company.

Tia was blocking Andrew's entrance. "We need to finish what we were discussing earlier."

He burned her with his stare. "I think you'd just get tongue-tied all over again. We wouldn't want that to happen, now, would we?" He chuckled.

I bolted back into the kitchen to search for something to eat. I opened the refrigerator and found leftover refreshments from the party. Jeremy sneaked in and kissed me passionately. He shocked me, but he gave me affection, and I showed him warmth as well. He locked his hands with mine. He pushed me against a wall in the kitchen. We stopped. Our breathing filled the room.

"I missed you." We French-kissed again. "A lot—I missed you a lot," he said, venturing underneath my robe.

"I missed you too," I said quietly.

"You have been here all this time?" He had undone the knot in Erin's robe, and I breathed out.

"Yes," I said as he undressed me.

"Let's go upstairs or into one of these bathrooms." He licked his lips, finger fucking me to change the mood.

I moaned, "No," into his ear. His hands were on my hips. He threw me onto the countertop. "Then let's do it right here."

I covered his mouth. "What if someone comes and sees us?"

He answered with my hands over his mouth, but I understood him. "Who gives a shit?" He attacked my neck, aiming for my hot spot. He found the precise location with no complications.

I laughed and then moaned. "That tickles, Jeremy."

He teased, "You talk too much. I'm trying to concentrate." He slid my lime-green panties to my ankles. Tia entered the kitchen. She was surprised to see us.

I stared. "Stop, Jeremy. Tia's in the kitchen," I mumbled.

He continued to try to fuck me. Jeremy didn't lose his focus, allowing Tia to watch us.

She opened the refrigerator to grab a green apple. "Just because I'm here watching doesn't mean you should stop knocking boots on my account." She gawked and bit her apple. I felt odd with her standing there as if she were viewing a porno. She left laughing, and he unzipped his pants. I pulled at his shirt in lust. Erin came into the kitchen and looked disappointedly at me while blinking. She walked out of the kitchen. I stopped Jeremy.

I hopped off of the counter. "Can we just talk? Because I'm not in the mood." I was concerned about Erin. I wanted to chase after her and leave Jeremy in the kitchen.

He breathed out deeply, giving me space to reposition myself. "Talk about what?"

I snatched my underwear from the floor and retied the knot in the robe. I was silent.

He respired deeply with frustration. "About what, Josephine?" He closed his zipper. "What is it?"

"Do you like them—Erin, Tia, and Jacky? You know, the competition."

"Sure, but I like you more." He leaned in to kiss me.

I pushed him back, leaning in the opposite direction. "Then is it such a bad idea for me to be a part of their team?"

He briefly covered his face with his hand. "We already discussed this a thousand times. How many other ways and in how many languages do you want me to say it?"

"Just in English." I touched his leg.

He removed my hand. "Do you know what BOTS stands for?"

I threw my hands up at the fact that he'd asked me a stupid question. "Yes, *BOTS* is the abbreviation for 'Battle of the Sexes.' Angelina's training me, so I had to know that."

"Training you?" He paused. "She's training you?" he asked, pacing slowly in the kitchen. What was his problem? "So what is this BOTS Association all about?" He tilted his head.

I hesitated. "Um, it's about doing projects and activities and hosting fun events."

He glared at me. "No, wrong—it's a secret sex club with the finest and most-popular male and female members, and it's sexist as hell. It's known as the Battle of the Sexes because the men are in competition with the women. And if you want to win, you have to do a lot of fucking. Do you understand that?"

I nodded. "Yes, I understand, and I already know this. Angel told me we have to complete sex tasks and projects."

He eyed me. "You're my girl, and I don't agree with the way they do things around here. If you join the team, they will one day assign you to have sex with someone else. I couldn't see you doing something with anyone but me. Stop the training with Angel. Drop it."

"You don't trust me!" I yelled.

"Playing this sex game automatically makes you a slut and a cheater! It's the game and the people in it that I don't trust. It's the girls you hang around and the dicks that follow them! Yeah, I like them, but they are certainly not girlfriend material—none of them! They use people, especially norms. That's all they do. That's all we do. They already have their circle of teammates!"

"That was quick." Tia tossed the remainder of her apple into the trash can with a *swish* sound. "We don't use people, not necessarily.

We haven't used your girlfriend, and that, my friend, must count for something. We have been nothing but nice to her." She leaned on the wall to support her weight.

Jeremy added, "Yeah, not yet!" He was serious as hell.

Why was he so angry? It was just a stupid club. He was part of it. Why couldn't I join them?

Tia responded quickly. "We really like Jo. In fact, she is already being trained to join the club—you know, our little circle of cunts that you're not too fond of. The female cheaters and sluts will take good care of her." She drew an imaginary circle with her finger.

Jeremy smacked his lips together at Tia, and then he looked at me with displeased eyes. Dillon situated her arm around Tia. He shook his head. Dillon said, "So you think we are a bunch of sluts, huh? How about that?" She leered.

"Whatever! You just remember that the decision you make will affect whether we are still a couple or not," he said. Dillon relaxed her arm over Tia's shoulder. He exited the kitchen and then slammed the front door to the house.

Tia comforted me. She pretended to cry and rubbed my shoulders. "I'm so sorry I interrupted. You didn't even get to finish." Dillon laughed, but Tia continued to make a joke out of the situation. "You made a wise choice, young grasshopper," she said, impersonating Mr. Miyagi from *The Karate Kid*. I hated that movie.

"You're so not funny, Tia!"

She covered her nose. "I'm not trying to be funny. But, Jo, you seriously need a breath mint or a strong Doublemint gum. No, make that two."

I covered my mouth and blew my breath into my hand. I didn't smell anything.

I screamed while entering the living room and seeing Amy and her guest. He was passed out on the sofa. I was quiet, just glaring. Amy was devouring him. Could she have been any rougher? I was surprised she was about to do this in the open.

It was disturbing. She was stripping him out of his clothes in public and kissing him on his neck. She was moaning on top of him. I looked around the house, avoiding Amy and her inappropriate state of affairs. I entered Erin's mother's room to think about how I would explain to Erin what had happened. There was so much commotion going on in the house. There was no silence, no peace anywhere. Pacing around her mother's room, I felt ecstatic when I noticed the details of her mother's walk-in closet. The carpet and walls were all white.

Her shoes were on shelves. The closet was huge. Her shoes were name brand and every color in the rainbow. Suddenly, I heard someone shut the bedroom door. I dimmed the closet light, looked into the room, and saw Andrew and Dillon. I darted out of the closet to watch. It was dark, but I was able to see what was happening.

"I thought you said we would just be friends, because I can't do this with you anymore. If I can't be with you, I don't want any of you—none of it. I want us to be together," Dillon said.

"We are friends, but I can't help that I'm very, very attracted to you. I don't think you mean that, not wanting some part of me. I want to be in a relationship, but a relationship is just going to stress you out even more. It's not what you need right now, and I want you to be happy, because I care about your happiness and your feelings. I want to be the guy who makes you smile. Being in a relationship will cause you to hate me eventually. I don't want that, because that's exactly what happens in most relationships."

"No, I don't want that to happen either, but I'm not stressed out. Is this what you really believe?" she said with a surprised expression on her face. She moved away from him as if she were afraid of being near him.

He moved closer to her, walking her straight into a corner. "Of course you are stressed out. It's obvious. Just look at you. Everything with Christian, the naked pictures on the Internet, and having someone replace your station have knocked your heart into your stomach. The rumors going around school aren't making it any better, and you are hurting." Andrew was unbelievable. He was too good to be true. Now I knew what all the fuss was about. He was about to unknowingly charm Dillon out of her panties. She didn't even see it coming.

"I am stressed, and I have been going through a lot." She wept.

Why was she agreeing with his lies? She didn't seem stressed out to me.

He lifted her chin. "By the way, how you outperformed Christian tonight was different but sexy. I liked it because you were in control, and he deserved everything you gave him for what he did to you."

"Really?" She arched an eyebrow, blushing. She inspected him as he started unbuttoning her dress from the front while their dialogued persisted.

"You're still hurting so bad, aren't you, Dillon? You're trying to fully recover but can't." He was progressing in between her legs.

"I am recovering. It is a slow process," she said, discouraged. He pulled her dress over her head. She had raised her arms.

"It doesn't have to be." He was serious.

Please, Dillon. Don't give in to his bags of bullshit.

"It doesn't?" She was clueless, and it was priceless to watch.

"No, it doesn't. I can help you, Dillon. All you have to do is ask me." There were no words to describe the skill of his persuasion.

"I do. Yes, help me." As she pleaded, he removed her panties, and then he stripped her out of her bra with one hand. He groped her breasts.

She paused and removed his hands. "Wait. I always fall for this bullshit and end up regretting it. Just stop. I think we should stop." Finally, I knew she had some sense.

He continued to undress her. He bent down to remove her heels, the left and then the right one. "See, that's your problem. You worry and overthink unnecessary things. You think too much, and you're overworked." He moved back from her, throwing his hands up. It was a trick but a clever treat I wouldn't easily forget. "Let whatever happens happen. If we are meant to be together, the universe will not disagree under any circumstances."

"I am not!" She shoved him friskily. He smiled in reaction to her playfulness.

"Learn to trust me, and stop caring so much. I'm your helping hand when you need it. Learn to struggle with no worries, and get out of your stage of thoughtfulness. Stop caring with me for one moment. Stop thinking, and just feel something unforgettable with me. I promise that after tonight, you will never feel like you're on your own. Our names are probably written in the stars, Dillon. You might be my soulmate and I'm just too stupid to recognize it, but you can help me see it."

He continued to seduce her. He was conversing with her to make her reconsider something she'd regretted before and soon would regret again. He had a tactic of disguising sex and making it sound like a dreamy relationship waiting to take place. He was tempting. I had to remember to stay away from him and his hypnotism.

"If we do this, I want to feel you like I never felt you before." He stuck his fingers inside her. "I like that you are always wet. You hardly ever disappoint me."

She peeled off his shirt. Instantly, they altered to a roughness of hard-core fucking. It was extreme. They were wild and out of control, knocking over items because they lusted for each other so deeply. The act, however, seemed difficult to bear. It wasn't sex or lovemaking. Not once did he reveal a personal or emotional movement during their sexual expression. They were fucking—nothing more and nothing less. It was everything but passionate.

I stopped watching to avoid getting aroused, but I heard him ramming her intensely. Every ram startled me lustfully. He was satisfying her with his sexual aggression. She moaned over and over again. The sound of her being pleasured as he fucked her did not aid in my composure. I couldn't help but get horny. Their heavy breathing proved how much he wanted her and how much she wanted him. I couldn't bear it any longer. I had to leave, so I crawled out of the bedroom. I quietly closed the door. I reentered Erin's bedroom. She was reading something—an old magazine or newspaper perhaps. She was lying on her stomach on top of her beige cover. It had lions, tigers, and cheetahs displayed on it. She was thoughtfully swinging her legs, separating them entirely. I looked elsewhere, but her movements didn't go unnoticed. I yawned, exposing my exhaustion. I lay on her bed and gazed up at the ceiling.

"Do you know that Andrew is banging Dillon in your mother's bedroom?"

She laughed. “What? You were watching them?” She sealed her legs together.

“Not really. I was in your mother’s magical walk-in closet, and they mysteriously appeared in that particular room out of all your other bedrooms.”

She was scanning a piece of mail of hers. “My mother talks about us starting over and fixing our family. My birthday is coming up, and she promised me we would go on a vacation.” She ceased her words to collect more information from a written letter from her mother. “Now she somehow concludes that our love and her present are no longer obligations for me.” She cried.

“What do you mean ‘fix’ your family? I didn’t realize it was broken.” I folded my legs in her bed. Her tears dropped onto her cover.

“I feel like I’m alone. This house was represented by love and tenderness, and now it’s nothing but emptiness here. My friends come over to reduce my suffering from loneliness. They can only do so much for me.” I heard her struggles in the lowness of her voice. She pulled the covers over her face. I followed her.

“I’m lonely just as much as you are,” I said, “except I had Jeremy there for me. I guess I should enjoy the peace I have at home, but I see it as me being empty on the inside.” My eyes looked into hers.

She hesitated with a smirk. “What’s up with you and him? What’s his deal? Because I think there’s something wrong with him.” She appeared to be concerned about him.

I stretched out my legs to prevent them from falling asleep. I removed the covers from over my head. “He hates this game and what it represents. First, he was in it for the sex. Now he has me, so he feels there’s no need for it.”

She swiftly became interested in what I had to say. “Then why is he still wasting his time participating?”

“You promise you won’t tell?”

She immediately rested her hand over her heart. “I promise. You can trust me,” she assured me.

I scratched my head. "He's stuck, Erin, because he's the leader of the group." Her eyes widened in surprise. She opened her mouth, so I closed it for her. She must have been shocked.

"No! You're not serious, are you?"

"I'm very serious." I quickly changed the subject. "Erin, I'm looking at you, and you're an amazing person. You're too beautiful to feel empty, and you're too caring to be lonely. I don't understand."

She touched my face. We paused. She leaned in to kiss me, and I copied her. The moment I closed my eyes, she hit me in the head with a pillow. I was not expecting that reaction to my seductive action. I fell off the bed. She laughed. It was cute. Restfully, I gripped the pillow from behind me and swung back at her. I giggled while we had a pillow fight in her bed. I climbed on top of her, laughing and hitting her. She liked it. She chuckled more eagerly; the sound was like gentle music to my ears. She had my preferred characteristics—beauty, brains, and tenderness. Those traits were the reason I was attracted to her.

She cupped her hands on my behind. She made the assumption her hands were prohibited from touching me. I deflated a large amount of distance between us while pressing my palms against the carpet on the floor. My left hand explored her right arm, rubbing her smooth skin. I assured her she had obtained a personal invitation to touch me. I leaned down to kiss her neck. Instead, she interfered with my plan and kissed me on the lips. I kissed her back slowly. Fondling my cheeks, she went for a firmer and more-demanding squeeze of both cheeks.

Her tongue was massaging mine. She was a great kisser. She tasted like Winterfresh. We rearranged our bodies. She positioned herself on top of me. *Mmm, yes. Dominate me,* my subconscious moaned. I caressed her buttermilk skin. My hands traveled from her stomach to her breasts. Her nipples were straining against her bra, and her lips were juicy. I detached her bra from behind. She had a slim and athletically toned figure, but it was curvy and thick. It was hot and caused me to become horny all over again. I started removing her underwear, and Andrew jogged into her room.

"Don't you knock?" I yelled. Why hadn't I locked the door?

He protected the door. "Jo and Rose, Rose and Jo, you two look gorgeous, as usual." He winked. "I would like to see you two French kiss, and don't be afraid to really squeeze or smack some cheeks. I like that," he said seductively. Erin covered her nipples with her hands.

"What do you want, Andrew?" Erin said.

"I want the two of you to continue doing what you were doing before I came." He absorbed our serious expressions and stiffness to his filthy response. "Okay. Jo, I really need a word with you—alone." He looked at Erin.

I took off Erin's robe and handed it to her. She left us so that we could have a private discussion. They shared a glance—a long one at that. He stared at her ass as if he wanted to ravish her. I stood in my underwear, not interested in having a conversation with him.

"Did you enjoy it?" He grinned.

"Not really. See, this idiot came and ruined it for me."

He came closer to me and shook his head. "No. I'm not talking about her. I'm talking about you watching Dillon and me from the closet." He smiled.

Why in the hell was he always smiling? It was distracting—but, unfortunately, in a good way. How did he know? I blinked with eagerness, stalling. "I don't know what you're talking about." I folded my arms with confidence.

"You're not a good liar, Jo. I don't like liars." He wet his lips.

"Okay, so what? What do you want from me? I was mistakenly trapped by you and Dillon. I saw a little, mainly Dillon. Are you happy now?"

"No, not yet. Who did you tell?"

Why was he questioning me? What had I ever done to him? I put on Erin's clothes, a white T-shirt and some shorts from her dresser. He was not distracted by my nakedness. "I told Erin."

He looked at me with disappointed green eyes. He approached me as if he wanted to seduce me. I was flattered, but I wasn't stupid like Dillon. "Now, why would you do that?" He exhaled severely.

"What's it to you? Why does it matter to you so much?"

He paced. What the hell was wrong with him? Then he said, "I don't want my business out there in the open. Don't tell Angelina. I would appreciate it if you kept my session to yourself. I don't want her to find out about this, and whatever thing you have with Erin, I would stop it before it gets out of hand," he advised.

"I think you should take your own advice. Don't worry about my business. Just like Dillon and you are none of my business, Erin and I are none of yours."

"You like Erin, so what—you're bisexual now? What about your relationship with Jeremy?" He twisted up his lips.

"What about him?" I said wickedly. I scratched my lower back.

"You don't even know Erin, so you are stupid if you really believe she likes you. Her pain and her emotions will send you running into the woods. Just leave her and it alone."

I laughed. "You're mad because I got to her first. You just want her for yourself." I smirked.

"Erin's got too many issues for my taste. I don't want her. But if I was you, I wouldn't want her either. I'm telling you to stay away. I'm not keeping her from you, but I'm keeping her from hurting you. Being with Erin isn't worth losing Jeremy. He might even dump you for what you are doing behind his back." He attempted to leave the room. I snatched his right hand. He faced me.

"Why? Why do you care so much about my choice?"

"Getting involved in this game, there's no way to avoid betraying someone who is participating. Mistakenly or purposely deceiving someone you shouldn't can lead to hurting yourself. You can play for the sex, the fifty-thousand-dollar prize, or the thirty thousand dollars, but there is no way you won't end up emotionally attached to the chaos. You end up doing almost anything to win when money is on the line."

He tried once more to conclude our discussion, but I wasn't finished. I yanked on him for his undivided attention. "I'll keep my personal interest in her composed."

I couldn't hurt Jeremy. My conscience would eat away at me. I still had not done one original assignment to finalize my membership. I pondered his speech about being betrayed, becoming disloyal, or eventually accepting and adapting to the corruption of the game. It would be my fatal attraction. I thought deeply about my current situation. Andrew abandoned me. I agreed not to hurt Jeremy. I knew the agreement was limited and would be soon terminated, but I figured I'd commit to it for the time being.

Erin returned. I yawned once more, unable to resist the natural urge to sleep. We were tired. She shut off the light. My eyes closed. In my dreams, Erin was mine, but was wanting Erin and Jeremy selfish? I believed it was possible to have them both without the interference of Andrew.

CHAPTER 17

Erin

Trapping Jeremy

Andrew was complicating my plans. Why was he discussing my intentions with Jo before acknowledging me, jeopardizing my mission? My purpose for her was sexual, but it was all a part of the game. He was going to ruin this for me. Having Jo around was beneficial. I wasn't emotionally attached to her or to anyone, nor did I plan to have any obstacles standing in my way, especially Andrew. Separating business from pleasure wasn't my difficulty. My mother was the only thing in my life I couldn't control. In my heart, all I needed was my family back, my father and Evan. Love would cure my bitterness. Hatred was a common emotion for me because I had lost them. Besides the bullshit picture of Evan on my dresser, the game was all I had left of him. This game was more than an amusement for me. He'd loved the game. It had been his tactic to keep the popular kids fascinated with school. We were fascinated all right.

I was in the hallways, rereading my mother's sad attempt at an excuse to abandon me once more for my birthday. For me, it was another sad and miserable day. For her, being at home with me was heartbreaking. For her, a five-thousand-dollar check and a shopping spree would assuage my pain and loneliness.

> Dear Erin,
>
> I know a thousand times I promised to take you on a vacation with me on a tropical island for your birthday. The truth is, I have made other arrangements for my modeling career. No way were you breaking down to

my proposal anyway, so I will save us the embarrassment of each other's company. Instead of my original plan, I figured you would adore spending time with your friends more. Here is a five-thousand-dollar check for your amusement because of my absence. It's my birthday gift to you. If my plans are somehow postponed, my stay in New York will be very brief. See you soon, sweetheart!

Sincere regards,

Your mother

Every word sent tears rolling down my cheeks. I smiled in public but cried in private. Saving "the embarrassment of each other's company" was the worst part. Misery loved company, I'd heard. On the other hand, I never had been fond of the company of my mother. She was as empty and as lonely as I was. The liveliness had disappeared the moment my father and brother became deceased. On the inside, Amy was also deceased—a walking, talking, wretched corpse. At least I was capable of pretending I had no issues. She was severely showered in them. She was too weak and emotional to bear her own pain.

Driving to school, I saw her busting out the windows to Mathew's black 2010 Hyundai Sonata GLS. She even keyed his car. It had been a beautiful Sonata before Amy vandalized it. This morning, he was yelling instead of calmly talking to Michael and Jeremy. He eventually grabbed the attention of three security guards as he complained about his car. Mathew was raging out of control. I thought he had been at his lowest point when he was enslaved in his cock cage, but he was ten times more hostile now.

Amy was disgusting. I read her misplaced diary. She deserved everything she was about to get. In the back of my head, I felt she had no station or future position for senior year. In fact, I would enjoy sheltering her into isolation. She needed to be expelled and needed her popularity points terminated permanently. How could I not have seen what she was doing to Mathew and to herself? In Mathew's shoes, I would have killed her. She had behaved in a selfish and horrifying manner. I couldn't tell Mathew. Even though Tia would put her in a casket or coma, I decided to allow her to do the honors. Again, we were having an essential meeting in our original location. The girls appeared weary and washed out of energy. They were seated in the first row. Amy, Angelina, and Dillon were to the left, and Jacky, Josephine, and Tia were to the right of the auditorium. I was front and center.

I couldn't stand still. "I have great news. Remember those benefits I was talking about a while ago? Well, they have finally arrived!" They were not happy; instead, my team was falling asleep and yawning uncontrollably.

Tia announced with exhaustion, "We're tired, Erin. We have a lot to do and a lot to prepare for, like original and bonus assignments!"

"Yeah, Erin," Jacky agreed. "We need to concentrate on project management and other personal issues. We do have a life outside of school, you know!"

"Look at how lucky we are. This game has given us such broad college opportunities. Have you not heard a word? We no longer have to do normal, boring homework assignments, quizzes, or project management—just our bonuses!"

They cheered and applauded poorly, not realizing their advantage. "I'm feeling a lack of synergy here," I said. "I went through a lot to pull this off! Your personal and individual bonus will determine your position for next year. Your popularity points will help this decision, with proof provided. For the lower-level station, we will vote for the better character!"

Dillon said, "Yeah, but what's the bad news?"

"Dillon, you're not even supposed to be attending this meeting! What did I say? Give everything time to heal!" I stared while waiting for a response.

"I'm still a part of this team. I might not have a voice with meaning. I still believe I need to be here."

"The bad news is that this is the time we reconsider not having all female members on our team and must temporarily assign a member over to our competitors!"

Amy woke up and stood. "No, Erin. No one wants to complete it, and no one ever does!"

I hoped she was correct, yet I wasn't looking forward to hearing her speak. I rolled my eyes at the nagging princess of the century. "The assignment that no one ever wants to participate in wasn't created by me, so it's far beyond my reach! We must do this! Who would like to make a sacrifice to be involved in this duty?" My brother had been the original creator of the assignment they hated. He'd loved it as well as the bonus. They avoided my glance. It was quiet.

Tia acknowledged me. "I will replace a competitor. I always felt like I was the misplaced piece to the males' puzzle anyway!"

I blinked, shocked. I should have seen that one coming. I had not expected a hero for the protection and leadership of my team. This act was not under my management. I should have known she would volunteer. I was supposed to be the conqueror of this assignment, but it was prohibited for a leader to establish permission to change teams. Every current leader was enslaved with his or her prior teammates. Doing this assignment meant I could have more time with Jeremy. It was the only excuse I had to get closer to him. Tia agreed to the transaction to be near Mathew. I was fucked, and I knew I couldn't make her rethink her decision, yet I didn't want to modify my stance. I wouldn't grant her permission. It was against the rules for me to perform this task, though it would bring me a step closer to finalizing my assignment against Jeremy.

"Tia, I have something more superior in store for you, so I will have to deny your request!"

"Is there any way I can make you reassess your refusal?" she said, standing eagerly to refute my decision.

I hopped off of the stage and paused to reveal the possibility of a modification. I swung my arms shortly. "Give me a good reason why I should reconsider my decision!" I said, rubbing my hands together to try to create warmth.

Jacky joined the conversation. "I think granting her permission will guarantee us the power and knowledge to unfold the discovery of our competitors' tasks!"

I breathed in and out to prepare for what was next. "Tia, your courage and leadership to guide us is a very rare and inspiring thing for this team to obtain. Your present mission to sabotage their most-valued and greatest individual and group projects would be unobtrusive for you. If only your infatuation and vulnerability for Mathew wouldn't cause you to be less cautious, granting you this wouldn't be a problem!"

She stood. "It won't be a problem. My vision is straight and clear toward my purpose. My eyes will not blind me of my duty," she claimed, eyeing everyone else. "Selecting me will not be an irrational choice!"

I said, "Completing this assignment will be a challenge if Mathew is not absent!"

She charged closer to me. "What?" she yelled. "What evidence do you have to support your assertion? None whatsoever—you have no proof of it!"

"Actually, Tia, there is plenty. Why was it so easy for Michael to plant the chastity belt on her?" I asked my audience.

Jacky answered, "Because of Mathew and her desperate state to secure his attention."

Tia exhaled and then extended her hand. "Who asked you, Jacky?" She rolled her eyes. "Butt out of it."

"Erin did, and we make these decisions as a team, if you have already lost sight of that!"

I added more to the conversation. "Who was the one that came over my house when I invited her to keep James busy but really came to steal Mathew's key to his chastity belt?"

"What?" Angel said in shock. "How could you do that, Tia?"

I crossed my arms. "Yeah, Tia, how could you?" I said in a displeased tone. "And how could I forget to add that one to our newsfeed?" I smiled. "Is this the person we want to be looking in the peephole for us? How do we know she won't further betray us to make Matt happy?" I said. "She might leave us to join them, and we need her the most! We can't allow that to happen!"

Her voice rose. "What makes you think I can't leave you now to join them later, huh?" she yelled as she threw her arms up uncontrollably. Suddenly, her face became red.

"Because it's the Battle of the Sexes and forbidden to do so in secrecy. As I was informed, no member has ever betrayed his or her team to this opportunity. Why would you want to start now?" Jo said, reminding Tia of the rules to the game.

Tia strolled closer to Jo. "Hi. Fuck you, you fucking Pop-Tart! What do you know about the history and the rules of this game?" she yelled, and then she giggled. "You're not even a member! You're just a dumb-ass freshman." Finally, she sat back down in her seat. "I know what this is about. It's racism." She wept. All of this was unnecessary.

"Shut up, Tia. I will not delay this meeting in hopes of a future acceptance, because refusal is still in place. All who agree with me, say, 'Aye,' and separate in an orderly fashion."

Jo stood proudly. "Aye." She then left the room.

Amy, Dillon, and Angel followed suit, leaving the auditorium seconds later. Finally, Jacky, after hesitating for a moment, said, "I agree." Her head was down. She barged out of the room to catch up with the others.

Tia touched my shoulder. "Why did you do this?"

I exhaled. "Tia, it's simply for the best, okay? Don't take it personally."

"It's best for the team or best for you?" she said, disgusted.

I stared into her eyes and rested my hands on her shoulders so that she understood that I wasn't against her happiness. "What do you want more? To join Mathew's team or to literally read Amy's secrets that you have been so eager to unfold for months?" I grabbed my belongings and attempted to walk past her. She stopped me.

She placed her hand up and paused. "You have her diary, and you didn't tell me?" she said, surprised.

I smirked. "Of course I do, silly, and I am telling you now," I joked.

"Give it to me," she demanded. We left the auditorium.

"Give it to you? No. That is not how I manage negotiations. It does not work that way. I will need something in exchange—a journal for a journal," I whispered into her ear.

"What?" She waited. "Whose book did you have in mind?" We stopped at the end of the hallway.

"I want Jo's book." I stared.

"For what, Erin?" she said.

What was up with the million questions? I snickered. "None of your business. Do you want the damn thing or not?"

"It's a deal." She marched down the hallway and bumped into Mathew, and I noticed Andrew was watching me as if he needed to speak to me.

I stepped up to him. "You know, if you continue to stalk people at a distance, you might be perceived as a stalker, and that, my friend, will stain your good and charming reputation, lover boy."

"So that's what you're calling me now—lover boy?" He grinned while running his fingers through his hair.

"Well, you surely have a little nickname for me. And hey, the shoe fits." I winked confidently. "I also think you should mind your business."

He followed me down the hall. "Your business, Erin? I don't know what you're talking about," he lied, trying to look clueless.

"Oh, really? Jo told me you warned her to stay away from me for her protection."

"Oh, that. Now I remember. Everything I said—you know I'm right, because I warned her for a reason."

"Look, lover boy, worry about your own nosy ass. What I do has nothing to do with you." I twisted my lips up.

I entered the tutoring center and closed the door, and he reopened it to enter the room. *Great, I was being stalked. Nice.* It was just what I needed—a stalker. He approached me again. "I can't talk right now, okay?"

He shrugged. "Why not?"

Why was he getting on my last nerve? I sat down at the desk. "Because I am working."

He rested his hands at the edge of the desk. His eyes scanned the room. "Work?"

"Yeah, work—you know, that place people go to make money," I said sarcastically.

He pulled out a piece of paper. "Well, that's great."

"Yeah, why is that?" I said in irritation, scooting closer to the desk.

"Because, Rose, I'm your first appointment. You must have forgotten to check the book—again. Do you mind signing me in? And for the record, you're five minutes late. Don't let that happen again."

Who in the hell did he think he was? I wasn't late. I suspected he didn't even need an English tutor. He just wanted to further piss me off and criticize me. I logged in to the computer and pulled up the sign-in sheet.

"What's your full name?" I stared.

He stood in front of the desk. "Andrew Maleek Walker."

"Who is your English 135 professor?"

"My professor is Ms. Harrison."

"What's your station and ID number?"

"Wait—let me think. It's D48010864. I'm in station five, code 5035."

"Okay, you're at a junior status. You can log in to one of those computers and pull up your information for your assignment or assignments."

He listened, and moments after, I was sitting beside him. I smiled. "So how can I help you today, Andrew?"

"Well, I'm writing a paper, but it's not finished. I need you to revise it for me."

"I can't do that." I blinked twice.

He frowned. "Well, why not?" He tilted his head to the side.

"The only thing I can do is help you revise it yourself. Is that okay?" I said, and he nodded. "Print it out, and let me take a look at it."

He printed his paper out and retrieved it. He handed it to me, and I handed the paper back to him.

"Read it."

He looked at me and then down at his paper. He started to read silently.

I exhaled. "No, lover boy, read it out loud, so I can hear you."

He then exhaled, staring into my eyes. I broke eye contact while clearing my throat. "Many girls have told me that they are in love with me, yet what about the girl I fell for years ago? For the others, I felt absolutely nothing. She was an elegant young woman who was autonomous. She went by the name of Angela Thompson. She was energetic as well as enthusiastic. Angela was social and the most optimistic individual I'd ever met. When I first saw her smile …" He paused to stare up at me. My heart leered from within.

I wanted him to finish. "Mmm, continue," I said.

"When I first saw her smile, she paralyzed me from head to toe. Her laughter was a continuous result and proof of her happiness. She had a spirit and energy that sheltered an entire room, coursing through every soul in her surroundings. Being exposed to her character brightened and redeemed all negativity. She maintained her positivity until someone she loved suffered a traumatic accident that ended in death." He coughed and covered his mouth with his right arm.

I breathed out, crossing my legs. "Well, go on," I demanded.

"This devastation—and, afterward, any other terrifying event—triggered post-traumatic stress disorder. It is a condition of persistent mental and emotional stress occurring as a result of injury or severe psychological shock, typically involving disturbance of sleep and constant vivid recall of the experience, with dulled responses to others. The three main symptoms Angela experienced were flashbacks, nightmares, and uncontrollable thoughts about the tragic occurrence her loved one faced." He exhaled and stopped.

"That's all?" I said, slightly leaning to the side.

He scratched behind his ear. "Yup, that is pretty much it for now."

I frowned. Our session was about to get interesting. "You said her name was Angela. What was her race?"

"She was white and African American," he said in a low tone of voice.

"You, uh, made her sound like an angel, or maybe it was her intent to be perceived as one."

"No, she was to me, but it was a limited definition, as I plan to clarify it throughout my body paragraphs thoroughly."

I stood. "Well, you certainly grabbed my attention as you read the introduction. As for the revision, we will work on the grammar errors, sentence structure, et cetera, when you finish the entire paper."

"It sounds good to me. See you." He leered.

Look at that smile. I couldn't help but wonder who Angela was and what kind of effect she'd had on Andrew's life. Surprisingly, Jeremy walked through the door of the tutoring center as Andrew exited. He was lost, in search of something or someone.

"Hi," I said energetically. My electrifying personality amused him and stole his interest. "You look lost, Jeremy. How can I assist you?" I asked with a cheerful grin.

"I need help with writing." He appeared embarrassed to ask for help.

"You need help with writing?" I couldn't believe it. Jeremy needed my assistance. *How cute.* "What kind of writing? Is it formal, informal, persuasive, or informative?" I asked in a sweet tone.

He came closer to me. "It's a five-paragraph essay. It's something about"—he paused, and I waited patiently for a complete response—"love, Erin," he said emotionally.

"All right, love. Should I sign you in?"

He grabbed my arm and pulled me into one of our private rooms. He closed the door. I was confused. "What's going on?" I asked, but he hesitated. "Spit it out," I said with my hands on my hips.

"Can you do me a huge favor?" he said.

I crossed my arms. I was curious what he was about to ask me. "I don't know. I may have to charge you for it later." He laughed. *Well, at least I got him to loosen up a bit.*

"Cost me what?" He leaned on the door.

I smiled while somewhat blushing. "Who knows? It could be an arm, a leg, or maybe even a foot."

"A foot?" he repeated.

I nodded. "Yeah, a foot—or just the big toe, if you just prefer that," I said, sitting in the chair comfortably.

"I didn't anticipate that you'd be so humorous," he said, gliding his finger against his bottom lip.

I lifted up out of my seat. "I bet you like it, don't you—a girl with a great sense of humor?" I got closer and closer to him. With one more inch, we would have been kissing.

He was nervous. Because he was shy, he took three steps back. "I guess I do, but I need personal help with my paper. Would you like to meet me somewhere outside of school?"

Hell yeah, I did. Let me know the time and place. I faced him. "Absolutely not, Jeremy." I opened the door.

"Come on, Erin. Please. You would be doing me a big one," he pleaded.

I waited for him to leave.

He continued. "We can meet anywhere you want, and I will owe you a huge favor."

I stopped to reconsider what he was offering me. *A huge one, huh?* It was flattering. It was exactly what I needed. "Anything I want?"

He said, "Whatever you want. I promise."

I was cheering on the inside. "We have a deal—starting tonight, right?" We shook on it. He left afterward, and I collected my brown jacket and purse, which had Amy's diary inside of it. I departed from the tutoring center. Amy rushed up to me.

"Hi, Erin. How are you?" she asked urgently.

I rolled my eyes. "I'm doing much better than you, as you can see," I said. "I know that for a fact." I marched past her.

She walked beside me. "I came over to your house to find something that belongs to me," she said in a concerned tone.

"Yeah, Amy, and what's that?" I had a serious look on my face.

She stopped me. "My diary," she said in fear.

I looked at her as if she were insane. All of a sudden, I smiled in her face vindictively. "That's too bad, because I haven't seen it anywhere." I proceeded to my destination.

"What the hell is your problem?" I said when she yanked on my arm. "Let me go, Amy!"

"Erin, you have to protect me," she said with wide eyes. "Some secrets in this world should never be out in the open."

I laughed at her, though I tried to hold in my giggles to not upset her. "I don't have to do a damn thing for you, Amy. Look at who you have hurt because of this. Who are you trying to protect other than yourself? You're a nasty, nasty person." I beamed. People stared at us in silence as they walked past.

Her eyes widened, and she moved closer to me. "You know, don't you?" She glanced at me as if I were Satan or something.

"Of course I know! Are you stupid? I'm the only one that does know, yet I bet there is more to it than what you wrote in your little diary." Not appreciating our closeness, I stepped away from her, attempting to enter the bathroom to redo my makeup.

Amy spoke loudly. "Just give me my fucking diary back, okay? Or I swear—"

I turned around, refusing to take another step. "Or you swear what, Amy? Are you trying to threaten me? Because if you are, you are off to a very poor start."

Amy marched up to me again while she asked unpleasantly, "Why did you have to fuck with me?"

I looked deeply into her wicked eyes and crossed my arms. "You have fucked yourself, and you don't even know it, but everybody will know the truth. I mean the entire school!" I threatened.

Her eyes had grown watery because of my response. "We are on the same team, you little bitch! You really are the shittiest leader, you know that?"

I had expected no less from an insane person. I arched my eyebrows. She walked away as Jo accompanied me.

Jo glanced at Amy, who headed in the opposite direction. "What's her problem?" she said with one hand on her hip.

I smiled at Jo as I shrugged at her. "How in the hell should I know? Maybe she got her period this week." Seconds later, I touched her face gently.

She leered back at me. Suddenly, she pulled my hand down to lock mine with hers. "Are you okay?"

"Aw, you're adorable. Yes, I'm perfectly fine. Thanks for asking." We kept staring at each other as we faced one another. She laughed because of the way I was looking at her. I couldn't help it, but I let go of her hand. Suddenly, we heard some students cheering down the hall; they were surrounding a table in the corner to our far left. I stared, wondering what the hell all the commotion was about. As I looked more carefully, I realized that mainly men were entertained by the hallway activity. It seemed as if they were conducting exchanges—as if they were purchasing something—but what could it have been?

Tia and Dillon barged up to Jo and me. Dillon started to rudely snap her fingers in my face to demand my attention. I grabbed her hands as I proceeded to beam down the halls. A few male students passed us, placing something black into their bags while they smiled. Dillon snatched her hand away from me, and all of them—Dillon, Tia, and Jo—watched me strangely.

"What happened with you and Amy?" Tia said curiously.

"Nothing. Amy and I just had a small disagreement. That's all."

Jo laughed while twisting up her lip at me and taking one step forward. She cleared her throat loudly. "Hmmmm, I thought you said she was upset because of her period."

I rolled my eyes. "It was both, okay? It's not even important. It was just a little catfight between us. It will pass."

Tia yelled, "Dammit! That sounds way more exciting than giving hand jobs in the bathroom! What the hell was I thinking? I can't believe I just missed a catfight." She touched Dillon's face. "Your skin is so smooth, Dillon."

We beamed at Tia. I was scared to ask, but was she honestly handing out hand jobs in the washroom?

Dillon thought about Tia's confession and screamed, "Did you wash your hands?" Dillon appeared disgusted by Tia's touch.

"Of course," she answered, continuing to rub Dillon's face, "not. I didn't have time."

Dillon smacked Tia's hand in the opposite direction. "You're disgusting, you know that?" Dillon wiped her face with her hands. She whispered, "Bitch," while looking at Tia, and Tia laughed at Dillon.

"Guys, something is going on down there," I said. We all ventured down the hall. Christian, Michael, and James were sitting at a table. As we stood in front of them, they all smiled wickedly at us. Jacky discreetly joined the group. A tall black guy was standing behind us. He then walked to the front of the table.

"I'll take one." He smiled.

Take one of what?

"It's fifteen bucks," Christian said.

The black guy looked at Dillon. "That's too steep, man," the guy complained.

Michael said, "Fifteen dollars is not steep when you're paying for the very best. Come on now. You were in the showroom at Jo's party. Do you want to see her in action or what?"

"Yeah, pal. I have to see it. Everybody has been talking about it all day." He reached into his back pocket. He passed James some money in exchange for an all-black DVD case.

"Enjoy," Christian said.

Jacky moved in front of me. "What is this?"

Christian laughed. "What does it look like?"

"She didn't ask you how it looks," Dillon said. "She asked you what this is." Christian ignored her.

Tia spoke. "Is this a part of an assignment?"

He responded to her in kindness. "No, not at all. I am just exposing the simple nature of love and how women should be more cautious of whom they sleep with, because well"—he laughed—"you know."

"What is this?" I repeated.

"Congrats, Dillon. You have completed an unforgettable assignment against me. That's all everyone talked about over the weekend, so excuse me for tainting and interfering with your fame and shine. Now you're really a star." He winked at her.

"What did you do?" she yelled. "You bastard!"

"It's a video," I said.

"Correct. That's ten points for Erin." He smiled.

Jo said, "It's a sex video of you and Dillon."

"Yeah, it is."

"I hate you!" Dillon screamed, moving forward in an effort to attack him. Jo and Jacky held her back. I didn't blame her. I hated him, too, for her.

Tia smiled. "Aw, wow, that's great," she said. "Oh my, Dillon, you are super famous now. Can I buy one, please?" she asked, moving closer to the table.

"Sure you can," Michael joked.

"Tia, you can't be serious!" What was wrong with her, asking to buy the sex tape?

"Yeah, I'm serious. Does it look like I'm joking?" She reached into her purse. "No!" she screamed desperately. She looked displeased. "All I have is a ten-dollar bill. I need five more dollars. Erin, can you help me out?"

She had to be fucking kidding me. "Come on, Tia—we are leaving," I said.

"No, we can't leave without the DVD!" Tia said. Jo grabbed Tia and pulled her down the hall. "No, I am Dillon's fan. I have to support her!" she screamed.

James lifted out of his seat. "And, Jacky, do you moan?" he yelled down the hall. She didn't respond. "Don't worry—we will find out soon if you do or not!" They all laughed.

What a bunch of kids.

CHAPTER 18

Jacky

Moaning in Class

Did I moan or not? What the hell was James talking about? I was confused. At the same time, my subconscious couldn't help but repeat what James had said to me. It was troubling. It meant that what they were managing next had my name written all over it. That day was a bad day for me and especially for Dillon. Christian always went too damn far. It was unnecessary. After I left the girls, I reported him to the dean, who was also the manager of our popularity club. I did what needed to be done. For evidence, I retrieved one of the sex videos from a male companion of mine. The first mistake Christian had made was mentioning that this wasn't a part of our sex game. He was not allowed to sell sex videos, especially not of a student on school grounds. Dillon was my girl, so I felt I had to look after her, and Christian was a fucking idiot. How stupid and ill prepared could he be? By far, he was the dumbest competitor in the competition. What was Dillon thinking? Because he wasn't charming, generous, or good looking, in my opinion. I couldn't let him get away with something so indecent. *No way.* As a result of his actions, Christian was terminated from the game and expelled from school. I made sure of it. I felt the game—male and female opponents—would be better off without him, and we were.

Christian caused Dillon to be nervous, but Professor Rodríguez and public speaking enhanced my anxiety. Those were the everyday things that raised my nervousness. However, with public speaking, preparation didn't work. I was bad at it for no reason. Over the weekend, I practiced my presentation consistently. It was possible I overworked myself in the process. I yearned for the presentation to be flawless. Erin was there to suffer along with me, listening to my performance. Even though it was unlikely I'd do well in front of the class, I developed false hope.

Before the night of my presentation, I received a package from a UPS man. I was psyched to open it and discover what was hidden inside. It was a card from Erin and a stunning strapless blue dress. She knew strapless dresses were my favorite, but I gave her five points off for choosing a royal-blue one. Lime or dark green, purple, or even yellow would have sufficed. It was short and puffy at the bottom but simple and fashionable. Underneath the dress was a brand-new all-white set of underwear from Victoria Secret. I screamed. Boy, I loved Erin. She was supportive of everyone. This was the nicest thing any girl had ever done for me. I felt special and jittery on the inside. The new outfit motivated me. What would I have done without her? I viewed her as my little sister, although she was teaching me a thing or two. I had much to teach her as well.

My new dress and underwear fit scrumptiously. Everything was the right size. Unfortunately, I hated the color royal blue—or any shade of blue, for that matter. I made an effort to contact Erin a few times but received no answer. I looked beautiful, yet I felt my nervousness would stand out over my beauty—and it did.

I sat with shaky fingers. I peeked down at them, not comprehending how to manage them. They had a mind of their own. The feeling was absurd. To make matters worse, Mr. Ford decided to merge all three of his classes together to deliver their presentations. I had four competitors in the room with me: Andrew, James, Jeremy, and Mathew. On the other hand, my teammates Erin and Tia pampered me with support. As another disadvantage, Professor Rodríguez entered my classroom. *Great, now he will also see me fall flat on my face.* There was nothing attractive about a nervous girl choking during her presentation.

"Erin?" I murmured. "Erin?"

She turned to the side. "What?" she whispered.

"I just wanted to thank you for everything—for the package, for the support." I exhaled with relief. "Just thank you, Erin."

"Jacky, what are you talking about?" she whispered. She gave me a confused look.

"What am I talking about?" I stared. "You know, the blue dress—and you know what else."

She had a clueless expression on her face. "Jacky, I never sent you a package."

"Are you sure?" I stated, twisting my lips up.

"Yes, I'm sure."

A student behind me shushed us. *Who would send me a dress and underwear to wear?* I looked around the classroom. Professor Rodríguez smiled at me. It was comforting and reassuring. I didn't understand. None of it made sense to me—an unknown person giving me a dress and buying me underwear. I pulled the card from my purse. I threw the card onto Erin's desk. She read it and quickly tossed it back to me.

"I didn't write that, Jacky." She sneezed loudly. "Excuse me."

Almost everybody said, "Bless you!"

"Thank you," Erin said. "This is James's handwriting."

Why would James buy me gifts?

I started reminiscing about the last words he'd said to me: "Do you moan? Don't worry. We will find out soon." Did I moan? "We will find out," he said. *We*. What did buying me material things have to do with me moaning?

Mr. Ford called my name, and the butterflies in my stomach flew around. This was it, the big delivery. I collected my note cards from my purse. I walked slowly to the front of the classroom. The other students were quiet. It was peaceful. I found it remarkable. They all watched me, ready to listen to what I had to say, ready to be educated on my chosen topic. I stood tall and proud; it felt good to have an audience willing to listen to me no matter what. I turned on the overhead, and I was prepared to inform everyone about Lyndon B. Johnson's war on poverty. I briefly stared at the screen. Tia dimmed the front lights for me. My subconscious thanked her. Tia winked at me. I winked back, smiling. All eyes were on me.

"We are ready when you are, Ms. Dickerson," Mr. Ford said.

"Good morning, everyone," I said loudly.

"Good morning!" the class said in unison.

"I hope everyone is having a great morning. I am going to talk about Lyndon B. Johnson, the thirty-sixth president of the United States, and why he declared war on poverty." With the remote, I turned to the second slide. I was feeling determined and motivated. Speaking and having people listen to me gave me a sense of self-empowerment.

As I informed my audience, I moved my arms assertively to reduce some of my anxiety. "Johnson declared …" I paused. "Aw, shit. Oh my," I groaned at full volume. I stopped briefly. My hands shook. My panties were vibrating aggressively and sharply massaging my clit. It felt incredible. I froze with my eyes sealed. I could have died from embarrassment. I covered my face with my hands. "No, no, no, Lord, this can't be happening," I whispered.

"Yes, Ms. Dickerson, believe it. It's happening. Please continue," Mr. Ford said.

Dammit, dammit, my Victoria Secret underwear fucked me up. Did I have to say something? I was mortified. Again, I covered my face as I listened to the vibration. I could hear the device forcefully massaging my pussy. I kept my eyes closed. *Someone, please hide me.* I wanted to become invisible. It seemed that the boys in the room were now more intrigued with hearing me discuss history.

"Ms. Dickerson, are you okay?" Mr. Ford said.

Someone increased the vibration to the maximum level. I moaned. "Yes, Professor, oh yes! I'm okay." I hesitated so that my voice wouldn't sound flirtatious and seductive. "It feels really, really great," I said softly but slowly, and then I immediately corrected myself. "I meant I'm great."

"Then you won't have a problem continuing."

The vibration made standing undoable. It seemed unbearable to maintain my position. Suddenly, the vibration stopped. Someone ceased it. I felt relieved for a moment.

I quickly managed a full recovery. "Our former president said, on January, 8, 1964—" The vibration startled me again; it was fondling my pussy at full speed. I bent over, quickly reacting in shock. "Oh Lord, why, why, why," I muttered. I breathed heavily. I crossed my legs as my body trembled. My body was excited and reacted accordingly.

"Ms. Dickerson? You are making a fool of yourself," Mr. Ford said, as if I hadn't realized that. The male competitors laughed at me and smiled.

"For the lives of many Americans who survived on the outskirts of hope—some because of their poverty, some because of their color, and all because of both." I moaned reluctantly. I couldn't help it. I formed two tight fists. My legs were now bewitched. They were most vulnerable to the feeling—and what a fabulous feeling it was. My breathing increased with the buzzing sound from my underwear.

Erin said, "Does anybody hear a buzzing sound?"

The students and teachers were quiet. I didn't want anyone else to hear the noise.

James said, "It sounds like buzzing—you know, like a vibrator."

"Or it could be someone's phone. You know, stupid kids forgot to turn off their phones," I said unconvincingly.

I continued while moving around to distract myself from the pleasure, which was astonishing. "Our task is to help replace their despair with pleasure." I was quiet briefly, and I shut my eyes. "Man, that feels"—I stopped—"really, really good." I murmured. I reopened my eyes. "And this administration today, here and now, declares unconditional war on poverty in America for the urge of being touched by this Congress in ways that I have been touched," I said, quivering more noticeably. I exhaled loudly and sealed my eyes. "That's the spot."

"That is enough, Ms. Dickerson. Come to your seat."

Michael stood up. "As a woman reaching her destination, I think we should let her come—I mean finish," he said, immediately returning to his seat.

Shit. Why was this happening to me? I instantly wrapped up my last words. "In conclusion …" I said slowly, crossing my legs again. I groaned. "Shit." I breathed. "And all Americans came as I'm coming now in that effort. Thank you."

No one clapped for me except James. I didn't blame them. "And I'm sure you came hard," he said.

I stared at him as I traveled back to my seat. It was embarrassing. They all looked at me as if I were a slut who couldn't compose herself in a professional environment.

Erin touched my shoulder. "What the hell was that?"

I didn't know where to start, nor did I want to answer her question. This incident was why James had asked if I moaned or not. Erin rose to deliver her presentation.

I rushed to the bathroom. I stared at my reflection in the mirror. I then entered the last stall and grabbed some tissue. There was no way I would return to Mr. Ford's classroom. I would rather have locked myself in that bathroom stall all day. I slid down my panties and wiped myself front to back. What the hell was I going to do? Someone knocked on my stall. I opened the door. I was stunned and speechless.

Professor Rodríguez and I shared a tight space as he entered the stall. He caressed my face with caution. He glanced down at me. "That was very courageous of you. I should fuck you right here, right now in this stall, for arousing me in public," he murmured. His voice was attractive.

"I'm sorry. I didn't mean to—"

He interrupted me. "Yeah, you did. You know that I don't like to be teased. I should punish you unquestionably for it."

I was scared of getting caught. "What if someone hears me?" I said with a pounding heart. His fingers had traveled up and between my thighs.

"Well, I guess you better learn to be utterly quiet. I love the way you moan, but self-control is a technique you should become familiar with starting now." He removed my panties.

My anxiety had trapped me in a corner. I watched him. He folded my panties up and put them in his pocket. I wasn't surprised he was stealing my underwear again.

"You don't need those—ever," he whispered into my ear.

"Professor Rodríguez? I can't." He paused, staring at me as if I'd said something wrong. Then I remembered. "Daddy, you're trying to fuck me at school inside a stall."

He covered my mouth with his hands. "Shush, Ms. Dickerson. I'm in control now, since you don't have any." He smiled.

I had control. I resented that statement.

He lowered down onto one knee, lifting my right leg up. My legs were open wide. With his head in between my legs, he kissed my inner thigh, and I dropped to the floor instantly. He never should have shown my body such affection, because it weakened me. My body wasn't suitably acquainted with the feeling of his fragile touch. He helped me up only to turn me around entirely. Behind me, he breathed lustfully onto the back of my neck. We exhaled heavily. I situated my hands on the wall to withstand my weight. He gripped my hair tightly for support. I tilted my head back. He began to finger fuck me. I moaned. He positioned his hand over my mouth again.

"Shush," he said seductively. "Because you haven't felt anything yet."

My mind considered all of the sexual possibilities. All I could think about was getting caught. I constantly imagined someone barging into the bathroom and acknowledging what was happening by the smell of sex in the air or the sounds of me moaning or us fucking. What if someone looked underneath the stall? Good girls like me were rarely in unfortunate situations such as this. I read books, wrote, and turned in my homework assignments on time. Well, I had until my professor started bending my ass over in bathroom stalls, as he was today. Why was he such a great fuck? He swirled his behind around and drew imaginary circles inside my pussy with his dick. It felt fabulous.

Someone entered the bathroom. We stopped quickly. She cried in the stall next to us. I laughed silently. I thrust my behind against his cock. I began gliding my clit against the head of his penis. From the front, I gripped him mildly. I glided against him repeatedly, back and forth aggressively with speed. I held his cock from underneath but in front of me. I massaged his dick while sliding him in between the lips of my pussy. The procedure became a routine. He groaned lowly. It was hot. He slipped. I had never heard him moan before until now.

The girl intervened by crying more harshly. She disturbed our erotic vibe when she farted randomly. The harsh smell instantly invaded my nostrils. She started dropping loads into the toilet. I covered my nose and mouth. I pulled my dress down. Seconds later, I charged out of the bathroom. Mistakenly, I bumped into James.

I rolled my eyes, stopping for a conversation. "Why did you do that?"

He ran his fingers through my hair. "It was just an assignment that was recently given to me. I found it quite amusing. Didn't you?" He gazed deeply into my eyes.

My eye contact wasn't as direct as his. "I would say it was bullshit. You humiliated me in front of everyone." I crossed my arms.

He laughed while walking around me. "No, you just were sexually satisfied while we all watched, and you moan beautifully, by the way." he admitted flirtatiously.

"Blah, blah, blah—save it for someone else who cares. I would never have sex with you, you dickhead, and that was the first and last time you'll ever hear me moan. That's for sure."

He laughed again. "You're funny and smart. I like that. I hope not smart enough to remove those vibrating panties of yours." He said bluntly.

I grinned confidently at him. "Let's just say that those panties won't be giving me problems." I chuckled. "Well, at least, not today, James." I worded strongly as I entered Professor Rodríguez's classroom. "Good-bye, James." I sat in the front row in the center. James sat in the seat next to me. *Do I ever get a fucking break?*

"Okay, class. You know the routine!" Professor Rodríguez was hot when he was serious. I still wanted to fuck him. I was willing to do anything to grab his attention. He hated being teased, so it encouraged me to be spontaneous and daring. I reached into my purse and retrieved my pen and notebook. He had written our homework and classroom assignments on the board, which were now irrelevant to all members in the competition.

I coughed hard for his acknowledgment. He gazed at me. I licked my lips and swirled my tongue around in a circular motion against my top and bottom lips. I grinned at him as I gazed in his direction. He cleared his throat loudly in shock. He then licked his lips. James interrupted our entanglement. He looked strangely at Professor Rodríguez, yearning to figure out why his gestures were so inappropriate and unprofessional in a public setting.

"Are you going to teach us or what, Professor?" James said.

Everyone shut up. Since when had he cared about our professor teaching us anything, let alone learning material that would be beneficial?

For a moment, his eyes were on James. "I'm sorry—are you deaf or blind, Mr. Gordon? Your homework and classroom assignments are on the board." he said aggressively. James had a look of frustration on his face. He stared directly in the eyes of our instructor, and suddenly he peeked over at me, but I unexpectedly caught his gaze. I then shrugged my shoulders at him. I believed that the manager of BOTS Association didn't converse with my favorite teacher yet. James cleared his throat, holding his pen, aggravated because of it. Professor Rodríguez sat down on his desk. Everyone was in the process of doing their work. Professor Rodríguez picked up the book *The Hunger Games*. He faced a constant struggle to avoid my erotic but private performance. I discreetly opened up my legs, slowly crossing them frequently to flash him at my convenience. *Yes, Daddy, no panties, just like you like.* I hoped he remembered his previous announcement to me. Who wasn't in control now? He would concentrate on his book for a few seconds, and then he would peek at me with his full concentration.

For a prolonged period, I let the appearance of my wet pussy amuse him. I sucked on my finger and grasped my breast without being noticed. He choked. We caught James's attention, especially me. Professor Rodríguez and I pretended to appear busy. James stared down at my legs. I watched him from the corner of my eye. The professor wrapped up his lecture for the day. Students rushed out of the classroom eagerly. I adored being enslaved by my professor. I locked Professor Rodríguez's door. We eyed one another. *Let's see who now has all of the control.* I stripped out of my clothes. He unbuttoned his shirt. He didn't know that I was his bitch.

CHAPTER 19

Tia

Rejection from Mathew

I remembered my elementary school days as if they were yesterday. Mathew was stuck on me, and I was permanently glued to him like wallpaper. He was my partner in crime, although as adolescents, we were not practicing the behavioral acts of criminals. After school, we would go to the park a few blocks from my home. We would later play board games or video games at his house. Sometimes I stayed longer than I'd planned. Mathew and I constantly lost track of time when occupied by each other's company. Because of our poor time-management skills when we were hanging out, my mother disliked him and disapproved of the time we shared. At nine years old, I felt as if my soul mate had already found me. There was no looking for him, because he was there with me and for me continually. He was my best friend and never disappointed me. My mother grew weary of our loyalty and friendship.

She forbid me from seeing him one day after she caught him kissing me with his hands wrapped around my torso. She went ballistic and snatched me away from him. She punished me for allowing him to lay his filthy hands on me. There was no more hanging out with him after school. I still had permission to watch TV and use the Internet, and I kept my phone privileges. My mother knew that excluding Mathew from my life was the only punishment that would influence my demeanor. During the summertime, our plan was to move to Florida. I didn't want to go, and I didn't want to leave Matt behind. My mother packed quickly. Someone rang the doorbell, but my mother was too busy stuffing our suitcases to care. I stared at the door, thinking that maybe Mathew had come to say good-bye and share a last kiss. I blew into my hands to check my breath. I opened the door in anticipation of greeting him, but a strange man dressed in casual all-black clothing stood there. I looked at him, and he looked back at me in curiosity. I blinked, and he mimicked me, blinking twice. I smiled.

"Hi, mister," I said with a grin.

"Hello there, little young one," he said, scooting down to my level. "What's your name?"

"Tia," I said proudly. "What's yours?" I asked, swinging my arms.

He stood outside the door. "Victor." He stared. "How old are you, Tia?"

"I'm nine years old," I said, twisting the doorknob.

He touched my pigtails. "And where's your father?"

I looked down while frowning. "I don't have a father." I shook my head.

"Yeah, you do. We all have fathers, Tia. Even you." He pointed at me.

I grinned wider. "How do you know?" I became excited with false hope.

"Because I'm your father."

My father—I had a father. Unfriendly thoughts about my mother's dishonesty filled my mind.

"Tia, where are you? Come help Mommy with the bags!"

I ran to her while the door remained unsealed. She dropped the bag that was in her left hand. She rested her hand on my cheek and smirked at me.

I felt hurt and disappointed. "You said my daddy was dead."

"Honey, I told you what happened. It's best that we let the memories of him that follow me fade away. Your father is dead, honey."

"But, Mommy, Victor is standing outside the door." I pointed.

Her eyes enlarged as I revealed my father's name to her. She instantly peeked outside the door. He entered our apartment and closed the door. I hugged him tightly. She pulled me from his grasp hostilely.

"Katrina, you told my child I was dead. That's a little low even for you, don't you think?" He was serious. His voice was dark, heavy, and deep. "I didn't even know I had a child until now. She'll be my special little angel."

I had never seen my mother afraid before. She was petrified, as if she had seen a ghost or Satan.

"She will never be your child. Tia, go to your room," she said politely. I refused to listen. "Tia, go to your room—now!" She seemed angry.

I stepped my way to my room and slammed the door. I went into the closet. Suddenly, I heard a strange noise. I listened cautiously. It sounded as if someone were throwing rocks at my window. I approached the window and lifted it up—it was Matt. My heart felt a sense of bliss and harmony. He made my life all right. Seeing him saved a piece of me. I held my head out the window and smiled at him.

He lifted his head up. "Are you coming down to spend one more day with me?"

Oh boy, there it was. "I can't." I frowned. "We are leaving in a few minutes."

He dropped his head. "I don't want you to go. You are always looking, but I'm always right here. Be with me. Be my girl for the day, Tia."

"Don't make this hard for me. Just say good-bye."

He paused. I could see the disappointment in his eyes. "Please, Tia. Come with me. I promise you won't regret it. I want to show you something."

I reconsidered my decision. I exhaled. "Okay, Matt." I smirked.

I climbed out of my window, and we walked down the street together. We were silent. The wind was blowing. He grasped my hand. I closed my eyes while the breeze comforted my skin. It felt compelling, the way it was pressing against my skin. We stopped to enjoy the weather. He hugged me spontaneously. His clothes smelled freshly washed. I wrapped my arms around him tightly. I refused to free him from my grasp. I would miss him and his company, which was irreplaceable.

I cried quietly on his shoulder. I watched my tears stain the back of his shirt. Our problem was letting go of one another. His grip seemed to be tightening seconds later. Everything was my fault because I'd made the mistake of leaving my mother in order to fulfill my selfish need and desire to accompany a dear friend. The requirements of my mother and my whereabouts didn't matter, so I kept her in suspense until I returned.

He held my hand nonstop. I smiled at him, and he kissed me slowly on my cheek as he walked me back home. As we got closer to my home, we saw police cars and an ambulance quickly stop in front of my home. The entire street was blocked off. Policemen and detectives were everywhere. Their cars were parked on my mother's property. My heart raced in my chest. I could hear it thumping in my ears. The sound was the only thing I could hear. I ran to the door of my mother's apartment. The door was unlocked. I turned on every light in every room.

"Mom!" I screamed as I searched the entire apartment. "Mama, where are you?" I yelled. Matt gazed at me, trying to get me to relax. I ventured off back into the streets. I shouted out, crying out at the top of my lungs, "Mama, Mama, Mama!"

There had been an accident on our block. I invaded the restricted area, crossing the yellow strips. I walked closer to the scene of the crime, where the detectives had begun to do their investigation. I marched up to where a man was loading a woman into the ambulance. The woman was my mother. My heart dropped. I was physically numb. My fingers were shaky.

"No, no!" I screamed. I ran to hold her, but a policewoman held me back. I just wanted to see her, but the woman wouldn't let me. "Let me go! Let me go! That's my mother. Please!" Tears dropped from my eyes as I gasped for breath. I couldn't control my tears. The policewoman collected both of my hands. Why wouldn't she let me see my mommy? I was so angry and sad.

"What's your name, sweetheart?"

I wept with a frown. "Tia." I wiped my nose. I felt numb and empty. "What happened to my mother?"

She knelt down on one knee. "My name is Detective Harris. According to your next-door neighbor, your mother was hit by a car. Apparently, it was a hit and run. She rushed out of her apartment, searching for you, Tia. Where were you?"

Where was I? I was with my best friend instead of my mother. Where was I? I was with the guy beside me. I'd left her. I'd left my mommy to be with a friend. If I'd stayed, if I hadn't been selfish and stubborn, she would have been alive. I should have called or texted, because if I had, I'd have still had a mother to hold me. Thinking of my mother in the past tense seemed unrealistic. Her death would be a nightmare that would last forever. At nine years old, how could I ever learn to forgive Mathew or myself? I didn't answer the officer. I watched them drive my mother's body away. It was dark, yet the blue and red police lights lit up the streets.

"Tia! Tia, snap out of it. Halo, come back."

Snap out of what? I breathed out. I wiped my face with my hand.

"Are you okay?"

"Yeah, Matt, I am fine," I said, observing my surroundings. Mathew and I were at a restaurant, waiting patiently for our meals.

He took a sip of his water. "You haven't called me that in a long time."

"What?" I said with a lost expression on my face.

"You called me Matt."

"No, I didn't." I couldn't wait to deny him.

He nodded slightly. "Mm, yeah, you did."

I cleared my throat, deciding not to start an argument. I exhaled with weariness.

"What are you thinking about?" he asked.

After his question, I envisioned us fucking on the tables. I stared off into space again. Jacky had warned me not to discuss sex or anything related to sex.

"Tia?"

"Huh? Oh, yes. I'm thinking about …" I paused to think of something that Angel would have said instead of the truth, which was Mathew fucking the lights out of me. *How I miss the special times we shared during childhood. Fuck, who said shit like that?*

"What were you thinking about before?"

The fact that my mother is dead because of you and me—and how I still hate you for it. I paused momentarily. "I was just reminiscing about our first kiss." Who cared what I was thinking about? Bringing up the past encouraged him to elaborate on the events we'd experienced.

"Do you remember the time when we went to the park, and your neighbor's dog chased me home?" He laughed.

I laughed as well. "Yes." I smiled.

This was fucking boring. I didn't want to talk or share my feelings. I just wanted to fuck. *What the hell?* I smirked, concealing my true thoughts. He continued to talk, and I pretended I was listening and caring about every word. *Is this how most guys feel when they want to just fuck a girl? Pretending to listen and pretending to care is what most men do, because expecting to have sex afterward helps them to accept the boredom.* I was so unamused that I started to wonder what color his underwear was. The waiter put our dinner in front of us. He was sexy.

"Would you like anything else?"

Yes, to sit on your face, I thought, eyeing him.

"Oh, jeez, do you eat a lot?" I said.

He was confused.

"I mean, how well you do, you know, clean plates?"

He tilted his head. "I don't know what you mean."

"What time do you get off of work? Because I would love to enlighten you."

"Tia?" Mathew said in a dark tone of voice, as if I'd mentioned something disrespectful.

"What, Mathew? What did I say wrong?" I scooted my chair closer to the table.

"We don't need anything else. She was just kidding, right?" Mathew said in a serious tone.

The waiter walked away. I guess I was pissing him off. Good. Maybe he would concentrate on fulfilling my needs.

"What the hell was that?" Mathew seemed angry.

I glanced at him in seriousness. "I don't have to explain it. We're not fucking," I whispered.

"I know that." He eyed me.

"So, what is this about, huh?" I said with a critical expression.

"You, Tia—it's all about you. Are you getting any sleep?"

"You know I'm not getting any sleep." It was a stupid question.

He said concernedly, "Why not?"

I rose. "Why in the hell do you care? A month ago, you didn't give a shit about me being sleep deprived." People started watching us.

"Tia, sit down," he said nicely. I was still standing. "Sit down!" he demanded. People stared more intensely. I slowly returned to my seat. "That's no way to talk to a friend."

"We're not friends, remember?" *You're not my father, so stop acting like it.* Why was he being so mean to me?

"Eat something," he said generously.

"I'm not hungry," I said while sucking my bottom lip in.

He breathed out. "Tia, I didn't ask you if you were hungry. I said to eat something."

I gripped my fork, picking at my spaghetti. I took a small bite of my garlic bread. "Since when did you become a demanding asshole?"

"Since you stopped listening to me," he said, eating his pasta from a bowl.

"I don't have to listen to you. Demanding me to do things won't get you anywhere."

"Well, you are eating, aren't you?" Mathew grinned.

Yeah, I was—but barely. I stared at him.

"What? Do I have something on my face?" He wiped around his mouth.

"Yeah, a dick," I joked, and I giggled.

He was serious.

"Sorry," I said sincerely. *He doesn't even have a humorous side.*

"I know why you can't sleep."

"I know what you can do to help me sleep, since my tiredness is troubling you," I said, swirling around the remainder of my spaghetti with my fork.

"I'm serious, Tia."

He was always so fucking serious. Why? The guy I loved and remembered was humorous and witty. I didn't know who the hell this man was, eating cold pasta, demanding I do things reluctantly.

"No, you're cranky," I said before sipping my pink lemonade.

A male waiter interrupted us. He wore an intriguing expression. "Would you like more lemonade?"

His voice was stimulating. No, I didn't want lemonade. I wanted to fuck, though. I was horny, and my hormones were racing out of control. I had grown tired of masturbating and using sex toys instead of having sex with an actual partner. Either Mathew was going to fuck the lights out of me, or I was going to find someone else to do the job for me. I didn't care if he didn't like it or not. I was who I was, and I wasn't about to change for him or for anyone. He could either accept it or fuck off.

I glanced into the waiter's charming light brown eyes. They were charismatic. In the corner of my eye, I watched Mathew stare as I gazed upon the handsome man serving me. "Yes, I'm glad you asked." With my finger, I placed a few strings of my hair behind my right ear. I sucked and licked my lips slowly.

When the waiter was finished filling my glass, he asked, "Is there anything else I can do for you?"

Oh yes, there was. There were plenty of things an attractive guy with a perfectly structured face such as his could do for me. I had a list. "Yes. As a matter of fact, there is something you can do for me."

Mathew stood. He grabbed his coat from the back of his chair. "You need to stop this. You hear me?"

I smiled. "Well, does this mean what I think it does?"

"No, it doesn't," he said.

What a cranky bastard. He didn't want to lie with me but didn't want me to sleep with anyone else. He was playing a dangerous game—a game I had invented.

I looked at the server. "Do you find me attractive?" He paused, looking at Mathew. I said, "Why are you looking at him? We're not fucking. We probably never will. I think he's gay or he doesn't find me attractive. Do you?"

"You are very much. He's a fool not to think so."

I wiped around my mouth with a napkin and rose. "I thought you would say that." I avoided Mathew, giving our waiter my full attention. "What time do you get off work?" I smiled, touching his chest gently. "You are strong. You must work out." The server leered at me.

"Fuck this. You're coming with me—now!" Mathew threw fifty dollars onto the table. He gripped my arm, pulling me toward the exit.

"You're hurting my arm!"

He was being hostile for no reason. He was pulling against my skin, holding me too tightly.

"Let me go, Mathew!" I said, and he released me.

We stopped in front of the car. "Where am I dropping you off?" he said.

Dropping me off? Oh no, he wasn't dropping me off anywhere. I touched his shoulder. He grasped my hand in anger. "I'm going home with you," I said.

"No, you're not. I'm taking you home!"

"Well, what if I don't want to go home?" I crossed my arms in all seriousness.

"Well, that's too bad because that's where I'm taking you—home!"

I rolled my eyes like a child. I didn't move a muscle, and I wasn't about to. I was quiet.

He stood in front of me. "You're acting like a child. Stop it, and listen to me."

Stop it, and listen to me, I thought, mocking him. He never listened to me, so why should I listen to him?

He exhaled as he stared at me. "Why are you being so difficult? It's starting to frustrate me." He leaned on his car, kicking small rocks from underneath his feet.

"I don't care if you are," I said, looking in the opposite direction. The wind blew.

He unlocked the doors. "Get in the car. I know you're freezing," he commanded.

I raise my upper lip. "No! I'm fine." I was freezing. Goose bumps appeared on my arms and legs. He gripped my arm again, opening the door and throwing me into the passenger seat. "You're such a dick," I said. He slammed the door and then entered the car and locked the doors. I stared out the window.

"My place it is, okay, Tia? So stop this." He breathed.

I turned to him quickly. I was surprised. I looked back out the window, smiling. I thought about Amy and the horrible things she had done. I wasn't finished reading her entire journal, but I had read enough. I needed to tell Mathew before Amy decided to plead guilty to all of her confessions. Since day one, I'd wanted to help. The truth was that I needed to help myself. Every night was the same. I suffered from night terrors. Why couldn't I sleep? Reliving my fear was an indication of my imperfections. I had too many to count. Being sleep deprived was a persistent situation for me. I had nightmares about the accident, about my mother, and about my father, involving every little disgusting thing he had done to traumatize and corrupt my life and me personally.

"I'm still helping you. Do you understand me? There is nothing you can do to change my mind about it." His eyes were fixed on the road.

I was immediately offended. "I don't need any help. I'm fine. Stop trying to fix me. I will never, ever be that little innocent girl you once knew. She's dead, she's gone, and she's not coming back, okay?"

We entered his apartment. It was still clean and smelled fresh. His apartment was spotless every time I visited him, even when my arrival was unexpected. My feet were killing me. I could no longer take another step without removing my heels. I sat down on the sofa, unbolting the straps on both sides of my shoes. I rested my legs on the arm of the sofa. My mind and body were now at ease. I decided to get more comfortable, waiting to be ravished. At least I was getting what I desired—Mathew's cock in my mouth. I undressed in the living room. I removed my underwear as well. He entered the room. He blinked and stared. I smiled, proud of my figure.

"So what do you think?" I said with my hands on my hips. He turned around. His reaction disappointed me. I looked at him in confusion. What did I have to do to get him to fuck me? I was a woman. It shouldn't have been so difficult.

"Cover yourself up, Tia." He left the room. Then he reentered and handed me a pair of his shorts and a black T-shirt. I concealed my body.

"Are you dressed?" he asked. He peeked into the living room.

I was frustrated. "Yes, sadly, I am." I sat on the couch, and he joined me. I faced him. "Are you attracted to me?" I said, fearing his answer.

"Very much," he confessed. "You are beautiful, Tia."

I caressed his face. He let me. "Do you want me?"

He held my hand. "I do," he said, not making eye contact.

I made an attempt to lift his shirt. He stopped me. "I can't, not until we get you straightened out."

Shit, help me. What do I have to do—roofie him or something? Shit, I sound like Amy. My heart was racing. "I have to tell you something about Amy."

He leaned back. "What about her? Because I told you—"

I stopped him. "You need to hear this. Do you understand me?"

He sat up straight and nodded. "I'm listening."

"I don't know how to say this to you." I hesitated. *This is not going to be good.*

CHAPTER 20

Amy

Meeting David

Maybe it was strange that I saw him as beautiful, but I did. He was lovely. *Fuck, where did he learn to French kiss like that? David, David, damn, baby. You got spunk.* We were getting heated in his car, a jet-black 2012 Chevrolet Camaro SS Coupe. His Chevrolet wasn't the only thing that was hot and funky. Why was I so attracted to David Saavedra? I personally liked calling him Dave. I found him attractive because he was himself around me, and he was social, so he often synergized off of other people. He was all about positive energy. Optimism was the only thing coursing from his body, and I wanted a taste of it, of him—just one piece. He had the kind of energy any girl would have wanted to absorb. Dave and I had a mutual attraction, although I'd failed to notice it in the beginning. In fact, he was the best of both worlds, good and bad.

Regarding the way people saw and described me, I hadn't always been that way. I was much, much worse. If someone didn't like me now, he or she wouldn't have liked me back then either. I was a bitch. When I looked into the half-broken mirror in my mother's master bedroom, which she'd claimed she would get fixed a week ago, I did not see the bitch I had been or still was—because I saw nothing. So what did they see? And by "they," I meant family members, friends, and ex-boyfriends.

What did Dave, the twenty-three-year-old Colombian guy, see in me? I was just a nineteen-year-old sophomore at Marshall S. King University. His appearance had stolen my complete concentration. I'd met him at a Chipotle on the north side of Chicago, near Belmont, where I'd been employed at my first job as a waitress about a year ago. I'd started my day off at a salon, the Finest Cuts, and gotten a trim because, well, I'd needed it. Other than the fact that I wanted to get fucked by David, my life was going great until I met him.

I didn't know what I liked most about him—the way he French kissed me or the way he kissed my neck perhaps. No, that wasn't it. It was the sound of his voice or that short, straight pitch-black hair with hints of gray. His imperfections were perfect. I wondered consistently about the gray spots of hair on his head. I inhaled and exhaled. His cologne smelled like Calvin Klein's fragrance Obsession. The scent traveled up my nose, and the smell was nice enough to catch my attention. On his neck, he had beauty marks, yet they made him more attractive. He was beautiful to me, and his skin looked beautiful to me. I couldn't help but stare at his beauty marks. They were like artwork—a masterpiece. Like a nonstop marathon, I envisioned him removing his shirt and having them all over his body. My insides were screaming at the idea of it. Seeing all he had to offer would have been extremely sexy.

I could tell he was serious about his personal hygiene. There wasn't a spot of dirt in sight. His plain T-shirt was as white as snow. Then I noticed his round, clear earrings. I loved earrings on men, but I loved them on David especially. I couldn't forget how handsome they'd looked on him one night when we were in a Jewel Osco parking lot. He put the car in park.

He looked at me. "Do you want anything?"

Every time I heard his voice, it got smoother and hotter. It wasn't too profound or lenient. I ran my fingers across my bottom lip as I glimpsed down for a brief moment, thinking of what I desired for the occasion. Eventually, I looked at him sexily. In all seriousness, he waited for an answer. I felt my shyness fold up into a beer bottle. I hated beer, but he was a big beer drinker.

I smirked and answered, "Some wine would be nice." I stared, crossing my legs and blinking mildly. "I really don't like or want any hard liquor." I thought hard liquor was disgusting. Not being able to handle my liquor might have been a factor in that decision.

He blinked. "Okay," he said, as if it were no problem. "What kind?"

I could have listened to his voice for hours. Why did almost everything about him turn me on? Maybe it was the fact that I was nasty but acting as if I were pure.

Many brand names popped into my head. *Decisions, decisions, and decisions.* I shrugged. "As long as it's fruity," I said with a half grin.

He turned to face me, and he surprised me when he leaned in and kissed me before exiting his car. Every kiss he planted on me aroused some new part of my body. We stopped locking lips, even though it felt amazing. His lips were pink and succulent. They were soft like pillows and sexy enough to suck on all night. He pulled away from me and opened the car door. It was chilly, and I was freezing until he shut the door. Smoothly, he strolled into Jewel Osco.

I smiled at the memory of our kiss. I touched my lips. Kissing him was my addiction, among many more I later discovered—addictions he helped me to expose. He thought I was looking for a relationship. Yet like him, I wanted to fuck, too, so I pretended to yearn for an emotional connection, because I didn't want him to think less of me. I bet he believed I was innocent. I wasn't. I bet he preferred hard liquor or beer. The first time he kissed me, we went bowling and played pool. I sucked at pool, and it was my first time ever playing it. I was a little embarrassed. He invited two other friends: a white girl named Michelle Whitmore, an old friend of his from high school, and his best friend, Ben. As I was standing there, trying to figure out my next move, Dave mistakenly touched my behind. I smiled the second it happened.

I faced him. "You just touched my ass." I wasn't complaining. Maybe next time he wouldn't touch my behind only by mistake. He could grab my ass all he wanted.

He gripped the pool stick tightly. He smiled and then looked at me. "Was that a bad or good thing?"

In a moment of flirtatiousness, I said, "It's too soon to say. I'll let you know at the end of the night."

He stared, listening to my response. He smiled, so I smiled back. As the game ended, we started our bowling game. He and his best friend bought drinks, and we did some shots. I wasn't much of a drinker. They left the table. I pulled a twenty-dollar bill from out of my bra. Michelle watched me for a second. She arched an eyebrow as if I were insane.

"Put that away. Let the guys pay for it!" she said.

I thought about what she'd said to me. I shrugged. *Okay*, I thought. I put my money back into my bra. *What was I thinking?* Dave returned with the drinks. The sight and smell of alcohol exhausted me. I figured he expected me to drink with them.

"Are you having fun?" he whispered into my right ear.

"Yes."

He sat down across from me. "Good, because that's what I'm all about—fun." He was fun and humorous.

I was curious; the word *fun* got me thinking. "What are you looking for?" I muttered into his ear. He relaxed his hand on my thigh. I looked down.

"I'm not looking for anything serious. I like to enjoy myself and hang out with friends."

At first, *How disappointing* ran through my mind. I frowned slightly without exposing my disappointment, though I respected his honesty. It wasn't the "I just want to fuck you" approach that concerned me. Without even granting me an opportunity to respond, he kissed me. It was the first kiss we had shared, and afterward, I received many more, but the first one was like a drug. Before fully accepting the first, I pulled away from him. Again, he leaned in to kiss me. The gesture, for me, was irresistible, because a guy such as this would maintain my interest and keep me entertained. I knew it. He looked like a big bowl of amusement.

My desire to be kissed by him overcame my urge to fight. I should have stopped him; I should have immediately told him a friend with benefits wasn't my thing and that relationships also weren't my thing, but I didn't. I was hypnotized by the kiss. It was a dream. Afterward, I had no concern about what was troubling me. His gorgeousness and intelligence were the reasons I let his lips touch mine. Being a total freak could have played a role in me tolerating the situation. I wanted to know him. Was there anything troubling about getting to know someone?

He entered the car. The coolness of the outdoors caressed my skin temporarily. I came back to reality. He was hot. I'd never had seen a guy so good looking before. He handed me wine in a white bag. He drove off somewhere quiet so that we could view the stars.

I glanced outside of the window. He was from Florida, and seeing Chicago's lights at night was something he cherished. For me, on the other hand, the view was a thing of familiarity and boredom. For him, it was more enjoyable. Again, he put the car in park. I looked up at the stars. They were beautiful. I rested my hand on the wine. The four small bottles were warm. I gave the beverages to him.

"It's warm." I laughed on the inside. I was sure he knew it already.

He removed them from the package, opened the car door, and then placed them on the ground outside. The weather was cold enough to chill our drinks. "I guess that should work." I smiled.

I uncrossed my legs and partook in my first mouthful of wine. The flavor lingered on my tongue. It tasted fruitful and sweet, like strawberries. I quietly smacked my lips together. Chucking down the first and second wine bottles made me feel awesome. Alcohol had a way of creating a relieving, courageous, and mellow feeling. It was the best feeling in the world. It was unexplainable. I leaned back. It seemed as if all of my difficulties and struggles lifted off of my shoulders. As strange as it was, I was happy. Love and joy were coursing through my soul. The feeling chilled my spine, but in a good way. I turned and watched him. He was already mellow, not drunk or tipsy. I exhaled loudly. When I finished downing my drinks, I longed for Dave to fuck me right there in his awesome Chevrolet.

It didn't take much to get me in the mood. He eyed me. Lustfully, I locked my hand onto the back of his neck. I gently fondled his head of hair. I kissed him, and he kissed me back, massaging his tongue with mine again and again. I wondered whose lips were bigger, his or mine. I pulled at the bottom of his shirt, imagining what was next for us. *Lord, Dave, take it off for me, please.*

My hands discovered what the darkness denied my eyes of. I made an attempt to touch all of him—his chest, shoulders, arms, and stomach. Shit, he was fit, evidence of him visiting the gym regularly. With gentleness, on the right side of my neck, he attacked me with light kisses while he leaned in closer and closer. I was instantly aroused. I was wet. The feeling was uncomfortable. He massaged my inner thigh. His touch was golden.

I could hear my heart thumping in my chest. While the right side of my neck was under attack, I duplicated the same act on his left side. To change it up, I sucked on the bottom of his earlobe and then headed for his neck. *What a fucking freak.* He liked it. His scent befriended my nostrils. It was nurturing. We then locked our hands on one another's neck. My lips again were entwined with his. We were stuck together like sex addicts as we lusted deeply to proceed. I began moaning while we continued to lock lips. I couldn't stop pulling at his shirt. I wanted to rip it off so that it would no longer be a concern. I hopped on top of him. My movements surprised him; I could tell by his face. He was adorable. I stopped suddenly. I grabbed and caressed the fingers on his left hand. I slowly sucked on his index finger, watching him watch me. His eyes were curious to view my nakedness. I kept moaning in his ear—I couldn't control it. He liked the sound of me moaning in his ear. I was positive it turned him on.

After the night we shared, he texted me every other day because, well, he wanted to fuck the lights out of me. He yearned for me to ride and suck his cock. He probably was also fantasizing about me. Valentine's Day was the best. He thought it was weird for us to hang out on Valentine's Day, because we were not a couple. I agreed. However, there wasn't a guy I preferred to spend my day with other than him. I had to dress up, although I told him that getting all dolled up was pointless. I looked into the mirror and discovered that I was too weak to resist. Getting compliments from Dave made me feel special. He was the perfect gentleman. He opened doors for me and held my hand. Dave was sweet to me, and his sweetness got me high on him. Dave was my drug, and I chased after the feeling he gave me. Seeing him became a requirement for me. I tried my best to hide it, but it was like covering an obese woman with a guy who was nothing but skin and bones. He would text me every other day, asking me about my day, what I was doing, and how I was feeling. He sometimes would text me to say good morning and good night. While he texted me the things of my dreams, I responded by telling him I was a constant masturbator, because I wanted to be honest with him, although I played a lot of games with him.

The more he was a gentleman to me, the more I thought I was getting to know him, yet I just wanted him to fuck me more. I needed to feel him inside me. I was addicted to masturbating, visiting pornographic websites, and watching sex films on television. My mind drew up sexual fantasies that frequently played in my head throughout my days. I was a girl who'd never had an orgasm before. I guess that was a good thing, because I would have certainly been addicted to sex, which I probably was anyway. One day, I woke up and went to class and then work, as usual. After I came home, I took a nice hot bubble bath, and I felt horny, so I masturbated in the tub to thoughts of Dave fucking me. His muscles, chest, and toned stomach came to mind. I was in bed naked. I was thinking about sex around twenty to thirty times a day, only with this one person. Dave was a sexual obsession for me. Every time I desired or fantasized about sex, Dave popped into my head. I couldn't control it—my longing for him was too strong.

I tried reading, writing, and going out on other dates to lose sight of him. I had never even seen him naked. I didn't know if he was big or small, a quick comer or a neck grabber. The fantasy of him and the thought of not knowing these sexual things got me high. As with the first encounter we'd experienced, it was the first high I chased. My behavior became possessive and obsessive. Eventually, he stopped responding to my text messages and calls, especially unknown numbers for a while. I was desperate to contact him. I would have done anything to get high on him again. He was avoiding me, and I couldn't accept the fact that he was rejecting me.

It had been a few months since I had heard from him. It seemed as if my fantasies had evolved after the rejection. He had been blunt with me about his previous interest in me: "I just wanted to fuck you, okay? I wanted to feel your lips on my dick, and I was just looking forward to you riding me. I never cared for you or about you. Good-bye, Amy."

Eyes Masked in Blackness

Don't cry, little girl, because this is a tough world.
Wipe away your tears since they don't stand dry.
Don't allow your fears to influence you and
mask your eyes in blackness.
Can you see yourself covered in your own unfeelingness?
Although your heart is shaded in dimness, do you
still consider yourself to be beautiful?
Even though you're a girl afraid of yourself, of your reflection,
of your own terrors, of the shadow that follows you, you
still manage to smile, dance, and sing in public.
I'm surprised you can hear your welcoming giggles,
your humorousness, and your pure tone of voice.
Have you convinced yourself that you look beautiful? Aren't
you perceived as an angel from numerous dreams?
It was because your father was your hero, your protector.
He saved you from the potential threats, and you
accepted him to be your savior forever.
He was the reason you could smile—until
he left you unshielded indefinitely.
You became lost in your uncertainties and drowned in endless tears.
Don't cry, little girl, because this is a tough world.
Wipe away your tears since they don't stand dry.
Don't allow your fears to influence you and
mask your eyes in blackness.
You are covered in bloody stains and shaped
by your own suspicions and filthiness
Although your heart is no longer beating, are you beautiful?
Your night unendingly fell on your innocence
and tainted your mental health.
You were deprived of your happiness as well as
your purpose for breathing in oxygen.
Your protector was a coward with no actual known face.

The consequence of his withdrawal was a fatal
action that led to a lethal result.
Your memories are the reason you became insane.
Your pain—oh, your pain—is your misery,
But it's no reason to mask your eyes in blackness.
This is a tough world, so no excuse for crying.
Dispose of your tears so that your eyes do stand dry;
Don't allow your fears to drive you into insanity.
Madness is your coverage—can you see it?
Although you're absent a heart and soul, you appear to be striking.
In secret, this has stolen your smile and laughter,
But look at how you sparkle in the eyes of others.
Look at the men who are persistently pursuing you
As you attempt to discover other false forms of substitution to
fill the emptiness of your father's departure so that your heart
can be redeemed, because your eyes will never stand dry.
Your loneliness has made your path to recovery seem unreasonably
idealistic, as you're desperate to keep a man in your grasp.
This has dictated your failure at love.
Who's that man resting underneath your sheets? The one
before and after him and the many more who follow?
Men are brought to your bed while you wear that mask in darkness,
so you feel no more pain, but your eyes are wet with tears.
You have been having much sex, wishing to
become a little closer to your reclamation,
But you've never felt more vacant on the inside.
You satisfy others in the belief that you can gain happiness,
but you've never been drunker with sadness.
You have persuaded yourself to believe a man is
the solution to the lost love of your father.
Have you seen yourself smile lately? Because
you frown when you are alone.
Have you heard yourself laugh? Because
collecting publicity has made you silent.

Can your soul give your energy some recognition?
Because you are dead in secret.
Have your spirits touched you, since you are soulless?
You are a woman mistaken for a child, a little girl with stunning eyes masked in blackness so that no one sees you cry.
You are fearful, trying to be fearless.
You are an angel, seen by the demons that surround you.
You are beautiful, but you've forgotten how striking you are.
Beauty is a thing in this world that a woman should never forget.

CHAPTER 21

Angelina

Who Needed Therapy?

That was insanity. Amy, Erin, Tia, and I were in one of the classrooms, standing in a circle, after school. It was a Wednesday. We all looked like people who were involved in a support group, such as Sex Addicts Anonymous. The guys always aimed far below the belt. *What a bunch of jealous and horny little male cheaters.* From that point on, I hated them all. I knew *hate* was a strong word, but they worked my fucking nerves. One of those competitors had written an anonymous tip to the manager that four female competitors—Amy, Erin, Tia, and I—required professional counseling. No one needed to be diagnosed—at least not that I knew of—because we were not suffering from any mental disorders.

I didn't understand why Amy was there—she was no longer a member of our sex group. I'd never presumed that Erin had psychological problems going on. Fortunately, we all comprehended that Tia needed some mental guidance from a psychiatrist. A gorgeous middle-aged redhead with porcelain skin walked in. She wore a silver Giorgio Armani suit and a pair of six-inch black leather Giorgio Armani heels. The lady, I could tell, wasn't a certified practitioner, although she dressed like one. She had a tiny notebook in her hand, and her legs were neatly crossed. The classroom was quiet. Amy's coughing shortly filled the silence.

The therapist grabbed her red pen. "Does anyone in this room know why they are here with me in this very room?" she asked after clearing her throat.

Tia rose childishly.

Here we go. I bet something stupid comes out of her mouth.

She breathed out freely. "That's none of your business. Who do you think you are—a psychoanalyst, a psychiatrist, a shrink, a therapist, a counselor, or something?"

"Tia?" I said.

She looked at me. "What?" she whispered.

"A psychoanalyst, psychiatrist, shrink, therapist, and counselor are the same thing." She was an idiot.

She scratched the nape of her neck. "Huh? No, it's not the same. Google it. We don't have to listen to this old hag. Who is she? Because she may scare the shit out of you, but not me—no way. That's why I'm the new leader of this group. Something is wrong with Erin, because I would never take this cheap, Walmart-suit-wearing pathetic excuse for a shrink seriously."

Erin warned Tia. "Sit down, and shut up! You don't know what you're talking about."

Tia glared at the therapist and then at Erin. "Don't shush me. You shush. I'm not shutting up or sitting down. I'm not listening to this, so I'm breaking out of here." She screamed, "Who is with me?"

The lady said with a stern voice and expression, "Tia may know me as your therapist today, but I'm also the manager of this little sex club here. If you're still clueless about my identity, I, the old hag with the Walmart suit, am the giver of the thirty-thousand-dollar and fifty-thousand-dollar prizes."

Tia arched an eyebrow at the counselor and us. I knew she felt stupid now. I laughed at her while covering my mouth.

Tia wrapped up her last thoughts. "You know what? I'm gonna sit down, listen, and shut my ass up, because I desperately need to be treated." Finally, she sat.

Our counselor spoke again. "Now everyone in this room knows of my importance and of the significance of my presence here. I can finally acknowledge the problem that each and every one of you is experiencing. Like I asked before Tia's useless announcement, why are you here?"

Erin said, "As a leader, I am honored to speak first."

"Please, do continue. You can call me Ms. Wright, by the way."

Erin's expression was solid. "Well, Ms. Wright, before my enrollment at Marshall S. King University, I lost my father in a plane crash. Months later, I lost Evan, my big brother, the creator of the sex club, not the sex battle."

Ms. Wright seemed curious. She had begun to write in her notebook. "I remember him, as I do you, Erin Wilson. How did Evan die?"

Erin shook her head while staring at the floor. "He, uh, committed suicide."

"In detail, what happened, Erin? How did he commit suicide?"

Erin's body was still, and tears smoothly dropped onto both of her cheeks. She didn't answer.

"It's okay, Erin. It's okay to tell me what happened to your brother."

She cried and rocked in her chair. I had never seen her like this before. It was as if her brain had malfunctioned and come crushing down. Spiritually, she was gone, but her body was present, as if she were a zombie or mutant. She was in isolation. Where had she gone?

"We wanted to throw a surprise birthday party for Evan. He had turned eighteen, so happy birthday and congrats to you, big brother, for graduating from Kenwood. My mother and I, as well as everyone else invited, were dressed in fancy clothes. Every time we heard someone coming, we turned off the lights and hid around the house. And every time, it wasn't him. I was growing impatient. Four hours had passed, and I sensed that something was wrong.

"I remember constantly dialing his number. What if he never left the house? Although he had a five-thousand-dollar check, he was too depressed to shop for whatever he wanted to purchase. While continuing to dial his number, my mother and I searched around the house. I heard his phone ringing and vibrating in one of the guest rooms downstairs, and I entered one of the rooms on the left side. I kept calling. The ring and vibration were louder and slightly startled me. I jumped briefly. I rested my left hand over my pounding heart. *Just relax, Erin,* my subconscious said to assist me. I walked closer to the closet. I slowly opened it.

"I shouted, 'Ah, oh my God!' at the top of my lungs. I lost my balance and fell onto the floor in shock.

"'Mama, Mama, Mama!' I yelled for assistance. 'Please!' I cried. 'Please. Someone, help me.' I think I was in shock. I just kept babbling and babbling. 'Oh Lord. Why would you do this?' I breathed out deeply. 'Get him down! Get him down!' I immediately got up. I shook and cried, attempting to remove the rope from around his broken neck. My tears dropped onto my sandals. Somehow, I managed to remove the rope from around his neck. His body fell on me.

"I cried out, 'Oh my God!' I rocked. 'Oh my God, oh my God!' I stated in shock. I screamed tirelessly. My body was still shaking. My big brother was dead just like my father. I had no one. Everyone I loved was dead. I yelled at the top of my lungs in hatred and confusion. I yelled over and over again. I hit him, and I hit him again.

"'No, Evan!' I shouted. 'You damn coward!' I stiffened. 'How could you leave me?' I screamed. 'How could you have done this? How could you?' I tried lifting him up again, again, and again, but I kept dropping him and falling back onto the floor myself. I stayed down on the floor with him.

"I started crying all over again. 'Get up! Get up!' I repeated. 'Everybody is waiting for you.' I rocked with him in my arms yet again. I placed my hands over his eyes and shut them. 'We got the yellow cake with the chocolate frosting that you like and vanilla ice cream,' I told him emotionally, wiping away my tears. 'And that girl you like—she's upstairs, waiting for you,' I muttered to myself.

"My mother burst through the door, screaming. 'Argh, my baby! What did he do? No!' She shook to the floor. Secretly I blamed her and hated her even more, because my father's and brother's death was her fault. And nothing could have convinced me otherwise.

"And that's what happened to him—he hung himself."

Ms. Wright was quiet for a few seconds. She wrote some things down in her notebook. She then shook her head. "It must have been a very tough time for you. I'm sorry about what happened to him, Erin. I know that it still hurts. Thank you for sharing with us."

Erin nodded. I felt bad for her. I gave her a napkin and walked back to my seat. "Thank you, Angel," she said.

"Amy, why are you here?"

All eyes were on Amy, possibly because she didn't belong there in the first place.

Amy stared at Ms. Wright. "I don't know why I'm here." She moved around in her seat as if she were nervous. I suspected Amy had a lot to be nervous about.

I said, "No one knows why you're here. You're not even supposed to be here, because—"

Amy interrupted. "As you all know, my mental health is more important than a game. I am ill, and it would be unethical if someone said something that would make it impossible for me to receive treatment."

After Ms. Wright cures her from her mental problems, then we won't have to put up with her shenanigans again.

Amy continued. "I feel abandoned because my father left my mother and me at an early age. I was thirteen years old at the time. He was my hero, my protector, my savior. When he walked out of my life, a small part of me left with him, the most crucial piece of a young girl. I had this emptiness—a huge hole in my heart. I tried to fill it with relationships, and you know …" She paused.

Of course we knew—at least I did. She was a whore. *Just say it already. Just continue.* She stared at all of us. We were waiting for a response, especially Ms. Wright.

"Amy, please complete your statement," Ms. Wright said.

Amy breathed out slowly. "I used relationships as a way to fill my loneliness. It would not fill it," she said. "I'm always depressed and frustrated. Without the love of a significant other, who am I?"

Our counselor gripped her pen. "Describe the perfect life for a young girl. This is whatever that may possibly be for you. Shut your eyes if this helps. Try to envision yourself living the life worth living."

Amy listened. She spoke with her eyes shut. "I'm at home. I wake up with an attractive guy at my side. Not just any guy, a gentleman—a guy worth loving, because he loves me the way he knows I want and deserve to be loved. Life is simpler for me with him there. If I come home from school or work upset, I have him to make me feel special, like an angel."

"What do you mean by making you feel special? Without this person in your life, do you feel special or beautiful?"

A tear fell from her left eye. "Without him, I feel like a zombie or mutant in the search for love. I am empty. I am insecure and have no reason to dress up or apply makeup to my face. But when I do, I hit the streets for attention, so I am seen and noticed. Without love or someone to love me, I am a ghost."

A ghost? She was fucking crazy. Love had never been that important to me. I knew who I was, whom I needed, and who I wanted to be. Amy had no identity. She'd lost herself, lost her way. She needed to better herself physically, mentally, and emotionally.

"With him, I am high off a fantasy I have created in my mind. It's a feeling I can't go on without. Thinking of it, the fantasy, takes me to another world. No matter what happens—like if he leaves me, disrespects me, and rejects me—the fantasy lingers, unless I meet someone new, but this new someone has to share most of the same similarities as the old guy of my fantasies."

She was a crazy person. I felt bad for Mathew.

"And, Tia, whenever you're ready." Ms. Wright smiled.

Tia cleared her throat. She opened her mouth, yet nothing came out. She was choking on her own words. "I, I, I, um," she said. "I can't!" She stormed out of the class. The door slammed behind her.

"Okay, last but not least, Angel."

I said, "I'm going to be perfectly honest with you, Ms. Wright. I don't have any problems, not like Amy, Erin, or Tia. The only thing I can say is that I like a guy who doesn't like me the way I like him. I don't even think about him like that anymore. I'm focusing on my bonus, and that's all. My cat, Grady, ran away. We call her Grady because, well, you know, she is a gray cat. We could talk about how I miss her, though."

"Okay, everyone, this is how everything is going to work. We will meet every Wednesday after school. If you fail to make your appointments, you will be terminated from the game. Leaders included. If Tia barges out of or doesn't make her appointments, remove and replace her. It's that simple. If someone seeks to have one-on-one sessions with me, they must inform me of this before our next group meeting, without Angel."

I exited the room. The hallways seemed empty. I bumped into Mathew. "Where's Amy? I need to speak to her!" he said.

Man, he was pissed. Why? Amy approached us. He gripped her arm and pulled her into the next classroom. I peeked into the classroom. Amy was seated. Mathew, however, was standing and yelling at her. The veins from his head were popping out. He turned red instantly. I listened carefully by placing my ear closer to the door.

"Were you pregnant with my baby?" He eyed her. I could tell he wasn't falling for any of her bullshit.

I bit my nails.

"I don't know what the hell you're talking about," Amy said, laughing.

"Aw, okay. You don't!" He tilted his head to the side.

She smirked at him. "Not a fucking clue," she said with wide eyes.

"That's funny, because I read your fucking diary—every single fucking page! I just want you to say it to my face."

She laughed. "Say what, Mathew? You cheated on me, and I cheated on you the same night. I slept with your best friend, Andrew. I was afraid you would leave me. Instead of choosing my unborn child, I chose you, because I loved you so much more. I didn't want to risk having Andrew's baby, so I had an abortion."

"You're a disgusting fucking person, you know that? Because now you have nothing and no one. I can't believe you and all this bullshit you put me through. But I know everything, even the shit you didn't write down in your fucking journal."

She rose. "No, Mathew, how do you know?" She fell to her knees.

"I know because I knew the guy that did what he did to you, Amy. I felt bad for you. I wanted to help you. He told me everything I needed to know, and your written confessions said it all! How could you do this to me? You have changed my life. No one will want you after this, you hear me—no one?" he yelled.

"I'm sorry, Mathew! I didn't know. I couldn't tell you, because I didn't know how to tell you." she cried. "I didn't even know I had herpes."

He immediately choked her up against the wall. "What the fuck did you just say to me?"

She gasped for breath and then spoke again. "I'm so sorry," she said with his hands suffocating her.

I stormed into the classroom. I charged over to them and locked my hands around Mathew's arms. "Let her go, Mathew! Let her go! She's not worth it!" He was staring at her in hatred. He removed his hands and tossed her onto the floor. He left the room.

While raising her arm to me to help her up, she said, "Thank you so much for helping me. I thought I was—"

I raised my hand at her and left her on the floor. "Fuck you, Amy. I heard everything you said to him. I didn't do this for you. I did this for Mathew."

I walked out of the class and Marshall S. King University. I caught Tia at the bus stop as our bus was approaching. Amy joined us. Tia and I sat at the rear of the bus. As Amy was paying her fare, I told Tia everything I'd overheard. Amy walked up to Tia as if they were still best friends. Tia balled up her fists with a serious expression on her face. She punched Amy twice with a left and then a right hook, once in the nose, but the second punch left Amy's right eye swollen. Some passengers made room for Amy as she hit her head on one of the poles on the bus.

I was in complete shock. "Oh my god, what the hell, Tia?" I yelled while Amy's eye started twitching from Tia's powerful blows. However, Amy could have had a serious concussion when she hit her head on the pole.

Everyone on the bus watched the incident. I couldn't believe Tia attacked Amy. Tia grabbed Amy and pushed her off at the next bus stop. She fell into the grass. Amy held her nose, which quickly started to bleed. "Walk home, bitch!" Tia yelled, and the driver drove off.

CHAPTER 22

Erin

Girl-on-Girl Action

I was worrying about too many things—attending the counseling sessions, getting Jo to dump Jeremy or Jeremy to dump Jo, joining the guys' team, and receiving my bonus. I was fucked. There was no way I would have time to finish everything by the time it was due. This was too much for me to handle, so I let Tia join the guys for a week after all. Honestly, I didn't have the patience for it. As long as she was on the same team as Mathew, she was happy. In addition, so was Jacky.

We were all comfortably sitting on my white leather sofa. Jacky and Tia were both facing me. I had on my purple pajamas. I crossed my legs on the sofa. Jacky was as stunning as could be. She was wearing a white fitted blouse and white jeans. Her smoky eyes were black, and so were her leather pumps. Tia was in an orange tank top and jogging pants. Jacky blinked and blushed.

I broke the silence while scratching my head. "So what's been going on?"

Jacky said, "We were just about to ask you the same thing." They smiled.

"Nothing is going on. It's the weekend. I am enjoying my few days of freedom. That is all."

"That is not what we heard," Tia said. "Just cut the act. Jo already gave everything away. Well, almost everything. She has been talking about it all morning, calling our phones."

Jacky said, "How did you get her all wrapped up around your little finger?"

I exhaled and then smirked. "Nothing! I just bought her red roses and took her to brunch." I fidgeted.

Jacky mimicked me. "I just brought her red roses and took her to brunch." The level of her voice increased. "No, no, no, you didn't just buy her red roses and take her to brunch. You did so much more. I just know it."

I walked around to stretch my legs. I stopped by the glass door.

"Did you fuck her?" Tia snickered.

My subconscious was grinning with aggression on the inside. I turned to look at them. "No. I didn't fuck her. I ate her out," I said, embarrassed.

They laughed at me. Jacky asked again to be sure. "You ate her out, Erin?"

I said reluctantly, "Yes, Jacky. I went downtown! Are you both happy now?"

Tia roamed over to me and pulled me back onto the couch. "Not quite. We want to know the story."

I was in the middle. Jacky was to my left, and Tia was plastered to my right. *Okay,* my subconscious agreed. If they yearned for a story, I would enlighten them with one worth telling.

"Yesterday after we went out, we came back to my place. She and I had a little chat about her relationship with Jeremy. Before our dialogue, she was blushing and smiling while we talked in my room. She must really like me. Although I am as straight as the red carpet, I was flattered. We were on my bed. I was as close to her as I could get."

"'Is there anything I can do for you or get you out of the kitchen?' I placed my other hand on her thigh.

"She exhaled. 'I'm comfortable, and I have everything I want right here,' she said shyly. Aw, how cute was she?

"I held and comforted her. I couldn't keep my hands off her. I said, 'I feel like Jeremy takes you for granted. You deserve someone who will be there for you. A girl like you needs someone willing to pamper you with love and affection—not when you want it but when you really need it the most. Jeremy can't handle a woman like you, Jo. I can, though.'

"She and I paused. Then she asked, 'What are you saying, Erin?'

"I said, 'I'm saying I want to be with you. I'm a woman that knows what she wants. I don't like games. I don't. I am mature, trustworthy, and honest as hell. Break up with Jeremy, and come be with me like you want, like we both want.'

"She said, 'I don't know, Erin.' She stood. 'Andrew told me—'

"'I don't care what Andrew told you. It's the oldest trick in the book. He wants me for himself.' She lifted up, and I grabbed her hand gently. 'Andrew doesn't know how I feel about you. It hurts being around you, knowing you're not mine.' I held her hand. 'I understand if you don't like me like I like you. It's the only explanation for this.'

"Jo immediately stated cheerfully, 'No, I do like you—a lot.'

"I shook my head in sadness. 'It's okay. I completely understand. You don't have to lie to protect my feelings. I don't think we should hang out anymore.'

"She touched my shoulder. 'I never realized how much you liked me until now. You really do like me, don't you?'

"I paused. 'Yeah, I do,' I said. 'Let me show you how much.'

"I found myself caressing her shoulders, because I was sure it would relax her. She smirked and stared at me. I licked my lips while crossing my legs on the bed.

"'Do you trust me, Jo?' I asked, running my fingers through her hair. She flushed again. Oh boy, she had it bad.

"She licked her lips. 'Of course I trust you. You're the only person that has been there for me.'

"I collected her hand. 'Then lay back,' I said seductively. She listened. She smiled while lying down on my bed. I stood over her.

"'Are you comfortable? Are you relaxed?' Jo was lying down at the top center of my bed, with her head on every pillow I had. She seemed tense, and it was my obligation to make her feel at ease. I could tell by her body's position and her facial expressions.

"She said, 'Sure, I'm comfortable, Erin,' readjusting her body a little more to the left. I removed some of the pillows from underneath her head, leaving her with three pillows. From below, I yanked on her legs to pull her lower, toward the center of the bed. I stationed the pillows properly underneath her head again. She watched me. 'Shut your eyes,' I said.

"She snickered. 'But why?' she asked. I then gave her a strong look. 'Okay, okay, Erin. Whatever you say, I'll do.' She suddenly sealed her eyes. *Good girl,* my subconscious proclaimed.

"'Allow your mind to journey off into another room, another place, another world and universe.' I guided her smoothly. I rested my fingers on her shoulders. She giggled. 'Relax, Jo. Relax your mind and body. Allow them to become one. Accept your thoughts, and embrace your feelings by letting them roam free of you. Feel yourself having no concerns or troubles about anything or anyone. Inhale and exhale, Jo,' I said sweetly.

"She listened. She was now practicing meditation. Jo breathed in and out roughly.

"'Breathe in and out slowly but deeply to release whatever it is that is knocking you out of focus. Do it much, much deeper.'

"I inhaled and exhaled as a demonstration. She copied me. I then let her continue on her lonesome. She did as she was told. I immediately removed my sandals. I joined her on the bed. I was on top of her, unbuttoning her lavender blouse. I unhooked her white sheer bra, and she lifted up slightly to assist me. I opened up her top completely, exposing her huge nipples. I glided my finger across her top and bottom lip. She grinned. I groped her breasts and sucked on her nipples with precaution. I swirled the tip of my tongue against her beautifully sensitive nipples. I continually twirled my tongue back and forth in urgency. They were very hard, and she groaned with control. I went from kissing her neck to her breasts to the lower half of her stomach. I mainly sucked on the sides of her tummy because it felt amazing to me, especially since my body is sensitive to touch. She moaned, exhaling in pleasure.

"I lowered myself onto my knees. She lifted up as she opened her eyes. 'Relax, Jo. Lie back down, shut your eyes, and just breathe in and out. Leave everything else to me. I am going to give you the best head ever, so enjoy it while it lasts.'

"My hands traveled underneath her long violet skirt. I pulled her underwear down gently. I opened her legs. 'Are you comfortable?'

"She nodded. 'Yes, Erin. I am very, very comfortable,' she said, blowing out her breath.

"Again, I yanked her closer to me. I wrapped my arms around her thighs. My hands were underneath her behind. I squeezed her cheeks. My head was in between her thighs. She smelled fruitful and sweet, like sweet-pea lotion. I remember her giggling a lot. It was sort of cute in so many ways. Her skin was soft and completely smooth. She stared, leaning forward slightly. I tried to remember the last time a guy went down on me. I considered all the things I liked and hated. My hands were still resting on her plump behind. I spit on her clit because natural lubrication was the best. I extended the lips of her pussy so that I could lick her clitoris efficiently. I wiggled my tongue on the edge of her clit with minor, teasing strokes. It was certainly a great tease for me. She loved my nibbling. Again, I was spitting on and nibbling on her cunt. The clitoris is the most significant yet delicate part of a woman's pussy. It had to be licked and sucked with carefulness, so I sucked on the top of her pussy.

"She screamed and repeat, 'Erin, Erin, oh my, oh my, oh my!' She got louder and louder as she shouted in pleasure. I built up a mouthful of saliva for moisture and continued to separate the lips of her pussy. In my mind and in different directions, I was spelling out all of the letters alphabetically and drawing my full name on her clitoris.

"She scooted upward while attempting to shut her legs. With a tight grip on her ass, I pulled her back to her original position. I squeezed her cheeks as my tongue swirled against her clit more quickly. With my left hand, I placed my index and middle fingers inside her pussy. She rose again, slowly dropping onto my bed. She groaned. 'Aye, oh, oh, oh, ooh, oooh.'

"I stopped to look at her. 'Don't stop. Don't stop, dammit!' she shouted. I smiled at her wish. With both of her hands, she quickly buried my head into her thighs. My fingers again pierced her pussy with aggression. I continued to finger fuck her. She lifted up, scooting back from me.

I followed her. 'Where are you going, babe?'

"'Erin, Erin, Erin,' she pleaded softly. 'Whoa, oh, nah, oh my Erin!' she screamed, and with both hands, she tightly gripped the sheets. She opened her legs wider and wider. She tilted her head to the right, biting the sheets. In fact, her toes curled up.

"She was trembling while resting both of her hands on top of my head. It seemed she had been holding her breath for years. She was now quiet and stiff as a fucking board. I didn't touch her, and I didn't move. She continued to shake. I allowed her to embrace it. Seconds later, I was beside her. She was exhaling genuinely. She kissed me spontaneously. I was shocked by it. She grinned at me in satisfaction. She lifted in happiness. She attempted to open my legs. I was alarmed by it. 'What are you doing?'

"She paused for a moment. 'Now I want to satisfy you.'

"I touched her face. 'Aw, how cute, but no, I just wanted to make you feel special and good for a change, since Jeremy is not doing his job right.' She refastened her blouse and readjusted her long skirt.

"'You are right. He has taken me for granted. If I have to choose between you and him, I choose you, Erin. I'll tell him the truth—that I want to be with someone else.'

"I thought for a second. 'Jo, don't tell him that you're leaving him for another woman. It will embarrass him. And plus, I am not quite ready to come out of the closet just yet.'

"She grabbed my hand. 'Okay, I don't mind for now. Take all the time you need.'

"I grinned. 'Thanks, Jo. All this means so much to me,' I said, breathing out severely."

Jacky and Tia blinked in surprise.

"Erin, tell me you are joking!" Jacky yelled.

"Does my expression say that I am joking?"

Jacky and Tia looked at one another and then at me. "No, she is serious," Tia said.

"Jacky, you look so beautiful. Why are you all dressed up?" I leered.

"Well, if you must know, Professor Rodríguez is taking me on a real date tonight."

Tia said, twisting up her lips, "Are you sure about this? I don't think going out in public is a good idea."

Jacky rolled her eyes. "We are just having dinner at his place and some harmless, wild sex," she said in a bubbly tone of voice. I knew she was smiling on the inside.

They left my house. I locked the door behind them. After my Saturday-morning bath, Jo came over to my place. I welcomed her with a hot breakfast. I made homemade French toast, sausage, and eggs. However, by the time she arrived, I had already eaten my breakfast. I pulled out her chair for her.

"Everything smells so good, Erin. I'm starving." She was wearing brown cotton shorts and a golden crop top with brown and gold diamonds on it. "Thank you," she said brightly. She was happy. I sat beside her, watching her eat her breakfast. She sipped on her orange juice. I displayed a look of sadness after she finished eating. She wiped her mouth with a napkin. I lowered my eyes.

"What is troubling you, Erin?" She turned to face me.

"I don't wish to trouble you with this. You look so happy. The last thing I wish to do is upset you. I don't want to take away your smile, when it's the most fabulous thing in this room."

She rubbed my shoulders in consideration. I closed my eyes at the feeling of her touch. I exhaled. She said, "Please, please, share with me what is troubling you. I am your girlfriend now. We have to take care of each other."

I relaxed my right hand on hers. She stopped massaging my shoulders. "Don't join the team. It's not too late. We both can walk away from this club. What do you say?" I beamed into her eyes.

"You are speaking nonsense. Are you going to tell me or not?"

"An assignment was mailed to me for you this morning, Jo," I said.

She leered with excitement. "Oh my God, oh my God, how marvelous. Isn't it?" She chuckled. "Finally, Erin—finally. I thought this day would never come!" She stood. She was blissful. "What is it?" she shouted in happiness. "What do I have to do?"

I stopped for an instant. I lowered my gaze to the ground. "Jo, the manager rewarded you with this task because you're a freshman."

"Because I'm a freshman? So? I don't care. I want to know what it is." She waited impatiently. "Come on, Erin. Are you going to tell me or not?"

I blinked and paused momentarily. "You have to have sex with two guys."

She faced me urgently. "What did you just say to me? No, no, no! I won't do it. No way, Erin—no way. I can't, and I won't! Why do I have to have sex with two guys? Why?"

"This is a fucking sex club. What were you expecting—something easy and filled with righteousness? There's not one assignment that is not complicated, especially for your situation! The manager believes that it is unjust for you to become a member after a few months, when we have been members for three years."

She roamed up to me. "I'm not a slut. I will never, ever be a slut, Erin!" she shouted.

Never say never, I thought. "Again, you're a freshman seeking a membership in a junior sex club! All our members are juniors for a reason! What do you think I had to do to get where I am in this game? What do you think Tia did? Why should you receive better treatment than us? You need to prove your worth and loyalty to our club, to our manager, and to me, as your leader."

"You had sex with two guys to join the club your freshman year?" She seemed bewildered by my confession.

"Yep, as a matter of fact, I did. It was two seniors. And after, I felt so belittled by it and the many other assignments that emerged to test my strength and devotion to this club."

"Erin, I can't. I'm not like any of you. I was wrong about this, about you."

I laughed. "Maybe you were, or maybe you still misunderstand me and my purpose for you. You're unique, just like me. I would understand if you feel that doing this isn't worth the money or gifts." Because she was disappointed, she ended up leaving early. Suddenly, I was receiving a phone call from Jeremy.

"Hi," I said, collapsing onto my bed.

"Hi, Erin. How are you?" His voice was assuring.

"I'm peachy. How are you?" I said, blushing.

"Not so good." His voice was unsettling. I could hear the pain in his voice. I wanted to help.

"What's the matter, Jeremy? What happened? What's wrong with you?"

"Well, it seems that Josephine selected this sex club over me. She just broke up with me."

"I am so sorry this happened," I said. However, I wasn't. I was pleased to hear this information; it brightened my day. "Is there anything that I can do to make all this better?"

"I doubt it, Erin."

"The storms will severely sabotage your shiny days with her; the rain will proceed to linger and pour cruelly. It will damage the petals that are keeping your flowers intact, as well as the plants beneath her and the grass below her feet."

He finished. "And so your blue sky will adapt to the clouds, as the skies are gray. True love will heal your gardens and renew your sky. Your love, if real, will never die. Even in confusion and pain, your garden of love will continue to blossom for a thousand years."

I was impressed he remembered the poem. "Actually, it will blossom for a century's time, not for a thousand years. But, Jeremy, you remembered some of it. I'm impressed."

"Of course I remembered it. I'm a good listener, Erin. Plus, your poem was the best part of our conversation."

I smiled, flushing uncontrollably. I laughed at how adorable and meaningful this made me feel. "I could just hug you right now." Man, I would have loved to remove his shirt and jeans. In fact, everything had to go, and I meant everything. I added, "And, Jeremy, you should forget about her. She doesn't deserve a great guy like you. She has taken you for granted. Jo made important decisions, like joining our sex club. You deserve a girl that will listen and respect your wishes, especially when it could jeopardize everything you and her have or had."

"Yeah, you're probably right."

I ran my fingers against my chin. I stood. "Love—I mean real love—is something that happens when you least expect it." I stared out the window in my room. It was raining. Eventually, it started to pour. "If you and Jo are meant to be together, the universe will bring you together like magnets, because nothing in this world can stop destiny."

"You are right, Erin."

"Of course I'm right, and while the universe is reaching for your perfect soul mate, just try"—I paused—"to have fun for me."

"Bye, Erin." It seemed by the sound of his voice that he was leering over the phone.

"It's not 'Bye.' It's 'See you later,'" I said, and he chuckled. I hung up the phone.

CHAPTER 23

Dillon

My Sex Tape

I hated everything. How could I have been so stupid? Everything to me now seemed childish. How could I have let things get so out of control? I didn't blame the sex club, and I didn't blame Christian. I held myself personally responsible for the mess I'd created and the embarrassment I was facing. I felt empty. I wished I could have worn a black mask so that no one could see me, all of the pain, and my reaction to this nonsense. That morning, I decided to take the bus to school instead of driving my car. I hated Mondays, but I loved Fridays, which meant that I could take a three-day vacation from the bitches and assholes of Marshall S. King University. Sadly, it was Monday, the beginning of my humiliation. I wouldn't have been standing in the hallways if my mother and father hadn't made sure I got out of bed that morning. Whatever I was wearing, it didn't matter. I was perceived as the most popular slut in school, even above Tia. No one whispered her name into friends' ears anymore. Wearing sunglasses, a black fitted cap, a hoodie, and a pair of jegging pants was pointless, because they saw through my disguise.

I was in the center of the hall. An attractive African American guy bumped me from behind accidentally. I fell to the ground. "I'm so sorry about that!" He apologized sincerely. "Are you okay?" It seemed his voice was welcoming me to a place beyond this world.

I looked up at him. He pulled out his right hand. "It's okay," I said as he helped me up. He was about six feet tall. He kind of reminded me of Jeremy.

He extended his right hand once more. "My name is Derek. And your name is …?"

I shook his hand. I couldn't believe he didn't recognize me from my naked pictures on the internet. I was even more surprised that he wasn't teasing me about my sex tape. Maybe he didn't see or hear the truth about me yet. Although this was probably true, I had to face that Derek would eventually see my pictures and watch my sex tape. "Dillon—my name is Dillon." I said, attempting to smile.

"Well, Dillon, it's nice to meet you." He grinned. "I'm looking forward to another hallway encounter with you."

"Likewise, Derek," I said as I bolted down the hall.

Students passed me as they stared, whispering and laughing. "Nice video, slut," someone shouted behind me.

A guy stopped in front of me. He strolled up to me. "Hi, Dillon. How are you? I was wondering if you would like to make a sex video with my friend and me. I'm trying to boost my reputation, and I figured you are just what I need. Letting everyone know that I am also the best fuck around will do me good." He leered at me.

I ignored him and entered my classroom. I sat at the back of the class as other students walked into the classroom. Professor Reed was late for logic and critical thinking. I lowered myself in my seat, folded my arms, and laid my head on the desk. My ears caught the sounds of my classmates' whispers, but I refused to listen to them, to anything. I shut my eyes. I then heard moaning and groaning in the background.

With urgency, I opened up my eyes. I heard myself say, "Oh Christian, yes, yes, yes, that's the spot!" I looked up bewilderedly. The entire class was laughing and glaring at me. I fought to hold back my tears. I promised myself I would not let them see me cry. "Christian, you're a king in the bedroom!" the recording of me said, breathing out. I listened carefully.

The guy holding the cell phone mocked me. "Yes, Christian. You are so, so, so big. Jeez, come inside me, Christian—come inside me," he said in a feminine tone of voice, winking rapidly. He let the entire sex video play during class. I grabbed my bag from the floor and marched to the front of the classroom as tears dropped onto my cheeks. I wiped my eyes and nose.

"Look, the slut is crying. Oh Christian, oh, why did you leave me? I still love you, although you put my naked pictures on the Internet and showed everybody in Marshall S. King University our sex video. Take me back, baby—take me back!" someone teased, giggling. "I can forgive you, Christian. You are my rock and the heart beating beneath my chest!" He threw his books into the floor. "Oh, Chris, baby, do me right here on the floor or on Ms. Reed's big desk before she comes," he sung while he was rolling onto the floor.

I left the class and stormed out of Marshall S. King University. I ran all the way home. Nothing mattered to me. I wanted to go home because it was the only place where I felt safe from everything. I slammed the front door when I entered.

"Dillon, is that you? Dillon, if it is you, say something, please." My mother's voice traveled from the kitchen to the living room. I smelled meatloaf cooking in the oven and perhaps some kind of vegetables, such as sweet corn and green peas.

I couldn't stop crying. I made an effort not to sound upset. "Yes, it's me, and I'm absolutely fine." I roamed upstairs and into my bedroom, and I locked the door behind me. With tears roaming down my cheeks, ten minutes later, I pulled the covers over my head. My mother later knocked delicately on my door. I heard three gentle, polite taps. Did I want to open the door? No, yet I did. Before I wiped the evidence of my tears from my cheeks, my mother entered with a concerned expression. I continued to conceal myself with my brand-new bondi blue and burnt sienna covers.

"What is the matter with you, Dillon?" I could hear her voice getting closer to me. She was probably standing right over me.

"Nothing. I said that I am fine—just perfect," I murmured underneath the covers.

"If everything is fine, why are you home from school so early?"

I coughed hard. "Because I am not feeling well." I threw the covers from over my head. "Can we please just talk about this later? Please?"

Her hands were on her hips. "Sure, later then, and your friend is here."

I stood. My mom left as Andrew entered my room. He shut the door and leaned against the wall. "I heard about what happened, so I came to see if you are okay."

I got into bed and turned onto my right side while resting my head on my pillow. I didn't answer him.

"Dillon, I'm sorry about what they did to you."

"Are you now? All they did was smile and laugh at me. I feel nothing. No, you know what? I have never felt more stupid in my life. I want everything to go away." I wept. I could hear him taking off his shoes and pants. He crawled into bed with me and held me tightly. I felt his dick rubbing up against my ass.

"Do a favor for me?" he said.

I hoped it was nothing sexual. I cried, "And what's that?"

He wrapped his legs around mine. "Stop worrying about what happened, because it is all in the past. Look forward to the future. It's important that you know who you are in all of this."

"Andrew? This is the present, and I can't."

"I know," he whispered. "You are remarkable. You can do whatever you put your mind to. For now, all I am asking you to do is dream for me."

"I don't know how to dream anymore. I can't remember the last time I had a dream. My fears have caused me to have nightmares." I turned around to face him. I looked into his green eyes.

He looked serious. "Those fears and nightmares are in your control, but you have to be the one to face them, especially the ones at school. Close your eyes, knowing that you are not alone. I am here for you always."

I lowered myself onto his chest. I listened to the sound of his heart pounding. I shut my eyes and went to sleep. I couldn't remember the last time I had dreamed. Where had my dreams gone, and how could I get them back? What did I have to live for in the absence of my hopes and personal visions? Andrew was right about one thing—I was in control of my fears and nightmares. Andrew was sound asleep. I needed to forgive Christian, because it was the only way I could conquer the power he had over me. Forgiveness was the conclusion to my suffering. I also needed

Christian's forgiveness for everything I had done to him. I needed my strength back. I wasn't in denial about my prior foolishness.

Going to his place was the only way to be strong, so I went to his house. I was dressed in all black. It was a little chilly outside, so I brought my hoodie along with me. The streets were dark. It was somewhere around ten o'clock. I knelt on the ground while stationed near his house.

I sealed my eyes, bowed my head, and placed my hands together near my face in prayer. "Lord, I am a sinner who is lost and trying to find her way. Although I was born in sin, I am a child of God. Please guide me in the right direction. I know that I have been misguided. I know that I have been confused and weak without you in my life. I believe that you gave your son, Jesus Christ, to die for my sins. He is my Lord and Savior. I accept Jesus into my heart. And tomorrow I will be righteous and morally sound. I will treat others right. I trust that Jesus will bring me home. Amen."

I stood. I raised my left hand to signal the mechanics I'd paid to go to work. They pulled up and exited the car. "Which car is it?"

I pointed. "It's the fucked-up gray convertible."

They retrieved their equipment from their truck. "Which tires?" one of them asked. He watched me, and I watched Christian's house.

"All of them—every single last one of them." I grinned.

They boosted his shitty gray convertible. I walked toward the back of his home, searching for bricks. Seconds later, I found two huge white bricks alongside his house. The men removed all four tires. They threw two into the trunk of my car, and I let them keep the other two. They lowered his car back to the ground. After I paid the workers, they left. However, I stayed around for a bit. At a fair distance and with a sturdy hand, I threw the first brick through one of his side windows. The sound was forceful and strong. There was nothing better than the sound of his glass breaking. It sounded like numerous vases and glass plates being tossed against a wall at once.

What woman would disagree that busting the windows out of her ex-boyfriend's car wasn't enjoyable, especially when she knew he deserved it? With more hostility, I tossed the last brick through his back window. The sound of the brick hitting his car window was loud. Most of the pieces of glass landed inside his car. Someone turned on the lights in Christian's house. I laughed aloud in aggression as I ran to my car. I immediately drove off and kept laughing.

After what I had done, I felt better, happier, and more confident. I had forgiven Christian for the naked pictures and the sex video. As Andrew had informed me, it was all in the past. My mission was to look forward to the future, and that was why busting the windows out of his car had been acceptable—because it was now all a part of the past. Wanting to be the leader of the female sex club, going up against Erin's authority, and belonging to the team were all pieces of the past. I would no longer participate. On the other hand, quitting the club meant I had to do regular homework and classroom assignments. The school year was about to end. Finishing up the regular leftover assignments within the small amount of time given would have been undoable and stressful. I might have acted childishly in the past, but I wasn't going to let my past ruin my future.

CHAPTER 24

Jacky

A Brief Separation

Not only was the entire school teasing Dillon about what Christian had done to her, but also, they were mocking Amy for everything she had done. She was known as the bitch with herpes, yet it wouldn't necessarily have been fair to presume that Mathew had herpes because Amy did. I'd once heard that women were less likely to give men sexually transmitted diseases than men were to give them to women. Either way, I felt bad for Mathew. Nonetheless, having Tia around made everything all right for Mathew like Professor Rodríguez made things better for me. I wasn't in love with him, even though I knew I was feeling something unforgettable.

I had butterflies in my stomach. Did I like them? I didn't know. Some days, I could barely think straight. I smiled for no reason. My laughter existed for no reason. I was okay with it, although my head was filled with random thoughts of compassion. It wasn't just the sex I liked. Perhaps I liked Professor Rodríguez as well. There was something about him that I couldn't quite put my finger on. Maybe it was the many ways I fucked up his hair during our unique sex sessions, maybe it was how he still found my presence worthy and necessary when we finished climaxing, or maybe it was his tenderness. He was a great listener, and I loved him watching me eat. I also loved his confidence and how he always made the cutest moves on me without my permission. Boy, they were something.

He gave me butterflies—too many to count. It felt scary at times, but he was my perfect distraction from everything and everyone. I felt that emotional feelings for a guy were dangerous because they were a potential threat, especially if this guy did things to harm me. My thoughts of him were all over the place—in my living room, in my bedroom, and even in his classroom.

My liking for him was deep. Surprisingly, I was okay with that. With him, it was fine to dream and yearn for him the way I did. I allowed myself to carry on with this notion, and I felt unstoppable and fantastic. I wondered where he had been all my life. As an individual, nobody would ever complete me. I was already whole, and I didn't need to be convinced that I was special. Professor Rodríguez made me smile and laugh. Feeling a sense of completion was for people who were mentally unstable, engaging in unhealthy relationships, such as Amy. I also thought Dillon was nuts.

Dillon stopped me in the hallway. She was wearing a pathetic excuse for a disguise. I chuckled at her. "Dillon, why are you dressed like that? I don't know who you think will fall for that little appearance of yours, but I think you are blowing things way out of proportion!"

She pulled me into the washroom. She was quiet for a second. "I have something amazing to tell you!" She was excited for some reason.

Why did she have that stupid look on her face? Had I missed something? Apparently, I had, but what was it? I looked at her as I waited for a response.

"I forgave him." She smirked.

I gently grabbed her arms in confusion. "Dillon, you forgave him? Him who? Who did you forgive?" I believed I was making her feel uncomfortable, so I removed my hands from her arms. She turned and walked to the mirror. Why was she acting weird?

She beamed at herself. "I forgave Christian, Jacky. It was beautiful." She looked at me and then back at the mirror. "You should have been there with me to see!" She was at ease.

I approached her. "What? You forgave Christian for everything?" I said as she kept staring at her own reflection. What the hell was going on with her? "I'm in the dark, girl. At some point, you have to pull me to the light. What is going on with you?" I had begun to worry. This didn't sound good.

"I got down on my knees, like in a kneeling position, and I prayed for God to send me a sign. When it was all clear to me, I forgave him as I stole all four of his tires that night and busted the windows out his car, but it's ok because it's all in the past now, Jacky!" she screamed with excitement while smiling.

This bitch was crazy. I waited for her laughter, expecting to hear her say at any moment that she was kidding. She didn't. I grabbed her face. "Please, please tell me you're joking! You are just kidding, right? Right?" I said with false laughter. "Dillon, any day now!" My heart was pounding.

"Does this look like the face of a joker? It's fine because all is forgiven, ok?" She eventually laughed to fill the silence in the area. She had sold her soul to the devil, I thought.

Oh Dillon. I didn't know what to say or do. My mind kept envisioning the damage she'd caused to his car. I could imagine the look he'd had on his face when he saw the destruction. She had picked the worst time to break loose her insanity.

I scratched my head, pulling her out of the bathroom. "So when did"—I paused and looked up—"God supposedly gave you a signal to disfigure your ex's car?!" I paused with a clueless expression.

"Yesterday—I got the signal yesterday." She nodded.

I couldn't believe she would refer to this incident as a means of forgiveness. Was she even listening to herself speak? I didn't know how to handle it—or her, for that matter. We entered class late together. She finished telling me the entire story. Maybe this was her way of coping with everything. I hoped that her break from reality would not last long. But why was any of this my problem? If Christian hadn't been such an asshole, his car would have still been in good shape. My morning started off nicely until I went to visit Professor Rodríguez after school.

When my last class of the day was over, I went to his classroom to see him because I was horny. Plus, I knew he would get my mind off of things. He was wearing a crisp gray suit, a baby-blue tie, and suede shoes. I was about to undress. "I really need a quickie. My hormones are rising off the charts," I said sexily.

He packed his things into his suitcase. "Just stop, Jacky. I have had enough of this. Just leave, and this stops now. Do you understand me?

I'm not playing any more games with you." He didn't even look at me during our conversation.

"I don't understand. Why are you doing this?" I tried touching him. He pulled away from me. "What happened? Everything was fine a minute ago!" I cried. "What did I do wrong?"

"This was supposed to be sex, and that's all."

I took another step closer. "We have kept caution in mind of this. It's just sex between us. I promise you, okay?"

Then his eyes were on me. "You don't get it, do you?" He collected his suitcase. "There are days when it's a challenge to not think of you the way I do, but I do every day because I like you so much, way more than I wanted and am supposed to, Jacky. I'm angry at myself for allowing this to happen. It's my fault."

Holy crap, I thought. I confessed, "I think of you, too. More than I would have ever anticipated, Professor Rodríguez. Everything you're feeling, I'm feeling, too. You are not alone." I smiled with assurance.

He shook his head. "We can't be together. We can't be in a relationship. I can't continue to do this with you, to you, and to myself."

"Do what? Huh? What are you doing to me? What? I'm not good enough for you? I'm not pretty, smart, or special enough for you to realize how much I care for you? Because I do! I know we weren't expecting this to happen, but it did."

We were close to the point of kissing. He looked at me, and I looked at him. "I care for you too, and I know in my heart you are good, pretty, and special enough for me." He rubbed my face with care and caution. "All I have to do is see your face. You make me laugh and smile when my bad days seem unredeemable, yet good things never last forever, Jacky."

He removed his left hand from my right cheek. I retrieved his hand. "You are leaving, aren't you?"

He glanced at the floor and was silent momentarily. "Yes." He nodded.

My eyes became watery. "Will I ever see you again?"

"No," he admitted.

I released him. Who would have thought my day would have ended like this? I understood why he was doing this. We were living in a dream. Now it was time to transition back into reality. With all my heart, I did care for him. How could I cry or be upset with him? He was a smart man. I was glad to have met him. Thinking about the moments we'd shared made me smile. I shut my eyes when he kissed my forehead.

He whispered into my ear. "Come with me if me leaving you is too painful."

What? What did he say? I couldn't believe it. My butterflies came back. I wanted him to stay there with me. But I knew we would get caught eventually. It was just a matter of time.

I opened my eyes. His last words had stunned me. "Come with you? You just said you couldn't be with me."

He glared down at me. "And I regretted it the moment I said it. I can't be with you like this, in disguises, sneaking around everywhere. Come with me so that we won't have to."

"I can't. I have school. What will I do?" I started thinking about the game and my position. I couldn't leave my only little sister behind. She needed me, and my mother needed me as well.

He opened his door. Before turning off the lights, he pulled out his hand. "Let me worry about that, Jacky. Plus, school is about to end in a few weeks. Do you trust me?"

I snickered. "Yes, with all my heart." I grabbed his hand before he turned off the lights. I shut the door.

CHAPTER 25

Tia

I Will Fuck You If …

Counseling was absolute bullshit. I didn't need to go to any fucking therapy sessions. Counseling was for insane people—like Amy and Erin. I was shocked that Dillon wasn't attending their group discussions on Wednesdays along with them. I wasn't going, and that was the end of it. Nothing could convince me otherwise, not even Mathew. If I was going to be removed from my station in the sex club, it was a chance I was willing to take. Nothing was scarier than sitting in that hot seat with that therapist in the room, questioning me about my devastating past. Hearing another person telling me I had a sex problem was the last thing I needed. I wasn't about to go for treatment, because liking sex wasn't unhealthy—it was normal. Everyone liked sex. I was obviously in control of my actions. Just because I was having sex with a complete stranger and Christian around the same time didn't mean I needed help. All of a sudden, I started to regret having sex with Christian, because he was grumpy the last time I went to see him.

He kept complaining about someone disfiguring his car. I hadn't come to hear about his problems or about his shitty, busted-out windows. So someone had damaged his car—so what? He mistook me for a girl who gave a shit about him. "Someone busted my windows; someone stole all of my tires" was the only thing he had on his mind. *What a little bitch.* He wasn't man enough to hold my interest. His behavior was a complete turn-off to me. Instead of listening to him finish complaining about his psychobabble bullshit, I left him to visit Mathew. When I reached his neighborhood, I saw a little girl who was about seven or eight years old going door-to-door to sell chocolate candy bars and cookies. An older girl was with her. She could have been fifteen years old. As I watched them sell candy and cookies, I knocked on Mathew's door. He answered the door in all-white boxers. His leer welcomed me. I entered. He began brushing his teeth in the bathroom. I waited for him to finish.

"Did the doctor call with your results yet?" I asked.

He shook his head while he brushed his teeth. I hoped everything was okay with him. I hoped he would be happy and not allow Amy to further upset him or me. Mathew and I would make some changes—just not the changes he was dreaming of.

"So are you going to your counseling session tomorrow?" he said, arching an eyebrow. A part of me felt he had too much faith in me changing.

I folded my arms and twisted my lips up at him. "No, I'm not going. I thought I already told you."

He was drying his hair off with a huge dark red towel. "Therapy is something you need, Tia," he announced sincerely. "I don't know why you don't understand that." He entered the bathroom again.

I finally decided to take a seat on his couch. "I don't need therapy. I told you I'm fine. Can we just drop this?"

He joined me in the living room. He smirked. "Oh, most certainly not," he answered in a cocky tone. "I'm sure there is something I can do to change your mind."

I twisted my lips up and rolled my eyes at the thought of it. "No, you won't hear about me being there. I promise you that," I said. He sat down next to me, smiling like a prince in a fairy-tale movie. "Why are you smiling? I said I'm not going," I told him.

He laughed with confidence. "You are going. You just don't know it yet, because I am about to make you a deal you can't refuse." He grinned charmingly. What a bona fide and confident bastard he was being.

I faced him. "I don't think that is going to happen, but I would love to hear your attempts," I said.

"My attempts?" He chuckled. "Tia, sometimes you forget how well I know you, from your laughter and tears to your very dark, dark desires," he said slowly. "You know, the kind that include me."

I stood over him. "I'm still listening. I'm all ears, Mathew." He rose and started slowly pacing around the room. I exhaled, watching him. It had been awhile since I'd seen him walking back and forth like that. What he had to say must've been good. I became interested in listening to him, especially because revealing his proposal to me was difficult from the beginning.

I rolled my eyes. "Would you just relax? Calm down. Nothing is that serious. Just tell me." He joined me on the couch again with a critical expression. Man, he looked good shirtless.

"If you receive treatment every week and show actual mental improvement, every time, we will do something sexual."

I was shocked. His blue eyes pierced my soul. I stared back at him in happiness. For the moment, he had me speechless. Finally, I said, "I, um, uh … It is an agreement." I shook his hand.

"Oh, and another thing—you can't have sex with anyone starting today."

I froze. *I can't? Well, why not?* I stood. "No, no deal. Only if you don't sleep around with other girls, and then we have an understanding."

He grabbed his black-and-white T-shirt off the arm of the couch. He smiled. "Okay."

"Okay? That's all you're going to say—okay?" I asked, twisting up my lips.

"Yeah, okay. I agree," he said cheerfully.

I couldn't believe this. What was today's date? I knew I would never forget that day. Were Mathew and I finally going to fuck? The idea of fucking only him would be a reluctant adjustment. I wasn't sure that I could just have sex with one person. Had I ever? Mathew needed to understand that I really, really needed sex. Without it, I felt something similar to Amy, but I didn't need love or to feel special to anyone. Sex made me feel alive and well, like breathing. During and after sex, I felt striking and superior. I was strong because sex gave me strength and power. Sex was my identity, and there was nothing wrong with it.

It was Wednesday. I wore my hair curled and pinned up. I had on my new Maybelline makeup I'd gotten from Macy's downtown. To make my eyes pop, I'd created a classic and dramatic smoky-eye effect with black liquid eyeliner and eye shadow. I was wearing a short, cropped sky-blue tank top; a short black suspender skirt with detachable straps; a felt hat; and patent-leather open-toed pumps. I was chatting with Jeremy.

"I know you are on my team for the moment, but you have to give me something to work with—something that shows you are trustworthy," he said.

"Okay, fair enough, Jeremy." I locked my hand on his collar, pulling him closer to me. I muttered, "I'm the reason why Jacky is missing in action. I wrote Professor Rodríguez an anonymous letter threatening to expose him and Jacky."

He laughed, briefly in shock. "That was you? Damn, girl," he said, impressed.

"Of course it was me," I said.

He took a few steps. "How did you know she would leave with him?"

I looked at him stupidly. "Because I know Jacky like I know the rest of them."

"Okay. We're good for now, but I want some more information, especially on Erin," he whispered into my ear.

"Actually, I do have something I can share with you about her."

He was intrigued with my willingness to cooperate with him. He smiled. "I'm listening," he said.

"She cares for you and about Jo. Erin respects Jo. She knows this popularity group isn't a place for someone as special and meaningful as Jo. Because they have become such good friends and because you care deeply for her, Erin has your best interest at heart. Jo is not on the team, and she never will be, but Erin has created a false assignment to reveal to Jo how she is making a huge mistake with wanting to become a member."

"I never realized how sweet Erin is." He smirked again. I rolled my eyes, and then I laughed at his statement about Erin. What the fuck was he talking about? Erin was everything but fucking sweet.

"Yeah, whatever. Make sure that when she asks you to help her with this specific assignment, you act surprised. The assignment requires sex between you and Erin while Jo watches."

He laughed freely. His laughter was filled with liveliness. "That's going to be awkward."

I rested my hands on his broad shoulders. I was in front of him. He started to understand what I was doing. He stared at me with confused eyes. I moved closer to mutter something sexual into his ear. "When you stop liking Erin, you can come fuck me anytime." I licked the bottom of his earlobe.

He wiped his ear with his hand. "You are something else. What about Mathew?"

"You just fucked up my moment. Fucking is fucking. It doesn't have to mean anything."

"That's disgusting. Just let me know if you discover any new and useful info, okay?"

"Aye, aye, sir. I will see what I can do." I winked my left eye.

The day went by quickly. Minutes before our group session, Amy and I had our own little private chat.

"Well, well, well, look at what we have here!" I wandered up to her, looking her up and down. I stared. "Wow, your eye is recovering quite well. It looks much better," I said with a grin.

I could tell she wanted to punch me, so I tempted her. It was highly entertaining.

"You did all this bullshit to me for Mathew, a damn boy?" she said.

"No. I did it because you hurt someone I care about. You didn't care about him. For you, he was just a rebound guy. Now, that guy you met at that Mexican grill—he really messed you up. I ran into him a few days ago, and now I can see what all the fuss was about. His name is David, right?"

"Great. That's just what I need—a slut getting everything I ever wanted! Stay away from him. Okay? It's just that simple," she said defensively. She made a fist.

"Okay, I will, little birdy. See, in my case, David isn't a guy you want as a boyfriend. He's a guy that you sleep with and have fun with. That's all he wanted from you, Amy. That's all he wanted from me. The difference between you and me is that I comprehend and accept it. We did fuck, and we had a lot of fun together—you know, the same kind of fun he denied you of. He still calls and texts me. What about you? Does he call you?" I asked her.

She shook her head. "You're lying! I'm not listening to you." She stormed off. I followed behind her.

"I'm not lying. He couldn't wait to sleep with me after he discovered I was your best friend. I only slept with him because I knew that you spent every minute of your day thinking of him. I bet you still do. I bet you even care about what he thinks."

She stopped walking. We were in front of our appointed classroom. She blinked with irritation and sadness. She had an empty expression on her face. I said, "We did talk about you. You know what he said? He said that you were thirsty and pathetic. Wait—what was my favorite part? 'She begged me please to not walk out of her life. She was like a desperate girlfriend texting and calling me from different numbers, and we were not even dating. I wanted to fuck her, but I have no intention of doing so. Although Amy is sexy, she's just too desperate for my taste.'"

She avoided me and entered the room. I laughed at her. Erin and our female counselor were already waiting. Amy sat in the center. Her eyes became watery instantly.

"If you don't mind, I would like to go first," she said politely. Ms. Wright agreed with her by nodding and smiling at her. "My name is Amy Robinson, but some days, I don't know who I am. Having someone in my life makes me feel lively." Tears poured down her face. "One day, I went to a bar with a fake ID. This guy walked up to me all cool-like. It was Mathew." She cried more intensely. "I'm not much of a drinker, but he bought me drink after drink. He told me he could tell I was special and that I had a good heart but I was just misunderstood by most people—not him, though," she said, fidgeting as she mildly swung her arms. "I finished my drink, and he, um, offered me a ride home. I agreed." I stared at her, watching her tears flow as her confession progressed. "I didn't know. I didn't know," she said again and again. "I just wanted to get this guy out of my head—David. I slept with Mathew. I wanted to stop thinking about David. I knew Mathew could help me forget. I was just using him—for sex, for security, and for company."

Ms. Wright said, "Is there anything else you would like to share, Amy?"

Amy breathed out. "It has been five months, and I still think about David. I still can't get him out of my head!" she confessed. "He won't leave—or the memories of us I use to keep him alive."

Ms. Wright asked, "How, Amy? How do you keep him alive in your head?" She crossed her legs.

"I know that I will never see or hear from him again, so my mind is insanely creative enough to revisit our past involvements. In my head, I form these hypothetical sexual situations that could have occurred when I had the opportunity. Like I go back and change the fact that I, um, didn't let him fuck me. Occasionally, every day, my head changes the past, although the probability of that is zero! I get high on these memories and erotic, made-up fantasies of David and I having sex! Because in reality, it would never, never happen, and I know it, so I often dream of it!" As she ended her last thoughts, she sat next to Ms. Wright.

"Thank you, Amy. I know that was very difficult for you. The first step is accepting or acknowledging you have a problem."

I raised my hand.

"Yes, Tia? Do you have something you would like to add to the conversation?" Ms. Wright asked.

"Yes, as a matter of fact, I do." I decided to remain seated during my moment of confession. "I am an addict of sex."

Ms. Wright gripped her pen and notepad. She looked at me comfortably. "And how so, Tia?"

"I have three sex partners. One, who I just met, goes by the name Dave. I knew and know nothing about him. Yet none of that mattered when I saw him shirtless. He's fit. I was mesmerized by the beauty marks he has on his neck and, of course, other unforeseen places. I mean a real nice body and face—you know, the kind women appreciate and unhealthy college women obsess about. I don't know him, and he doesn't want to know me, but there are girls who would kill to have him. You see, guys like that just want to have fun with us—isn't that right, Amy?" I said, touching my neck in pleasure to piss Amy off. She rolled her eyes at me.

Ms. Wright looked at me and then at Amy. "I'm sorry, Tia. Are you two both referring to the same person? Is Dave David?"

Amy stared at me in hatred. "I hate you!" she said as she stood. The veins in her neck popped out from all of her yelling.

I laughed and looked up. I clapped with joy. "Then my purpose for living is complete."

She stormed out of the classroom.

"What is this confrontation with Amy and you about?" Ms. Wright asked.

"There is no confrontation. It is just a misunderstanding among us. It will pass, or maybe it won't."

"This sex addict in you has numbed you like ice, Tia," Erin said wisely.

"I believe Erin is correct, Tia. Having three sex partners is nothing to be proud of. The best thing for you to do is go to rehab so that you can begin recovery, Tia," Ms. Wright said.

I didn't know which was worse—being a sex addict or being a love addict. A love addict was exactly what Amy was. I never forgot what Erin told me: "The sex addict in you has numbed you like ice." I was numb. This was their perception of me. They presumed I was buried by sex. I wasn't. I was just looking forward to my treat from Mathew for attending these boring group sessions. I went back to his place. I ran hot water in the bathtub. I felt filthy, and I wanted to freshen up for him. I took a nice long bubble bath, soaking away my sins from that morning. I left the tub, drying my hair with my hands. I entered his room. He was sound asleep. I opened his top dresser drawer, which was filled with his T-shirts. I grabbed one and slid it over my head. I ushered myself over to him. I ran my fingers through his long, curly hair. I rested my body next to his. I liked messing with him when he was asleep, but he eventually woke up.

"How did the session go?" he said, wiping his face with his hands. He looked into my eyes.

I inhaled and exhaled before I responded. I said cheerfully, "It went great, Mathew. It really did. Ms. Wright, my counselor, said that I did a really good job today! I told her that I was a sex addict. She said that many people are in denial about their problems."

He leaned up, interested in what I was saying. "Really?" he said, as he was happy to gain some more information.

"Yeah, really. She announced that the first step to recovery is admitting your addiction or whatever the case may be."

"Good, and I'm proud of you, Tia." He touched my right cheek. I flushed.

"Thanks, Matt. I really feel positive about this now! I am really glad I went. This will be good for me, and not just because you're offering me sexual favors to do it. This can change my life for the both of us."

He kissed my forehead lightly. "Hearing this has made me happy, and did you just call me Matt?"

I responded quickly, "No. No, I did not!" I joked.

He laughed. "Yeah, Tia. Yeah, you did."

I randomly grabbed his ears and locked my hands on them firmly. We were quiet. I kissed him. We breathed in deeply. He massaged his tongue with mine. He put his hands on my behind. My hands, on the other hand, were roaming down into his shorts. He was aroused enormously. I groaned at the start of something good. I leaned closer to him, pressing my nipples against his chest. He kept kissing me again and again.

I was about to get on top of him. He stopped me. "Tia, let's just slow down—it's late. I have a job interview in the morning."

I was shocked. "What?" I said in confusion. How more irritable could he get? "You said if I went to my group sessions and made progress, we would have sex."

"No, I didn't. I said if you receive treatment every week and show actual mental improvement, every time, we will do something sexual. Kissing is sexual. The bigger the improvement, the better the sexual reward."

Isn't that a bitch? Fuck me. I felt stupid. He was dumb to think that holding out on me would stop me from having sex with someone else. It just meant that I wasn't having sex with him. However, I didn't know whose situation was worse—mine or Amy's. Could a person be an addict of both love and sex?

The Love and Sex Addict

Out of the many faces in the world, the expressions of love
and sex addicts fade within the crowds around us.
One is staring back at you directly.
Just look at yourself.
But remember, I want you to take a glimpse at that kid of mine—her.
You know, my daughter, who is staring at the love
addict in the mirror, and my youngest, who is blowing
kisses at the oldest sex addict she knows.
Stand up against that face of bitterness and
rudeness, and spit on that sex addict.
Love and sex addictions do not shape a woman, nor
are they the face or outline of her identity.
Don't let addiction to sex or love further manipulate or
damage the many components that define you as you.
Don't be frightened of what you don't understand.
You are in love with love and in love with sex, but the
sex and love don't love you, because your sex has failed
to please you, and you never actually loved another.
Jeez, my poor daughter.
I almost didn't recognize you with brown hair, that full
coverage of makeup, a short black crop top, high heels,
and that tiny black-and-white zebra-print skirt.
As a love addict, you won't accept the nerd with glasses,
the best friend of eight years, the white guy with the
briefcase, or the guy who would jump in front of a
bullet for you to make sure you got home safely.
You deny the gentlemen who do nothing but care.
You turn your back on love and true lovers.
Yet you care for the dishonorable men who show
you nothing but carelessness and suffering.
They are quick to deny you affection,
Although you despise being neglected.

The rejection is intolerable for you, so they run for their
freedom, and you chase their inability to commit to you.
But abandonment is a magnet that is your reluctant attraction.
You go back to being my youngest when
you're the oldest daughter I have.
Rejection is your obsession.
The more they neglect you, the more you're aroused
by the fantasy of separation and refusal.
But note that the departure is not your stimulation.
It heightens your desire for them.
You've been alone so much that your mind is preoccupied
by the notion of love in music, books, and movies.
It's not the love you seek, although it's driven
you to the edge of obsession.
It's the fantasy of love that gets you high like cokeheads
snorting cocaine, potheads smoking marijuana, or
shopaholics going on an endless shopping spree.
The love and sex addictions will be deeply regretted.
You know, my daughter, who is staring at the love
addict in the mirror, and my youngest, who is blowing
kisses at the oldest sex addict she knows.
Stand up against that face of bitterness and rudeness, and
spit on that sex addict, because you can do better.
These fictional thoughts of being loved or
touched intimately elevate you.
You're not challenged by love, just by their doings.
It's the concept of the fantasy.
It's your reason for dreaming of such notions.
Your fantasy is a workaholic's workload, the drinks in the
possession of an alcoholic, or the dope for a dope fiend.
Oh jeez, my poor daughter.
It's the fantasy of love that gets you high like cokeheads
snorting cocaine, potheads smoking marijuana, or
shopaholics going on an endless shopping spree.
The love and sex addictions are deeply regretted

She is my daughter, being watched by the love addict in the mirror.
But what about my youngest, who has kissed
the oldest sex addict she knows?
You have a face of bitterness, and it's rude;
take a bite out of that sex addict,
Because she has become you—all of you.
I don't know how you can get over your desire to be touched,
But say no to all of those sexual urges.
The consequences for your sexuality will forever be your burden.
The pornographic sites won't help, so bury them, my dear darling.
The masturbating won't ease your inner depression,
so stop all the private touching.
Sexual fantasies won't bring you any closer to love.
Having sex won't cause you to feel less emotional pain.
I doubt you feel good afterward.
You have organized your world around sex;
Therefore, you are a true sex addict.
You're like an alcoholic drinking, a man with a cigarette, a crackhead
with a pipe, or a porn addict watching his or her pornos.
Don't get addicted to the medication; drop the
blue, yellow, green, and purple pills.
You get high already enough as it is.
Just remember all of your nasty fantasies.
Sex now transports you to the white clouds.
How rude, because I know she is you.
But spit, kick, and bite that sex addict.
Tell her that sex isn't worth missing out on opportunities.
Tell her she will be denied affection because she is an addict of sex.
As your mother, I have protected you against the world.
I kept you away from the strangers who sought to hurt you,
the drugs wanting to control you, and corrupt friends.
Mama forgot one thing: to save you from your biggest threat—you.

CHAPTER 26

Erin

Happy Birthday

I went shopping with the money my mother had given me for my birthday. It had been awhile since I had gone shopping at the mall with my friends. I started my birthday off by jogging around my nice neighborhood. Running felt amazing. For a minute, I'd forgotten how good it felt to me. It was the best form of stress alleviation and freedom. While jogging, I listened to music to occupy my mind. Twenty-five minutes later, when I was back at home, like a goldfish, I drank some water from the sink in the bathroom as the hot water filled the tub. I took a quick bath and got dressed. I straightened my hair. I didn't feel like wearing any makeup. I decided to go natural for my birthday. I was wearing a sexy long-sleeved and backless golden dress and some glittery nude floral-and-lace platform boots. It was finally my twentieth birthday. My doorbell rang. Tia and Jo had arrived. Tia looked upset and held a brown plastic bag in her hand. Jo was grinning ear to ear with lilies in her right hand.

Tia wandered past me immediately. "Here's your shoes back." She threw them onto my sofa. She made herself comfortable and shrunk onto the sofa. "We didn't even have sex! Man, this is starting to frustrate me to death. I just want to have sex! That's all!" she shouted.

Jo entered, and I shut the door. "You look naturally stunning, and I love those laced platform boots on you," she said, flirting. "Here—these are for you." She handed the flowers to me innocently. I hated lilies, but I went along with it.

I forced a smile. "Aw, you are so sweet. They're so lovely," I lied. "Thank you." She kissed me lightly on the lips. I entered the kitchen to place them in a vase with water. I situated the vase at the center of the table.

Tia followed and whispered, "So did she agree to the assignment or what?"

I lowered my eyes. "No. I'm still working on it. She's a tough one to break," I muttered into her ear.

"When she does do it, I will come back for it, but I want you to take credit for the train-the-girl assignment. I don't want Mathew to think anything of it. What guys are helping you to finish your task?" she said.

Certainly not Mathew—that was for sure. "Maybe James and Michael," I said.

"This is evil even for you, Erin."

I shrugged. "What? They both slept with this hot girl from school because of me a few days ago. They owe me, okay? Yeah, this is evil, but the way you have been treating Amy is bullshit too and you know it," I teased.

Jo decided to join the conversation. "Yeah, I heard about the cruelty. How can you just sleep around with her man like that?" she asked.

"Easy there. Just bring Jeremy over here, and I will show you with no hesitation," Tia said, toying with Jo. Jo murmured something under her breath. Apparently, she still had feelings for him. Then Tia added, "And off the record, he wasn't her man. They weren't even dating anymore." Tia snorted while laughing.

I changed the subject. "On the record, has anyone seen or heard from Jacky? I haven't talked to her for days."

Jo answered, throwing up her hands, "No, I haven't seen her either."

Tia opened up my refrigerator. "Wait," she said energetically. "I just saw her yesterday. She's fine, still attending and everything. She told me not to trouble her, so I didn't. She's just super busy."

"Erin?" Jo paused. "I'm ready," she said nervously.

"Jo," I said, walking over to her, "ready for what?"

She looked down. "I'm ready to do my first assignment."

I was surprised to hear this. I glanced over at Tia. She was beaming at me behind Jo's back. I discreetly signaled Tia to call Michael and James to come over. We were on the same accord. Tia left the kitchen.

"I don't know what to say, Jo." I rubbed her tense shoulders gently. "You're my girlfriend now. I care for you deeply," I said. "This is not something I want you to do! It will bring me to tears to allow two guys anywhere near you in that way! I know this was what you were assigned, but I can't and won't let you go through with this, not like I did!"

She rested her hands on mine. I stopped massaging her shoulders. She faced me and glared into my gray eyes. "Erin, do you trust and believe in me?"

Of course not, my subconscious replied. "Sure, I believe and trust in you. You are unique just like me, like all of us, yet I don't want you to do something you will regret."

She hugged me tightly. "I already agreed. Please, please don't fight me on this."

My subconscious laughed as I wrapped my arms around her firmly. I breathed out, pretending to be upset about it. "Okay, okay," I said. "If this will make you happy, then I'll make the arrangements today."

She was stunned at the urgency of the assignment. "Today?" she asked loudly, shaking. "Today is your birthday! I was hoping we would go out somewhere special!"

"Yes, today. This assignment has been delayed for a while, Jo. If you want to be a certified member, the completion of the task must take place today. And don't worry about us going out for my birthday." I smiled shyly. "Just make sure you make it up to me another day, okay?"

She hugged me again, excited. This was too easy for me. She kissed me passionately on my lips. "Okay! I will. I promise!"

"Go upstairs to my room, and get ready. I don't want them spanking or biting you, okay?"

She wandered upstairs, shouting, "Okay! You got it, babe!"

I walked back into the living room with Tia. I removed my boots because my feet were hurting. Tia gave me credit where it was due. "Nice, Erin." She sat beside me. "So how has your assignment been going?" She laid her head on the arm of the sofa.

"Actually, I have some news for you."

"I'm listening. I heard from a reliable source that he has something planned for the leader of our group. He knows you are our leader, just so you know. I don't know when it will happen, though."

"I don't care that he knows. I want him to. Just as a piece of enlightenment for you, it doesn't take a rocket scientist to get Mathew to sleep with you either."

She rose up desperately and startled me. "How and what do I do? Oh, guide me, for I am lost in all things boring."

The doorbell rang. I stood to answer it. "Change your attitude and behavior, and wear some real clothes for a change, or tempt him to the point that he finds sex with you irresistible. Look for a moment of vulnerability."

I welcomed Michael and James into my house. Boy, they smelled and looked good. "Happy twentieth birthday, Erin," James said, kissing my right cheek. He then approached Tia to accompany her.

"Yeah, beautiful, I almost forgot—happy birthday," Michael said. "You're finally twenty years old." I smiled eagerly as he added, "So where is she?" He looked around.

"She is upstairs, getting ready," I said as we headed over to Tia and James.

James asked, "Getting ready?"

Tia responded, "Yeah, getting ready—you know, dolling herself up. She's nervous as shit. She can't handle the two of you like I can."

James looked down at Tia with lustful eyes while he grinned.

The doorbell rang again. I ran to open the door. I wondered who it was. Tia ushered Michael and James up to Jo.

"Hi, Jeremy," I said, hugging him passionately.

He muttered into my ear while he held me, "Happy birthday, and you look nice in that dress of yours." His breath smelled minty. I proceeded to hold him. I didn't want to let him go. I collected his hand and guided him into one of the guest rooms downstairs.

He chuckled. "Where are we going?"

I opened the door, and we entered the room. I shut the door. I wrapped my hand around his arm. We sat down on the bed and faced each other. "I have something that I want to get off my chest. If I don't, I will probably go crazy," I said.

He grabbed my hand. "I'm all yours."

All mine. I liked that statement. I repeated it to myself. "I like you a lot, and I want to be with you."

We smiled at one another. "I like you too, and I also want you to be my girl."

"There's just one problem," we said at the same time. I looked away in shock.

"You go first," he said like a gentleman.

"I can't be with you like this, under these circumstances. I hate this sex club. I do," I said.

"You do?" he asked.

I stood. "Yes, I do. I'm not this person, and I don't need to be in this sex club. All I need is that one special person for me. I haven't been with anyone. I won't, because I want you—all of you. Just you." I started pacing. "I'd choose you over this club any day. It's just …" I stopped to look at him. "It's just that I …" I froze up.

"You can't leave the team yet, can you?"

I stared at him, and he stared at me. "Yeah, I can't leave—not right now at least."

He stood. "I can't leave either, but I'm just as ashamed of this as you are." He rested his hands on my hips, slowly moving to my stomach and breasts.

"I think about you every day and how Jo did you. I told myself that if I ever got the chance, I would never hurt you. Do you understand me?" I said.

"Yes, I understood." He grabbed my behind, and then he kissed me.

I pulled away to speak. "There is something I want you to do with me," I said.

"Wow, okay. You don't want me to butt fuck you with my fingers, tie you up and whip you, or anything like that—do you?"

While laughing, I said, "Oh no, nothing like that."

He wiped his face. "Thank God, because that is really disgusting," he said with relief as I placed my hands around his neck. "I forgot, Erin, but I actually have a surprise for you. It's back at my house."

"Wow, oh my God, really?" I said loudly and energetically. I smiled.

"It's a surprise. I'm not telling you," he said in a serious tone of voice.

I pleaded sweetly and kissed him on his cheek. "Aw, please? I really want to know. I'm so anxious right now," I said, slightly hopping up and down.

He stared and said, "So anxious, yeah, and so was Ginuwine. But relax—you still have to wait. I'll be back in a couple of hours." He kissed me slowly and softly. "Okay?"

I exhaled loudly. "Okay, okay," I agreed unwillingly. I leaned in to kiss him again.

"Your lips are as soft and juicy as they look," he said. His hands were on my hips again. We stopped and smiled at each other.

"Well, thank you. I think," I said as I blinked twice.

He let go of my hand. "I will be back," he said.

"I know you will," I said confidently.

I rushed down the stairs to search for my phone. I couldn't find it. I entered the kitchen and looked on the table, and there it was.

Just as I picked it up, it started to ring. The call was from a number I didn't recognize.

"Hey," I said as I marched back into the living room.

"I heard it's your birthday today, gorgeous," a male voice said with confidence.

I was lying down on my sofa. "It is. Who is this?" I asked, listening carefully.

"In due time. But first, I have five birthday wishes for you," he said pleasantly.

Is that so? I readjusted my body by turning onto my right side. "Five birthday wishes for me? Are you sure? What are they?" I smiled in suspense.

"The first wish is that I hope you remain as beautiful as you are today, a beauty that will last a lifetime, which includes your inner and outer beauty."

"Really? Okay, I like where this is going." I smiled.

"For the second wish, I wish you great success in wherever your sweet dreams take you, because I want to let you know that it is okay to dream."

I laughed with pleasure because I found his words pleasing. "Wow, oh my God. Stop it. No. Keep going. You are starting to make me blush," I confessed with a grin.

"I wish you happiness in all of your choices, because a stunning girl such as yourself deserves to smile and be happy."

I leaned up slightly. "Who are you? I have to know. I'm curious."

He chuckled. "In a minute, but don't interrupt, Erin. I'm finishing up." I could hear him smiling on the phone. I could tell he was enjoying his moment of anonymity. He said, "For your fourth wish, I don't wish that you find love but that the guy of your dreams finds you, because we all need and want love. However, not all of us are ready for it."

I shut my eyes, listening to the sound of his voice. "What about my last wish?"

"Your final wish will remain a mystery until—"

My doorbell rang once more. I approached the door, waiting for him to finish. "Until what?" I said as I turned the knob to open the door.

It was Andrew, and I would have never guessed. "Until you open the door for me, Rose." He smiled as I lowered the phone away from my ear. "Your last wish is that before you leave this world, there will be something to remember you by. Smart women like you always find ways to be remembered by the world," he said flirtatiously. He put his cell phone into his front pocket. "What do you have planned for today?"

"Nothing, lover boy. I've never been much of a planner. I just do and live in the moments I create."

He looked at me, and his glance traveled to a place within me that was unreachable. I hid my face to smile in secret. He lifted my face with his finger. "Well, as a creator of memorable moments, this will be a creation worth remembering."

I leaned in closer to him. "What will be a creation worth remembering?"

He raised his hand out to me. "It's a surprise. Come with me and find out."

I ran over by my couch to get my shoes. I then grasped his hand. I went with him because I was curious what he was referring to. I loved surprises. I shut the door, but I left it unlocked for Jeremy. Andrew took me to a fancy seafood restaurant downtown.

We sat in a nice booth with a beautiful view. The tablecloth was red and long. Andrew was talking to our male waiter. It seemed to me that they knew one another. I waited patiently for him to return. He eventually sat down with me. I crossed my arms on the table comfortably.

"It's nice of you to join me. For a second, I thought you'd forgotten about me," I teased, making crazy faces at him. He laughed.

He replied in a silly voice while arching his eyebrows, "Never, Rose. So let me in on a secret about you—something no one knows."

I scratched the back of my neck. "Nothing sexual has ever surprised or embarrassed me before."

He stared into my eyes. "Really?"

"You are questioning my secret right now, and yes, really. What? You don't believe me?"

He drank some of his water. "In all honesty, no, I don't." He briskly extended his hands.

"And in all honesty, I don't give a shit what you think," I said bluntly, smiling at him.

He quickly observed the menu. "I'm going to have the lobster and smothered potatoes and a Coke. What about you?"

I glanced at the menu and the pictures. "Whoa, that looks good. I will have the grilled fish and chips and a salad."

He quickly ran his fingers through his straight blond hair. "Okay, are you ready for your surprise?"

I gave him a confused look. I looked around the restaurant. "I thought taking me to this fancy seafood restaurant was my surprise."

"Well, Rose, you thought wrong." He paused for a minute. "Again." He signaled to our waiter. "Do you mind ordering for us? I shouldn't talk with a full mouth."

A full mouth? His mouth wasn't full, but I said, "I guess it's not a problem."

He immediately went underneath the table. I opened my mouth as my eyebrows rose. I blinked nervously. My face revealed how shocked I was at what he was about to do to me.

"What the hell are you doing?" I asked, but he didn't respond. *Oh boy, oh boy, oh boy.* He opened my legs. "Stop it," I whispered. "Are you trying to embarrass me?" I shooed him away with my right hand. I almost kicked him a few times. He struck me back with minor taps. I scooted as far back as I could in resistance. He yanked on my legs powerfully to pull me closer to him every time. The waiter eventually reached the table. He opened my legs wider. It was embarrassing, knowing what he was about to do.

"Are you ready to order, miss?" The waiter smiled delicately at me.

"No, not exactly," I said shyly.

"See, your boyfriend told me that you were ready to order, so I'm not leaving until you do."

"Well, then it sounds like I am ready to order."

"And what would you like?" He grabbed his small notebook and pen and listened.

Andrew yanked on my legs. The waiter stared at me bewilderedly, since he saw me being pulled underneath the table. "Are you okay?"

Andrew pulled my underwear completely off as I looked back at the waiter. I nodded, making silly faces as Andrew removed my underwear. "Yes, yes, I am fine. Just getting comfortable." I exhaled seductively. "I would like the—oh my!"

I gripped the tablecloth firmly with both hands. Andrew began slurping my clit and licking all over my pussy. "Oh, damn those cramps! It's that time of the month, you know. I'm sorry. Please excuse me."

The waiter rolled his eyes in disgust, as if I had given him too much personal info. "I'm just waiting for your order."

I slowly rolled my eyes to the feeling of Andrew's tongue on my clit. *Whoa, that's the spot.* I rocked my hips a little to the left. *Right there, oh, right there, Andrew,* I thought as I briefly forgot to respond to my waiter. He knew how to swirl his tongue on all the right places with just enough spit. I gritted my teeth. I was breathing heavily. I scooted over the menu with my now balled-up fist. I stared at it. I again gripped the tablecloth.

The waiter became impatient. "Miss, what would you like? I don't have all day."

I leaned forward to hide my face from him. I said, "I would like the grilled thing—" I stopped, trembling, clenching my teeth once more. I shut my eyes. "With the thing on the side with the wet stuff."

"I'm sorry. I don't know what you mean by 'the thing on the side with the wet stuff.'"

I covered my face. I tried groaning discreetly, but the waiter might have heard me. I made a fist once more as Andrew swirled around his tongue. I could hear him spitting and sucking on my pussy. I muttered, "Holy cow, holy fucking cow." I groaned. "You're absolutely right."

I placed my hands over my mouth. The waiter watched me in irritation. I flushed even more. I moaned. My body trembled. The waiter walked away rudely. Andrew jerked my legs forward another time and wrapped his arms around my upper thighs. He suddenly squeezed and rubbed my cheeks together as he ate me out. I folded my arms on the table. I relaxed my head on my arms while leaning forward. I respired overpoweringly. "Oh, oh, oh," I moaned, covering my mouth. Shit, he could eat pussy well.

The waiter turned. My hand traveled underneath the table and landed on Andrew's head to stop him. For about a second, he did stop. "I'll have the grilled fish and chips and a salad and another glass of water," I said urgently.

"Okay, and for your partner?" he said, writing down my order.

Andrew spanked my hand like a child. We were fighting underneath the table. I yelled in pleasure. "He will have the … the … the …" He proceeded to lick and suck on my pussy. I could hear him gulping and spitting. I wiggled my hips, opening my legs wider and wider. I remembered being so wet.

The waiter's eyes lowered. He was glancing down at the table. Now he knew what was going on. My eyes revealed the truth to him. He laughed at me. "Oh, oh, miss. I see, I see. I'll be back with your order."

I screamed into my hands as I hid my face from customers. They stared, and I was embarrassed, of course. Some stopped to watch my inappropriate act, attempting to guess what was going on with me. Andrew inconspicuously came out from underneath the table. He sat in his seat across from me. He wiped around his mouth. "Happy twentieth birthday," he whispered. I looked underneath the table for my underwear. I didn't see them. "Are you looking for this?" he asked. He showed me my balled-up panties in his hand. I stood and snatched my underwear from out of his hand. He smiled. "Come on. You know you liked it."

I stared at him aggressively. "Don't you ever pull this shit with me again! Do you understand me?"

I rushed out of the restaurant with my underwear balled up in my hands. He came rushing after me. I stopped by his parents' car. "I'm sorry, okay? I didn't mean to upset you. I wanted to make you feel good." He collected my hand. "I promise I will never, ever do something like that again," he said, and he kissed the left side of my cheek smoothly.

I exhaled. "Okay, okay. I forgive you." And I did forgive him, yet I also, in some way, provoked him.

CHAPTER 27

Angelina

All about a Book

I'd trapped myself in my room. I was sitting down at my desk, staring at my computer screen. I pressed the start button and searched for my saved documents and notes. I opened the files. I scrolled down to the section titled "Amy." I was writing a story about our lives. Her section gave me writer's block. I had written as much as I could about her, but her story was incomplete. Now that I thought about it, I didn't know Amy that well. I had many questions to ask her. What had happened between her and the Colombian guy? Had they ever had sex? How had she gotten herpes? How long had she had it? How had the condition changed her life? Had she learned anything from it? Did she plan to join Sex Addicts Anonymous? I made a note of all of these unanswered questions.

Someone tapped on my door. "I'm busy right now. Come back later!" I said, typing my final unanswered question.

"It's Amy. Your mother let me in."

I immediately stopped typing. I turned and looked at my door. I unlocked the door and opened it. Amy entered and shut the door behind her. I stood there, waiting to know what the hell she was doing in my house. "What do you want, Amy? I'm busy," I said aggressively.

She peeked over by my laptop. "Yeah, I see that."

I moved in front of my computer. "What the hell do you want?"

"I just need someone to talk to. Everybody hates me." She frowned.

You got that right. "You think? Your flat ass shouldn't have ever done what you did! You're a stupid, selfish, ugly, and dirty person! I bet the walls of your vagina are like hallways. I can throw tennis balls straight through it."

She twisted her lips up at me. "Take that back!" she yelled, frowning more painfully. "My ass is not flat! You, you, you come gargler. You glory-hole slut!" After a minute, she and I laughed together. Then it was quiet, and we just relaxed and grinned in peace.

"What section are you working on now?" she asked as she sat on my bed.

I scrolled back to my original spot. "Yours—and I have nothing to work with."

She stood up. "What do you mean you have nothing to work with? I have already given you a fair amount of material." She was standing over me, reading what I had written about her.

"Hmm, huh," she said. She arched an eyebrow. "I like it. It's interesting, but you are leaving out the best parts of my story."

I stood in amazement. "I don't know about the best parts of your life, Amy. That's what you're all about—lies and secrets."

"Ask me anything, and I will answer it honestly."

I reached into the drawer of my desk and grabbed my voice recorder. I then pulled my chair closer to my bed. I sat down, and she sat on my bed again. I pushed the red start button.

"Did you and that Colombian guy ever have sex?" I said.

She looked at me in confusion. "You mean David? Why is everyone asking about this lame guy and me? No, I never had sex with him, because I wasn't supposed to take it that far. My job was to drive him away, just like I did Mathew. David was so judgmental of me, but who could blame him?" She giggled. "He thinks I am fucking crazy, boy, which I am. He convinced himself he knew everything about me. I really, really hated that."

I could see that. "But didn't he? You wanted to sleep with him, though. But instead, you drove him away—why?" I had many questions for her. It wasn't my mission to overwhelm her with them, yet it was unavoidable.

"There were moments when I wanted him in every which way, but I knew him well enough not to spread my thighs for the liking of him. Sex with him would have been irrelevant. One phone call with 'Where are you?' attitude secured the fact that I would never see him again.

Saying please don't walk out of my life took away his urge of wanting me." She had a blank and disturbing look on her face.

"Did he keep in contact with you after you begged him to?"

"Of course he did. I made him feel like he was obligated to do so. He would text me reluctantly sometimes, although he wanted nothing to do with me." She laughed at the thought of it. "I found it funny the way he was playing it cool with me, waiting for me to make one more mistake."

"When did he give up on you?"

She said wickedly, "When I wanted him to. Being an obsessive and desperate girlfriend, in my definition, helped him to finally avoid me altogether. Calling and texting Dave from different numbers set everything in motion."

"I don't understand why you would do something like that. What's your malfunction, girl? Do you even regret any of it?" She was one of the crazies I needed to avoid having in my life.

"I regret not waiting until he begged for it. I don't regret walking into that restaurant, although some people, I believe, are not meant to meet one another. Some people should never shake hands, have sex, or share a kiss. No more questions about this guy, okay? I don't want to hear another word. He's not special. I am. I'm sick to my stomach of talking about him, but hearing you ask questions about him now depresses me. Ask about me, since my experience with David was for your book." She coughed. "A silly, silly story."

"For my book?" I grinned. "Much of everything was for my book, Amy. I need to hear you say it to me."

"In reality, people want their lives to be perfect, a happy ending, especially women. They want nothing to go wrong. But everything that creates stress and depression in novels and movies grabs their attention, because perfection bores them. They want to see and hear about lies, secrets, cheating, stealing, betrayal, and all the drama they can handle, because it's remarkable."

"What about Mathew?" I attempted to alter the direction of the dialogue.

"What about him, Angel?" she asked irritably as I changed the direction of the conversation.

"Do you have herpes, or did you lie about it like you did everything else?"

She clapped as her eyes watched me. Her giggles were unbearable to listen to.

"What's so funny? I don't think herpes is a laughing matter," I said, displeased.

She said sarcastically, "Of course not, ma'am." She chuckled. "I don't have herpes, Angel." She laughed maliciously. "I don't take pills or get breakouts. Since I am being honest with you, yes, I did care about Mathew. I really did, but I care about myself more than anyone. Unquestionably, when people read this book, they are going to love my section. From readers' standpoints, they are going to want to know who I am before they determine whether they hate me or not. It won't matter, because it is all fictional bullshit anyhow. It's a character, like the kind that is assigned to actors and actresses."

I stared at her as if she were suffering from numerous forms of mental illnesses. "Why would you want people to think you have it? What could you get out of it? And to be totally honest, I think you are crazy!" I backed away from her as I gave her my opinion.

"Don't you worry your pretty little hairs about it. Yeah, but of course, you do. I can't blame you for that accusation. Yet as irrational as you believe I am, why are you still listening to me?" She paused as I searched for an answer. "Because my story is intriguing, so your ears can't help but suck the information up like a sponge."

"What was real?" I said. "What is true? Because I know everything wasn't fiction."

"You are right. Everything wasn't made up in my diary. I did have an abortion, but I didn't know who the father was. It was between Andrew and Mathew. I just wasn't ready for twins. I'm not a believer in love or love at first sight. I did search for it, and everyone already knows that when you go searching for things, you never find what you're looking for. Someone once told me that I will never find love but that someday he would."

"Do you believe that was true, Amy?" Maybe it was, but maybe it wasn't.

"It must have been, because I remember feeling the pain of every word, so yes, I thought it was true. It brought me to tears," she announced with moist eyes. She cleared her face with a wipe of her hand across her eyes.

"Amy, what's the scariest thing that ever happened to you?" I asked, and she glared at the carpet. She had begun fidgeting, and she was hesitant for some reason. I repeated the questioned. "What was the scariest thing that ever happened to you, Amy?"

"I heard the question the first time. Before I met Mathew, there was Eric. He was the true definition of tall, dark, and handsome. I thought he was so sweet and cute. The day I met him, I was at a party. I went alone.

"A guy with broad shoulders came up to me as I stood. The sound of his voice lingered in my ears. It was staggering to me. 'Hi. My name's Eric. What's yours?' he whispered into my ear over the loud hip-hop music.

"'Amy—my name is Amy.' I gazed into his eyes.

"'Amy,' he repeated. I loved the way he said my name. I leered unintentionally as I shook his hand. He smoothly pulled me closer to him to kiss me slowly. His kiss was so unexpected. I told myself to stop him, but he was an excellent kisser. I gave into it really quick, like a one-second decision.

"He was so confident. It was what I found most attractive about him. He held my hand and walked me into the living room by the couch. 'I'm getting a drink. Do you want anything?' he asked.

"'I'm not much of a drinker,' I said.

"He kissed my lips gently and said, 'I will bring you a little something just in case you change your mind, okay?'

"I was in a corner. 'Okay. That's fine with me.' I nodded. When he left, I started dancing to the words in the song. I only liked dancing in private. In my mind, I imagined I was by myself.

"He muttered into my ear to grab my attention. He tilted his head to the right. 'You dance beautifully, Amy.' He could compliment me all night.

"I turned to face him with raised eyebrows. I blushed. "Well, thank you." I continued to move my hips in a sexual motion.

"He bit his bottom lip fragilely. With confidence, he looked me up and down. 'This is for you.' He handed me my drink as I danced in front of him. He drunk it all, every last drop. I stopped dancing to drink. I drank as much as I could bear. After the alcohol traveled down my throat, I started coughing straightaway.

"'Are you okay?' he shouted over the loud music. I nodded and continued to drink the rest of it. He watched me as he cheered with the other people around us. I cheered along with them. The rest of the night was a blur to me. I couldn't remember much of anything. I do recall dancing and drinking, and I also couldn't forget Eric's hands being all over me at the party. The last thing I noticed was Eric carrying me to his car, putting me in the backseat, and shutting the door. The next morning, I woke up in a motel room. While I stood, I searched for my clothing. My underwear was on the floor, and my red bra was on top of the nightstand."

"He drugged and raped you. How do I know you are not lying about this?" I said.

"Because I wouldn't have made a night up like that— a night that I can't even remember. That took away my humanity and everything that made me happy and innocent. I may be a liar—and a great one at that—but I was drugged and raped. That is something no woman should ever lie about," she said emotionally. Her eyes showed fear. It seemed that the memory of her terrifying experience still horrified her in ways I'd never been exposed to before.

"Did you report him?"

She shook her head as she wiped her nose.

"Why not? Why didn't you turn him in?"

Amy stiffened as she screamed at me. "Because I just didn't, okay? I didn't. I couldn't, not alone!" She lowered her voice. "That's actually where I was—or how I felt—until I met Mathew. I felt so empty and alone." She froze up. Her facial expression was as cold as ice. I hugged her while holding her hand.

"Thank you for sharing your story with me. I think that maybe you should still report his ass."

She rose and walked to my window. "What is your purpose for writing this book?" She stared outside the window.

"It was the same reason why we joined the sex club—for the money and gifts. Let's be real. Not all of us are going to win that money in the end. I'm just thinking of this book as plan B for me. If you help me get the story of every member involved, you are welcome to your fair share when the book gets published."

"I'll help you for a fair share, like you said."

"Okay," I agreed.

"Who is your next section on?" She faced me.

"It's Dillon."

My heart went out to Dillon. Amy and I decided to go to her place, but her mother said she was ill. It wasn't the kind of sickness that gave people headaches, dry coughs, or sore throats. According to her mother, she had been lying in her bed for days, not eating or speaking to anyone. I didn't understand what was going on with her. I watched her, trying to communicate with her, but there was no response. I took her diary without her mother noticing. Her mother wouldn't let us stay long. She said she was taking Dillon to the hospital or to see a professional therapist. During my ride back home, I read a few pages of her diary.

> Dear Diary,
>
> I have been crying for hours, days—a week. When was the last time I laughed in goodness? I can't recall, because it has been awhile. Happiness is not me. Some days, I find smiling impossible. I remember it being as easy as tying my shoes. Perhaps smiling and laughing were dreams. They are things that steer clear of me. I don't understand the pain I have been feeling recently. I am consumed in so much sadness. I have lost all interest in the things I found most pleasurable. I tried washing and wiping away my unexplainable mood, but it left the

> shower with me. I tried leaving it at home, yet it follows me everywhere I go. Something in me has changed—the way I think, behave, and, most importantly, feel. I am in a position in life where I have allowed my emotional and physical problems to cause me a great deal of grief. I have the blues, and the blues are stuck on me like my skin. Something or someone, put me out of my suffering, for I am too weak to inflict pain upon myself. I just want this sadness to end.
>
> All I see are death and darkness around me. I just want to be free of this world, of sadness, of stress, and of these mental chains on my shoulders, for they weigh so much. Trouble with obsessing about my past failures was the one true chain weighing me down. Freedom is happiness, and only death will bring me bliss, because life is one big tear. Death would be the only escape from my downheartedness. I am crying and screaming in silence for help. Where did all of these frequent thoughts of death come from? When did it first begin? Because it was the day I truly died on the inside.

Dillon had to be suffering from a mood disorder or something. It was the only explanation for her feelings of sadness. It had to be some type of clinical depression. It wasn't something Dillon would easily snap out of. I wanted her to. There were a variety of different levels of depressive disorders. The main ones I had knowledge of were double and major depression. Who knew what form of depression troubled her? Reading her diary made me visit her often.

According to her mother, she was at the second stage, or level, of depression and might require long-term treatment. She was placed on medication and attended weekly therapy as well. I was there for her, and so was Amy. All I could do was provide her with my wisdom and words of courage.

CHAPTER 28

Tia

A Proper Closure

Erin and I had gotten rather close since Jacky's sudden absence. I visited Erin to collect my bonus assignment she'd awarded Jo to complete for me. Perhaps having Jo around and manipulating her was unethically sound, but it was convenient and beneficial for us. I'd never had sex with two guys before, and surprisingly to everyone and myself, I wasn't about to start, especially not with the dicks of James and Christian. I was planning to stay away from any dick that didn't belong to Mathew. I was still masturbating to porn continuously, even though it wasn't enough for my sexual cravings. I had numerous foreplay essentials, such as an original blue-and-white Magic Wand massager, a gemstone body wand, and Euphoria, a G-spot attachment. The Euphoria always gave me pleasure, possibly because it stimulated my G-spot and clit simultaneously. I had to give the credit to the dual-petal silicone, since that essential aided me in reaching my destination. For this reason, it was my favorite, along with my new dildos, the purple Wild Rabbit and my black-and-silver clit simulator.

I loved to watch two people fuck on a huge television. Hearing them moaning and groaning gave me a tingling sensation. I would think about two attractive people fucking, since watching a guy's penis frequently going in and out of a girl's pussy made me orgasmic, especially the aggressive I'm-tossing-you-up-against-the-wall kind of fucking. Sex like that seemed always to have a guy pinning a bitch's hands up together while saying all sorts of nasty and dirty shit into her ear. I got wet thinking about it. The excitement and tension traveled from my brain to my pussy. Even the thought of Jo doing my train-the-girl assignment aroused me, and I often visualized them both being inside her, ramming her tight little ass into a corner.

I felt bad about how I was treating Amy. Sure, I hated her passionately. I hated everyone. Nonetheless, Amy and I made a personal arrangement that encouraged proper closure between us. My guts were warning me that Amy was highly untrustworthy, but I believed that some things she'd revealed to me were true. For some reason, I didn't think she had herpes—no fucking way. Amy was too intelligent for that. Amy was different from me. If people thought she was a lesbian, murderer, slut, or sex object on the Internet, she didn't give two shits whatsoever. What people thought was what people thought. I was convinced she was the reason I wasn't getting closer to Mathew. There was a possibility that Mathew wasn't sleeping with me because he believed he had herpes. He was probably being protective of me. That was my theory, and Amy had something I wanted. *What does she want?* I wondered. Was it still David—to have, touch, and kiss him? He was my only chance of getting the truth out of Amy, and I was her hope of getting David. I'd never actually met David or slept with him. I'd only read about him in her diary. I had Angel text me his number from her phone one day. I called him.

"Hi," I said optimistically.

"Um, hello," he said uncertainly. "Yeah, who is this?" he asked. I could see what Amy found attractive about his voice. It was deep but in an appealing fashion.

"My name is Tia. I am a friend of a friend," I announced sweetly.

He laughed seductively. His laughter was breathtaking. "And who are you referring to as a friend I know?"

I could listen to him speak while fucking me. I was curious how he looked in person. "You know an Amy, right?"

He hesitated as he laughed a bit. "Yeah, but we are not friends." His tone changed. It had been frisky and optimistic and was now serious. It seemed Amy was a serious topic of discussion for him.

"Well, I'm sorry. I thought you and her were friends."

"No, your friend is crazy. I mean obsessive and desperate-girlfriend kind of crazy."

Yup, that was my Amy. *Desperate* and *obsessive* were the best words to describe her. I giggled. "Well, I've heard so much about you. I saw your pictures on Facebook. I think you look like all kinds of fun, and that is exactly what I'm all about." I paused. "Having fun."

He chuckled at my unexpected statement. He said, "Really? Well, I think it's unfair that you know how I look but I haven't seen you before. Do you have a Facebook?"

"Sadly, no, but I can send you pictures of me, if you want."

"Ok send me a few," he said quickly.

"I'm sending them to you now."

He was quiet for a moment. "You're cuter than Amy. Did you know that?"

I blushed. I couldn't believe it. He really believed I was cuter than little old Amy? "So when will I see you in person so that we can start having some fun together?"

"What are you doing tomorrow?" he asked. To me, that was a stupid question.

"I'm going to be busy hanging out with you tomorrow." I could hear him grinning on the phone. I smiled.

He said, "I guess I will see you tomorrow. Text me your address, and I will let you know what time I will be on my way to get you."

"Okay. It sounds good to me." I hung up, thinking he was hot.

I was at the home of my foster parents and their two children. I rarely came home to them. I was probably just another liability to them. They stayed out of my way, and I stayed out of theirs. It was Monday. My foster parents were likely gone, and their children were probably in school. I knocked on the door in case they were there. No one answered. It was great. I searched for the key under the brown mat. I let myself in. The house looked as if no one had been there for days. It was sparkling clean.

An hour later, Amy was ringing my bell. I welcomed her in as I shut the door behind her. She stayed by the door.

"You can make yourself comfortable."

She shook her head. "There is no need for acting friendly, because I have something you need or want."

"Look, Amy. We both have been through a lot, okay? I know we haven't been real friends for a long time. And I do have your best interest at heart."

She rolled her eyes. I hoped she would roll those motherfuckers to the back of her head and get them stuck there. "My best interest at heart?" she said. "You don't give a fuck about my best interest."

"You know what? You are absolutely right. I don't give a fuck about what you are interested in. I just want to know the truth about your condition. Do you have something, Amy?"

"Of course I do. I have a lot of things. What kind of fucked-up question is that?"

"I don't think you're being honest with me."

"I don't care what you think, Tia. If you forgot, I don't care what anybody thinks." I grabbed her hand to pull her into the living room. She dragged her foot. "Let me go!" She leaned in the opposite direction.

"Relax, Amy. I have a little surprise for you. That's all."

She finally stopped resisting. "A surprise?" She faced me. "A surprise for me—from Tia to Amy?" She couldn't believe it, so she grinned innocently.

"Yes, from me to you," I said as I rushed her into the living room.

She blinked. "Is that," she said with a tied tongue, "you know?" She watched him.

"Yes, it's David on my foster parents' couch." I mocked her, as it was a dream for her to see him. I figured she knew she would never have seen him again if it weren't for what I had done for her. It was all thanks to me. I patted myself on the back. "Good job, Tia," I murmured with a grin.

She sat next to him eagerly. She suddenly slid her fingers through his hair. "It's just as soft as I remembered." Amy stared at him curiously. "What's wrong with him? What did you do to him?" she asked, looking at me directly. She touched his face. She liked it. I didn't know why she was fronting.

"You know that's how you wanted him—vulnerable and too weak to fight you off?" I said. "I see why you find him irresistible, Amy. I do.

He's special, but I think you only find him attractive because you're a love addict."

She stood. "A love addict? What's a love addict?"

I marched closer to them. "A love addict is a person, man or woman, who is only attracted to people that neglect or avoid having a relationship with him or her." I pointed at Dave while I stared at her. "David will never give you the affection you want. That's why you chase him. You can't bear to accept that you finally can't have something you want. He took away that power you have as a woman. You want the power and the control back because you're no longer the gatekeeper of sex when it comes to you and him. It drives you insane that David now has to say yes to it for it to happen, but you know the answer will always be no."

"For your information, women like me will always get what they want," she said, "with date-rape and enhancement drugs or no drugs, with them conscious or unconscious. It's just what I like, and seeing him lying on your couch just for me because of you is evidence of that." Her tone of voice was cocky. "I am not a love addict, okay? Don't call me that. How would you like it if I called you a sex addict?"

"Okay, fair enough. Now there is something I need from you." I crossed my arms. She removed her white blouse. Damn, couldn't she at least wait until I was gone?

"I don't have anything, okay? You already knew this, though. I only said it because I didn't want to see you with Mathew. I knew I could get back at you through him. He would never put you at risk like that if he thought he had gotten it from me. I had always known in my heart you guys would more than likely end up together."

"I will be back in an hour or two," I said. She didn't respond. I guess she did get everything she wanted. She kissed him on the lips. I left.

Keeping my promise, I came back later. Amy didn't say much after. We left him in his car, and she drove away with him.

The next day, I went to school. As usual, I didn't want to go. While walking past Mathew, I whispered to him, "If you want a blow job in the boys' bathroom, you better follow me." I waited. "I promise to take good care of you."

In reaction, he said deeply and seductively, "Whoa."

I winked at him, and then I fiercely proceeded to head to the washroom with Mathew right behind me. I could feel him leering behind me, with his blue eyes on my ass. *You got him,* my subconscious cheered, celebrating too early. My heart began pounding because this wasn't like going downtown on Michael, Christian, or James, though I'd never gave James oral before. There was a massive difference since it was Mathew. I cared and wanted him to like it. He caught up with me, stretching out his hand to grip mine. My heart was now in my stomach.

Sex was a fun and natural activity for me. I'd never longed for anyone as much as I longed for Mathew. We were in the last stall together. He leaned against the door with one leg slightly extended to support some of his weight. I looked up at him while he crossed his arms. I got on my knees, and he watched me. The tile floor was firm and cold, but it was nothing I couldn't manage. I gripped his belt. I stared up at him with innocent eyes.

He grabbed me and lifted me. "What are you doing?" I asked, shocked at him still refusing me.

He blurted out, "I'm sorry. I can't." He fastened his belt, unlocked the stall door, and stormed out. He then paced back and forth.

I exited the stall and shut the door. "It is because you think you may have herpes?"

He ran his fingers through his hair as he exhaled. "No, my doctor called me this morning with my test results. I don't have it."

I smiled in relief. "Thank God." I beamed at him. He didn't seem happy about it. "That's a good thing, right?" I said.

He nodded. "It is." He winked delectably.

I moved a little closer to him. "Then what's the problem, Matt?"

Some guys aggressively entered the bathroom. They were screaming while smiling. "No, man! She wants all of us—same time, man. Same time!" They quieted down once they saw a woman present.

Another one entered behind them. "Tag-team that little bit—" He stopped his sentence to begin a new one. "Hi. Um, how are you doing, beautiful?" he asked me. He paused and stared at me, waiting for a response. The guys pretended to go about their business, but they seemed to be more interested in why I was in the boys' bathroom, as if they hadn't seen me there before.

I stared back rudely and faced them. "Why in the hell are you staring at me?" I got louder. "What the hell is wrong with you guys? Haven't you ever seen a woman in a men's washroom before?"

His friend beside him chuckled strongly. One laughed at my distastefulness. "No!" He then hesitated. "Well, yeah, but just you." He winked and looked me up and down. Mathew gripped my arm and pulled me into an abandoned classroom.

"Hey, wait! What's your fucking problem? Let go, Mathew—now!" He listened. I rubbed my arm. I glanced at him in confusion. He paid attention to the ground. I said, "What's going on with you? Why are you acting like this?"

He muttered under his breath, "You make me this way." He didn't face me. Instead, his eyes glared into the halls. He leaned against the door of the classroom.

I looked through the glass to see what he was looking at. "Huh? I can't hear you," I said, but he was quiet.

Then he suddenly spoke. "Jeremy asked me where I saw this thing going between us," he said in a serious tone of voice. "I told him there wasn't a 'you and me,' because there isn't—because I'm ashamed of us being together, of people seeing us. I listen to the bullshit people say about you, and it all makes me sick. Being with you would be bad for me, a thing that I would regret."

"Why are you doing this?" My body started to tremble in reaction to his words.

"You're not a girl I would ever bring home to my mother, Tia! Girls like you are only good for an easy lay, and that's your only purpose in life. And for me, I'm not even attracted to you. I wouldn't even sleep with you, and that's why I haven't." I couldn't move. "You're just like one of the guys. The thought of being with you is a dream of yours, not mine."

Tears fell onto my cheeks. *I disgust him—really?*

I slowly walked up to him as more tears fell. I looked down, breathing; they felt like my last breaths.

I crossed my arms, weeping. I tried to hold back my tears, but I couldn't. Mathew couldn't bear to see me cry. I believed it was the reason he refused to look at me. Instead, he gazed at the floor with low shoulders. "Don't ever—and I mean *ever*—speak to me again!" A tear had fallen from his cheek. In that moment, I knew he cared. He was just trying to discover ways to deny it. Maybe, just maybe, I felt it was a little too late.

I left the room. He stormed out after me. "I'm sorry, Tia, but it has to be this way. It just does!" He collected my left arm, and I punched him. He let me go as he fell to the ground. He looked up at me slowly. While we stared at each other, his nose started to bleed. He was surprised to feel something roaming down to his mouth. Mathew wiped his bloody nose with his hand. I lowered to his level and looked straight into his eyes with a rocksolid, revolted expression. "You don't mean shit to me—shit, okay? Did you not hear me clearly? Well, just in case you had crust in your ears, I said to never speak to me again! Trust me. You have lost that privilege!" He glanced up at me as I left him where he belonged.

My nose began to run. I wiped it with my hands. My tears stained my cheeks. I went on with my day, and I'd never felt so empty. I kept crying and couldn't stop. I kept telling myself, "You are not in love with him. You are not in love with anyone." Before I went to class, I paused at the door. "You don't love him. You hear me? You just don't," I muttered recurrently. I looked into the window of my classroom. I entered the room, and the class was having a discussion about relationships.

I quickly sat in my seat. "Tia," Mr. Ford loudly blurted out, "it's nice of you to finally join us." The old bastard had startled me. "So what are your thoughts about love and how it relates to relationships?"

The class was silent, but I was numb from head to toe. I felt as if I were somewhere else mentally. Perhaps my state of mind was in another room or on another planet. "Love and relationships …" I said, standing as I stared at Mr. Ford and the class. With a blank look, I asked, "Love—what is love, Mr. Ford?"

He laughed playfully. "Tia, you tell me and the class what your view is on this emotional subject."

"I think …"

Mathew, surprisingly, came into the classroom, passed Mr. Ford a note, and sat in his seat. Mr. Ford briskly glared at him untrustworthily. Seeing him entering the class stole my breath, so I shut my eyes for a minute because I didn't want to see his face or feel him glaring at me.

"I'm waiting," Mr. Ford said. Boy, he was terribly impatient. I opened my eyes and told them everything I knew and felt about loving Mathew.

"Love is making personal sacrifices over and over again for the one that you share that deep emotional connection with. It is an unconditional care that a person can't break him- or herself free from overnight. Love is being selfless, yet it is also tears, laughter, pain, and joy. Love makes you fight when you feel you have no more fight left in you. Love is difficult, and it makes you do the craziest things that never really make sense to others. Love is accepting the person for who they are. And those that have fallen in love sometimes are willing to change for the person he or she loves for the sake of the relationship or connection. You wanna know what hurts more? Being in love with someone since you were a child who still doesn't love you because you're a slut!" I said intensely. The class laughed, yet Mathew just watched me with a blank look on his face. "And though I'm a slut, even I know a relationship is just a title or a word. It's the people in them, like you and me, that give relationships meaning, but most people say sluts are incapable of love, so what would I and other women like me know about love or relationships?" I said in a confident tone. I immediately rushed out of the classroom.

"You can't just leave my class, Tia!" Mr. Ford yelled behind me.

I ignored him. My eyes got watery again. I covered my face, wiping the wetness from my eyes, and I exhaled severely, trying to collect myself. I was a fucking mess. I tried my best to subdue my feelings for Mathew. For the last time, before continuing my day, I whispered once more, "You only care for yourself. What you're feeling is only sexual. That's all. Get over it, Tia." I dropped to the floor hopelessly. My phone vibrated in my right pocket. I pulled it out.

"Hi," I said, depressed.

"Hello, Tia. It's your counselor doing a simple follow-up. Are you still interested in going to rehab for the summer?"

I took a breath. "No. I had a change of heart."

"And why is that, Tia? You seemed so sure."

"I love myself just the way I am. Why or who am I changing for? I am happy," I stated miserably.

Students exited their classes. I remained motionless.

Uninvited Thoughts

I don't want to remember you, nothing whatsoever
about you, especially that smile that awakens me,
Those dimples indented into your cheeks, the curl of
your lips, and perhaps the color of your skin:
The liveliness in your voice sounds sweet
to my ears, unpredictable even,
So I fearfully seal my eyes tightly because I am petrified
my sweet dream will melt away like warm butter.
I'm liquid.
My humanity will drown and slowly sink to the bottom of the sea.
I'm dying.
Give me life, or give me death.
Call me breathless.
Implant a reason for my breathing.
I remember you.
You are the disease that is damaging my worried parts.
You are my fats and proteins.
I can't dare to function properly in your exclusion.
I have eaten too much of you.
Call these my sickening bites.
A dying fragrance to the nostril, you are indeed.
The smell is highly unwelcoming, and the taste is
bitterly sour, though it looks enticing, of course.
But I don't want to remember you, nothing whatsoever
about you—not that dance or those jokes.
I'm drunk on you.
I've drunk too much. Intoxication.
I am filled with an appealing laughter,
Occupied by the unpredictable and unbearable
feeling of being fixated on you.
I remember that smile that awakens me, those dimples indented
into your cheeks, the curl of your lips, and the color of your skin.
The liveliness in your voice sounds sweet to my ears.

Erase me.
If I open my eyes, you'll be gone, and I will certainly
shatter into bits and pieces. I'm fragments.
Call me totally unfixable.
Some things that are broken will never be fixed.
Do you remember me?
I remember you.
Do you miss me since I'm oppressed because of you?
Cleanse me, my sinner.
You're no good.
I was happy, but happiness rarely lasts, because I'm miserable.
You're jolly.
But I remember—do you?
Do I run through your mind?
Am I going half crazy? Is this insanity?
I have memories of you.
How come I remember you, but you seem to have forgotten me?
The girl who cared on the daily,
Who satisfied and loved unforgettably.
The girl who lived in the gates you opened, since she aimed to please.
How can I refuse to forget?
Your words weakened me, made me vulnerable.
I unsealed my thighs to your presents, penetration.
Suddenly, I'm the lost one without a map.
I was betrayed by the very thing that generated my hopes, failure.
I remember you, memories.
I hate you, lies.
I trusted you, regret.
I'm finished, unlikely.
I'm moving on indefinitely.
Rewrite, take away, and erase the permanent feelings I have of you.
Let's just call them unwanted thoughts.

CHAPTER 29

Erin

Letting Go of Jo

It bothered my subconscious that Jo didn't grow weary of me. I couldn't understand why Jo still longed for me. It would have been fabulous if she had stopped texting and calling me the way she did. I would have done anything to cease the link between us that she did everything to conserve. Ignoring her wasn't easy. I answered almost every call and message from her. If I didn't reply to her calls and text messages, she knew ways of getting around the miscommunication. Showing up unannounced, calling from unknown numbers, and finding out where I was were no issues for Jo. She had fallen in love with me in ways I'd dreamed a man would, but I wasn't bisexual or anywhere close to a homosexual. Being around her made me tired of pretending that I was. If I had liked women, Jo still wouldn't have been my type. It was time that she knew our relationship was over, there hadn't been a connection between us from the beginning, and Jeremy had volunteered to help me get rid of her without even knowing. He was upstairs, preparing for the task.

Jeremy knew I needed to execute one more final sex project, which involved three people. He made it obvious that this other individual had to be a female, of course. Since he was now my boyfriend, it was felicitous to have him aid me in the accomplishment of my last duty. He agreed to support me, because I convinced him that I would no longer be a member of the BOTS Association. In reality, I wasn't going anywhere. I wrapped my purple robe around me. I was downstairs, waiting for Jo to accompany us. A few minutes later, she showed up. Her kisses were proof that she'd missed me dearly. They were soft and comforting. I looked at her. She was wearing a long all-white dress and white sandals. I had a feeling she'd rushed to my place. I hugged her as if I'd missed her, too.

I asked her while I squeezed her tightly, "Do you have the assignment you completed?"

She nodded, handing me the sheet. I scanned down to the bottom of the sheet. James's and Michael's signatures were at the bottom. I folded it. She smiled shyly. "So what's next for me?" she asked.

I stared into her eyes with a devilish smile on my face and then winked as I exhaled out of my nose. "Surprisingly, you were awarded another task. I guess the manager is in your favor, Jo," I said, lying.

She jumped up and down. "Really?" For some reason, she got louder and louder. "What is it? What is it?" she repeated loudly. She reminded me of a spoiled child.

I reached into my robe and pulled her task out of my corset. I handed it to her. She silently read every word. "I have to watch two people have sex. Are you serious? That sounds so exciting!"

Yeah, isn't it? I thought.

She leered in suspense. "I've never watched two people have sex before. Who are they? Do I have to join them?"

I grabbed her hand. "It's a surprise, and I just know you are going to love it."

"I like surprises!"

Wow, just look at her reaction to all of this. "I like surprises!" I thought, mocking her. *I don't know what Jeremy saw in her.*

She easily swallowed the bullshit I served her. "I know you do. In the room next to mine on the right, he and she will meet you in like five minutes. In the nightstand, there is a beige blindfold that you will wear for a short duration," I said while she journeyed up the stairs.

She screamed as she ran upstairs. "Wow, I'm so anxious right now!"

I heard a boom by the stairs. My eyes widened. I was concerned, so I ran to see if she was okay. She turned around in embarrassment as she attempted to recover from her fall. She forced a smile and chuckled to hide her shame.

"I'm okay. I'm okay!" she shouted. I managed to suppress my giggles. She'd tripped up the stairs. That was a first for me. I had never seen anyone trip while running up the stairs before, though I'd witnessed many people falling backward.

I entered my room, and Jeremy greeted me with a welcoming smile. I smiled back at him. He chuckled in response. I sat beside him. "I wanna say something to you, Erin."

I readjusted my body to face him. I hoped it was all good. I nodded and said, "Okay, Jeremy."

He touched my chin. "I think you're an amazing person. You are so selfless and caring toward others around you."

I covered my face. "Stop, Jeremy. You are making me blush."

He removed my hands and glanced into my eyes. I rejected his eye contact. He said, "You are so shy, and I think it's absolutely adorable of you. I hope it doesn't scare you away, but I want to know everything about you."

I laughed. "You don't mean that." I shook my head. He lifted my face with his finger.

"I do. I mean every word," he said confidently. He held my hand passionately. I looked deeply into his eyes.

I stood. "You make me feel …" I paused. "You make me feel alive—so alive that my heart is literally pounding in my chest."

He rose to kiss me. I shut my eyes as I wrapped my arms around his neck. He said, "Being around you makes me feel alive, too. Don't worry. I feel the same way about you as you do about me."

I grabbed his hand. His grip was comforting. We left the room to enter the next one with Jo. He shut the door forcefully. Jo jumped when she heard the slam. "Oh my God," she said, placing her hands over her heart.

We could hear her breathing deeply. She was seated in a chair next to the bed. She smiled. Her giggles filled the room, and unexpectedly, her energy entertained me and sparked feelings of joy and anxiety. Jeremy gently gripped my neck with both of his big, muscular hands. We kissed. With one hand, he stripped me out of my robe. He stared at my lingerie from Lover's Lane. It was an all-white Dream Corset with built-in boning, a lace bust, ruffle trim, satin bows, a ruffled hemline, and attached garter straps. I wore no stockings, though. I didn't need them. Jeremy seemed to like my lingerie very much.

We went over by the bed. I sat on the edge, and he knelt on one knee. He lifted my right leg, holding my ankle. I looked down at him. He rested my leg over his shoulder. Meanwhile, he started kissing my ankle while watching me. This act was something special coming from Jeremy. It tickled to the point that it tingled like hell. It felt electrifying. The feeling ran through my entire body. While continuing to watch, he proceeded to kiss my ankle. Suddenly, his kisses traveled up to the middle of my leg and then the center of my inner thigh. My body was shaking. Like a nerd, I rose and giggled at the feeling of it. I exhaled deeply. I couldn't remember the last time my body had been treated this way. I moaned.

"What in the hell?" she shouted while removing her blindfold as Jo stood conflictingly. Jeremy and I both turned our heads in result of her unfortunate outburst, but I had never seen someone glare at me in such disappointment. Her eyes became watery as she shook her head in sadness. She exhaled profoundly in anger and pain. "How could you?" she screamed, staring in my direction. She then exited the room and slammed the door. Jeremy lowered his head. "Erin, I have never seen her so upset like that before." he mentioned subjectively. He respired deeply. "Maybe we went about keeping her from this club the wrong way. The last thing I wanted was to hurt her." I gripped the sides of his face gently as I looked into his eyes. "We were just trying to protect her. That's all, Jeremy. Maybe this was wrong, but all of this came from a good place," I said genuinely. I lowered my hands. "Did you see the way she looked at me?" He nodded smoothly. I shook my head. I rose. "I can't let her leave like that. Please stay here, and let me talk to her. It would be awkward for you to do it, when we have grown so close and you and she have grown so apart."

He relaxed on the bed. "Sure. That's fine with me. Just make sure she's ok." I agreed.

I then rushed down the stairs to catch up with her. She had to have heard my footsteps. She was sitting by the front door, crying. I eased a little closer to her. "What was all of this?" She wept.

"All of this? All of what, Jo? What, you mean your ex-boyfriend and me?" I stopped and lowered myself onto the floor to face her. "Well, I have to admit that I was jealous of the two of you being together. To be honest, jealousy isn't my thing." I rubbed her shoulders. "But let me explain this to you, Jo, I'm not a lesbian. I'm as straight as the red carpet. I'm guessing you wanna know why I fucked you over the way I did. Well, Jo, because I receive pleasure from sabotaging healthy relationships in exchange for simple fucks." She lifted as she aggressively knocked my hands from off her shoulders. Jo beamed down at me. Her lips tightened while her eyes fluttered in fear.

She stuttered a bit. "I don't—we were—I-I—" she paused. "What, why, huh? I don't understand!" she shouted. "It was just so easy for you to pretend to be something your not!" she cried dramatically. "What girl or kind of person would do that?" She shook her head in tears. "I trusted you and you—and you—" she couldn't complete her sentence.

"Well, Jo," I giggled. "I see your taking all of this kind of personal. How about this? When he's done slurping up my pussy—you know—like a pineapple smoothie, I'll call you. I promise." I teased. "Just make sure you wait patiently by the phone, for my call, ok?" Jo didn't respond. She glared at me like I was a psycho. I lifted myself up from the floor, moving closer to her. She wiped her face and her nose. "I'm not going to let you get away with this! I will tell him everything. You hear me?!" I chuckled at her.

"Tell on me. What are you—Twelve? That's funny. You don't have a man and nor are you in our sex club. As you probably know, you completed Tia's train-the-girl assignment, which I will be getting credit for because she doesn't want Mathew thinking she let two guys fuck her at the same time, like you did. Don't worry—she thanks you, as do I." She raised her hand and smacked me. My eyes widened. I was surprised she had the balls to hit me. After she smacked me, I stopped laughing and smiling at her. My cheek stung for a while. I rubbed the left side of my face, hoping and waiting for the sting to cease. "I'm going to let that one slide since I was the man of this relationship. But smack me again"—I pointed my finger at her—"and I will hit you back. I promise you it will be a fucking punch in the nose!"

She was disgusted, and I liked it. "You think Jeremy is going to want you after I tell him the truth about you?"

"And you think he is going to accept you back, knowing you willingly let two guys fuck you at once? He is going to think you're a dirty little slut—because you are."

"I am not a slut. You're the real slut. You did the same thing to join the sex club your freshman year!"

I laughed at her again. "You are just a stupid little girl, like Tia and Amy said. None of my teammates has slept with two guys before, at least not that I know of, nor have I. If you tell Jeremy about me, I am going to mention how you let James and Christian train you like the little slut you are. Believe me. A smart woman like me always has proof." I watched as more tears dropped from her face. I listened to her weep while she shook her head at me. She slowly backed away from me. I crossed my arms as I moved closer to the front door. She left, slamming another door of mine.

Jeremy came down the stairs. "Is everything okay?"

I wiped my eyes as if I had been crying about the situation. "No. Everything went so badly. I don't know what to do. She thought I was a lesbian because I told her I'd dated a girl before, like I mentioned to you at the party. She had a crush on me, and I feel stupid. I told her that you and I were together. She just went ballistic." He held me from behind. "She even smacked me after I told her that she wasn't a member of my club. This club isn't good for her. She just doesn't realize she's better than this game we're playing, like I am."

"You are. You both are, but maybe it isn't a good idea for the two of you to be friends." I agreed by nodding as he added, "I'm surprised you didn't hit her back. It says a lot about you, Erin."

I grinned. Of course it did.

Life was not complicated. It was comfortable, and I liked it. Jeremy and Andrew had redeemed me. My heart was no longer broken with them protecting it. Surprisingly, Andrew had been the first one to assist me with my recovery, though I couldn't have achieved it without Jeremy. I started to want them both, because I was vindictive like that. I became their responsibility—something they couldn't shake off. At that time,

I was spending more time with Andrew. From time to time, he would visit me, and so did Jeremy.

Andrew found my home captivating. "I'm always coming here and finding you in this huge, empty house by yourself." He was concerned about me. I didn't understand why.

"No." I frowned at him. "The emptiness always finds me somewhere and somehow." I froze. "I'm stuck with it."

His eyes did another evaluation of our surroundings. "Where is everyone—your family members? Better yet, what of your giggles? I see you pretending with me. None of your smiles I see and laughter I hear are real, Erin. They're pretend. Where did your smile go? How do I get it back for you?" He stared into my eyes. I felt trapped by his eyes. Maybe it was because they were green.

I faced him more directly. "My family? I don't have a family, Andrew. As for my smile, it abandoned me a long time ago." I lowered my eyes. "I don't know where it is." I paused, waiting to exhale. "Yet I know it's in a dark and unforeseen place. You should know. I stopped searching for it. It's just me, myself, and I," I said.

"What happened to your family—your father, sister, or brother?"

"My father—he was my joy and hope in everything good, but my brother was like my twin. When they died, my love and laughter died along with them."

"Erin," he said, "you may feel alone, but you aren't. You are not stuck or imprisoned by loneliness. I don't ever want you to feel alone, hopeless, or unhappy. I'll bring your real laughter back to you somehow. Fortunately, I don't need to search in the darkness to do it or touch you to make you laugh or smile. I'm going to create new memories for you."

If I had been innocent, he would have melted my heart, and I would have fallen in love with him. How sweet was this? Familiarity was a thing I quickly had become accustomed to. On the other hand, I had never been good at understanding his ways, although they were generous.

Irritably, I said, "You can't. I have already given up on it. I have accepted it for what it is, lost somewhere within me." Was it really? Who knew?

"None of this makes sense to me. I don't believe it. Have you not heard a word I have said?"

My proclamation seemed to trouble him; I could tell by his expression. For the moment, he was serious but caring.

I said, "I have—every word. Your words hold no meaning for me. Words are useless, because it is people that give them power when they decide to take action." My father used to tell me that when I was little. My subconscious endured the memories of his voice feeding my ears with knowledge.

"My words, Erin, hold much purpose because I am a powerful and active person. Take my hand. I want to show you something, because I am ready to change my words into actions, but are you?"

He couldn't have known, but on the inside, I was as bright as a star in the night sky. I took his hand. It gave me a settled feeling. He was patient with me, although I didn't leave him with a choice.

Together, we enjoyed the streets of downtown Chicago. He held a large black bag. While we roamed down the sidewalk, a black homeless man begged. It was the same homeless man Angelina and I had seen on the bus several months ago. His grieving was even more sincere than I had remembered. "Please, please, sir and ma'am. Don't you have any food or water to give? I haven't eaten in two days."

We stopped. Andrew let go of my hand. He ventured into his huge black bag and pulled out a small brown bag. "Here you go. I hope you enjoy the food."

The man peeked into the bag. He then smiled as if Andrew were his hero. "Thank you, sir! Thank you. May God bless you."

"No, bless you." Andrew smiled like a true child of God. "You have a good day."

We kept walking, and I was speechless. I was impressed. In response to his selflessness, I eagerly grabbed his hand. "What was that for?" I asked. Our grip was unbreakable.

"That was nothing. Every Sunday, I go downtown and pass out lunches to homeless people."

"You do this every Sunday—always?"

He grinned pleasantly as he pulled me closer to whisper into my ear. "Every Sunday—always."

I lowered my eyes and smiled. Seeing this act of kindness caused me to smile as I never had before.

We stopped at the next red light. He stared down at me. "I hope you don't think I missed that sumptuous smirk of yours."

I moved in on him, teasing him confrontationally. I shouted while attempting to conceal my bliss at the occasion. "I did not," I lied as the sides of my mouth curled up.

"You did too," he said playfully in response, wrapping one of his hands around my lower back from behind while he held the black bag in the other.

I confessed with laughter, "Okay, okay, okay. I give up. I give up. I surely did. I smiled for a moment. What's so special about that?"

He answered, though it was a rhetorical question. "It showed true pureness. It was nothing like your other smiles of vindictiveness. It was a smile of excitement and hope for another. You are beautiful, and I'm glad I was the guy to see it tonight." He blushed for the first time. It caused me to smile wider. For the rest of the night, we proceeded to pass out the lunches he'd packed. During those moments, he wasn't lying, as I'd thought he was. He made me smile all night.

After I relayed this story in my next counseling session, Ms. Wright said, "Thanks for sharing, Erin. However, there are a few questions I have for you. How are you sleeping now?"

I cleared my throat. "I am sleeping a lot better than I was before."

"What factors have contributed to this, Erin?"

I smiled. "Many factors, Ms. Wright. My team has recovered from a lot by doing things to help themselves, like Dillon. Things have been better because of Jeremy and Andrew, we have completed our bonuses, and this is the end of our junior year."

"Interesting. So who have you chosen?" She stared.

I raised an eyebrow. "What do you mean?"

"Between Jeremy and Andrew, who have you picked? We're all curious."

I began daydreaming about what I'd said to them. They had both shown up unannounced at my house one day. They'd found out I was seeing both of them. They'd asked me to choose. I couldn't and had refused at first. I'd demanded to talk to them individually. They wouldn't agree to it. They had forced me to choose between them, and I had chosen Jeremy. Andrew had been disappointed. The truth was, I had never chosen between them. A day later, I had taken the bus to school to see Andrew. Surprisingly, I had spotted Andrew sitting alone. I'd sat beside him as he looked straight ahead. I hadn't known what he would say, and my heart was pounding, of course. I had tried not to look at him.

Like Andrew, I'd stared straight ahead as well. He, luckily, had reached out his hand to me. I'd grabbed his hand and held on to it tightly. In that moment, he had run his thumb against my fingers. Some tears had fallen from my eyes, because I'd known I could never choose Jeremy over Andrew or Andrew over Jeremy.

I wanted and needed them both in my life. Andrew, as he'd promised, gave me unforgettable reasons to smile. He gave me a purpose for my laughter. I knew he wouldn't let me slip through his fingers. With him, I would always have a warm place in his heart, as he would in mine. He wasn't the guy I wanted. He was the guy I needed. Jeremy was different. He listened to me and believed in my dreams. He was my purpose for breathing.

"That answer is still unidentified," I lied.

"What about you, Amy? What has changed?" Ms. Wright asked.

CHAPTER 30

Amy

An Ending to Begin

I paused to organize my thoughts. "Um …" I laid my finger on my bottom lip. "Where do I start?" I blinked with a grin. I sat back to get more comfortable in my seat. "I have made a list of everything that's healthy and unhealthy for me. I have decided to go to rehab for the summer with Tia." Erin, Tia, and Angelina applauded. Ms. Wright clapped formally but kept her composure. "Tia was the other person who helped me to realize something big besides Ms. Wright," I said, smiling at Tia.

"And what was that, Amy?" she asked as she nodded.

"That, uh, I'm a love addict. Even meeting David made me realize how mentally unhealthy I am. I used to wonder if I would ever see him again. I often would fantasize about what I would do if I saw him one last time, just once." I didn't really believe that I was a love addict, but I needed my teammates and Ms. Wright off my back. Accepting that I had a problem was the first step toward recovery.

Ms. Wright asked while giving me direct eye contact, "And did you?"

"I did. I was only thinking about him because of the chase—you know, the challenge. The fact that he was neglecting me influenced me to want him even more. It was all because I knew I wanted something I couldn't have, when I always got what I wanted. The rejection was my sense of motivation. When I saw him again, I knew I had him right where I needed him to be. I was given a second chance to sleep with him, and I didn't, because in that moment, I no longer wanted him." I did still want him. Although I didn't want to fuck him while he was unconscious, I knew my opportunity to have sex with him was extremely limited. Therefore, I licked, sucked, and fucked him in every which way. Because of this, my obsession was over. I just couldn't tell the truth to them. It was better this way.

"You no longer wanted him?" she asked. "What else possibly aided you in that decision, Amy?"

"Wanting him was pointless and miserable for me. It hit me that I had to work on me. I'm not in a place where I can be in a relationship with anyone until I am more confident and happy on my lonesome. And plus, knowing that his package was little also changed my final decision." His package was everything but little. I couldn't stop lying even if I needed to.

They all laughed, except for Ms. Wright. I was happy, and that was all that mattered. I felt a sense of joy in my heart that I'd never known before. The feeling had me glowing, though everything I did was all a part of my performance.

She smiled lightly at me. "I am extremely happy for you, Amy. I look forward to you returning to my sex club for your final year!" Her tone was filled with liveliness.

I rose in excitement, because Erin had informed me that I couldn't return next year. "Oh really? Are you positive?"

She nodded. "Um, yeah, Amy, I'm serious. I definitely want to see how you have grown. I think having you around would be a great thing for the sex club."

I exhaled in relief. I wiped my face, returning to my position. I looked toward Tia.

"Okay, Tia. I see that unique smile of yours, and it's stunning," Ms. Wright said.

Tia grinned even harder. "Thank you, Ms. Wright." She tilted her head slightly.

"I have to ask. What has aided in this happiness of yours?" She stared at Tia.

Tia hesitated. "Where do I begin? Hmmm, um, well, I'm no longer okay with being a sex addict. This addiction is not a part of me, of who I truly am. It is important to me that I am true to myself. This addiction has taken over my life, and it has made it difficult for me to be loved."

Ms. Wright restated our good news. "If I heard correctly from Amy"—she pointed at me—"and I'm sorry for pointing, but you and Tia are going to rehab to get help together?"

I looked at her. Tia looked back at me and then said, "Yes. That is correct, Ms. Wright."

"Okay, okay, okay. What of you and Mathew?"

"I thought long and hard about this. After our confrontation at school last week, I promised myself I would never speak to him again because of everything he said to me. He kept finding reasons, which I called excuses, to call, text, and see me. For a few days, I ignored them altogether."

"One day, he showed up to my foster parents' house unannounced. It was early in the morning. My foster parents' two children were already at school. My foster dad went to work a few minutes after, and my foster mother wasn't feeling well, so she stayed home. I let him in because I didn't want him to wake her. Wanting to know why he wanted to see me so desperately was another reason I listened to him. I stared at him in curiosity. My expression revealed the pain he'd put me through.

"He stared back and said, 'Why are you looking at me like that?'

"'I hate to say this to you, but I'm disgusted by you and everything you said to me. It makes it hard for me to look at you,' I confessed.

"He listened. 'I thought I wouldn't have cared how you viewed me. Unfortunately, I do. I heard you are going to rehab for the summer.'

"'Yup, I am. This time, for the right reason—myself, not a silly boy.' He nodded and I said, 'What do you want, Matt? I have more important things to do with my time.'

"He spoke immediately. 'I'm so, so sorry that I hurt you, Tia.' He attempted to touch me. I pulled away from him.

"'Please, don't touch me! Okay?' I blurted out aggressively. I opened the door to let him out. 'Are you finished?'

"He blinked. 'I miss you, Tia. I never missed a girl as much as I missed you. I was only trying to protect you from me. I learned that you don't need my protection. I don't think you ever really did.'

"Tears randomly dropped from my eyes. 'Now are you finished?' I asked hurriedly.

"'Say something other than asking if I'm finished. Say something real from your heart.'

"'Why, huh?' I paused and looked into his eyes. 'Why do you stress yourself out for me? Why would you do that for someone you already said isn't special to you? Just leave me alone. That's all I want from you now. There is no point in being with someone you are ashamed of and who disgusts you. You care about what people think of us and of me. This will never work, and I don't think I would want it to either,' I said, approaching him. 'Good-bye, Matt.' He backed himself out of my house. I shut the door behind him. Before going about my day, I repeated, 'I don't love him. You are not in love, okay?' I breathed out.

"I put on a summer dress in shades of light purple, hot pink, and white and a pair of four-inch heels. Surprisingly, I didn't have any dark makeup on, because I wanted to change my appearance. In the hallway after I took my finals, students were hugging, kissing, and conversing with their friends and associates. I couldn't wait to get home. I started to leave the school, when I saw Mathew all dressed up in a white and baby-blue tie, vest, and dress shoes. I stopped instantly. His hair was curlier than I was used to. I liked it. He looked good. He was watching me as I watched him. He walked up to me as I stood in the center of the hallway.

"'Would you like to know why I'm all dressed up?' he said. It seemed that everyone in the hallways had grown silent, listening to our conversation.

"I twisted my lips up at him. 'No. I wouldn't,' I said, giving him a hard time.

"As he fragilely caressed the lower part of my face, he said, 'Well, I am telling you anyway. I'm all dressed up for you because you are special to me. When I hurt you, I learned that I hurt the best part of myself. Because I am not ashamed to say I'm in love with you, Tia. I always loved you. I am not ashamed of loving you and letting everyone know you are the woman I wanna wake up to every morning. I love you more than I love myself, Tia.' He quickly placed one hand gently on the left side of my neck and wrapped the other around my waist. He kissed me in front of everyone passionately. I mildly gripped both of his ears and

French-kissed him back. We slowly stopped locking lips. I looked at him as if I were impressed.

"I had watched him confess his love for me in front of the entire school. All eyes were on us. I couldn't believe he'd said he was in love with me around a crowd of students. I saw just him and me, no one else. Everyone in the hallways applauded. I wrapped my hands around his neck and shut my eyes, smiling. 'I love you too, Mathew.'

"We kissed again and again. Angel walked up to us with some beautiful red roses. 'Here are the flowers you ordered.' She handed them to Mathew and winked happily at me.

"He stared into my eyes and said, 'These are for you.' All of the other students went about their business. I grabbed the roses from his hand. I sealed my eyes and buried my nose in them.

"'You did all this for me?' I said with a half grin.

"He looked down at me, rubbing his fingers up and down my arms. 'I've said "I love you" to a lot of girls, Tia, but with you was the only time I ever meant it. I hope you're impressed.'

"I rubbed his face. 'I am,' I said emotionally.

"Two hours later, he took me to a fancy restaurant downtown. When we arrived back at his apartment, he went into the bathroom. I removed my dress, leaving my underwear on. All of a sudden, my eyes grew heavy. I was so exhausted from that day. I dropped onto the bed to rest my eyes. I found myself dozing off. I fell asleep altogether in a few minutes or so. I had on my full-coverage and strapless gray cheetah-print bra with the panties to match. It was my favorite set, but Mathew liked cheetah print for some reason. Later on that night, I heard a woman moaning in the background and a squeaking bed. It sounded like she was receiving great pleasure. I was tossing and turning to the sounds of her moaning.

"Hearing and watching people fuck got me wet. She groaned and said something like 'Yes, yes, oh, oh, yes, fuck me—shit!' She screamed loudly.

"I could feel his friendly fingers against my skin. Mathew turned me around on my stomach with my ass in the air. Of course, I let him. I kept my eyes shut totally. From underneath me, he scooted in between my legs. He swirled his tongue around and against my clitoris. I jumped at the feeling of it. Whoa, it felt so damn great. I managed to hold in my groans for about a second. But all fuck, I screamed on the inside. Meanwhile, he spit and slipped his wet fingers inside my pussy. My ass jiggled as he violently finger fucked me while sucking on my clit. I then opened my legs wider and wider.

"The woman continued to moan. Her moans outclassed mine. His suckling got louder. It sounded good to hear him eating my fat pussy. He unexpectedly spanked my cheeks. I didn't mind, though—not with him, oh no. It turned me on even more. The juices from my pussy tickled as they ran down my thighs and legs. I respired deeply. I wanted us to fuck like gorillas. Although I was in love with him, I wasn't the make-love-to kind of girl. I was a complete fucking freak.

"I rose somewhat and opened my eyes when I moaned. 'Oh, na, na, shit!' I screamed. 'Whoa, don't stop! Don't you fucking stop! Dammit!' I leaned back down.

"He spanked me again. 'I knew you were pretending to be asleep. I knew you wouldn't miss out on this one,' he said, continuing to finger fuck me.

"'Talk dirty to me while you touch me!' I shouted to him.

"'No, not until you beg me for it first. Stay please,' he muttered. 'I want to hear you beg for it.'

"I grabbed his arms in pleasure, as I was pleased with his words. 'Please, please, please,' I pleaded seductively while his fingers proceeded to fuck me. 'Talk dirty to me.' He leered with confidence. However, his confidence could have been mistaken for cockiness.

"'What do you want to do to me?' he asked erotically.

"I nodded and turned to face him. 'Yes.' I grunted in excitement. 'I want to suck and to get fucked by you!'

"'Oh yeah?' he asked. 'You want me to fuck you, huh? How badly do you want this dick inside you?' he yelled.

"I whispered, 'Desperately.' I paused, looking into his eyes. 'I want you so, so bad.' He kissed me, massaging his tongue with mine. 'Mouth fuck me, Mathew,' I said. 'I want you to mouth fuck me.' I listened to the porn star getting fucked by a black guy with an enormous cock.

"He stared in shock with wide eyes. 'Really?' he asked while pausing.

"Then he moved his fingers deeper inside me. My pussy started to make noises because of it. 'Yes, oh yes!'

"I rose and kissed him on the lips. We collapsed onto the bed with him on top of me. I laughed, and he chuckled at my reaction to the fall. He unfastened his belt and undid his zipper. My sexual tension built up during the wait. He moved to put his dick in my face. I loved it, so I stroked his dick around my lips while glancing up at him. He was extremely stiff. He was huge. I spit on his dick.

"'Yeah, spit on it just like that, babe,' he said. I spit on it again and again. I bit my lips as I poked them out for him. I lowered myself onto the bed, opening my mouth.

"He leaned down slowly, putting every inch of his dick into my mouth. 'Aw, shit. Aw, fuck!' he shouted. 'Damn, Tia.'

"He fucked my mouth, rocking back and forth as if he were inside of my pussy. Spit dropped from my mouth because his dick was covered in saliva. This was the first time I'd ever let a guy mouth fuck me before, and I enjoyed every moment of it. I tightened up my jaws to enhance his pleasure. His cock almost reached the back of my throat. He increased his speed after he gripped the top of his headboard. I rested both of my hands on his behind. I sucked more aggressively as he forced every inch of him inside my mouth. Before he finally penetrated my wet pussy with his hard and powerful python, he placed a condom over his dick. He swirled his ass around with his dick in me. The more he fucked me, the deeper he went inside me and the wetter I got. He went at a quicker pace. I dug my short nails into his back. I grunted. He took the pain.

"During the process, the bed squeaked and squeaked as I screamed, practically moaning to us fucking, and he groaned. 'Damn, Tia—shit. You feel so fucking good.'

"He kissed my lips and neck. It felt fabulous. He breathed out. I suddenly moaned rapidly. I was severely breathing in and out while the bed rocked wildly. Us bouncing on the mattress made the headboard bang against the floor and walls. I ran my fingers through his curly hair and ended up grabbing both of his ears. He then put his hands behind me to grip my ass cheeks. He squeezed them firmly and really stroked his anaconda in and out of my pussy. Boy, I was so wet for him and his huge fucking cock. Again, my pussy started to fart, but I wasn't embarrassed by it, like I was with Michael. Mathew slowed down. I guessed that he was tired. I lifted up to get on top of him. Mathew and I were sweaty. I loved it. All good, hard-core fucking ended up with people sweating, so I was grinding on his stick, gently bouncing on the tip.

"He grunted. 'Oh, oh, right there. Don't move. Stay right there.'

"He began to suck on my small nipples. For the finish, I made an exaggerating and sexy moaning sound as a result of my orgasm being released. I stopped. He came the second I did. He was quiet and stiff for about one minute. Mathew and I then took breaths. He spoke while exhaling and inhaling.

"'You sound sexy when you moan, but I'm sure you already knew that,' he said.

"We had sex, but he called it making love. It was weird at first and uncomfortable for me because he kissed me on my neck and lips so much during the time we were having sex. It felt awkward to me. Looking me in my eyes deeply showed me that I had been fucking all my life. No one had ever made love to me before. It was like connecting on another mental and physical level altogether."

"Okay, Tia. That was not what we all were expecting, but thanks for sharing anyway," Ms. Wright announced.

I guess my confession to the group was a little much. I didn't care, because I'd needed to get it off my chest.

"Okay, everyone." Ms. Wright stood. "I have two surprises for you." She opened the door, and Dillon and Jacky walked in. We all screamed when we saw them.

Erin eagerly rushed to Jacky to hug her tightly. "Oh my God, girl, where have you been?" Erin said loudly.

Jacky smiled at her and at us. "With you-know-who."

Erin let her go. "We've missed you!" She hugged Dillon.

I approached Jacky and wrapped my arms around her. I eventually held Dillon. Angelina and Amy greeted Jacky and Dillon as well. We all stood beside each other. Ms. Wright said, "We are all here to vote for a leader for next year." We all applauded. "We will all start with your vote, Tia."

I hesitated. "I renew my old vote. I select Erin as leader for our final year." I glanced at Erin and smiled happily. She returned the friendly look.

Dillon said, "I vote for myself."

Amy disagreed. "I'm in agreement with my last vote of Erin being leader next year."

"I vote Erin," Angelina said.

Erin nominated another. "I move from my station as leader and speaker for senior year. All votes for me—the votes of Amy, Angelina, and Tia—I transition and lock down for my selection. Out of respect for my previous authority, I would like my inferiors to nominate Angelina as our new leader."

I laughed loudly. They looked at me. "I'm sorry," I said sincerely. "Out of respect for Erin's past station, I vote for Angel."

Amy said after me, "Out of respect, I vote for Angel." Amy then glared at Erin.

Angelina said, "Because of Erin's initial authority, I accept the position as your new leader for senior year."

Jacky disagreed. "I'm sorry, Erin. I respect your former ability and station as leader. Forgive me for my disagreement with your selection. I vote for myself."

Dillon said, "Well, shit. I still vote for my damn self, but I'm outvoted. So out of respect, I vote for the virgin."

Ms. Wright declared, "Well, it looks like we have a new leader." She approached Angel. "Please raise your right hand, Angelina Smith, and repeat after me." Angel lifted her hand, and Ms. Wright said, "As leader, I first announce that during next year, at any time until the year has ceased, I realize that it is prohibited to remove myself from my position as leader."

Angelina repeated, "As leader, I first announce that during next year, at any time until the year has ceased, I realize that it is prohibited to remove myself from my position as leader."

Ms. Wright added, "As leader, you understand you are stuck with this powerful station until all sex assignments have been completed by all group members."

Angelina agreed. "As leader of next year, I understand that I am stuck with this powerful station until all sex assignments have been completed by all group members."

"When leading your team, you are responsible for the completion and guidance of all female members. If they fail, you fail as their superior. As our new speaker, you will not accept failure. Do you agree not to confide in the male competitors in BOTS Association?"

"When leading my team, I am responsible for the completion and guidance of all female members. If they fail, I fail as their superior. As their new speaker, I will not accept failure. I agree to only confide in my female members, not the male competitors in BOTS Association."

"And lastly, do you agree to sustain the secrecy of our sex club? We must not reveal the purpose of the sex club unless you have a new member joining the club. Cheating is forbidden. Stealing the credibility of another's assignment or allowing others to complete your assignments for you or your members is unjust and will not be tolerated. Do you understand, Angelina Smith?"

"Yes, Ms. Wright. I completely understand." She grinned.

"Do you understand and know your authority and the benefits that come along with it?"

"I do." She nodded.

"Okay. Congratulations, Angelina." She extended her arm to Angel and shook her hand with pleasure.

"Thank you," Angel said. We all hugged Angelina individually as a show of respect for her and her new station.

Then we marched down to the auditorium to join the males. Yesterday the manager had set up a meeting with the boys to discuss the same boring bullshit and to keep everything properly organized to reduce confusion and misinformation. I entered, and the guys were waiting for us. I searched for Mathew. I found him sitting on the lower left side of the auditorium. I ran to him; he was now standing tall. I held and kissed him. "I missed you," I said with sealed eyes.

I opened them, and he said, "I missed you, too."

I sat beside him. I was the only girl who sat with the males. The guys were to the left, and the girls were to the right. Ms. Wright stood in the center of the auditorium.

Our manager announced, "I would like to give recognition to all members within both groups and shed light on the assignments each person has completed. With pleasure, I would first like to give credit to Christian. He completed most of his tasks and projects against Dillon, the Internet- images-of-Dillon assignment and the who-I-am sex-tape assignment, which was improperly executed on school grounds." The men clapped for Christian, who was not present. "Next, I would like to mention the success of Dillon's missions, the live-sex-performance assignment in the showroom against Christian, and the major-depression assignment." Dillon rose with a smile on her face.

All of the females applauded, especially me. Mathew stared at me. I looked at him. "Sorry, babe," I said, and he shooed me away with his hands as he peeped in the opposite direction. I moved to sit with the girls.

"James, I give you credit for the strange-birthday-sex assignment with Tia and the moans-during-a-presentation assignment against Jacky." James rose shortly to do a cool little dance.

"I would like to now acknowledge Jacky for finishing the you-got-herpes assignment and the teacher-and-student-sex assignment in the class!"

I screamed, "Yeah! Go, Jacky!" We cheered even louder. "Go, girl!" I repeated.

"I'd like to recognize Michael for finishing the female-chastity-belt assignment shared with Mathew," Ms. Wright said, and Michael clapped for himself.

Ms. Wright continued, "I'm giving credit where it is due for Angelina for the popping-my-cherry assignment and the process of writing a novel, *An Old War among the Youth*, which is all about the sex battle."

Amy, Angel, and Dillon stood together and cheered.

"This next person accomplished the pretend-rape assignment on Amy and the reject-Tia assignment." The guys applauded for Mathew for a brief moment as she finished her sentence: "Mathew!" The manager clapped.

"Let's next acknowledge the work of Tia," Ms. Wright said, and I screamed for myself. "The cock-cage assignment against Mathew with the assistance of Amy, the male-chase assignment, the fantasy-sex assignment, and the join-the-males-for-a-week assignment." The females cheered loudly.

"Andrew," she called out, "I give you recognition for accomplishing the player-gets-chased assignment, the oral-underneath-the-table assignment, and the asshole-of-the-week project." They stood for Andrew, clapping and shouting his name.

"Amy Robinson," she said, "you completed the I-got-herpes assignment, the secrets-to-keep assignment, and the I-got-punished assignment.

"Let's acknowledge the leader of the male sex club, Jeremy Waters! It was all about the big-threesome assignment, the resisting-Tia project, and the sex-with-a-stranger assignment." All of the males rose out of respect for Jeremy and applauded for him.

"Lastly, let's mention the leader of the female sex club, Erin Wilson." We all stood out of respect for Erin. "She has completed the train-the-girl assignment, the I-got-your-man assignment, and the girl-on-girl-action task." We all applauded for the team leaders of our junior year. "It is my pleasure to introduce the winners of this year's sex battle, the female competitors!" We all jumped up and down, giving a standing ovation to our team members and the leader, Erin. "With that being said," she said in conclusion, "out of all of our female competitors, the thirty-thousand-dollar prize goes to Erin Wilson!"

Erin screamed. I didn't shout for her, because I'd wanted to win the $30,000. *Boo, boo,* my subconscious said after Ms. Wright announced her as the winner. But I wasn't too upset, not when I was the only girl who had Mathew. Seconds after, we left the auditorium. Jacky held Erin's hand. I was behind them, listening to their conversation. I tried being as discreet about it as possible.

"Erin, I have something I need to ask you," Jacky said.

Erin was extremely happy. I would have been too, if I had just won $30,000, yet I was looking forward to the $50,000 prize, a gift for next year's winner. Boy, I was excited just thinking about it, especially because our junior year's sex assignments could have never outclassed the sex tasks we were expecting for senior year. Then again, I was prepared to give everyone a taste of what was coming. All of the members of the BOTS Association had to be participants in a senior orgy as our final project.

Jacky's speech to Erin now had my full attention. "After senior year, I'm moving to Florida to live with Professor Rodríguez. I would like you to move to Florida with me."

She glared at Jacky awkwardly. "I love you, Jacky. I really do, but why would I leave Illinois and Shante?"

Jacky stopped Erin and put her hands on Erin's shoulders. "Well, as your big sister, Erin, you don't have much of a choice. I don't care what you say, because you are coming with me whether you like it or not."

Erin froze with wide eyes, as did I. She stared back at Jacky in shock. I hadn't seen that one coming. I stared at Jacky and blinked as Erin's bitchy attitude emerged. I thought, *What the fuck was Jacky talking about when she called Erin her little sister?*

Printed in the United States
By Bookmasters